Regency Brides
Collection

2 Sparkling
Regency Romances

True Colours
by Nicola Cornick

The Youngest Miss Ashe
by Paula Marshall

Regency Brides

A collection from some of Mills & Boon
Historical Romance's most popular authors

Regency Brides

Collection

Nicola Cornick & Paula Marshall

MILLS & BOON®

*MILLS & BOON and MILLS & BOON with the Rose Device
are registered trademarks of the publisher.*

*First published in Great Britain 2004 by
Harlequin Mills & Boon Limited,
Eton House, 18-24 Paradise Road,
Richmond, Surrey TW9 1SR*

REGENCY BRIDES COLLECTION © Harlequin Books S.A. 2004

The publisher acknowledges the copyright holders of the
individual works as follows:

True Colours © Nicola Cornick 1998
The Youngest Miss Ashe © Paula Marshall 1997

ISBN 0 263 84079 4

138-0704

*Printed and bound in Spain
by Litografía Rosés S.A., Barcelona*

TRUE COLOURS
by
Nicola Cornick

Nicola Cornick became fascinated by history when she was a child, and spent hours poring over historical novels and watching costume drama. She still does! She has worked in a variety of jobs, from serving refreshments on a steam train to arranging university graduation ceremonies. When she is not writing she enjoys walking in the English countryside, taking her husband, dog and even her cats with her. Nicola loves to hear from readers and can be contacted by e-mail at ncornick@madasafish.com and via her website at www.nicolacornick.co.uk

Also by Nicola Cornick
in Mills & Boon® Historical Romance™

A COMPANION OF QUALITY★
THE RAKE'S BRIDE
(short story in *Regency Brides*)
AN UNLIKELY SUITOR★
THE EARL'S PRIZE
THE CHAPERON BRIDE
WAYWARD WIDOW
THE PENNILESS BRIDE
★*The Steepwood Scandal* series

Look for

THE NOTORIOUS LORD

August 2004

Prologue

Had matters fallen out differently they might never have met again. If his ship had not reached Plymouth early with a westerly wind behind it, or if she had not chosen that particular day for the journey into Somerset, or even if the hunt for Miss Frensham's lost reticule had taken just five minutes longer, the accident would have been averted and they would have passed on the road none the wiser. And later during the London Season, in some hot, airless drawing-room, an inquisitive matron would have fixed her with a sharp, avid gaze and said eagerly, 'I saw Lord Mullineaux driving in the Park today. Did you know that he was back in Town, Lady Carberry? You used to have some…small…acquaintance with him, I believe?'

And Alicia, Lady Carberry, would have put down her glass with a steady hand and responded in a colourless voice, 'Lord Mullineaux? No, I was not aware that he was back in England. But then, our acquaintance was not such that I would be likely to have heard of his return.'

And Mullineaux, hearing in his club the name of Alicia Carberry toasted on all sides as an Incomparable, would have said nothing, but reflected that money could buy much, even respectability, in a society that delighted in scandal.

But that was not the way that it was to be, as fate, which had first brought them together only to tear them apart again, took another decisive hand.

Chapter One

The accident happened on a stretch of road the locals called
Verney Drove, on a bend where the track—for it was little more—
abandoned its straight course across the Somerset Levels and
skirted a small hill. Both carriages had been going too fast and
neither could see the other before it was almost too late. The curricle grazed past the travelling chaise with less than an inch to
spare and such was the shock and noise of its sudden appearance
that the carriage horses took fright, rearing and plunging violently,
and the chaise almost overturned. It lurched off the road into the
water-filled ditch and there was a loud crack as the front axle
broke.

For a few moments, all was panic and confusion whilst the
groom leapt down to try to reach and calm the terrified horses,
and the coachman found both himself and the team dangerously
entangled in the reins. The groom had reached the horses' heads
but was finding the frightened animals difficult to hold single-
handed, and was shouting for assistance. The coachman cut the
reins and tumbled down from his perch into the ditch.

Meanwhile, the driver of the curricle had pulled up his own
team with an expertise that might have been admirable under other
circumstances, and had passed the reins to his groom with instructions to drive on to the nearest village and warn them of the accident. He turned back and reached the scene at a run, just as the
coachman, shaking the water off him like a dog and swearing
horribly, joined the groom and grasped the reins.

The gentleman materialised beside the two of them as the horses were beginning to quieten and the groom cast a first dubious glance towards the carriage, uncertain whether to stay or go to the rescue of its passengers. The February afternoon was unseasonably mild after a long, cold spell and already the first heavy drops of rain were starting to fall from a leaden sky, threatening to turn the track into a rutted quagmire. The gentleman summed up the scene in one swift glance and turned to the coachman.

'Stay with the horses,' he instructed tersely. 'Keep them steady whilst I go to find your passengers. How many do you carry?' The rain was already running in rivulets down his caped driving coat and he pushed the soaking dark hair back from his forehead. In the sudden darkness of the storm the groom and coachman could discern no more of his appearance than a dark countenance with lowering black brows, and neither of them had the courage to ask him who he was; they simply responded to the voice of authority.

'There are two of them, sir,' the coachman volunteered. 'Two ladies.'

The gentleman swore briefly under his breath and turned his attention to the carriage. It was of the newest and most elegantly comfortable design, though it carried no crest. Leaning at a drunken angle, two wheels in the ditch and two on the road, it was immediately evident that it could not be moved without help. The horses were also of a high quality, though not so highly bred as his own team, and they were calm now and looking rather dejected in the rain. One, the left-wheeler, whickered softly and put its head down to pull at the sparse grass at the side of the track.

The gentleman had reached the carriage door when he was fore-stalled by it being scrambled open from within. The figure of a little old lady appeared in the aperture, raising her voice above the wind in querulous protest. Her actual words were lost but their meaning was plain—she was unable to get down, for the carriage was tilted at such an acute angle that the steps could not reach the ground, and she was diminutive of stature and far too elderly and proper to even think of jumping down.

'Oh, I am shaken all to pieces!' As he drew closer he could

hear the quaver in her voice that denoted the beginnings of hysteria. 'This is quite intolerable! Jack Coachman, where are you? Help me down at once before I swoon!' Her gaze fell suddenly and suspiciously on the stranger—little more than a tall shadow in the darkness as he stood beside the carriage—and he could tell she did not know whether to faint with fright or appeal for help. In the event, common sense won.

'You, sir, whoever you are, help me down at once!' Her words came out imperiously but with an edge of fear, and she looked about her a little wildly. 'Oh, this is not to be endured! The steps will not reach to the ground!'

Sensing the real panic behind the lady's words, the gentleman stepped forward to the rescue. Without further ado she was picked up in a pair of strong arms and swung down onto the road in a flurry of petticoats and outrage.

'Sir, you are importunate!'

She made a desperate grab for her bonnet as the wind caught the brim, dropped her gloves in a puddle, and looked round forlornly for her reticule. She was shaking with both fear and reaction, and the stranger felt an immediate pang of compunction at having caused the accident in the first place and given anxiety to one so frail.

'I ask your pardon, ma'am.' He sketched an elegant bow which was incongruous in such inclement conditions. 'Pray accept my apologies both for the accident and for any further distress I may have caused you. You must allow me to make amends by helping you.'

His voice was low and attractive, and Miss Frensham's ruffled sensibilities began to feel a little soothed. Though at heart a timid woman, the necessity of earning her own living had trained her to be practical. She was still very shocked at the accident but decided that little would be achieved by succumbing to a fit of the vapours. She even allowed the gentleman to take her arm gently and draw her against the side of the carriage, which afforded a little shelter from the wind and rain. His attentions were all that was proper, she assured herself; he was clearly both reliable and, more importantly, well-bred.

'Allow me to present myself and my apologies to you at the

same time, madam,' the gentleman continued. 'I am James Mullineaux, entirely at your service. We must see you conveyed to shelter, but first—am I mistaken in thinking that there was another lady with you in the carriage?'

There was no trace of urgency or alarm in his voice, but Miss Frensham froze and clapped her hand to her mouth with a squeak of horror.

'Alicia! Oh, how could I be so thoughtless?' She grasped James Mullineaux's arm in urgent entreaty. 'Oh, please, sir, could you see what has become of her? We were both knocked to the floor when the coach overturned and I could not rouse her! How could I forget so? I am the veriest monster!'

Her words dissolved into a wail of misery and once more she looked round hopelessly for a handkerchief.

'Do not distress yourself, madam.' Mullineaux pressed his own large handkerchief comfortingly into her hand. 'You have sustained a great shock, you know, and could not be expected to think of everything. Wait here—I will find your friend.'

'She is my charge,' Miss Frensham sniffed, inconsolable, 'and I should have taken greater care of her! Oh, whatever will Lady Stansfield say? I shall never be able to face her again—never!'

Her words had an extraordinary effect on the gentleman, although Miss Frensham was too distraught to notice it. There was a moment of absolute stillness, then he asked expressionlessly, 'Lady Stansfield, ma'am? Would that be the Dowager Countess of Stansfield?'

Miss Frensham sniffed assent, dabbing her eyes with the handkerchief, which was already soaked with rain. She was still too upset and preoccupied to realise that a digression onto rank and title was rather odd in the circumstances.

'Her ladyship is Alicia's grandmother, and much attached to her,' she confirmed. 'I promised to take care of her!'

'Lady Carberry is hardly an infant in arms,' James Mullineaux commented dryly, with more truth than tact. 'Surely she can be expected to take care of herself? She has always managed to do so extremely well in the past!'

This time there was no mistaking the sarcastic edge to his voice.

Miss Frensham looked up, startled out of her preoccupation, but it was too dark to see his face.

'Are you acquainted with Lady Carberry, sir?'

Mullineaux returned no reply, and for a moment Miss Frensham had the oddest feeling that he was about to turn on his heel and walk away. The impression lasted only a moment, then he spoke brusquely. 'I knew Lady Carberry before her marriage.'

Miss Frensham stared in puzzled incomprehension, but Mullineaux said nothing more, merely turning back to the carriage and leaving her standing a little despondently in the road. A moment later, she saw him swing himself up easily into the darkened interior and disappear from her view.

Inside the coach the floor sloped sharply forwards and into the ditch. It was slippery with rain and there was almost no light at all. Nor was there any sound. Mullineaux steadied himself with one hand on the door jamb and paused for his eyes to adjust to the darkness.

Alicia Carberry was lying tumbled in the far corner. A faint glimmer of light touched the pallor of her face and he edged his way cautiously down the sloping floor towards her, bracing himself against one of the thick velvet seats. The creaking of the coach as it settled more deeply in the ditch was hardly reassuring. The rain drummed constantly on the roof.

After making cautious progress for a few moments, Mullineaux was able to kneel down beside Alicia Carberry's recumbent figure and reflect on what he should do next. She was unconscious but still breathing normally and he doubted that she was seriously hurt. However, it would be impossible to check her injuries until he had managed to get her out of the carriage. It seemed a little undignified to drag her across the floor, but he could not safely pick her up inside the carriage in case it toppled over completely. Anyway, in her current state she would scarcely be in a position to notice and he was disinclined to treat her with any particular care or consideration.

Mullineaux managed to get a grip on the material of Lady Carberry's travelling dress and manoeuvre her body back up the sloping floor to the doorway. Once there, it was a simple matter to jump down onto the road and scoop her up into his arms. She did not stir at all, which was probably just as well since it made his job easier and spared her the distress and confusion that would have inevitably followed had she regained consciousness.

She was surprisingly light, and Mullineaux found himself thinking with a certain grim humour that her years as a wealthy widow had evidently not taken their toll in rich living. He could not see her face clearly in the darkness. No matter—he knew exactly what she looked like. More disconcertingly he also recognised the feel of her in his arms, even after the passing of seven years.

'I knew Lady Carberry before her marriage...'

It was a ridiculous understatement from the man to whom she had once been engaged and from whom she had parted in such extraordinary and scandalous circumstances, when she had jilted him for a rich man old enough to be her father. Mullineaux, who had been out of the country since that time, reflected dispassionately on the ironic quirk of fate which had decreed that almost the first person he should meet on his return to England was the woman he wanted at all costs to avoid.

He had known that he would probably have to meet Alicia Carberry again some day. He had every intention of taking up once again his place in society, and he was well aware that Lady Carberry was one of its greatest ornaments and had been so for many years. However, he had anticipated that it would be easy to avoid her and to treat her with cold civility if their paths did cross. The past, after all, was dead, and with it any warmer feelings that he might have held for her.

Now, holding her reluctantly in his arms, he was conscious of an immense irritation at the situation in which he had been placed. But that was not all. Treacherously, dangerously, he became slowly aware of the scent of her skin, the brush of her hair against his cheek, the way her head rested so confidingly in the curve of his shoulder. It was intolerable to still feel an attraction towards her, particularly when his rational mind was telling him how much he disliked her. With a very forcible effort he blanked out the past and shut the door very firmly on his emotions.

As he stepped away from the wreck of the carriage Miss Frensham emerged from the shadows and hurried forward. She had retrieved her reticule, which had gone a long way towards restoring her composure, but she had started to shiver with cold and reaction and looked woefully frail.

'You have found her! God be praised! But—' she peered closer through the rain, pushing Alicia's wet hair off her face '—is she badly hurt, sir?'

'I have no doubt that she will survive,' Mullineaux stated coldly. 'Lady Carberry appears to have sustained a blow to the head, but I think it will not prove too serious, and I doubt that she has broken any bones. You may rest assured that she is strong enough to cope with worse than this.' He gave Miss Frensham a comprehensive look and his tone softened.

'But you are soaked to the skin, ma'am, and no doubt badly chilled, too. This benighted village must surely have an inn of sorts. Let us repair there and see what can be done. If you are able to walk a little way, ma'am, I shall carry Lady Carberry—' was there the slightest of hesitations on the word 'Lady'? '—and we may call a doctor once we are there.'

Miss Frensham did not dissent from this plan. The village of Ottery was a mere five hundred yards distant, and, though it was little more than a hamlet, there should surely be shelter there. James Mullineaux carried his fair burden along the muddy road with a cautiousness born of distaste, not care, while Miss Frensham trotted along by his side. She shivered as the wind hurled flurries of rain in her face and every so often cast anxious glances at Alicia's unconscious form.

The coachman had managed to extricate the carriage horses from their harness and had led them on ahead whilst the groom was now retrieving as much as he could of the luggage. Little could be done for the carriage itself, however, and the coachman and groom, after a muttered discussion, had decided to abandon it until daylight might bring the chance of salvage or at least the opportunity to consult with their employer.

The ill-assorted group had gone about half the way towards the village in silence when Alicia Carberry stirred. The chill of the rain against her face was the first sensation she recognised. She had no notion of where she was, or what had happened to her but she felt the arms about her tighten in response to her involuntary movement and was obscurely comforted.

'Lie still,' Mullineaux instructed in a low voice. 'You are quite safe.' The last thing he wanted at this point was for her to regain consciousness for it would make matters too complicated. The sooner he could deposit her at the inn and leave her, the better.

Alicia immediately relaxed and did as she had been told. She did not know who had spoken and did not really care. There had been something reassuringly familiar about the voice although she could not place it. Her head ached abominably and it was pleasant to rest it against the broad shoulder so invitingly close. For the first time in a long while she relaxed into an unfamiliar feeling of safety and security.

Mullineaux glanced down at her nestling so confidently in his arms. Old passions and memories stirred instinctively within him again and he could not avoid a rush of protectiveness, followed swiftly by a greater rush of anger. Damn it, after all she had done to him, how could he still feel this way? He had not even seen her properly yet, but already he could feel that insidious pull of attraction there had always been between them reasserting itself and threatening to make a fool of him again.

He had been a man of twenty-five when they had first met, no mere stripling, and for some reason the fact that she had so thoroughly duped him then rankled more than if he had been a youth in his salad days. James, Marquis of Mullineaux, with his looks, title and reputation for wildness, was hardly a flat to be taken in by the pretty face of an adventuress. For that was what Alicia Carberry had been.

An adventuress. He faced it squarely. She was the granddaughter of an Earl and under the patronage of her redoubtable grandmother, she was the heiress to a fortune, she had beauty and to spare, but it had not been enough for her. He could still recall with bitterness the last words she had written to him to terminate their betrothal:

'...and so, dear James, I fear I must end our betrothal for I am sure we should not suit. Carberry will make me a much more comfortable husband, and though one should not refine too much on the value of a good financial match it is better than being poor as a church mouse. Your title is worth a great deal, my dear, but sadly not enough...'

As evidence of a grasping nature it could scarcely be surpassed, and after the first blinding flash of disillusionment James Mullineaux had had time to be shocked by both Alicia's sentiments and the fact that she had damned herself so eloquently in writing. That she had only loved his title, not his person he could just about accept, although if he had not seen the letter with his own eyes he would not have believed it of her. She had seemed so innocent, so devoid of conceit or greed. He had thought that he had found a kindred spirit in her, recognising instinctively a bond between them, and yet he had been totally mistaken.

The Mullineaux title was an old one and although in recent years the family's fortunes had dwindled considerably James had still been hunted exhaustively by the matchmaking mamas and their resourceful offspring. He had thought Alicia Carberry different and had been sadly disenchanted. He had been in love for the first time since his youth and not only had his feelings been engaged but his pride had been seriously dented by her defection. His judgement had always been good and he'd found his confidence severely impaired by the way in which she had so cleverly duped him. She had snared him, then ruthlessly dismissed him when a richer prize had come her way.

Such bitter reflections on the past served only to reinforce his antipathy towards Alicia, and by the time they reached Ottery he had his feelings well in hand and viewed her with nothing but strong dislike. The village itself hardly lifted his spirits, for it was the merest huddle of cottages down each side of the road, and though there was indeed an inn its peeling doors were very firmly closed. This did not dissuade Mullineaux, however, who was resolved to rid himself of his burden, and strode firmly up to the main entrance and pulled the bell with determination.

A harsh peal sounded somewhere in the depths of the building and it seemed an unconscionably long time to Miss Frensham, shivering on the doorstep, before there was the sound of footsteps on stone and the bolts were drawn back reluctantly. The door opened a crack to reveal a villainous-looking individual.

'Horses! Carriages! And now this!' the man began indignantly.

'I tell you, we're not open—' But James Mullineaux cut him off ruthlessly.

'There has been an accident on the road,' he began, in tones which brooked no refusal, 'and we are in sore need of shelter. Be so good as to show us to your best parlour and call your wife to attend to these ladies. I take it that my groom and curricle are already in the yard?'

Then, as the landlord still stood gawping on the threshold, he lost his patience.

'Come along, man; we are like to die of cold if you keep us standing here any longer!'

Whatever alarm had previously been raised by the arrival of the curricle, it had not stirred any concern within the landlord, who now sniffed loudly and opened the door only a crack wider. He stumped off down the dimly lit corridor, grumbling at the whims of the gentry and leaving them to follow if they chose. With ill grace he opened one of the doors off the hallway to reveal a dark, mean little room with peeling walls and the unmistakable sound of mice in the wainscot. The stale smell of beer seemed to have seeped into the very fabric of the building. The light was faint, and there was no fire in the grate. Mullineaux looked about him with incredulity, distaste, and a sinking heart.

'It's the best I 'ave to offer,' the landlord said, with no trace of apology. 'Curricle an' horses are out back, but they ain't in no state to travel. Soaked through, the lot of them!'

He gave the bedraggled trio a look which clearly told them that beggars could not be choosers, turned on his heel, and disappeared down the corridor.

Mullineaux, meanwhile, won a brief but violent battle with his temper. It could be some miles to the nearest alternative hostelry and they currently had no means of transport. Lady Carberry might well require the services of a doctor, and Miss Frensham was beginning to look decidedly unwell. He could go out in the rainstorm to search for shelter in a vicarage or sympathetic manor, but he did not know the area well and to approach strangers in that way would involve him in precisely the complicated explanations he wished to avoid. Anything which associated him with Lady Carberry or kept the two of them together for any length of time was anathema to him. He would have had no compunction about abandoning her there and then had it not been for the miserable spectacle of Miss Frensham, dripping onto the taproom floor as she waited in vain for the arrival of the landlady.

No, all he could do for the present, Mullineaux thought with resignation, was to make sure that the ladies were attended to and see what better alternatives presented themselves. He had still not given up hope that he might be able to leave them and travel on further, thereby avoiding all embarrassing confrontations with Lady Carberry, but for now he could not in fairness abandon Miss Frensham alone to the mercies of the landlord.

He deposited Alicia Carberry somewhat unceremoniously in the parlour's only armchair and straightened up. It seemed that she had either lost consciousness once more or fallen asleep, for when Miss Frensham hurried over to her she did not stir. After hovering ineffectually for a moment, Miss Frensham had the happy idea of extracting her smelling salts from her bag and waving these vigorously under Alicia's nose. A few moments later their pungent smell began to have the desired effect.

'She's awake!' Miss Frensham exclaimed excitedly and somewhat superfluously as Alicia moved slightly and opened her eyes, only to close them again immediately. 'Oh, sir—' she turned to Mullineaux, who had been watching her efforts with sardonic amusement and no offer of help '—do you think we should send for the doctor? My poor Alicia, she will be very shaken you know, and perhaps the best thing would be for her to lie down at once!'

'I am perfectly well, Emmy.' Lady Carberry spoke for the first time, making her companion jump. Her voice, normally low and unhurried, sounded a little strained. 'Pray do not trouble to send out for a doctor. You know how I hate fuss! A little rest and perhaps a cup of sweet tea will suffice. I shall feel completely better directly.'

She rested her head on one hand and kept her eyes closed. Miss Frensham, used to her ladyship's decisiveness through long experience, did not trouble to contradict her but pursed her lips with disapproval. She caught the tail-end of an ironic smile from James Mullineaux, which prompted her to look at him more closely. It had begun to dawn on her that the gentleman appeared in no hurry to offer Lady Carberry any further assistance, but still she felt a sudden shock as she assimilated the expression in his eyes as they rested on her charge. She was used to gentlemen surveying Alicia with every shade of expression from shy admiration to blatant lust. She could remember no one, however, who had looked at her with such a very cold, hard dislike. Miss Frensham unconsciously drew herself up straighter.

It was the first opportunity that the companion and the gentleman had had to consider each other properly, and there was some curiosity in the look which they now exchanged. The dim light revealed Miss Frensham to be a little wisp of a lady. Of indeterminate age, she was sensibly dressed in a practical grey cloak over a black bombazine gown, which spoke her calling more clearly than any words. Fussy rows of beads, her only concession to adornment, clashed with each other about her neck. Her hair, which had no doubt started the day neatly curled, was now hanging in damp white strands under her bonnet. She was shivering occasionally and appeared soaked to the skin. Her eyes, large, anxious and grey, moved from Alicia Carberry to James Mullineaux with a puzzled appeal.

Mullineaux turned abruptly to the doorway and gave vent to his feelings by shouting peremptorily for the landlord to come to light the candles and make the fire up immediately. That might at least be achieved, though the cup of sweet tea was looking an increasingly unlikely prospect.

Miss Frensham, for her part, desiccated spinster though she was, was not completely indifferent to the appearance of the gentleman before her. She was familiar both with the gentlemen of *ton* society and with the heroes of the marble-backed books from the circulating library, and James Mullineaux appeared to combine the attributes of both. He had a tall, broad-shouldered physique which any man of fashion would envy, setting off to perfection his immaculate tailoring. Both his eyes and hair were black, which combined with his tanned face to give him an almost piratical air, Miss Frensham thought, a little faintly. She had never seen any pirates, but she knew they would look like this. He might almost be said to possess classical good looks, were it not for the fact that some air of arrogance suggested that he would scorn such an accolade.

His bearing had both the easy assurance of authority and a latent elegance in its economy of movement, but the hint of amusement showing in his eyes at her scrutiny was belied by the hard line of that firm mouth, which betrayed no humour at all. Indeed, there were lines around his mouth which suggested bitterness and unhappiness, rather than a willingness to laugh. Yet a moment later Miss Frensham was obliged to revise that opinion when he smiled at her with quite devastating charm.

She dropped a prim, disapproving curtsey. She was a stickler for convention, and felt instinctively that this man would not conform to any recognised conventions at all. The knowledge was disturbing, but good manners had still to be observed.

'I do not believe that I have thanked you, sir, for your prompt rescue of myself and Lady Carberry,' she said, a little uncertainly. 'Nor have I introduced myself properly. I am Miss Emmeline Frensham, one-time governess and now companion to Alicia, Lady Carberry.'

The gentleman took her hand and raised it to his lips in a gesture so gallant that Miss Frensham felt a most unexpected shiver along her nerves. His smile, she reflected dizzily, was wickedly attractive.

'Although I deplore the circumstances of our meeting, I am most happy to make your acquaintance, Miss Frensham,' he murmured. 'As I mentioned earlier, I am James, Marquis of Mullineaux, very much at your service.'

Miss Frensham's memory had always been tiresomely unreliable, and now at last it suddenly presented her with the reason why James Mullineaux's name had seemed vaguely familiar to her. Her recollection of who he was and his precise connection with Alicia Carberry followed swiftly. Her hand fell from his grasp, her eyes widened to their furthest extent, and her mouth formed a perfectly round, horrified 'O'.

It was at that exact moment that Alicia opened her eyes.

Alicia Carberry was generally held to be a diamond of the first water, although her looks hardly conformed to the accepted standard of beauty of the day. Even James Mullineaux, who held her in such strong dislike, could not deny her physical beauty and now found to his annoyance that he could not tear his gaze away from her.

The hood of Alicia's bronze-coloured cloak had fallen back and her mass of dark auburn hair had escaped its pins and tumbled in glorious profusion about her shoulders. She had inherited the distinctive heart-shaped face that was a feature of her grandmother's family and with it the high cheekbones and determined chin which gave fair warning of her temperament. But it was her eyes that compelled attention, for they were a vivid emerald-green, brilliant and direct, framed by thick black lashes. Not even the unfashionable sprinkling of freckles across the bridge of her small nose could mar Alicia Carberry's looks, for they merely made her seem more endearing, less remotely beautiful.

The faint colour was returning to her face now, and to James Mullineaux she looked at once the same and poignantly different from the nineteen-year-old debutante he had known. Her looks had, if anything, improved with age. There was a sophistication and air of aloofness about her which had replaced the innocence of the country girl fresh to London. Temperamentally too, he sensed that she was far more complicated and interesting.

Alicia raised her head and their eyes met and held for a long moment.

'I thought that it was you,' Alicia said slowly, 'but then I thought I must have imagined it.'

Mullineaux's expression was as blank and unwelcoming as a stone wall and as he seemed disinclined to say anything appropriately gallant or charming in reply to this Miss Frensham rushed into the breach.

'The Marquis was good enough to stop and help us after the carriage accident, my love, and has conveyed us to this inn, where we hope to find refuge!' She looked a little forlorn on this point, since the landlord had not yet reappeared to light the fire and the room was as bleak and unwelcoming as when they had entered it.

Alicia sat up a little straighter, unwrapping her sodden cloak with distaste. She tried to rise, but winced and fell back, closing her eyes for a moment and resting her head against the back of the chair. Miss Frensham made a sound of distress at Alicia's evident discomfort and hurried back to her side, but Mullineaux did not move at all. A minute later, Alicia opened her eyes again and her gaze swept comprehensively from the anxious face of her companion to the Marquis's blank one.

'His lordship stopped to help us, indeed!' she marvelled sweetly. 'How very chivalrous of him! I remember little about it, of course, but was not he the cause of the accident in the first place? I am sure that I recall something of the sort—assuming that he was the driver of that curricle which flashed past us with such wicked speed!'

This outrageous statement threw down the gauntlet with a vengeance, and the direct challenge in Alicia's eyes only served to underline it.

She had been aware of Mullineaux's antipathy from the moment that she regained consciousness; the air positively crackled with it. The suddenness of the encounter had left her with no time to examine her own feelings but she responded instinctively to his animosity. So he held her in contempt, did he? She had no very high opinion of him, if it came to that! Here was a man whose protestations of love had meant so little that when her father had forced her into marriage with another he had stood by and said not one word against the match. Worse, he had damaged her reputation irrevocably with his denouncement of her as a fortune-hunter.

Pride had always been the besetting sin of the Mullineaux family, Alicia thought resentfully. James Mullineaux had been unable to bear the whispers and gossip of the *ton*; he had moved to disassociate himself from her immediately it appeared he would be tainted with scandal. Her disillusion had been intense; helplessly in love, hopelessly inexperienced, she had waited stubbornly like the heroine of a romance for James to arrive and rescue her. Even after her father had forced her to send the letter breaking the engagement, she had confidently believed that she and James Mullineaux were so close, so attuned, that he would instantly know it for the fraud it was.

It had not been so. As the days had stretched to a week, Alicia had begun to realise that something was wrong. Finally her father had triumphantly shown her a copy of a scandal sheet in which her own identity was very thinly veiled indeed in a cruel story relating how the lovely, duplicitous Miss B had been scorned as an adventuress by the handsome Marquis who had previously been at her feet.

Alicia determinedly pushed her memories back into the past where they belonged, and met Mullineaux's contemptuous look with an equally acerbic one of her own.

'Your own carriage, madam, was travelling at a pace hardly considerate to other road users,' Mullineaux said coolly. 'I had no time to react to your sudden appearance other than in the way I did. I am, however, relieved to discover that a knock on the head has in no way impaired your faculties. You appear to be remarkably resilient, but then I already knew that to be so!'

'You, on the other hand, are no more gallant, sir!'

Such an inimical look immediately flashed between the pair of them that Miss Frensham once more attempted to be conciliatory.

'It's true, you know, my dear, we were travelling very fast! We were late leaving Glastonbury, if you recall, and you did tell Jack to spring the horses!'

'So I did.' There was a glint of amusement in Alicia's look which did nothing to calm her companion's fears. For a moment Miss Frensham indulged in the uncharitable wish that Alicia had been completely incapacitated by her injury. This miraculous recovery of hers was proving to be most uncomfortable. Miss Frensham knew Alicia very well and had already divined that her ladyship intended to be very difficult indeed. As for Mullineaux, he was looking so forbidding that Miss Frensham doubted she would get any help there.

She pursed her lips. She had been Alicia's governess until her charge had been sent to Miss Hannah More's school in Bath, and had later assumed the role of companion upon Alicia's widowhood. In the intervening years had occurred Alicia's London Season, under the aegis of her grandmother, Lady Stansfield—and the ill-fated betrothal to the Marquis of Mullineaux. Alicia had never spoken to Miss Frensham of her broken engagement and subsequent hasty marriage, and Miss Frensham had been far too well-bred to pry, but she could tell that some very painful memories still troubled Lady Carberry. As for the Marquis of Mullineaux, he had gone abroad immediately after Alicia had jilted him and tales of his exploits on the Continent and in Ireland had filtered back to Society over the years. As far as Miss Frensham knew, this was the first time he had returned to England since then.

'What a very great surprise to meet with you here, Lord Mullineaux,' Alicia was saying with a syrupy sweetness which somehow managed to convey that meeting him was the least pleasant aspect of their current situation. 'I am sure everyone had thought you settled abroad this past age... Italy, was it, or perhaps France? What can have brought you back to England? Your grandfather, perhaps... He is quite well?'

Her words were courteous but Mullineaux chose to read into them an implication which was in all probability there. Despite his lengthy sojourn abroad he was still heir to his grandfather, the Duke of Cardace, whose health had taken a decided turn for the worse recently. The Duke was one of the premier landowners in Britain. Mullineaux flushed at the suspected insinuation, but managed a tolerably polite reply.

'His Grace is well, I thank you, ma'am.' His tone showed how plain was his dislike of having to converse with her. 'I am, in fact, on my way from Cardace Hall now. I landed at Plymouth but two weeks ago, and made my grandfather my first call.'

'Such devotion,' marvelled Alicia in dulcet tones. 'I do not wonder at it. Your grandfather is very rich, is he not?'

Now the implication could not be missed, and Miss Frensham drew her breath in sharply at such pointed bad manners. She hurried in with a question of her own. 'And do you intend to settle back in England now, my lord?'

Mullineaux's face immediately lightened as he turned to her. 'I hope to do so, ma'am. Now, by your leave, I will go and rout out the landlord. You need some light, a fire and a warm drink, not to mention rooms for the night. Then I shall go to the stables and see how matters progress there.'

Miss Frensham opened her mouth to thank him but was forestalled.

'So eager to escape us, Lord Mullineaux?' Alicia asked, mockingly, from her armchair. 'No time for pleasantries, and such indecent haste!'

This time she had the satisfaction of seeing James Mullineaux provoked into anger. His dark eyes narrowed in a way Miss Frensham could only describe as murderous. 'I would not choose to stay here a moment longer than I must,' he ground out and, turning on his heel, stalked from the room.

'There now,' Miss Frensham said exasperatedly into the sudden silence, 'look what you've done! Was there any need for that, Miss Alicia? I didn't know you had it in you to be so ill-bred!'

Alicia had the grace to look a little ashamed. Such strictures were very uncommon from her normally timid companion, but she knew she had behaved extremely badly. She leant against the chair-back for a moment and closed her eyes. Her head was aching and she felt very close to tears. She had dreamed plenty of times about meeting James Mullineaux again. Why did it have to be like this? She turned her head to look at Miss Frensham, who was fussing with the ribbons of her cloak and laying it out to dry over a chest in the corner of the room.

'I know it was very bad of me, Emmy, but he evidently despises me and I cannot abide being treated in such a way!' Alicia's face took on a mutinous look. 'I will *not* allow Mullineaux to judge me, not when he was as much at fault as I! If he had ever cared a jot for me he would have known that the breaking of our engagement was none of my doing!'

She warmed to her theme, her eyes flashing. 'But he chose to believe the worst of me—and did not scruple to tell everyone else so! Oh!' It came out with a vehemence she could not hide. 'Of all the pieces of bad luck—to be obliged to spend some time in enforced contact with Mullineaux!'

This somewhat jumbled speech led Miss Frensham to conclude that Alicia was genuinely upset and she relented a little. Lady Carberry was normally the most serene of characters, at least superficially. But then, Miss Frensham thought a little sadly, she had never seen anyone move Alicia beyond the superficial. No man had had the power to affect her in all the years Miss Frensham had acted as her companion—until now. The Marquis of Mullineaux had achieved in five minutes an impact no one else had even approached in five years.

'Well, to be sure it was very bad of him to behave so, but that is all in the past now!' Miss Frensham observed, in an attempt to console. 'Can you not at least *try* to be civil to him? After all, he has done us a considerable service in rescuing us both! I had not the least idea he was back in this country,' she added reflectively, 'but if the two of you are to meet at all in future, my love, you will need to preserve at least a semblance of politeness!'

'I see no reason to speak with him at all,' Alicia returned, sulkily, but there was the glint of tears in her eyes and Miss Frensham sensibly chose to let the matter drop. It was very unusual to see Alicia put so out of countenance. Although she was renowned for possessing the fabled temper of the Stansfields, this loss of control was quite another matter. No doubt she had been more shaken by the accident than she would care to admit.

'Let me have that sodden cloak, my dear,' she urged, changing the subject and coming across to help Alicia to her feet. 'Indeed, I am sure I do not know how long it will be before we get a fire in here! This really is too bad! No fire, no bedchambers, and no doubt no one to go for a doctor!'

'I do not need a doctor,' Alicia repeated fretfully. 'Truly, Emmy, I shall be very well with a little rest.' She let Miss Frensham take the cloak from her and place it across the back of the chair, shivering slightly in the damp air. The matching bronze travelling dress beneath was not damp, for Alicia had not been out in the rain for as long as Miss Frensham, but her right wrist was starting to ache badly. She was determined not to mention it and add to her companion's anxieties.

Shaking out her skirts, Alicia cast her first critical glance around the room and gave a silent sigh. Not only mental turmoil to contend with, but physical discomfort as well! Her gaze moved thoughtfully on to Miss Frensham and she was concerned by what she saw. There was a hectic flush in that lady's cheek and a glitter in her eyes which Alicia did not like the look of at all.

'It looks as though you are the one in need of a doctor's attentions, Emmy,' she observed judiciously. 'You must have taken a chill. Since Lord Mullineax has evidently failed to raise the landlord, I shall do so myself. We must see you to a bed immediately!'

Miss Frensham gave a muffled groan. She had suddenly started to feel very unwell with the combined effects of the soaking and the worry of it all, but it made her feel even worse to contemplate

Alicia wandering the corridors of an alehouse alone. Not that Lady Carberry, being a widow, required chaperonage in the sense an unmarried girl would, but Miss Frensham was a dragon for preserving the proprieties—it was one of the reasons that Alicia had employed her. She sat down rather suddenly in the chair Alicia had recently vacated.

'Oh, no, my love, you cannot go looking for the landlord! I feel sure that he will be here directly, and only imagine if you should meet anyone; we should be quite undone!'

'Nonsense, Emmy,' Alicia said robustly. She was already halfway to the door. 'This is no time to be worrying about the conventions! I am well able to take care of myself, and besides, there is nobody else here!'

Whatever reply Miss Frensham might have given was drowned out by a sudden noise outside the inn. Alicia moved across to the grimy window to try to see what was happening but the rain was lashing down so violently now that it was too dark to see anything at all. A moment later the doorbell pealed sharply. Alicia and Miss Frensham exchanged a look and Miss Frensham stifled another moan. This was the worst thing that could befall them, alone and unprotected in a seedy alehouse—she had temporarily forgotten the dubious protection available from the Marquis—with goodness only knew what kind of disreputable travellers about to burst in on them.

'Who could possibly be out on such a night? Oh, Lady Carberry, I fear we shall be ravished in our beds—or worse!'

Alicia forbore to point out that they did not even have any beds in which to be ravished, for she did not think this would help. In silence they waited. Once more it was an extraordinarily long time before they heard the sound of the landlord's reluctant footsteps and the drawing back of the squeaky bolt. There was a swift, decisive but indistinguishable altercation in the corridor, and suddenly the parlour door was thrown open and the room appeared to be full of people, all talking at once.

The landlord was in full flow, involved in a heated exchange with a large and forceful lady. A portly, middle-aged gentleman was also present, talking and gesticulating wildly. Just as matters appeared to be getting out of hand, the lady made a dismissive gesture and accosted Alicia across the room.

'So it *was* your carriage, Lady Carberry! I thought I recognised it, and obliged John to stop here to see if there was aught we could do to help!' She was a plump, comfortable-looking woman of middling years and she shook the nerveless Miss Frensham by the hand with the warmth of an old friend, before turning back to Alicia with a quick look of concern.

'My dears, are either of you hurt in any way? Lady Carberry, you are looking a trifle pale, if you will forgive me! Can we be of service to you?' She cast an unfavourable look around the room. 'Indeed, you cannot possibly stay here! John, tell them they must not stay!'

'Indeed, my dear ma'am, you cannot stay here!' her husband echoed obligingly.

The landlord, who had at last lit the candles and started to make up the fire, glared at them, but Mrs Henley ignored him with superb indifference. As the wife of the local squire she considered all village matters to be her business and made no secret of the fact that she thought the Crown and Anchor inn a disgrace in terms of hospitality. She repeated her offer of help energetically and it was a moment before Alicia could get a word in.

'We are well enough, thank you, ma'am,' Alicia replied, with a smile, when at last the flow of words had ceased. 'Neither Miss Frensham nor I too much the worse for our accident, but I am afraid that she may have taken a chill.'

Mrs Henley had just turned back to Miss Frensham with an exclamation of alarm and sympathy that had that lady shrinking back in her chair, when the parlour door opened again and James Mullineaux strode in. He seemed unperturbed to find the room so full of visitors and strolled forward with easy charm to make their acquaintance.

After a swift glance at Alicia, who was standing stubbornly silent, Miss Frensham struggled to her feet and made the introductions in a failing voice.

'Mrs Henley, this is the Marquis of Mullineaux, who was so good as to assist us after the accident.' She ignored Alicia's snort of disgust and ploughed on. 'My lord, may I make you known to the Squire and Mrs Henley, who have stopped to offer us their help?'

Mrs Henley's shrewd brown eyes opened a little wider as she registered Mullineaux's name, but she was too well-bred to show curiosity. She also noted that Alicia's mouth was set in lines of obstinate dislike, and that, for his part, Mullineaux viewed her with no less antagonism. She became even more interested as Mullineaux launched into an easy explanation of the presence of so ill-assorted a group in such a small village on such a bad night. No inquisitive questions were required on her part whatsoever, for Mullineaux seemed determined to make the details of their unfortunate encounter crystal-clear in order to avoid the suspicion that he and Alicia had intended to meet.

Alicia stood listening to his admirably factual explanation of their accident with growing irritation. He showed nothing but the most impersonal concern for Miss Frensham's welfare and none whatsoever for her own. Mrs Henley missed none of the nuances, and, watching Alicia covertly, concluded that there was a very interesting by-play going on between the two of them.

'And so, ma'am, sir, if you would be so good as to recommend a more reputable hostelry, I should have no further worries about the safety of these ladies,' Mullineaux finished smoothly. 'I, alas, am fixed here for the night as my cattle are chilled to the bone and it is now too late for me to continue my journey. However, I am sure that the landlord could muster a gig to convey the ladies a short distance.'

'Lord Mullineaux is anxious to be rid of us, ma'am,' Alicia said with so much honey in her tone that Mrs Henley was barely able to suppress a smile. 'We are a sad burden on him.' She looked down at Miss Frensham drooping in her chair and added silkily, 'There is one aspect of Lord Mullineaux's commendable speech with which I would disagree, however. It does not seem to me desirable to subject Miss Frensham to the rigours of another uncomfortable journey. I am sure we shall do very well here.'

There was a flash of irritation in Mullineaux's eyes and as he drew breath for a scathing remark Mrs Henley hastened into the breach, much as Miss Frensham had done earlier.

'I will not hear of you putting up at this or any other inn tonight,

Lady Carberry,' she said decisively. 'Ottery Manor is but a short distance from here and I am happy to convey you both there immediately as our guests. Nonsense.' She cut across Alicia's protests decisively. 'It will be a pleasure!' She turned courteously to Mullineaux. 'You are also most welcome to join us at the Manor, Lord Mullineaux!'

Alicia watched with malicious pleasure as Mullineaux tried to think of a way to decline without giving offence. She knew full well that only his dislike for her was prompting him to stay at the inn and refuse Mrs Henley's invitation.

'Alas, ma'am,' Mullineaux was saying with every evidence of sincere regret, 'I would be honoured to accept were it not for the fact that I must continue my journey at first light. I would not wish to inconvenience you in any way, and I am sure I shall do very well here.'

He could not be persuaded otherwise and eventually Mrs Henley accepted his refusal with resignation, not in the least fooled as to the reason for it. Bowing to them all but Alicia, who got the curtest of nods, Mullineaux went out to bespeak his lonely supper.

A smile twitched Mrs Henley's lips. She had never met the Marquis of Mullineaux before, but rumour certainly had not lied about him. He was without doubt a very attractive man and a formidably determined one. It was also beyond doubt that Lord Mullineaux wanted nothing more to do with Lady Carberry and viewed this whole incident as a profound nuisance. Meanwhile Lady Carberry herself, unaccustomed to being disliked, resented such cavalier treatment and could be very provocative when she chose. Lady Carberry was not spoilt, Mrs Henley reflected fairly, but it was unusual for men not to fall at her feet. Even the squire, who had never given Mrs Henley a moment's worry in twenty-five years of marriage, was gawping like a foolish schoolboy, ready to leap to Alicia's aid if required.

Alicia was looking particularly lovely in the candlelight, with her hair drying in tangled curls and the fire bringing a glow of colour to her almost translucent complexion. But clearly James Mullineaux was immune and, remembering the past history of Alicia and the Marquis, Mrs Henley could not really be surprised at it.

She had heard all the slanderous talk—the hastily arranged marriage to the grossly libidinous George Carberry, the sudden death of the bridegroom on the wedding night—from over-excitement, so the wags said—the bitter denunciation by James Mullineaux of his former betrothed, the wild tales that had circulated in the clubs... Alicia Carberry's name had been dragged through the mud so thoroughly that it had been thought she would never recover.

Mrs Henley had always had her own theory about the hastily arranged marriage to George Carberry. She gave no credence to any of the wilder tales about Alicia, but suspected that the Carberry match had been forced on her by her father. In the county of Somerset, Bertram Broseley's ruthless dealings were known at first hand, from the money he had made from the slave trade to the hard-driven land deals which had enabled him to expand his own estate immeasurably. Broseley was quite the most unpleasant man of Mrs Henley's acquaintance, and she was sure he would not scruple to use his own children as a business asset.

Time could bring about great changes, Mrs Henley reflected. The enormous social power of the Dowager Countess of Stansfield had been brought into play to help rebuild her granddaughter's place in Society, and after a while those who had been disposed to censure Alicia had seen only a rich and beautiful widow who had made an improvident marriage. Seven years had passed in which the lovely Lady Carberry had been courted by Society's most eligible bachelors, but had shown no sign of remarrying.

Mrs Henley frowned slightly, drawing on her gloves. Mullineaux's return from Ireland would whet the appetites of even the most jaded of society's gossips, she thought, with a certain degree of speculative interest. He was a vastly handsome man with a certain reputation as far as women were concerned, and there would be any number willing to put it to the test. And then there was the delicate matter of his future relationship with Lady Carberry. This unexpected meeting must have been embarrassing for both of them, and no doubt the fur would fly in the future. It was going to be a very interesting Season.

The door closed behind Mullineaux and Mrs Henley turned her warm smile upon Alicia, who was still looking a little dubious at foisting both herself and Miss Frensham unexpectedly on the Henleys' hospitality.

'I have guests already, Lady Carberry, and shall be happy to augment the party,' Mrs Henley reassured her comfortably. 'However, therein lies the only problem—my visitors are in the carriage outside, neglected shamefully, I know, but I hope they will forgive me! However, it means that I have room to take up only one more person at present. So perhaps—' she turned to Miss Frensham '—if you do not mind waiting, dear ma'am, I will take Lady Carberry to the Manor now, and send the coach back for you directly.'

Miss Frensham, who had been in a feverish doze in her chair, started to agree, but Alicia interrupted quickly. 'By your leave, ma'am, Miss Frensham has been exposed to the rain for longer than I, and is of frailer disposition. I should be happier if you could take her up first and return for me.'

Mrs Henley and Miss Frensham exchanged a look. Miss Frensham stood up shakily.

'It would be most singular, my love, to leave you here alone,' she observed carefully, worry reflected in her grey eyes. 'I am grateful for your consideration, but I will do very well here for a little longer. Perhaps—' her face brightened '—we could both wait, ma'am, if you will be so good as to send the carriage back for us when you have delivered your guests.'

It would have been the best plan, but Alicia was so used to taking decisions that she hardly hesitated.

'Stuff and nonsense, Emmy—you are shivering with ague,' she said strongly. 'You must get into the warmth as soon as possible. As for the proprieties—for I take it that is what concerns you—I doubt Lord Mullineaux will even return before the carriage comes back to collect me, and even if he does the landlady may stand my chaperon for five minutes! I beg you, ma'am—' she turned to Mrs Henley '—do not let us delay you any longer!'

Mrs Henley nodded. 'Very well, it shall be as you wish, Lady Carberry! Come, ma'am—' she took Miss Frensham's arm '—we will have you right in no time! I have a herbal mixture which is sovereign against the ague!'

So it was settled, and, whatever her private qualms, a secretly grateful Miss Frensham went out to the carriage.

Chapter Two

Ten minutes later, James Mullineaux re-entered the parlour from the direction of the stables, whistling under his breath.

Whistling! How very pleased he must be to be rid of us! Alicia thought crossly. Nevertheless, there was a hollow feeling in the pit of her stomach as she contemplated having to deal with him without Miss Frensham's soothing presence, and she smoothed the material of her dress down in an unconsciously nervous gesture.

Mullineaux stopped dead on seeing Alicia sitting alone before the fire and a swift frown descended on his brow. His dark hair was ruffled from the wind and he brought with him from outside the scents of fresh air and leather. The casual shooting jacket fitted his broad shoulders to advantage and despite the events of the previous hour his buckskins were clean and fitted to perfection. Only his topboots indicated that he had spent some time wading through the mud outside. Realising suddenly that she was staring, Alicia removed her gaze to his face and surprised there a look which could only be described as antagonistic. Her nerves tightened.

'What's this? I understood you to have gone to the Manor with Mrs Henley!' There was a dangerous control in the Marquis's quiet voice.

'Miss Frensham has gone with Mrs Henley,' Alicia said, with more composure than she was feeling. 'There was only room for one in the carriage and Miss Frensham has, I think, already started to develop a chill. The carriage will return for me shortly, my lord.'

Mullineaux appeared to be having difficulty in grasping what she was saying. He ran a hand through his dishevelled black hair, which only served to make him look even more attractive. Alicia noticed, and chided herself for being so susceptible. Unfortunately it seemed all too possible to find someone physically attractive whilst simultaneously disliking them intensely.

'You have sent Miss Frensham on ahead and stayed here alone?' Mullineaux repeated, carefully expressionless, looking at Alicia with something approaching incredulity. He crossed the room and turned to face her, his back to the fire.

Alicia, feeling intimidated and determined not to show it, rose to her feet. She met his eyes squarely. 'That is correct, my lord. Miss Frensham is not feeling at all well and it seemed only right that she should be taken to shelter immediately!'

The astonishment in Mullineaux's dark eyes was turning swiftly to anger. 'It may have been the right thing to do, but it was hardly wise!'

Feeling her own temper rising, Alicia decided to be deliberately obtuse. He really knew how to bring out the worst in her. 'Why, whatever can you mean, my lord?' she enquired coolly.

Mullineaux looked exasperated. 'I cannot believe you so naive as to fail to understand me! It would be unexceptionable for a lady of advanced years to be alone here with me. It is rather more singular for you to choose to stay here unchaperoned!'

He was, of course, quite correct. As a widow Alicia had a certain latitude of behaviour allowed to her that was denied unmarried girls, but even so she could not expect to retain her reputation for virtue by spending time alone with a man in an isolated inn. Given the circumstances of their previous relationship it was particularly unfortunate. Alicia mentally acknowledged this, but she was scarcely going to give Mullineaux the satisfaction of agreeing with him. She shrugged with every appearance of nonchalance.

'Oh, I do not have such a slavish regard for the conventions! You refine too much upon this, my lord!'

'I see.' His expression was contemptuous. 'I can only assume that your reputation was lost so long ago that it is of little consequence to you. Or perhaps—' he looked at her thoughtfully '—you deliberately contrived to stay here with me?'

Alicia had inherited her grandmother's temper along with the red hair. Normally it lay fairly well-buried, but now she could feel her control slipping away rapidly. Damn his presumptuousness! 'What a very good opinion you must have of your own attractions, Lord Mullineaux!' she said scathingly. 'Alas, I must disillusion you. There is no basis for your arrogance—I scarce chose to stay here in order to be with you! And you may acquit me of any attempt to compromise you! I assure you, you are quite safe with me!'

'Thank you for your reassurances, madam,' Mullineaux snapped. 'It is gratifying to know that you are more concerned for my reputation than for your own! I suppose I should not be surprised by your comments. Seven years ago you made it abundantly clear that you did not wish for my company. At least you are consistent!'

Even as he spoke, half of Mullineaux's mind was marvelling at the speed with which they had jettisoned polite convention and slipped into conflict. He was well aware that Alicia had been deliberately trying to provoke him all afternoon and that she had succeeded in getting under his guard very easily. Her unwanted company was a complication he could well have done without. His anger was intensified by the discovery that he was hardly indifferent to her. He might reasonably have expected the passage of seven years to have weakened, if not destroyed, any appeal she had once held for him. It was infuriating that this was not so.

Alicia herself was both angry and confused by their mutual antipathy. Whilst it would have been impossible to imagine that they could ever be on friendly terms, this instinctive antagonism was difficult to deal with. An icy reserve would have been more her usual style, but, shaken out of her habitual cool composure, she was unable to get back onto the sort of footing with Mullineaux that might at least have enabled them to preserve the minimum of cold civility. Whilst she struggled to regain lost ground, Mullineaux pushed them further into conflict.

'You say that I am safe from your attentions, ma'am.' He gave her a dispassionate look that was so indicative of scorn it brought the colour up into Alicia's face. 'Have you considered that you may not be safe from mine? Behaviour such as your own is an open invitation!'

'It might be construed as such by a man of your stamp!' Alicia pushed the heavy waves of burnished hair away from her face with a hand that was shaking. 'You never could believe yourself resistible, could you, Mullineaux?'

The tone of this extraordinary conversation could only degenerate further.

'I had heard that you were enjoying to the full the licence your widowed state allows you!' Mullineaux took a step towards her. 'It is what I would have expected. And it ill becomes you to play the innocent now, Lady Carberry. Had I realised that all candidates for your hand in marriage had to be old, rich and degenerate I should never have troubled you with my attentions! Not,' he added coolly, 'that it is marriage that is on my mind at the moment—far from it! But now that I understand you better, perhaps we could find a more interesting way of passing our time here?'

Alicia whitened. Her own comments had been provocative, but she was shocked by the ruthless cruelty of his response. He evidently considered her to have lost every shred of reputation and to be fair game for his advances. She had been in society long enough to recognise that she had tested his precarious self-control to the limit by the attitude she had assumed. He could not know that her apparent lack of regard for the conventions was mere bravado. In fact, she had reinforced his own prejudices by her wanton disregard for propriety. She struggled to regain some lost ground before it was too late.

'Your comments are both inaccurate and discourteous, sir! Pray do not make arrogant assumptions when your knowledge is so incomplete! Added to which, I find that strictures on behaviour come somewhat strangely from you! A man who abandons his responsibilities for seven years for the pursuit of pleasure is not in a strong position to criticise the behaviour of others!'

'Pray do not make arrogant assumptions, madam!' Mullineaux said, through his teeth. His look of scorn swept over her comprehensively, from copper curls to kid slippers. He did not even hesitate. 'At least I have never sold myself for a fortune!'

Even as he was speaking, he knew that he had gone too far, but her false protestations of innocence had infuriated him, and her comments on his own behaviour had touched a raw nerve. The tension that had been building between them from the very first moment had reached such an intensity that it had to defuse itself somehow.

As for Alicia, she was conscious only of her anger and resentment building with searing intensity. She wanted only to hurt him for the pain he had so carelessly inflicted. She raised her hand to strike him, but Mullineaux read her intentions quickly enough to prevent it finding its mark. He caught her wrist in an unbreakable grip. Their eyes locked in furious confrontation.

And then it happened. Mullineaux's hand slid from wrist to elbow in a caress that made Alicia shiver, but no longer with nerves. It had always been like this—like recognised like and reacted instinctively, and the conflict between them gave the attraction an edge that had not previously existed. Rational thought was suspended as he drew her closer. She could not tear her gaze away from his, realising that whatever it was that drove her also had him in its compulsive grip.

A corner of Alicia's mind acknowledged that in another second he would kiss her and she would not be able to resist, would not want to resist, and then God alone knew what might happen....

The door of the parlour opened and the landlord entered. Mullineaux dropped Alicia's wrist and stepped back unhurriedly, and the landlord smirked meaningfully in their direction.

'Road's flooded over by Ottery Down,' he said with gloomy relish. 'Ain't no ways they'll get a carriage through there from the Manor.' He peered out of the parlour window at the dark sky. 'Still rainin' too,' he remarked with obvious satisfaction. His gaze darted from James Mullineaux to Alicia and back again. 'Reckon you'll be needin' that room, sir!'

'Make that two rooms, please, landlord,' Alicia said hastily, and turned away from both the landlord's knowing leer and James Mullineaux's too penetrating gaze. She felt sick and shaken with reaction after what had just passed between them. Her injured wrist had started to ache badly and she put the other hand up to it, wincing as she touched it. It was nothing to the pain she felt inside.

How could they have quarrelled so horribly when they had only just met again? And then for her to almost fall straight into his arms as though she were as promiscuous as he suspected her! And the final and all too predictable disaster of them being stranded together... Everything in the world felt so irrevocably wrong that Alicia was sure it could never be right again.

James Mullineaux did not appear similarly disturbed. The driven quality of a moment before had left him and he seemed once more the cold, remote stranger. He put up a hand to halt the landlord as he was leaving the room.

'Bring me some bandages, if you please,' he instructed quietly, then, at the landlord's look of dumbstruck amazement, he added with an edge of sarcasm, 'You do have such a thing in the house, I presume?'

'A horse bandage is the best I've got,' the landlord said churlishly. 'Will that do for your Honour?'

Alicia could have sworn that Mullineaux nearly smiled. 'That will have to do,' he said. He caught her look of mingled surprise and hostility, and added expressionlessly, 'Your wrist clearly pains you. You will do better with it bandaged up until you can see a doctor.'

His consideration had the effect of making Alicia feel even worse. It would have been more in character, she thought numbly, for him to tear her off a strip for her folly in causing this whole disaster. She hoped fervently that she would soon awake from this nightmare but it seemed unlikely.

James Mullineaux was standing before the fire watching her with an incalculable expression she found most disconcerting. He did not say a word about their recent argument or about the coil they now found themselves in, no doubt believing that the facts spoke for themselves. Perversely, Alicia wished he would say something, anything, to break that intolerable silence. She did not wish to feel beholden to him.

'Thank you for your thoughtfulness,' she said, trying not to sound ungracious, 'but surely the landlady could tend to my wrist?'

Mullineaux raised a sardonic eyebrow. 'I have not even seen evidence that there is a landlady, let alone assessed her ability to minister to the sick! If my help is so repugnant to you, you will just have to suffer the pain! Make your choice!'

Alicia's face flamed. For once she floundered for words.

'I did not mean...I did not say...I am grateful to you for your offer of help, but—'

'The landlord is returning with the bandage,' Mullineaux interrupted her laconically. 'You had better make up your mind! What's it to be? Common-sense or pride?'

Alicia acquiesced with ill grace. Somehow he had made her feel like a gauche schoolgirl, and an unappreciative one at that. She sat down and watched him untie the bandage, extending her arm unwillingly, as though his touch would burn her. Her wrist showed faint marks of bruising and was already beginning to swell. Mullineaux probed it gently, looking up as Alicia could not avoid a small gasp of pain.

'Not broken, I think,' he said thoughtfully, 'but a nasty sprain. If you will bear with me a little longer whilst I bind it up, that should ease the discomfort.'

His long, tanned fingers were deft and gentle as he bandaged the wrist with impersonal skill. To her horror, Alicia found her throat had closed with tears—tears which she was determined not to shed. She looked down at his bent head as he knelt next to her chair. The candlelight turned his dark hair the blue of a raven's wing and cast the exaggerated shadow of his eyelashes along the line of his cheek. Alicia was swept by a physical longing so intense it hurt her. All the feelings she had buried deep had been exposed in the most sudden and cruel way possible. She wanted to throw herself into his arms and cry away all the pain and misery of the last seven years.

She bit her lip viciously to hold back the tears and pulled her sleeve further back out of his way. As she did so, the slender bracelet she always wore slid down her arm and caught the light, the glow from the fire sliding over its intricate gold and silver tracery. Mullineaux's gaze fastened on it, drawn by the sudden glitter. For a moment he stared at it, completely still, then he looked up into her eyes with the dawning of puzzlement and disbelief in his own. It had been his betrothal gift to her and she always wore it.

True Colours

It was too much. The accumulated shock of the accident, the strain caused by seeing Mullineaux again and his evident dislike for her, the impossibility of ever having the opportunity to explain the past to him—all these combined to drown Alicia in a huge wave of grief. With a sob she tore her arm half-bandaged from his grip and ran out of the room to seek sanctuary, any sanctuary, away from his astonished gaze and disturbing presence.

Alicia got very little sleep that night. The best bedchamber the inn had to offer was a bleak garret facing north and battered by the storm which raged outside. The walls were cold and damp to the touch, and the sheets were no better.

At first Alicia curled up on the bed and cried as if her heart would break, too unhappy to think of anything at all except the huge weight of her own misery. Such a flood of tears could not last for ever, though, and when she was at last drained and exhausted she looked up and shivered at the grim, grey room with its icy chill. The solid warmth and comfort of Ottery Manor, a mere half-mile distant, could only be imagined but even though she was desperate Alicia rejected the idea of trying to walk there and no doubt developing pneumonia in the process.

She got up, lit a candle and washed her face in the stale water from the pitcher, peering at her unprepossessing appearance in the speckled mirror. Alicia was not vain, for Miss Frensham had successfully managed to instill in her a respect of person, not appearance. However, the red-rimmed eyes which looked back at her from a deathly pale face did make her shudder. She felt suddenly hungry, but was too tired to bother with the effort of requesting a meal which would as likely as not be inedible. She wrapped herself in her cloak, blew out her candle and lay down on the bed. She found that she could not think at all; her mind appeared to be completely frozen. Soon she fell into a light doze.

Some unmeasurable time later Alicia was disturbed by a tapping sound and before she awoke sufficiently to enquire who was there the door opened and a thin, pale woman entered carrying a tray. She marched into the bedchamber and deposited her load on the chest of drawers with something of a crash, then turned to Alicia rather defiantly.

'The gentleman below insisted that I bring this to you, miss. He thought you might wish to partake of some food but prefer not to come downstairs. I'll leave it here for you.'

Her sniff and the toss of her head were indicative both of her unwillingness in performing the errand and her opinion of members of the so-called gentry who managed to get themselves into such compromising situations. She gave Alicia a look full of contemptuous curiosity and did not wait for any response but marched out in the same manner in which she had entered.

Alicia moved the tray onto the small bedside table and looked at its contents dubiously. The game pie was cold, but it turned out to be tasty enough to tempt her into eating a little and she found the wine pleasantly reviving in its effect. After she had finished she sat quite still, trying to decide what to do. The process took a long time, for her head was still aching with the aftermath of sleep and her mind was understandably reluctant to face the facts of her situation. She could get up and go downstairs, but the prospect of confronting James Mullineaux again so soon filled her with horrified embarrassment.

Although she acknowledged his kindness in thinking of sending her some food, she scarcely felt able to sit down with him to a game of cards to while away the evening! She had no books or needlework with her and there could be little else the inn would offer in the way of entertainment. Besides, she felt suddenly tired and light-headed from the wine, and her wrist, which she had finished bandaging inexpertly herself, was aching badly. In the end she merely wrapped the cloak about her again and lay down on the threadbare bedspread.

It seemed that the thoughts and memories which she had kept at bay whilst she was awake could not be denied, for as soon as she was asleep she began to dream almost immediately.

The scene was familiar: the ballroom at Stansfield House, lavishly decorated as it had been seven years previously on the night of Alicia's come-out ball with a richly coloured fresco of harvest fruits and an extravagant display of real, exotic fruit and flowers. The room was full of music and chatter, rainbow colours and ostentatious jewellery, as the cream of the *ton* mingled and gossiped, all so eager to see the new sensation that they had begged, borrowed or stolen an invitation. Alicia herself, slender in a white dress overlaid with silver net, moved through the crowded rooms and could feel the thrill and excitement of the evening almost tangible on the air.

The dream continued in a blur of laughter and music. Alicia had no concept of time passing as she danced every dance. Then suddenly everything slowed down and became sharper than crystal as she relived moment by moment all that had happened next...

It was the supper interval and Alicia was swept up into the group of people surrounding her friend, Caroline Oxley. She felt immediately welcome in the circle of friends, included in their light-hearted banter and with several of the young men making their admiration for her very plain. The food was delicious, the company great fun, and Alicia was thoroughly enjoying her introduction into society.

There was a lull in the conversation, and Alicia looked up to see a girl seated further down the table who was simply sitting staring, her spoonful of strawberries suspended inelegantly halfway to her mouth. Following her rapt gaze, Alicia realised that her eyes were riveted on a man who was threading his way between the tables and was being hailed on all sides. His tall, broad-shouldered figure seemed to draw all eyes and Alicia's neighbour was not the only lady who was frankly staring.

The stranger had reached Lady Stansfield now and was bowing elegantly over her hand before straightening up to give her a wicked smile. Alicia was amazed to see her grandmother positively preening herself—she who reduced most fashionable young men to stammering incoherence! Still, Lady Stansfield was not completely immune to good looks and this was a very personable young man indeed.

At that moment, Caroline Oxley looked up, gave a shriek and dug her brother Charles painfully in the ribs with her fan.

'Charles, only look! It's James Mullineaux, of all people! He never usually attends these affairs!'

'Too afraid of being pounced upon!' her brother agreed caustically. He turned to Alicia. 'You must know, Miss Broseley, that James Mullineaux is considered one of the biggest catches on the marriage mart and is always fighting off eager women! He came into the Marquisate last year, and has been under siege ever since! But I suppose one can't blame him for that and he's a capital fellow, really!'

Caroline tutted. 'Really, Charles! Must you give Alicia the wrong impression from the very start? James Mullineaux is all very well as long as one does not take him too seriously!' Her perceptive blue gaze swung back to Alicia, and there was the tiniest shadow of concern in her eyes. 'James is a reckless but charming flirt. He has an air of careless arrogance which many women seem to find fascinating, but, Alicia—' again, there was that hint of concern '—do not believe a word he says, I beg you!'

The Marquis had reached their table by now and was greeting Caroline's cousin, Charlotte Anstey. Watching Charlotte blush becomingly, Alicia felt a hitherto unexperienced emotion sweep over her which she had no trouble at all in placing as pure jealousy. Judging by the expression on the faces of other ladies nearby, she was not alone.

Fool! she chided herself, but it was without heat. The impact of this man hardly lessened at close quarters, and she could scarcely expect herself to be immune when all about her were devastated by his charm.

Then he was beside her and was demanding an introduction. There was an odd moment of tense silence before Peter Weston complied—as Alicia's self-constituted beau for the evening, Weston was not best pleased at the sight of such a rival. James Mullineaux noted his friend's reluctance and the possessive way his arm lay along the back of Alicia's chair, and his smile deepened.

'Miss Broseley, this is James, Marquis of Mullineaux.' Weston sounded even more sulky than he looked. Charles Oxley caught his sister's eye and they exchanged a meaningful glance.

The Marquis took Alicia's hand. His dark eyes trapped and held Alicia's startled green gaze for what seemed like forever. Then he smiled and spoke as though they were quite alone.

'My grandfather told me once that he had been one of Lady Stansfield's greatest admirers in their youth. He said that she was the most beautiful woman he had ever met and he fell hopelessly in love with her. They say that your resemblance to her at that age is very strong, Miss Broseley, and as soon as I saw you I realised how my grandfather must have felt.'

There was a long silence. Seeing Alicia's complete inability to reply in kind, Caroline Oxley came to her rescue.

'A pretty compliment indeed for my friend, sir!' she observed pertly. Her smile encompassed the whole group. 'Pity me that the Marquis of Mullineaux has always viewed *me* as a sister!'

Mullineaux relinquished Alicia's hand reluctantly and joined in the general laughter at this.

'Allow me to tell you that you look very fine tonight, Caro,' he offered, with a smile.

'Pah, a paltry piece of flattery!' she replied, with laughing disgust.

'Then you must rely on Marcus for the necessary compliments, I think,' Mullineaux commented with a sideways glance at his friend, Marcus Kilgaren. He drew up a chair beside Charles Oxley and the conversation became general again, but Alicia was all too aware of that dark, intense gaze resting thoughtfully on her face from time to time. Her heart was still beating erratically and she felt a frightening breathlessness. Well, she had been warned. She was not to believe a word he said.

Later, Mullineaux cut Peter Weston out for a dance with her and continued to pay her the most outrageous compliments whilst doing so. Alicia had regained sufficient composure to parry his comments quite effectively, but it was proving quite impossible to remain indifferent to him. She was young and fresh from the country and whatever her sensible intentions had been she was hardly proof against the sheer overwhelming magnetism of the man.

What was perhaps more surprising was that James Mullineaux, cynical and notorious breaker of hearts, should have found himself so genuinely drawn to her. Yet he had felt exactly the same as she had. Alicia had known that from the first moment he had looked into her eyes. The feelings wrapped themselves around her again as she slept. It had been recognition and danger, excitement and warmth, security and elation, all mixed up together. It had been perfect...

Alicia woke with a start. The damp and heavy bedspread had somehow managed to tangle itself around her in her sleep and was pressing down on her like a shroud. She struggled out of it and discovered that her face was wet with tears. The warmth of the dream fled, leaving her feeling cold and bereft. Shivering a little, Alicia crossed to the chest of drawers and washed her face again. There was a bitter taste in her mouth and she felt a little sick. The inn was quiet and the storm had died down, no longer battering the corners of the building. The candle had burned down and the room was dark and lonely.

The dream was still in her mind and all thought of sleep had fled as she contemplated the past. What a naive innocent she had been in those days, convinced that because she and James loved each other all would be well! Her father had had different ideas. To him, Alicia's undeniable beauty and social lustre had just added to her value as a marriageable asset. He had never had any intention of allowing her to choose her own bridegroom. Summoned hotfoot to London by the news of his daughter's imminent betrothal to one he considered entirely unsuitable, he had wasted no time in acquainting her with his alternative plan for her future.

Alicia stood by the window, staring out into the windy dark. She swallowed painfully. She had resisted his plans with all her strength, but the things that he had done to coerce her into finally agreeing to marry George Carberry were best left unremembered. Strangely, it was not her father's brutal treatment which had distressed her the most, but the slow, lonely disillusionment about James Mullineaux...

At first, the pain of loss had been excruciating and she had not known how she would survive it. She had lain awake for night after night, going over in endless detail the time she had spent with James, his every word, her every feeling. Every emotion had flared into vivid and unbearable life and when the searing pain had finally died down she had been an empty shell, a shadow of her former self.

A tear trickled down Alicia's face, mirroring the raindrops on the pane outside. Widowhood had not been unpleasant for her. She was rich, beautiful and much courted, and though she knew there were those who would always consider her bad *ton* because of the scandal of her marriage they would never say so to her face. She had her friends, her charitable works, and her grandmother.

She had enough money to do whatever she wanted and if there was a monotony and emptiness about her life it was at least materially comfortable and undemanding.

She would never marry again. Alicia had known that already, before the unexpected encounter with Mullineaux had opened up wounds which had never truly healed, but could perhaps have been tacitly ignored. Unconsciously she had always compared every man she met with him and found them all wanting. And now he had come back... She shuddered at the prospect of meeting him socially in some dowager's drawing-room and being obliged to treat him as the merest acquaintance. A moment later, her mind presented her with the even less palatable picture of Mullineaux choosing one of the approaching Season's debutantes as his wife and she could not prevent a shudder of misery. Jealousy, long dormant, stirred in her again.

Shivering in the draught from the ill-fitting window, Alicia groped her way back to the armchair and drew her cloak about her for comfort. She was stiff and tired, but her mind stubbornly refused to rest. Huddled in the chair, she thought about their quarrel.

It was all too obvious now that Mullineaux considered her to be without a shred of honour. Briefly she tried to imagine explaining it all to him and gave up almost immediately. They were as strangers after seven years—she could never tell him the terrible events which had overtaken her.

Emotionally exhausted at last, Alicia settled herself to sit out the rest of the night. The inn had a long-case clock at the foot of the stairs and she heard it chime every hour through the night.

Alicia did not look her best the following morning, although she had done what she could with no clean clothes, no hot water and no maid to help her. Jack had managed to retrieve her valise the night before, but it was both crushed and soaked from resting in the ditch and its contents were largely unusable. Alicia knew she looked wan and pale in her crumpled dress, and about as young as a schoolroom miss with her hair in one long plait down her back. Looking and feeling scruffy gave her none of the confidence she needed to face James Mullineaux over breakfast.

She pushed open the door of the breakfast parlour somewhat apprehensively and found Mullineaux moodily eating buttered eggs and toast. He rose to his feet, unsmiling, as she entered.

His immaculate appearance made Alicia feel both dirty and resentful. There was not a mark on the close-fitting buckskins and his boots had a high gloss again. The coat which fitted his shoulders without a wrinkle was not of Weston or Stultz's making, but had an indefinable continental elegance for all that. He had not shaved and the stubble already darkening his tan only served to emphasise the piratical air Miss Frensham had observed the previous day. It did not detract from his spectacular good looks. Alicia, feeling as tongue-tied as a new debutante, looked away and hoped her colour had not risen.

'Good morning.' Mullineaux's observant gaze did not miss the violet shadows beneath Alicia's eyes, nor the fine lines of fatigue on her face. 'I trust that you slept well and are feeling better this morning?'

'I feel very well thank you,' Alicia responded with obvious untruth, but in tones that dared him to argue. It won her an assessing glance, but he did not comment and she almost immediately regretted the impulse which set her on the defensive and made her snap at him when she was barely in the door. Fortunately the landlady came into the parlour at that moment and with her customary good grace slapped a plate of eggs and toast down in front of Alicia. There was also a pot of coffee which both smelled and tasted surprisingly good.

Mullineaux showed no inclination for conversation, simply staring out of the window in an abstracted sort of way, and it was Alicia who finally broke the silence between them when it threatened to become prolonged.

'Do you plan to continue your journey today, Lord Mullineaux?'

'I do.' The dark gaze focused back on her in a most disconcerting manner. 'I have sent to enquire after both Ned and Jack this morning, and they are both well despite their soaking. Ned tells me that my horses are none the worse and have taken no chill.' He smiled suddenly in a way that Alicia found immediately familiar and her heart gave a little jolt. 'Indeed,' Mullineaux added,

'I believe Ned takes better care of them than he does of himself and would count it a personal insult were they to come to harm!'

'Do you have far to travel?' Alicia asked, determined to show she was perfectly able to pursue a civil conversation.

Mullineaux reached for the coffee pot and poured himself another cup. The strangeness of sharing breakfast with him suddenly struck Alicia forcibly; its intimacy made her abruptly aware of the sorts of rumours which would no doubt surface as a result of their enforced stay. She put her hand up to a head which was suddenly aching. She really was not feeling capable of thinking about that at the moment.

'I am going to Monks Dacorum for a few days,' Mullineaux was saying, effortlessly casual. 'I own a small property there which has been let for the last few years. I wish to make sure all matters such as tenancies are in order before I leave, as I do not intend to spend much time in these parts in future.'

That, Alicia thought as she bent her head over the buttered eggs, could be interpreted in several ways, none of them favourable. Mullineaux was as aware as she that his estate of Monks Dacorum bordered on her own at Chartley, since it was the Marquis's father who had sold that part of his estate to George Carberry some twenty years before. The Mullineaux family had never seemed fond of the house, however, preferring their homes in London and Oxfordshire. It could certainly not be wondered at that James Mullineaux would not wish to make his home so close to her! Alicia chewed the bitter crusts of misery and wished that the effort to make polite conversation, which so obviously came easily to him, were not such a trial to her. But then, he simply did not care, whereas she cared too much. Every moment in his company was a torment which Alicia hurried through in order to escape him as soon as possible.

Mullineaux put down his empty coffee cup and rose to his feet, crossing to the window where a sliver of watery blue sky was visible above the bare trees.

'Lady Carberry, there is something that I must say to you.'

He was standing half turned away from her and had his back to the light, but she could still see that he was frowning. Alicia's first thought was that she disliked intensely the sound of her married name on his lips. Her second was that she did not in the least wish to hear what he wanted to say. Whether he was about to resurrect ancient history and demand an explanation for her behaviour seven years ago, or merely to ring a peal over her for her behaviour as recently as yesterday, she simply could not cope. She had no wish to dissolve into tears yet again. However, she had no opportunity to make a graceful excuse and retreat, for Mullineaux had already started to speak.

'Circumstanced as we are, madam, I feel obliged to ask you to do me the honour of becoming my wife.'

For one dazed moment Alicia wondered whether she had misheard, or misunderstood his pompous words. It seemed unlikely, however, that one would mistake a proposal of marriage for anything else, and as Mullineaux merely waited silently for her reply Alicia found her indignation growing. He could at least have waited until she had finished her meal before he put her off her food so completely! Her appetite fading rapidly, she pushed her plate away and gave him her full attention.

'How can you be so ridiculous, my lord, as to offer marriage to one you hold in such complete dislike?' she demanded, with characteristic candour. 'I declare I cannot believe that you would do anything so ill-judged! But perhaps I misheard you? Indeed, your enthusiasm was so half-hearted that I fear I may not have understood you properly!'

She watched with no little satisfaction as the angry colour came into his face. He already looked as though he would like to strangle her.

'You did not mishear, Lady Carberry, nor misunderstand, as well you know!' Mullineaux spoke through gritted teeth. His hands were clenched tightly by his sides and his whole body was taut with anger. 'Nothing but the situation in which we find ourselves would induce me—' He broke off and resumed as politely as he was able, 'In short, I am making an offer in an attempt to limit the damage of this discreditable escapade, and would hope that your own sense of propriety would prompt you to accept!'

Alicia would not have believed that she could feel so furious so quickly. Normally she had her temper under tight control. She reluctantly rejected the idea of responding as her grandmother might have done—Lady Stansfield would no doubt have said, 'A pox on your propriety, sir!' or some such well-chosen phrase. That would not really help matters, tempting as it was. She bit her lip, trying to regain control of her temper.

'I believe that it is customary for a lady to express herself honoured by a proposal of marriage,' she said carefully. 'However, I cannot find myself grateful for a proposal which clearly caused you as much pain in the offering as it did myself in the receiving. So I thank you for your chivalry, my lord, but I fear I must decline.'

Too late she wished she had been a little more conciliatory, for Mullineaux looked no less furious as he came across the room to lean on the table in front of her in a way Alicia found completely intimidating. His mouth was a tight, angry line and Alicia could sense his rage, elemental in the tense lines of his body. She shivered, unable to help herself.

'You have no choice.' Despite his anger he spoke softly, which was somehow even more chilling. 'You must see that you have compromised yourself!'

'I have a choice.' Alicia met his gaze very steadily. 'I accept that my reputation is compromised, but I cannot regard that as good enough reason to marry you. To accept your reluctant proposal would surely cause more speculation than to continue as though nothing important had happened.'

There was a moment of silence as Mullineaux held her gaze, his own thunderous with disapproval. Then he straightened up and turned away.

'Very well, madam! Let me put this another way! You may reject my proposal with scorn, but have you really given any thought at all to our situation here and the gossip which will inevitably arise as a result? You think that you can ignore it? Think again, before you condemn us both to yet another infamous scandal!'

His arrogance took her breath away. Once again Alicia felt her temper rising and made a grab for her self-control. How dared he insult her by his insistence on doing the honourable thing when his dislike of her was so obvious? Only the previous night he had suggested that she no longer had a good reputation to protect, and whilst that might have been said in the heat of the moment his opinion of her was scarcely high. In her book it would always be better to face the scandal and ride it out than tie herself to so reluctant a suitor.

'You are overstating the case, sir,' she said, as calmly and coldly as she could. 'Certainly it is unfortunate—'

'Unfortunate! The most damnable mess imaginable!' Mullineaux strode back to the window. 'You may feel that you have the—"licence" was the word I believe you used last night—to do as you wish, but even your credit will suffer from a story that you spent a night alone in an inn with a man whom you once knew exceptionally well!'

He swung round to glare at her again. 'And the story which goes round will not be that we were marooned here as a result of a carriage accident and inclement weather—a far better tale would be that I returned from a long stay abroad and arranged a secret rendezvous with you.'

His tone took on a wealth of anger and bitterness. 'Then they will say that you deliberately sent your chaperon away and chose to spend the night with me—how romantic; how deliciously scandalous! And how does that suit your ladyship?'

It suited Alicia very ill and she could hardly deny it. Knowing society as she did it was impossible to believe that there would not be a great deal of speculation about the two of them and that the story which circulated would not be highly coloured; it was so much more interesting than the truth. Even so, she thought stubbornly, that was no reason to consent to a marriage where her feelings were still hopelessly engaged, and his were based on nothing but contempt. But how ironic! Alicia grimaced. She had just rejected the only man she had ever considered marrying!

She dared to raise her eyes to meet that furious dark gaze, and tried to speak composedly.

'I take your point, my lord. I might even apologise for unintentionally causing this situation. However, I would have thought that to become betrothed to you so suddenly would only give rise to a great deal of speculation on its own account! It is no solution! No, I still would not marry you were the gossip twice as loud!'

Mullineaux ran his hand through his disordered black hair in a gesture she knew well.

'You seem to take a perverse enjoyment in making life as difficult for yourself as possible!' he exclaimed. 'Of course there would be conjecture over our betrothal, but it would not be nearly as harmful to you as the gossip which will inevitably suggest that we are lovers!'

Alicia lost her patience. His scorn seemed to make a mockery of the feelings which she had tried so hard and so unsuccessfully to suppress. His persistence when it was obvious that he detested her was the veriest insult.

'Lovers! I would imagine that anyone with half an eye would quickly realise that there was no truth in that and that we could not bear each other!' she retorted unwisely. 'And for my part I cannot see that it would make my life any easier to be betrothed to you! Are you suggesting that we should break off this false betrothal after a respectable time has elapsed, or do you feel we should go through with the charade and actually get married? I am sorry, my lord, but I find the whole idea nonsensical in the extreme!'

'I thank you, madam; you have said quite enough!' Mullineaux interposed with exasperation as she paused to draw breath. Their gazes clashed and held, both bright with anger. After a moment Mullineaux shook his head slowly in disbelief. He was not at all clear how they had managed to get into such a situation of conflict yet again. Why did she always bring out the worst in him?

He knew that the terms of his proposal had scarcely been flattering and was not even sure what quixotic impulse had led him to make it. He'd had no intention of doing so until he had seen her that morning; indeed he blamed her recklessness for compromising them both. Yet she had seemed so small and tired when she had come down for breakfast and so in need of protection. How misleading, when she had proved as little in need of protection as a tigress!

Her spirited rejection of his suit had perhaps been deserved, and, of course, she was right in that to become betrothed would be madness. He had no wish for their names to be linked, and his reputation would suffer far less than hers by the gossip that would inevitably follow this escapade. Nevertheless, her refusal rankled with him. And, confusingly, some element of him felt an obscure disappointment, but he knew he could not afford to examine why. Already his emotions were becoming dangerously involved.

'I thought that you would be glad to add a better title to your fortune,' he said, to give vent to his feelings, and almost immediately felt ashamed that he had allowed his distaste for her past behaviour to force him into rudeness. He watched the hot colour flood her face at the insult. How amazingly good she was at playing the hurt innocent! But what was the point in pretending to him?

Not for anything would Alicia show him how much his accusations hurt her. They cut through all the protective layers she had painfully built up over the years and exposed the unhealed scars beneath. This man had once held her in his arms and murmured words of love in a tone so far removed from his current one that it seemed like another world, another time... That man and this... The change was too great. She rallied all her forces to defend herself.

'You may consider me an adventuress, Lord Mullineaux,' Alicia said, getting up to leave the room, 'but had you thought that *you* might be seen as a fortune-hunter in proposing to me? After all, you would be regaining a piece of your lost patrimony. And I am so very rich, you see,' she added sweetly, 'that no doubt people would quickly recognise the temptation my fortune, if not my person, presents to an impoverished Marquis!'

Well, Mullineaux thought, smothering a sudden grin, he had asked for that. She was quite capable of countering his ill-bred accusations with her own. At nineteen, Alicia Broseley had had plenty of spirit, but a sweet nature to accompany it. Now she seemed both decidedly outspoken and unfashionably quick to offer an opinion.

'Well, then, no doubt I should simply be grateful to have escaped marriage with a shrew!' he stated unforgivably, and once more they were left glaring at each other with bitter hostility.

The sky was a pale washed blue later that morning as Alicia trudged along the road to Ottery Manor. The road was still damp underfoot, but most of the flood waters had receded beyond the ditches, and lay across the low flat fields like a silver mirror. The faint, plaintive call of the curlew floated across the drowned landscape, and a single buzzard wheeled high overhead. The fresh breeze had brought a little colour back into Alicia's cheeks, but she was less inclined than usual to pause to enjoy the scenery.

Only the coldest words of farewell had passed between herself and the Marquis of Mullineaux. He had gone to the stables to oversee the preparation of his curricle, eager to be away, and Alicia had consulted Jack about the salvage of her carriage before setting off to the Manor. Jack had been hopeful that the repairs might be effected that day, which left Alicia with the dilemma of how to pass the time before she could resume her journey. The thought of whiling away time at Ottery Manor under the curious eyes of Mrs Henley's guests was almost intolerable, but the prospect of spending more time at the inn was equally unacceptable.

Alicia's thoughts turned back to Mullineaux and she felt sick at heart at what had passed between them. He was worse than a stranger, someone to whom instinct persistently drew her, whilst fate placed apparently insurmountable barriers between them. It was horrible that she still found him so undeniably attractive when he held her in the deepest contempt. For the sake of her sanity she would just have to keep out of his way in future. This melancholy reflection brought her to the stone gateway of Ottery Manor, and the low, rambling building came into view.

If Mrs Henley was taken aback to receive a visitor when her guests were still at breakfast, she hid it well. Shutting the breakfast parlour door in the frankly curious faces of Mrs Eddington-Buck and her daughter, she drew Alicia into a charming, sunlit drawing-room and settled her in a chair by the fire. Her shrewd brown eyes appraised Alicia's face with concern.

'You look a trifle out of curl this morning, Lady Carberry, if I dare say so,' she ventured at last. 'I am so very sorry we were not able to return for you in the carriage; indeed, John did try, but the Lilley had burst its banks, and the road was under several feet of water. We were at a loss as to what to do, and Miss Frensham was nearly beside herself with distraction!' She did not add that Miss Frensham's usual discretion had deserted her and that her wailed lamentations had added immeasurably to a scandal which her guests had been quick to seize upon.

Alicia looked up, her tired green eyes meeting Mrs Henley's observant brown ones and seeing nothing but kindness there. The urge to confide in someone was overpowering. Alicia swallowed a lump in her throat.

'Oh, my dear ma'am, do not apologise! The fault was all mine for thinking it best to send Miss Frensham on ahead, although—' she shuddered '—I would hardly have wished to condemn her to a night in that appalling inn! But now Miss Frensham has probably taken a chill anyway, and I have lost my reputation—which is, I suspect, a longer-lasting handicap!'

It seemed that her granddaughter resembled old Lady Stansfield in plain speaking, Mrs Henley reflected. Certainly Lady Carberry was very likeable, and one could not but sympathise with her predicament. Even so, Mrs Henley hesitated to offer advice and chose to address the easier part of Alicia's comments first.

'Well, I fear Miss Frensham is rather poorly this morning, my dear. She did not feel able to take any breakfast and has stayed in bed to rest. I expect the news of your arrival will cheer her, though. As for your own dilemma...' she took a look at Alicia's expression and decided to risk it '...well, it is rather difficult, is it not?'

Alicia managed a smile at this masterly piece of understatement whilst still looking despondent. Watching her unconscious grace even whilst she was drooping with tiredness, Mrs Henley felt grateful that her impressionable younger son was not at home. At nineteen he was ripe to fall in love, and Alicia was the perfect romantic heroine.

'You are very welcome to stay here as we had originally planned,' Mrs Henley ventured, with complete truth, 'but I fear that it might be rather uncomfortable for you. Mrs Eddington-Buck is an unkind creature, and as for Mrs Evelyn—well...' She did not need to complete the sentence, for that lady's lack of discretion was legendary. 'I imagine,' Anne Henley said carefully, 'that they may be capable of inventing all kinds of fascinating tales for public discussion. Not that I do not believe you able to cope with such tabbies, Lady Carberry, but—'

'But it would be poor repayment for your kindness, ma'am, to cause you such trouble,' Alicia finished. 'No, I will not stay. If I may trespass on your hospitality further and beg to borrow a carriage, I will continue the journey which was interrupted yesterday. My own vehicle may be ready on the morrow, but I have no wish to delay my business. Miss Frensham may have told you, ma'am, that we were on our way to my father's house.'

'Indeed, my dear,' Mrs Henley murmured. Now she was very surprised. To her knowledge, Alicia and her father had not met for seven years.

'Nothing could be simpler than you borrowing a carriage,' she added, 'if that is what you wish. And perhaps you are right in thinking that the scandal will die down in your absence. Certainly I will do all I can to squash it. Does the Marquis of Mullineaux have plans to travel on today?'

Alicia smiled faintly. 'I believe he does, ma'am, although I know little of it. Believe me, the Marquis was too displeased by my folly to think of indulging in much conversation!' She stared miserably at a bright square of sunlight on the carpet. 'Not,' she added suddenly, 'that any blame for this situation can lie with him. He was generous enough to offer me the protection of his name, but I declined.'

Mrs Henley's eyes opened very wide at her words. What sudden impulse could have prompted Mullineaux to offer for Alicia Carberry when he so clearly despised her? And why did Alicia feel that she had to refuse him but still make it clear that he had behaved as a gentleman ought?

'I had no choice but to refuse his offer,' Alicia was saying softly, more to herself than to Mrs Henley. 'How could I accept, knowing that he detests me so?'

Their eyes met and what Anne Henley saw reflected there made her think that perhaps she understood. Lady Carberry's predicament was worse than she had originally imagined, for, whatever Mullineaux's motives had been in proposing, Anne Henley knew Alicia had refused him because she had the misfortune still to be in love with him.

Chapter Three

Alicia slept for most of the journey from Ottery to her father's home north of Taunton and woke only as the carriage turned in at the black iron gates of Greyrigg. Despite the wonders worked on her appearance by Mrs Henley's maid, who had both dressed her hair and miraculously removed all dirt from her clothing, Alicia felt both worn and tired. Her eyes were gritty from lack of sleep and she already had a slight headache which she wryly ascribed to tension. Her first meeting with her father after seven years was bound to be difficult and she did not feel best prepared to face it, but having got this far she was determined to go through with it.

A line of bare chestnut trees bordered the gravel drive which led up to the house. Greyrigg had once been the home of an impecunious Viscount but had been purchased some twenty-eight years previously by Alicia's father, Bertram Broseley, who was a fabulously wealthy nabob. Broseley had made his fortune in trade with both the Indies and the African continent, and the Viscount, who had considered him to be an upstart of the most encroaching sort, had nevertheless seized the opportunity to turn the least favoured part of his estate into hard cash.

It was easy to see why the Viscount had felt no attachment to the house. On this wintry day the grey bulk of the building was uncompromisingly ugly as it stood amidst its park. Not even the carpeting of wild snowdrops beneath the trees could lend it any charm. It was as though the house had absorbed some of its owner's characteristics over the past decades, and now it had an air of gloom and neglect.

As the carriage drew up outside the imposing portico, the door of the house opened and a liveried butler emerged. The groom jumped down and opened the carriage door for the occupants to descend. Alicia tilted her head to gaze up at the massive edifice and could barely repress a shiver. Taking a deep breath to sustain her, she turned to greet the butler, who was advancing across the gravel with an unctuous smile on his face.

'May I welcome you to Greyrigg, my lady.' Obsequiousness did not become Castle, who had the physique of a prizefighter and, indeed, was more at home in dealing with the unsavoury side of Bertram Broseley's business affairs than in greeting his guests. His black boot-button eyes flicked over Alicia with an unpleasant expression which reminded her of their last meeting. Things were different now. She raised her chin.

'Thank you, Castle.' She sounded as coldly regal as the Dowager Countess of Stansfield herself. Nothing would induce her to say that she was pleased to be home.

Alicia preceded the butler up the steps and into the gloomy entrance hall with her borrowed maid trotting along behind, seemingly awed into silence by the oppressive atmosphere.

Although Alicia had been nineteen when she had left Greyrigg for her London Season, the house now looked smaller, as though she had previously seen it through a child's eyes. There was a smell of mustiness and decay in the hall which she did not remember. Huge cobwebs festooned the grimy central chandelier and there was a spartan emptiness which suggested the recent removal of various pieces of furniture. Alicia wondered briefly if her father's business affairs were ailing and the neglect of his house was a direct result. Certainly the marble floor had not been cleaned for an age and the air had a stale smell which made her wrinkle up her nose in disgust.

The front door closed and Alicia had the oddest idea that a trap had closed with it. She shrugged the fanciful idea away impatiently. It was natural that she should feel uncomfortable, for she associated her father with the unhappiness of her marriage and her recent meeting with James Mullineaux could only put such matters back at the forefront of her mind.

Even before the meeting at Ottery, she had never had any intention of staying long at Greyrigg, having come reluctantly at Broseley's behest only to take her sister to London for the forthcoming Season. It would be pleasant, Bertram Broseley had written, for Annabella to have the opportunity for a come-out, just as Alicia herself had done. This had seemed perfectly reasonable, but Alicia had felt both hurt and manipulated. Three years before, when Annabella had been fifteen, Alicia had tried to mend the breach with her father so that she could see her sister again. Her approach had been brutally rebuffed by Broseley, who had never contacted her again until the day three weeks before when his letter had arrived out of the blue.

Despite their past differences and the fact that all Alicia's letters to Annabella had been returned unopened, she had unwillingly bowed to her father's pressure, anxious to prevent a fate similar to her own from befalling her sister. Broseley's letter had pointed out urbanely that Alicia's home at Chartley was close enough for her to come to Taunton to collect Annabella, and Alicia had not been able to find a gracious way to refuse. Now she wished she had tried harder.

Suddenly the door of her father's study was flung open and Bertram Broseley himself came striding across the floor to greet her, hands outstretched as though she were the prodigal daughter.

'Alicia! My dear! It is a happy day for us now that you are once more beneath the roof of your home!'

He met his daughter's sardonic eye but did not falter. Castle smirked. Alicia, overwhelmed by a feeling of revulsion, found that she was utterly unable to respond in kind. In fact, she was unable to respond at all and simply stood, struck dumb. She had underestimated how unpleasant it would feel to be confronted with her father again. Old fears and memories were stirred up, confusing her. As she struggled to frame a suitable response, Broseley spoke again.

'We expected you yesterday and were somewhat concerned when you failed to arrive. I hope you did not experience trouble on the journey?'

'Merely some damage to my carriage on the Ottery road,' Alicia replied, dismissing all the events of the previous twenty-four hours in one fell swoop. She was already feeling profoundly uncomfortable. She had hoped that Annabella would be ready to leave immediately, yet there were no trunks in the hallway, no signs of imminent departure. Suspicion stirred, faint but disturbing.

'It's a bad road,' Broseley commented, his shrewd grey gaze making an inventory of his daughter's appearance as though totting up exactly how much her clothes and jewellery had cost. An indefinable hint of satisfaction entered his manner. He had already calculated how expensive her outfit was.

'Never mind, you are here now. And you are looking very...' He paused, and for an insane moment Alicia thought he was going to say 'rich'. 'Very well indeed. I hope that you will feel able to stay for a little time.'

Nothing would have pleased Alicia less. She tried to think of a polite rebuff, but once again the effort of framing the appropriate words defeated her. Fortunately the silence, which was already threatening to become strained, was broken by the sound of running steps on the stair and by Annabella's voice.

'Lud, sister, can it really be you?'

Alicia could have said much the same thing. The voluptuous beauty who had reached the bottom step and was now pausing for effect bore little resemblance to the skinny little sister of eleven whom Alicia had not seen in seven years. Annabella Broseley justified the term statuesque and her clinging scarlet riding habit made her charms abundantly clear. Unlike Alicia, who had, of course, inherited the glorious but unfashionable copper hair of their maternal grandmother, Annabella was blonde. Her eyes were of a paler green than her sister's and hers was a bold, flaunting beauty which she used to advantage on all the men she met.

Annabella's gooseberry-green eyes were now appraising her sister with a patronising regard. She was deeply jealous of Alicia, though she would never have admitted it. Not only was her sister very wealthy in her own right, but she was also an acknowledged beauty who had earned the sobriquet of the most desirable widow in Society. Society's opinion mattered a great deal to Annabella and it seemed unfair to her that a widow of twenty-six, who should have been at her last prayers, should have such an enviable existence.

Both sisters had the same heart-shaped faces, but the dramatic lines of the cheekbones and the determined chin which gave Alicia both beauty and resolution were already blurring into fat on Annabella's face. Her mouth was accustomed to droop with bitter discontent and her low voice was cultivated to be deliberately sultry.

Alicia's taste in clothes was far too subtle to appeal to Annabella, who, unlike her father, dismissed the superbly cut bronze travelling dress as plain in a single glance. Mrs Henley's maid had taken Alicia's hair up beneath the elegant bronze wide-brimmed hat and this, with its contrasting ribbon, was again too simple to win her sister's favour. Patting her own be-ribboned and flower-decked hair with complacency, Annabella walked around Alicia, inspecting her as one might the points of a horse.

'La, Alicia, you are so thin!' This was not a virtue in Annabella's eyes, for she saw her sister's slenderness as ugly. 'And so pale!' She eyed Alicia's porcelain skin suspiciously. 'I see you do not favour cosmetics to improve your looks. Oh!' She gave an affected little shriek. 'Never say those are freckles on your nose! Are freckles become the fashion in London, then?'

The words were naive but the look which accompanied them was anything but simple. Belatedly she offered her own enamelled cheek for her sister's kiss and stood back to watch the effect of her words.

Alicia merely smiled at her sister's malice. Annabella had always been like a kitten sharpening its claws, although now the kitten showed signs of having developed into a fully grown cat. For a brief moment she wondered how the two of them could possibly coexist peacefully during the next London Season, at the end of which she hoped Annabella would be safely married and off her hands. It looked as though it was going to be a difficult prospect.

'You are looking very well, Annabella,' she observed peaceably. 'Are you intending to go riding? I had hoped to be away as soon as possible, for it is a few hours' journey back to Chartley, and—'

'Oh, but you must stay for refreshments at least!' Annabella had flashed a look at their father who had stood silent throughout this exchange. She slipped her arm through Alicia's, steering her in the direction of the drawing-room.

'Unfortunately I have a prior engagement to go riding, but there is plenty of time, and I know Papa hopes for the chance of a chat! Perhaps we might stay until after dinner? Or indeed until tomorrow, since I do not suppose you to wish to travel after dark?' She made it all sound comfortably domestic and cosy, and her gaze was bright and innocent. There was no reason for Alicia to feel the same vague uneasiness stir within her, but she did and she could not place the reason. Perhaps it was Annabella's deliberate insouciance, or perhaps she was simply imagining things.

'I would prefer to leave today,' she said, a little stiffly. Above all, she wished to be home at Chartley to achieve a little peace. 'I had made no arrangements for an overnight stay.'

'Oh, very well.' Annabella seemed to dismiss it as of little importance. 'But tell me about London! We hear much about you, even buried here in the country! We are so dull.' She pulled a face. 'I saw Severn's heir when he was staying with the Milburns at Stoakely Manor. You must have had windmills in your head to refuse his proposal, sister dear—a Viscount, and so handsome! Thirty thousand a year! Why, I declare, if I had half your chances I should not waste them as you do! Lud, to think—'

'Annabella—' There was something in Bertram Broseley's voice which brought the colour rushing to Annabella's face. She paused in the drawing-room doorway.

'La, here I am running on so, and you must be fagged to death after your journey! I will ask Mrs Rivers to send in refreshments, and—' she turned to the maid with a dazzling smile '—Castle will escort your maid to the housekeeper's room whilst you wait. Until later, then, sister dear!'

She swung out of the main door, shouting for her groom, and Bertram Broseley took Alicia's arm in a firm grip and guided her into the drawing-room. She found that she had to make a conscious effort not to brush him off, so strong was her feeling of distaste. The atmosphere of constraint in the house seemed very strong; this visit was proving even more difficult than she had imagined. She had seldom felt so uncomfortable, although her father seemed quite unaware of her feelings.

'Do you ever see your cousin Josiah?' he enquired sociably as they crossed the threshold and the door was shut on Annabella's demanding voice.

Alicia sighed. It was scarcely a happy choice of question with which to start the conversation rolling after seven years. Josiah Broseley, the son of Bertram's younger brother, was foolish and feckless, and aspired to live the life of a gentleman in London. Alicia seldom saw him unless he came begging for funds, but despite her exasperation with him she found she could not dislike him, for he had a surface charm that was engaging. What worried her more was the knowledge that, in his more impecunious moments, Josiah had undertaken some work for Bertram Broseley. He was not discriminating when it came to funding his more questionable habits, nor was Broseley selective if he felt he could use someone to his advantage.

Alicia returned some slight, negative reply to his enquiry and looked about the room with interest. It was dark and oppressively hot. There were heavy curtains which all but hid the windows. It was an ugly room, and Alicia realised that it had not been altered since the last time she had been in it. Now the furnishings looked old and outmoded, the wall-hangings a threadbare shadow of their former rich show. An huge fire was burning in the grate and added to the overpowering warmth. The heat and tension between them were combining to make Alicia's headache much worse, but Bertram Broseley seemed totally unaffected. He had spent much of his life in tropical climates, and no doubt felt the cold, particularly during an English winter.

Alicia took a seat on one of the puffy sofas which had looked so elegant twenty years previously, but now were merely lumpy and uncomfortable. Since she had been manoeuvred into spending at least a little time at Greyrigg she would try to make it tolerable, though how she would manage this defeated her. She would have wished to avoid a tête-à-tête with her father above all things. She watched his easy confidence as he moved to pour her a glass of Madeira, then helped himself to brandy from another decanter. He seemed completely at ease. Alicia could even hear him humming under his breath. She accepted her glass with a stiff word of thanks but could make no attempt to initiate conversation.

'May I repeat what pleasure it gives me to see you once again at Greyrigg?' Broseley began pompously, seating himself at a right angle to her and crossing his legs. 'You have been too long away, Alicia.'

His shrewd grey eyes met hers with an expression of guileless innocence. Any daughter should have been moved by the paternal sentiments, but Alicia had learned in a hard school just how far he had her interests at heart.

'My absence is hardly surprising,' she said coldly.

'A difference of opinion, perhaps...' Broseley sounded vague, waving his hand in an indeterminate gesture of dismissal. He took a sip of his brandy, eyeing her over the rim of the glass. 'I am sure that time must have gone a long way to healing the rift between us, and today we have a chance to further that process.'

Alicia almost gasped in disbelief. How could he assume that a reconciliation would be so simple? She set her glass down with a snap that made the delicate crystal shiver. This was intolerable. Her nerves were already on edge from the other events of the day and she felt utterly incapable of sustaining a travesty of politeness.

'Let us be quite plain from the start, Father, and avoid any insincere sentimentality. It was my intention never to set foot in this house again and I am only here today because you suggested that it would be good for Annabella to spend the Season in London with me. As you know, I have always been anxious to re-establish my relationship with my sister.'

Broseley winced at such plain speaking but his daughter did not relent. She eyed him thoughtfully. 'I am beginning to think that there was more to your invitation, however. I do not see much urgency on Annabella's part to be on her way!'

Broseley's expression was one of hurt innocence. 'My only other motive in inviting you here was an earnest wish to see you again, my dear Alicia!'

His daughter raised a cynical eyebrow. 'Come now, Father, do you expect me to believe that? Annabella may well wish for a Season in London, and you may well be pleased for her to go, but there is more to this than that! Do you take me for a complete fool?' She bent over to pick up her reticule. 'I have no wish to effect a reconciliation between us. If it is indeed your intention that Annabella have a Season, I suggest that you send a groom to find her and bring her back so that we may leave immediately. I asked for my carriage to be ready within the hour. If you do not want her to go with me, I will take my leave now.'

'You are too hasty, my dear.' Broseley looked pained at her lack of finesse, but managed to summon up a wintry smile. The light fell across his face as he leant towards her. He looked much thinner than Alicia remembered, for his face had lost a lot of its fullness and the portly figure—the result of years of good living—had become almost gaunt. Only the slate-grey eyes were as sharp as ever beneath their lowering brows and the mouth was a thin, cruel line. He steepled his fingers and spoke weightily.

'I'll allow that a Season in London for Annabella was the reason I gave to ask you here, and, of course, I wished to heal the breach between us. But as you are so perceptive, my dear Alicia, I'll admit that there are other options which I wished to discuss with you.'

He paused, but Alicia remained silent, looking at him with nothing more than polite enquiry. It was as she had suspected. Bertram Broseley wanted something but he could never approach his objective directly. She was deeply distrustful, but it would be far safer to know his intentions now rather than to get an unpleasant surprise later on.

'It was always my intention that Annabella should have the benefit of a Season in Town—as you did, my dear,' Broseley was continuing, 'but the little minx is hot to marry Francis St Auby, and pesters me night and day for my consent.'

Alicia raised her eyebrows, but managed to keep her tone neutral, revealing none of the agitation she was starting to feel. The suggestion of a Season for Annabella was looking more and more like an excuse—hence the lack of luggage and Annabella's reluctance to make plans for departing. So where was all this leading?

'Is it St Auby that Annabella is riding with today?' she asked.

Broseley nodded. 'It is. He is a reckless youth, but I can see that they would be well-matched. Annabella would like to join the accepted ranks of the local gentry and she and St Auby have much in common.'

'And does this marriage have your blessing, Father?'

'Not yet.' Broseley looked secretive. 'But it would be quite a good match for Annabella—she would like to be Lady St Auby—and besides, she wants Francis.'

'I am sure that she wants both the man and the title,' Alicia observed dryly. She knew Francis St Auby to be a handsome young man with an unsavoury reputation. She also remembered the St Auby family, and privately reflected that they must be desperate indeed to consider an alliance with Broseley when they had always considered him to be a jumped-up nobody. But poverty made for strange bedfellows and the St Aubys possessed endless debts as well as an old title and an overweening pride. Perhaps they had been consoled that Annabella's grandfather had been an Earl and that her pedigree, on her mother's side at least, was immaculate.

'You know the St Aubys a little,' Broseley was saying, in a conciliatory way so far removed from his usual manner as to be suspicious in itself. 'What is your opinion of them?'

Alicia paused. 'I should say that Francis St Auby is a dissolute youth and his father thinks of naught but his hounds and his women, no doubt in that order,' she observed after a moment. 'They have no money and are snobbish and small-minded. It amazes me that you are considering an association with the gentry, father. I thought that as a class you despised them.'

Broseley flushed angrily, but managed to shrug with an approach to nonchalance. His hatred of the aristocracy to which he had once aspired was notorious and his dislike of the landed gentry, amongst whom he had never been accepted, was almost as strong.

'To tell the truth it was not my intention originally,' he admitted grudgingly. 'But, as I said, Annabella is keen to have him.' His gaze flicked over Alicia, and it was not kind. 'She wishes to have a title to outrank yours, amongst other things.'

His taunt missed its mark, for Alicia only laughed. 'That would not be difficult, poor Carberry being a mere knight! But a baronetage is scarcely more and Sir Frederick St Auby may live for years if he does not break his neck on the hunting field.' She paused. 'If you are willing to buy a title for Annabella, could you not make more sure of one? Or buy a better one? Annabella would improve her chances immeasurably by coming to London with me. If I make it known she comes with a fat dowry she might even catch herself an Earl!'

It was a comment very close to the mark and Broseley held onto his temper with an effort. He had always considered his elder daughter to be a headstrong chit with a regrettable tendency to speak her mind. Annabella he understood, for she was very like him, but Alicia had always been a mystery to him. He knew that she was the image of her grandmother and that did her no service in his eyes. Of course, she was considerably older than when they had last met and no doubt possession of an independent fortune had only strengthened this deplorable attitude of self-assurance in her. He schooled his features to a semblance of pleasantness, and struggled to regain lost ground.

'Come, come, we must not quarrel, you and I. After all, this is supposed to be a reconciliation! The truth is that Annabella and St Auby...' He paused delicately. 'Well, they are very close. They have already—'

'Anticipated the pleasures of the marriage bed?' Alicia finished for him sardonically. She was not particularly shocked, for she knew Francis St Auby's reputation. Nor did Annabella seem concerned over her apparent fall from grace. 'Is she expecting a child?'

'No!' Broseley snapped, abandoning subtlety in the face of his elder daughter's outspokenness. 'At least, she assures me that she is not! The little madam—she came and told me as bold as brass—' He got a grip on himself and finished grudgingly, 'You must see that it changes matters...I am obliged to agree to her demand that they wed!'

Alicia thought that she saw rather well. No doubt Broseley had mooted some arranged match for Annabella and her sister, preferring Francis's undeniable attractions to some middle-aged libertine, had acted on her own plans rather than her father's.

'I am touched to see that you are more solicitous for Annabella's happiness than you were for mine, sir,' Alicia said smoothly. 'But in what way does this paternal dilemma affect me?'

Broseley seemed not to notice her sarcasm.

'I simply wanted to discuss my predicament with someone I could trust,' he said with a plaintiveness that was so ludicrously uncharacteristic that Alicia almost laughed aloud.

'And so you chose me?' she said incredulously. 'Pay me the compliment of believing me less gullible than that, sir! It seems that my sister has made her own decision! Francis St Auby's attributes were clearly more attractive than a Season which could not guarantee a richer prize! You knew that, but still you chose not to disabuse me! You used Annabella's future as your excuse to bring me here—now, what was your true purpose—those other options to which you referred earlier?'

It never occurred to Bertram Broseley that some part at least of Alicia's tenacity could only have been inherited from himself. He abandoned his attempt at pathos but still tried to pin on a friendly smile.

'How very direct you have become, my dear!' It was not a compliment. 'Since we are being so matter-of-fact, I will not waste any more of your time! It occurred to me recently that we might be able to do business together, you and I. I know that you have considerable capital which could be invested wisely, were I to advise you. Or, alternatively, you might wish to consider marrying again. I have a business associate who is much taken with the idea of an alliance. It could be an advantageous financial match!'

Alicia's overriding reaction to this crassly insensitive suggestion was blind fury. He evidently thought that, having benefited so handsomely from the forced marriage to Carberry, she would be willing to enter a second arrangement of her own free will!

'I am surprised that you did not offer him Annabella!' she said wrathfully. 'That would be more in keeping with your usual style, would it not, Father?' Her eyes narrowed as she considered his flushed, furtive face. 'Or perhaps you did, only to be circumvented by her conduct with St Auby! I cannot believe that you truly thought that *I* would consider either of your suggestions seriously! I have no interest in going into business with you, and I certainly have no intention of marrying to oblige you again! What conceivable benefit could there be to me from such a match?'

'The prospect of enlarging your fortune?' Broseley suggested, still hopeful.

Alicia was not impressed by this evidence that he thought her as venal as he.

'My fortune is already too great, sir, and achieved by means that I detested!'

Too great a fortune was not a concept Broseley could understand. By now he was rigid with the effort of holding onto his temper in the face of his daughter's defiance.

'I do not believe that one can ever have too much wealth, my dear Alicia,' he said, condescension just winning over annoyance in his tone.

'Then that is the difference between us!' Alicia snapped furiously. Her headache was worsening and she took a sip of the unwanted Madeira in an effort to help clear her thoughts. It had never been a favourite drink of hers and the taste of the wine was strong and cloyingly sweet. Already her head was starting to spin and the edges of the room were beginning to blur in the dark and the heat from the fire. Sweet wine, but with a slight, bitter aftertaste which was almost undetectable... She put her glass down again with such a jolt that some of the liquid splashed onto the table.

She might be mistaken, of course, but her father appeared to favour such drinks as this. He had given her a sweet, drugged wine to soften her resistance once before: when she had refused to marry George Carberry. Alicia looked at the glass pensively. There was no way of telling if this drink had been doctored, but drugged wine and an overpoweringly hot room would combine to make her feel very ill...so unwell that she would probably be unable to leave Greyrigg and would be vulnerable once again to Broseley's machinations for her future.

Alicia shivered convulsively. The shock had helped to clear her head. She could see the gardens outside in the pale sunlight and hear the birds twittering in the gutters, but here in this dark room it was possible to believe that Bertram Broseley was capable of anything. To him it would only be a means to achieving an end. He was watching her intently.

'I do not care much for your taste in wine, Father,' she observed as coldly as she could. 'And I care as little for your plans. Now let me be quite plain. I do not wish to invest in your business and

I do not wish to remarry. You may tell this mysterious suitor that I have no desire to be treated as yet another commodity!'

'Indeed, my dear, you wrong my colleague,' Broseley murmured, with a smile Alicia neither liked nor understood. 'You are fair and far out in thinking that he would have taken Annabella— it was always you he meant to marry!'

'My money, you mean!' Alicia snapped, refusing to fall for this appeal to her feminine vanity. 'How fortunate that you broached the subject with me first, Father—I have a dislike of being rude to complete strangers!'

'But no compunction over showing your father a most unfilial ingratitude!' Bertram Broseley was now letting his anger get the better of him. 'Your duty as my daughter should at least prompt you—' He broke off as Alicia made a noise indicative of her contempt.

'Come now, sir, that is taking it too far, even for you! You lost the right to ask for such filial respect seven years ago!'

Broseley's nature had always been choleric, especially when crossed. He had been keeping a hold on his temper for a long time, but now his face suffused with blood and he brought his fist down on the arm of his chair with a force which made the dust rise in a choking cloud.

'I see that you are still the same ungrateful chit you were those seven years ago, miss! To whom do you owe your pretty little title and your fine fortune? Had I not exerted myself for your benefit you would have thrown yourself away on that wastrel who was wild to a fault and spent all his money at his tailor's or in the gambling clubs! Who was it who arranged the wedding settlements so that you would inherit all George Carberry's wealth and property? And how did you repay me?' He did not wait for an answer. 'By running to your grandmother when my back was turned and destroying all that I had worked for! And now that you have the opportunity to redeem yourself you throw my generosity back in my face!'

Alicia stood up. The heat, the sticky sweetness of the wine and her own anger had combined to give her a blinding pain behind the eyes. She could barely tolerate being in the same room with him, but there was something she had to do before she left. She locked her hands together to prevent them from shaking.

'How you delude yourself, Father! No—' as he made a move towards the bell-pull '—you will hear me out! That may be your interpretation of events seven years ago. Let me tell you mine!'

She gripped the back of her chair to steady herself, her fingers digging into the faded brocade, and cut across his bluster incisively.

'You refused to allow my betrothal to the man of my choice and told a farrago of lies as to how I preferred George Carberry. You made my name a byword for scandal in the clubs and finally you forced me into marriage with that…that disgusting old man! Throughout it all you were motivated by nothing but commercial gain! Oh, no,' she corrected herself angrily, 'I mistake! You had another purpose—to make my grandmother look a fool because you had never forgiven her for refusing to accept you as her son-in-law!'

'You always were a sentimental fool!' Broseley was on his feet, vicious in his anger, his rage matching her own. 'All that happened was that I arranged a good match for you and you were headstrong enough to think of opposing me! If Carberry had not died, he would have knocked this ingratitude out of you—'

Alicia rounded on him, her eyes blazing. 'You tried that when I refused to marry him—do you remember? How could you forget? Beating your own daughter into submission and starving her, and worse—' Her voice broke. 'But Carberry *did* die and you were too drunk at the time to stop me from going, and I thank God that I will never be drawn into your wicked designs again!'

The hot tears filled her eyes and overflowed down her cheeks. She dashed them away with an impatient hand. Broseley's expression had changed suddenly and miraculously from a convulsion of fury to a rather calculated and sickening look of concern. He came to her side, taking her arm in a proprietorial grip.

'My dear, you are distraught.' His sympathy was far more objectionable than his anger. 'I will send for Mrs Rivers at once to take you to a room. You cannot possibly travel in this condition—'

'You mistake, Father.' Alicia shook him off abruptly. 'I intend to leave directly.'

True to her word, she marched to the door and wrenched it open and Castle practically fell into the room, demonstrating all too clearly that he had been listening at the keyhole.

Alicia glared at him. 'Castle, summon my maid and my carriage. I am leaving.'

There was a moment of silence and indecision as Castle looked to his master for guidance. Broseley himself was looking at Alicia's barely touched glass of wine and frowning heavily. Alicia could read his mind all too easily.

'I may be a foolishly sentimental chit, Father, but I am not so green a girl as to be caught by the same trick twice. So you see I did learn something from the experience of my first marriage! Now, will you let me go, or are you intending to restrain me by force?'

She knew quite well that he was capable of doing so, but would he dare? Even now, she could hear the spattering of the wheels on the gravel outside as Jack, following her earlier instructions, brought the coach round. Broseley heard it too and made his decision.

'Really, my dear, I would have expected more courtesy of you! Such a breach of manners!'

'It's the company I keep,' Alicia snapped. She turned to find Mrs Henley's maid hurrying to her side, drawn like half the other servants by all the noise in the hall. 'Come, Joan, we are leaving!'

The carriage drove off moments later at a spanking pace and the door of Greyrigg slammed shut behind them. Broseley and Castle were left standing silently in the hall as the sound of its wheels died away down the drive.

'Your daughter has turned into a formidable lady, sir,' observed the butler to his master after a moment, with his habitual smirk.

Broseley glared at him. 'I'll bring her down,' he ground out, his West Country accent thickening as it always did under stress. 'Aye, and her grandmother with her, that old troublemaker!'

He retired to the privacy of the drawing-room where he smashed the offending glass of Madeira in the fireplace. He had had no interest in mending the breach with his daughter for the sake of it, but he had devised an opportunity to regain control of both her and her fortune and to use both to further his own ends. He stared furiously into the pier glass. So he had misread her. He had hoped—believed—that inheriting such a huge fortune would have made her more materialistic. How many people in such a situation would not see the benefit of increasing their wealth? Not many that he knew! Unfortunately, Alicia had proved to be one such and the prospect of augmenting her fortune held no interest for her. The nineteen-year-old girl whom he had forced into marriage had been replaced by a woman of considerable character who could not be either persuaded or threatened.

For the umpteenth time Broseley reflected bitterly on the malign fate which had caused George Carberry to die on his wedding night. He could hardly have anticipated such bad luck. To have worked so hard, only to lose it all! He allowed himself a moment to dream of the ventures he and Carberry had planned together. What he could have done with such money! Carberry had been as rich as Croesus.

Broseley turned to stare unseeingly out of the window. It gave him a bitter satisfaction that he had managed to sabotage Alicia's relationship with the Marquis of Mullineaux so thoroughly. Alicia had never known that Mullineaux had come round to Bruton Street day after day, demanding to see her. Impetuous hothead! Broseley's mouth twisted with cynical disdain. Mullineaux had represented everything he had grown to hate about the privileged classes.

Broseley's train of thought turned back to his commercial dealings. His business associate would not be pleased with the day's outcome. Mr Wood, as Broseley liked to think of him, had never been interested in Annabella and had only ever wanted to marry Alicia. She had divined the reason correctly—her money—but she had never thought to ask his name. This had saved Bertram Broseley the trouble of inventing another lie, for his associate was actually known to Alicia and was very anxious that his connection with her father remain a secret, at least until the marriage contract was signed.

Broseley sighed. He hated to be proved wrong. His associate had warned him that his approach was misguided. He had correctly predicted that Alicia would reject both an invitation to a business partnership and a marriage of convenience. Further, he had pressed

Broseley to allow him to try his fortune under his own colours. Broseley had been dismissive. Now it seemed that he would have to allow it. He moved over to the fireplace and rang the bell vigorously for Castle. There were matters to attend to.

Alicia, exhausted by the scene with her father, had quickly resolved that she could not bear to return to Ottery Manor and the malicious whisperings of Mrs Henley's guests. Instead, she decided to throw herself on the mercy of one of her grandmother's oldest friends, the Reverend Theophilus March, who held a country living which included the parish of Ottery as well as several others. An elderly bachelor with a fearsomely respectable housekeeper, he inhabited a spacious and well-appointed vicarage in the village of Ashlyn, some five miles from Ottery.

The vicarage was warm and quiet, a haven after Greyrigg. The Reverend Theo was delighted to see her. Stooping slightly, he came forward to greet her warmly and kiss her on both cheeks.

'Alicia, my dear child! What a splendid surprise! No, do not apologise for intruding; I could not be more delighted! Mrs Morland will see your luggage taken up. I must apologise, but the green room is already taken—I have another guest, you see...' He was ushering her into the library as he spoke. 'The grandson of an old friend...called this afternoon, after a considerable time abroad...I persuaded him to stay for dinner...'

Alicia had a presentiment of disaster a second before the library door swung wide to reveal the Marquis of Mullineaux, a tattered copy of *The Meditations of Marcus Aurelius* in his hand. He was smiling as he looked up from the book, and for a heartbreaking moment he looked exactly like the boyish young man she had known all those years before. Then he saw her and an expression of complete astonishment was followed swiftly by incredulous disbelief, before he assumed a carefully cultivated indifference.

Alicia, horrified to find herself confronted with such an unexpected problem, was already backing out of the door and bumping into Theo, who was trying to follow her into the room.

'Oh, no! Dear Theo, I did not realise...' She took a grip on herself as she saw the faintest hint of amusement touch Mullineaux's mouth at her discomfort. 'I would not dream of intruding

on your reunion! It is of no consequence...I can easily stay elsewhere...'

The Reverend Theo, a scholarly and spiritual man, was rather
unworldly and seemed completely unaware of her very real reluctance, and of Mullineaux's sudden withdrawal.

'My dear Alicia, do not think of it! I could not be more delighted by your unexpected arrival, and I am sure James shares
my sentiments! James, dear boy, may I introduce Alicia, Lady
Carberry? Alicia, this is the Marquis of Mullineaux, whose grandfather was up at Oxford at the same time as I. I used to coach
James on his Sophocles during his school holidays!' He smiled
reminiscently.

Mullineaux took Alicia's reluctantly proffered hand with an
equal lack of enthusiasm. This was, she knew, the moment to
reveal to the Reverend Theo that they knew each other already,
but she felt a curious reluctance to do so, aware that the attendant
explanations could be difficult. Mullineaux seemed equally reti-
cent. He dropped her hand with a murmured word of greeting,
and went to return the copy of *The Meditations* to the bookshelf.
Alicia remembered, at least ten minutes too late, that Lady Stansfield had once mentioned that Theo was a mutual friend of herself
and the Duke of Cardace, James's grandfather. Alicia mentally
conjured up as many unladylike epithets as she could muster.

'We are dining early,' the Reverend Theo was continuing, in
blissful ignorance of the turmoil affecting Alicia, 'for James could
do with a good square meal and a proper night's sleep! Do you
know, my dear, he had the misfortune to be involved in a tiresome
carriage accident yesterday with some careless fellow traveller?'
He tutted loudly. 'Too many people drive with a total lack of
consideration these days!'

Alicia's eyes met James's for a long, silent moment. He was
looking studiously blank.

'I always say exactly the same thing myself,' Alicia said
sweetly. 'Do you know, Lord Mullineaux, by an extraordinary
coincidence, I too was involved in an accident on the road yesterday and I believe the other party was very much to blame?'

A muscle twitched in Mullineaux's cheek. 'Indeed, ma'am,' he said colourlessly. The Reverend Theo beamed to see his guests in such harmony.

As she dressed for dinner in the blue bedroom, Alicia took stock of her situation. It was the most confounded nuisance to meet Mullineaux again so soon and unexpectedly, but she had to manage as best she could. Her preferred strategy of avoiding him was obviously impractical, so she had a choice between languishing over her feelings like the heroine of a bad melodrama, or taking her courage in both hands and the battle to his camp. She knew which she preferred. She raised her chin defiantly at her reflection in the mirror and went down to dinner.

Mrs Morland, privy to the servants' gossip, might have been able to enlighten her employer as to the relationship between his two guests, but she never offered an unsolicited comment. Wrapped up in his world of parish matters, the Reverend Theo had never paid much attention to events in the outside world, and since neither Lady Stansfield nor the Duke of Cardace had mentioned the broken engagement between their grandchildren at the time he remained in happy ignorance.

'And so I told him to send the creature to the horse-coper!' he finished triumphantly, coming to the end of a long anecdote which had taken up the best part of the first course. He roared with laughter and both his guests smiled politely.

Alicia had been studying James Mullineaux covertly since the beginning of the meal. Immaculate in a coat of black superfine over a dove-grey waistcoat, there was something austere in both his dress and manner. She had already divined that he intended to ignore her for the most part, for he never looked at her directly and addressed not one word to her. Invited by Theo to take Alicia in to dinner, he had graciously seceded the privilege to his host in a manner so charming that Theo had suspected nothing, whilst Alicia had been left fuming with indignation. He had taken a seat opposite Theo, which kept her out of his line of vision, and for the most part they had all talked on generalities such as the weather before Theo had begun his anecdote about the horse.

Alicia swallowed the last of her turbot and watched entranced as the dressed capon was brought in, accompanied by asparagus and new potatoes. For a country parson, Theophilus March certainly did not stint himself. She remembered that he had a private income and also assumed he would be killing the fatted calf for the return of this particular prodigal. Her attention was caught as she realised Theo had started off on another of his unpredictable trains of thought.

'Excellent shooting at Monks Dacorum in your father's time, my dear James,' he was saying, through a mouthful of rich sauce. 'The woods between Monks and Chartley were always flush with pheasant. Why, I remember—' He broke off as an idea appeared to strike him for the first time. 'I say, Alicia, do you realise that this chap is your near neighbour? Well, I declare, what a happy coincidence! You will be able to show him around the neighbourhood!'

Alicia thought she saw James shudder slightly. 'I should be delighted,' she said warmly. 'Lord Mullineaux has been so long away, has he not, that I dare say he can scarce remember where his own tenants live!'

That earned her a look at last, dark and direct. Theo did not notice, for he was nodding enthusiastically. He leant towards James confidingly. 'You should know, my dear boy, that Lady Carberry is a considerable benefactress to this neighbourhood!' He waved his fork about in vague description. 'The schools she has started, the businesses saved from closure... Her work has given employment to plenty of young men who might otherwise have gone to the bad, driven by a want of education and honest toil! I always preach her example from my pulpit!'

James Mullineaux's lip curled slightly. 'Very commendable, I am sure, my dear sir! Lady Carberry must be an example to us all!'

Theo missed the sarcasm completely, but Alicia did not and flushed with mortification. She began to perceive that Theo's ignorance of their situation might be awkward. She had no wish for him to sing her praises to James Mullineaux of all people.

'Dear Theo, you exaggerate,' she said gently, hoping to stem his flow. Unfortunately it had the opposite effect. He looked injured, peering at her short-sightedly from under his thatch of grey hair.

'Alicia, dear, do not hide your light under a bushel! His lordship should know of your good works!'

'You need not praise Lady Carberry to me, sir,' the Marquis of Mullineaux said smoothly. 'I already know all I need to form my opinion!'

Only Alicia saw the dismissive look of contempt in his eyes. She felt her temper rising with the unfortunate effect his scorn always had on her. Arrogant, overbearing man! She took several reckless mouthfuls of Theo's excellent wine.

'Your reputation precedes you also, Lord Mullineaux,' she observed with saccharine sweetness. 'I imagine the county has not had so much excitement in an age! Your...pursuits are legendary!'

Mullineaux's gaze touched hers for a brief moment, then he looked away with an apparent lack of interest.

'Plenty of country pursuits here!' Theo was chuckling, oblivious to the undercurrent running between them. 'Hunting, shooting, fishing... Take your pick, my boy!'

'And what pursuits do you indulge in, Lady Carberry?' Mullineaux asked suddenly. Only his tanned fingers, drumming a ceaseless rhythm on the table, betrayed his irritation at her subtle provocation. 'Other than the exercise of your benevolence, that is! Balls and parties, perhaps? Or would a masquerade be more to your taste?' He put the very slightest emphasis on the word and Alicia's over-sensitivity did the rest. So he thought her charitable activities were all a pretence, did he? She had never boasted of her philanthropy but it infuriated her to think that Mullineaux was judging her a fraud.

'My favourite activity,' she said, determinedly squashing her anger with a demure smile, 'is my gardening, sir.'

It was such an innocuous reply. Theo beamed again and Mullineaux almost choked on his wine. He cast her a cynical look. She met it with a defiant sparkle in those green eyes.

'Alicia's garden is a joy to the whole neighbourhood,' Theo commented as a redcurrant syllabub and the dessert wine were brought in.

'Are the village children permitted to play there?' Mullineaux enquired innocently. 'It would seem a charitable act to allow them to do so!'

Now it was Alicia's turn to choke on her food. She took another draught of wine, regarding him thoughtfully over the rim of her glass. Mullineaux had turned to Theo, courteously praising the quality of his wine cellar.

'And that is a genuine compliment from Lord Mullineaux, who is a connoisseur of such matters!' Alicia observed smartly. 'Of all the areas of Lord Mullineaux's expertise, that is surely the only one suitable for *your* ears, dear Theo!'

Even the Reverend Theo was not so obtuse as to misunderstand that comment. He swallowed convulsively, his baffled gaze travelling from Alicia's flushed face to Mullineaux's politely expressionless one. Mullineaux might, in fact, have been forgiven for administering the set-down which Alicia so richly deserved for this, but he said not one word. Theo wriggled uncomfortably, greeting the butler's arrival with the port as though he were a long-lost cousin.

'Alicia, my dear, the port...would you mind? Mrs Morland has tea served in the drawing-room... Perhaps you would be so good... We will join you later...'

The relief on his face as he saw her rise to her feet was almost comical.

Alicia was suddenly feeling very light-headed. Her poor night's sleep the previous evening and the strain of her day had led to an immense, unexpected lassitude. She found that she had to enunciate her words very clearly.

'Please excuse me. I am very fatigued and would retire. Thank you for your hospitality, Theo.' She nodded distantly in Mullineaux's direction. 'Goodnight, sir.'

Mullineaux put down his napkin and rose to his feet. 'I will escort you to the stairs, Lady Carberry.'

Hysteria rose in Alicia. She realised that she was feeling very odd indeed. Why should she need his escort? Did he think she would get lost? The vicarage was a sizeable house, but not that large! She almost laughed, and just managed to swallow a hiccup.

Mullineaux was holding the door for her and somehow she found herself standing with him in the relative darkness of the hallway. He was lighting a candle for her with grave concentration, the flame catching and illuminating his face from beneath with its soft light. Alicia's mouth dried. She could not look away. His dark eyes were hooded and the candlelight shadowed the hard, determined line of his jaw, his mouth...

He looked up and shattered her mood.

'Do you always drink too much at dinner?' he asked casually.

Alicia stared at him in outrage. 'How dare you insinuate—? I am not drunk!'

'No?' Mullineaux looked at her with cool disinterest. 'Then you have even less excuse for that ill-bred display in there! Be careful, Lady Carberry! Drinking too much and failing to realise it is the first sign of danger for a lonely, middle-aged widow—'

'How dare you?' Alicia's voice was rising. 'I am *not* middle-aged!'

She saw his sardonic smile and could have slapped him. 'Maybe not,' he agreed readily, 'but you are becoming repetitious! And as to how I dare, well, it seems to me that no one else does dare tell you any home truths, my lady!'

Outrage and misery struggled for ascendancy within Alicia. She had had enough of his officious, interfering ways! Here he was again, judging her with such insufferable arrogance! She glared at him speechlessly.

Mullineaux seemed completely unaffected. He handed Alicia the candlestick, but when she would have taken it and marched off upstairs he did not let go. She looked up into his face, confused. What new indignities was he about to heap on her head?

'Lady Carberry, tell me one thing.' There was an odd note of urgency in Mullineaux's voice. 'The schools...and the businesses...is it all true?'

Alicia felt as though she was looking into his eyes for ever. A welter of thoughts tumbled over themselves inside her head. Tell him the truth, one voice urged. Damn his presumption, said another. Well, damn him, and damn her as well. Some imp of perversity prompted her to confirm his poor opinion of her.

She gave a little, catlike smile. 'Oh, it is true as far as it goes, my lord. But you should know that sound businesses make more money than ones that are poorly run! I never invest where there is no profit to be made!'

She took the candle and swept off upstairs, but not before she had seen the disillusion and scorn return to his face. It was his habitual expression when regarding her, she thought.

She slept heavily and woke with a headache, heartache, and a severe case of guilt towards Theo, who did not deserve his hospitality to be abused in the way she had done the previous night. She need not have worried about meeting Mullineaux again. He had left before she even came down to breakfast.

Chapter Four

For a week after her return home, Alicia had been pondering whether she dared venture near Monks Dacorum now that she knew that the Marquis of Mullineaux was in residence. She felt so bruised by their recent encounters that she had no wish to see him again for a very long time. Unfortunately, a short while before Christmas, she had accepted an invitation from Mrs Patch of Monks Farm to take tea that very Thursday and she was loath to cancel the engagement and give offence.

In the event the hour she spent at Monks Farm was very enjoyable. She admired the small Patch children and received Mrs Patch's assurances that the yield from the estate had increased since she had been so kind as to lend them the money for drainage of the five-acre field. The tea was strong and the home-made cake delicious. It was only as Alicia was leaving the farmhouse with her arms full of fresh vegetables and two small children clinging to her skirts that disaster arrived in the shape of the Marquis of Mullineaux on what was evidently a tour of the estate.

It was perhaps to be expected. It was the first fine day of the week, with a fresh, crisp feel that made it perfect for riding out. The hedgerows still glistened with frost and the puddles in the farmyard were slippery with ice. Mullineaux, on a raking grey hunter, looked formidable and every inch the lord of the manor as he rode slowly into the farm courtyard, glancing round with evident approval at its trim tidiness. Then his gaze fell on Alicia, defiantly clutching a large marrow, some sprouts and a bag of potatoes, and a less easily definable expression crossed his face.

Mrs Patch was curtseying clumsily, drawing the children to her side like a protective mother hen. She was horrified at the unexpected intrusion.

'My lord, if only we'd a' known you were coming to visit! Farmer Patch is down the five-acre field—I'll send to fetch him at once!' Belatedly she realised that she did not sound very welcoming, dropped another hasty curtsey and added, 'We're most honoured by your visit, my lord, to be sure!'

Mullineaux had dismounted and was quick to put her at her ease. 'I was just passing, Mrs Patch, and thought to stop and renew old acquaintances. Don't trouble to disturb Patch now—Tadcaster and I will drop by in a few days for a proper chat with him about the farm. And these must be your children.' He smiled at them, and they smiled back, completely dazzled. 'What a delightful pair! I believe your daughter favours you, Mrs Patch.'

Mrs Patch looked overwhelmed by such magnanimity. Tom Patch, a sturdy six-year-old, stood braced, gazing up at the Marquis as though he had seen a god. Four-year-old Matilda looked more dubious, but was coaxed into a smile again as the Marquis squatted down beside her and asked her gently if she enjoyed living on a farm. Alicia, feeling distinctly *de trop*, tried to edge away only to be thwarted as her bag of potatoes burst and scattered its contents all over the cobbles.

Tom whooped with glee, chasing them round the yard. Mullineaux straightened.

'Your servant, Lady Carberry. It is something of a surprise to see you here.'

Alicia was immediately on the defensive, as was Mrs Patch who was quick to detect the hint of disapproval in his tone. In her haste to smooth matters over she stumbled into disastrous speech.

'Lady Carberry has always taken an interest in the farm, my lord, ever since we had that terrible flooding last year and she advanced Patch the loan to drain the five-acre field! It's made such a difference to us, my lord, you would not believe! Why, if it hadn't been for her ladyship...' Her words trailed away, conscious of Mullineaux's sudden silence.

'Monks Farm is now the best purveyor of fresh fruit and vegetables in the locality,' Alicia added, knowing she sounded completely inane but anxious only to prevent Mrs Patch from making any further damaging disclosures. Judging by the black frown on Mullineaux's brow, it was already too late.

'Thank you, Tom,' she added as the young Patch solemnly presented her with her potatoes. She turned to Mrs Patch with a warm smile. 'And thank you for your hospitality, Mrs Patch. I hope to see you again soon. Good day, Lord Mullineaux.'

It was not to be supposed that she could escape so easily. As she turned to walk away, her arm was caught in an iron grip.

'Let me escort you to your carriage, Lady Carberry,' the Marquis of Mullineaux said, in tones which brooked no refusal. 'This ice is most treacherous and I would not care for you to slip and hurt yourself.'

Alicia looked up suspiciously, but the dark face above her was completely bland. She was acutely conscious of his gloved hand beneath her elbow, holding her lightly now but in a grip that nevertheless made her nerve-ends tingle. They crossed the courtyard in silence and reached the gate, where Alicia's coach was drawn up to one side of the archway.

'Now,' Mullineaux said, very pleasantly, as they paused beside the hawthorn hedge, 'we can either talk here or in the relative privacy of your carriage. Which do you prefer, Lady Carberry?'

Alicia looked mutinous. 'Neither suggestion would seem appropriate, my lord,' she said coolly. 'I have nothing to say to you.'

'You are mistaken, however.' Mullineaux still sounded pleasant but there was an expression in his eyes that belied his tone. 'You will tell me, if you please, exactly how much the Monks Dacorum estate owes you for the drainage of Patch's land. I do not care to be indebted to you.'

Alicia almost gasped at his words. He had wasted no time on polite conversation. The gloves were off with a vengeance.

'I shall do no such thing,' she said hotly. 'The arrangement between Farmer Patch and myself was a private transaction and nothing to do with the estate!'

Mullineaux was tapping the end of his riding crop impatiently in the palm of his other hand, and Alicia wondered suddenly if he was about to use it on her. He looked angry enough to be thinking of it.

'I do not care for you to be making private transactions with my tenants,' he said, with silky politeness. 'Tell me the figure and I shall see it repaid at once.'

'I doubt it!' Alicia flashed, stung into fury by his desire to be rid of all obligation to her. 'Having been away so long, you may not realise, my lord, that drainage is prohibitively expensive. The reason Farmer Patch approached me in the first place was because your agent had told him the estate could not afford to pay!'

Mullineaux's eyes narrowed. 'You are telling me that Tadcaster knew of this transaction and permitted it? Good God, how could he allow Patch to be bled dry by a private loan?'

Alicia felt a spark of triumph prompt her to provoke him further. 'He permitted it because a man's livelihood was at stake, my lord! And,' she added sweetly, 'you quite mistake the case! The loan is interest-free and based only on Farmer Patch's ability to pay! But now that you are aware of this obligation on your estate perhaps you would wish to take over the repayments to me?'

Murder flared in Mullineaux's eyes. 'You little—!' He got a grip on himself. 'You sound like a cursed money-lender, madam!' He flung away from her, to turn swiftly back and view her with a narrow, contemptuous gaze. 'Devil take it, that's what you really are, isn't it? Tell me.' He came to stand menacingly over her. 'What other insidious little arrangements have you made to undermine my estate? A loan here, a business started there... Buying the loyalty of my tenants because that's the only currency you really understand, isn't it? Well, hear this! I will not tolerate your damned interference any more!'

A great wave of desolation hit Alicia. No matter what she did now she would never be able to alter his opinion of her. Whenever she tried to avoid him, a malign fate seemed to cast her in his way just so that they could argue again and part on bad terms. Remembering their previous encounter, she blushed with embarrassment. Not only did he view her as mercenary but as a sad, lonely woman whose fondness for drink led her to make ill-bred observations! She knew that there was little she could say now to counteract his bad opinion, but at least she could try.

'Whatever I have done for your tenants has been done with the best of motives, my lord,' she said, so quietly that he could only just hear her words, 'and perhaps I was wrong to interfere. Are you sure that your anger springs from genuine concern and not mere resentment? I bid you good day.'

In the silence that followed, she turned on her heel and would have got into the carriage without another word had not Mullineaux caught her wrist again to stop her. This time Alicia gave a gasp of real pain, and too late he saw the new white bandage below the sleeve of her dress, and remembered the accident at Ottery. He dropped her wrist as though scalded and stood back.

Alicia was shaking now. The pain had pierced the artificial calm which she had managed to preserve under his last, furious attack and now she felt horribly close to tears. Not again, she thought despairingly. She was turning into a complete watering pot.

'Lady Carberry...' There was a note in Mullineaux's voice she did not recognise, did not understand, but she knew she could not cope with it now. She ignored his half-outstretched hand and brushed past him to the carriage where Jack, his ears pink-tipped with the embarrassment of overhearing their argument, was waiting to help her inside.

James Mullineaux stood in the road watching the carriage disappear. He had just remembered Alicia telling him that she never struck a bargain unless it was to her financial advantage. And yet she had apparently offered Patch a loan whose terms were generous in the extreme—terms he could substantiate simply by asking his agent. Mullineaux frowned. Perhaps it *was* time he asked a few questions. There was something going on here that he needed to understand. He stood in the empty road until Tom Patch emerged from the yard to tug on his hand and offer to show him the sheepdog's new puppies.

It was evening, and in the library of James's house at Monks Dacorum sat the Earl and Countess of Kilgaren, playing at chess. They had arrived earlier in the day and had been highly diverted to discover that their host was absent, having been held up by estate business for longer than expected. Caroline Kilgaren had wasted no time and taken charge in her usual capable fashion.

Soon the servants were eating out of her hand, the beds were aired, the fires lit and a delicious cold supper was resting on a side table, for Caroline was certain that James would be sharp set after a day out in the fresh air.

Monks Dacorum was a small house, tranquil in atmosphere, and retaining many of its original fifteenth-century features. Over the centuries it had become an appealing but rather inconvenient muddle of medieval and modern, with a great deal of charm and individuality. The library was a cosy room panelled in dark wood with shabby, leather-bound volumes filling its oaken bookshelves and similarly shabby leather armchairs set before the huge stone fireplace. Caroline and Marcus sat in front of the fire, the chessboard spread out on the table between them.

The rainstorms of the previous week had returned with the dusk, but in the room there was a companionable silence as they concentrated on the game. The candlelight burnished the fair heads of both players and cast flickering shadows across the chessboard. The only noise was the tap of the pieces on its wooden surface and the ticking of the ormolu clock on the stone mantelpiece.

The clock had just chimed seven when there was at last the sound of an arrival.

Caroline finished her move with a flourish which suggested that she had checkmated her husband very neatly, then both of them rose to their feet as the door of the room opened and James Mullineaux strolled in. Caroline, always demonstrative, gave a shriek and flung herself into his arms, careless of the fact that he was still wearing his caped driving coat and that rivulets of water were making their way down from it onto the carpet.

'James! It's wonderful to see you!'

Caroline was tiny, and it was easy for James to pick her up off her feet and spin her round, before planting a kiss on her cheek and holding her at arm's length to take a closer look at her. It was several years since they had met and they had known each other well, even before Caroline had married James's closest friend—and he had almost married hers.

The sparkle in Caroline's bright blue eyes owed as much to tears as pleasure, but it did not prevent her frank appraisal of him. She had always been very fond of James Mullineaux for they had grown up together, and it was probably that very familiarity which had preserved her from the danger of ever falling in love with him. Others had done so with an inevitability which she had felt was tiresome and predictable, but her feelings had never been remotely threatened. This had not prevented her from admitting, however, that he was quite devastatingly attractive, and whilst it had always been difficult to quantify this attraction it owed something to his height and presence, as well as his expressive dark eyes, carefully disordered black hair and immaculate tailoring.

Not that he made any pretensions towards high fashion these days, Caroline thought, but time had transmuted the arrogance of a young nobleman into an unconscious self-assurance, and age—he and Marcus were both almost thirty-three!—had done little to diminish his spectacular good looks. Perhaps he appeared to have a harder, more incisive edge to him, but he was indubitably the same James Mullineaux.

James let go of her and gave her an approximation of the wicked smile which had set so many hearts fluttering in the past.

'Well, you haven't changed at all!'

It was Caroline who spoke, but James could have said much the same about her. Caroline Kilgaren might now be a society matron, the proud mother of two delightful offspring, but her diminutive figure had not altered and the only difference he could see in her piquant face was a becoming gravity. He was willing to lay bets, however, that this solemnity would soon be banished by the same irrepressible high spirits that had led her, as Caroline Oxley, to be one of the toasts of her generation.

Marcus Kilgaren was waiting quietly to greet him, his casual calmness as much of a foil for his wife as ever. It had always been Marcus who had counselled against the wilder escapades of their group of friends and who had soothed the ruffled feelings of disapproving dowagers with his charm and apparent good sense. The same spark of humour still burned in those shrewd blue eyes as he shook James's hand.

'My apologies for not being here to greet you,' James said as he handed his sodden coat to a hovering footman with a word of thanks. 'I spent far longer out on the estate than I had intended. It was all very interesting—' He broke off as a small, wet bundle of black and white fluff streaked into the room with a triumphant barking, and sat down at his feet to gaze up as adoringly as Tom Patch had done.

The hapless butler arrived a moment later, out of breath. 'I'm sorry, sir! I had him down in the kitchen and he suddenly took off when my back was turned! Shall I take him away?'

James was laughing as he bent to scoop the puppy up in his arms. 'Don't worry, Russell! He may stay here with us for the time being.'

'I don't think he is house-trained, sir...' Russell continued with a worried frown, but James waved him away airily.

'House-trained or not, I'll swear he is as hungry as I am!' His eye fell appreciatively on the table, groaning under the weight of the supper dishes. 'I detect your influence here, Caro! Let's eat, shall we?'

There was much news to catch up on during the meal. They ate informally on their laps and James entertained his visitors with some of the more light-hearted anecdotes from his time abroad. They had stayed in touch during the past years and picked up the threads of their old friendship without any trouble. The conversation ranged widely from the French political situation to the latest fashionable plays, and the time passed agreeably for them all. The puppy, which Tom Patch had solemnly assured James was called Nod, sat beneath James's chair and ate the bits of food surreptitiously passed to him by all three.

The last of the cold chicken and ham pie was finished and James rose to put more logs on the fire whilst Marcus poured the port and rang for a pot of tea. Caroline had stated with characteristic frankness that she had no intention of withdrawing whilst the men drank and chatted together. Thus they settled themselves in a circle before the fire and a contented hush fell upon them which no one felt inclined to break. After a few moments, however, Caroline stirred herself. She could never sit quietly for long.

'I do like this house, James. It has a very restful atmosphere.'

'Yes.' James looked around him with surprised approval. 'I have scarce been here since I was a boy and could hardly remember it, but it is rather charming. I had intended to let the place shortly,' he added thoughtfully, 'but it's usefully placed between

London and Cardace Hall. If I am to visit my grandfather much, it might prove a convenient staging post.'

'How is your grandfather?' Marcus enquired. 'Did you find him improved?'

'Fortunately I did, although he was out of charity with me!' James smiled, albeit ruefully. 'Not surprisingly, he was ill-disposed to forgive me my neglect of him over the past few years! I shall have to work hard to regain his approval. I wish now that I had not stayed away so long.' He remembered suddenly Alicia's searing indictment of him as a man who had cared nothing for his responsibilities, and shrugged irritably. She had an uncanny aptitude for finding out his weaknesses.

Caroline and Marcus exchanged a look. 'Why did you not come back sooner, James?' Caroline asked, tentatively for her. 'We have all missed you, you know!'

James's face softened and he smiled at her. 'Thank you, Caro! To tell the truth, I never planned to be away so long; it just turned out like that.' He looked sombrely into the flames. His confrontation with Alicia was still at the forefront of his mind, the urge to talk about her was strong.

'I suppose,' he said slowly, 'that I left in the first place for all the wrong reasons. I was young and I had too much pride.'

'You mean because you could not tolerate what Alicia had done?' Caroline asked directly. 'Don't glare at me, Marcus! We both know that's what James meant!'

James smiled, a little reluctantly. 'Near enough, Caro! And, once away, I found that I had no inclination to come home. Until now.'

'So you went to Paris and plunged into two years of dissipation and dangerous living,' Marcus observed, deliberately cheerful, and after a moment the tense lines on James's face eased and he laughed.

'Well, Paris is the best of places for that!'

'So I'm told!' Marcus looked at him with speculative amusement. 'The whole of London Society heard of your exploits with Ghislaine de Fleuriot, *and* Marguerite Santony, *and* that delightful actress...'

'Not forgetting that Italian opera singer,' Caroline added mischievously. 'The one who apparently entertained her guests one evening wearing your pearls and very little else, James!'

'I see you know more of it all than I do,' James commented, undisturbed by their teasing. 'It was an...educational two years, one might say, but there were pressing matters relating to my father's estate which still needed to be dealt with, so I went to Ireland to sort them out.'

'And exchanged a life of dissipation for one of seclusion?' Marcus prompted, with a grin.

'Hardly that,' Caroline objected. 'They say Dublin Society is very fast—is that not so? And remember the tales of Jane Clancy and that heiress—Elizabeth Daubenay? Rumours reached us that you were to marry her, James!'

James managed to look amused and cynical at the same time, and for a moment there was an expression in his eyes which led Caroline to reflect whimsically that she could perfectly understand why the besotted Elizabeth had tried so hard to fix his interest. He seemed so dangerously attractive, she thought soulfully; the temptation would always be to try to reform him. Then she smiled at her own fanciful ideas.

'There was never the least possibility of my marrying Elizabeth Daubenay!' James was quite definite. 'Such stories were much exaggerated, Caro! I was too—'

'Exhausted?' Marcus suggested wickedly.

'I was going to say busy, actually!' His friends' teasing was having the desired effect and James appeared to be relaxing. Both the Kilgarens had noticed the latent tension within him earlier and were curious to learn its cause, but they also knew well enough that he would tell them in his own time if he wanted them to know.

'Turning the stud farm around so that it became profitable again took both more time and more work than I had anticipated,' James finished, by way of explanation.

'Well, you've been remarkably successful,' Marcus commented. 'The pair of greys you sent to Tattersall's last autumn were sweet goers and I know Saltburn paid a fine price, so keen was he to secure them. But what do you plan to do now that you are back in England, James?'

The arrival of the tea tray provided a short distraction at this point and Caroline poured for herself whilst the port decanter made another round. Once the footman had withdrawn, James tossed another log on the fire and turned back to the question.

'I've made arrangements to sell the stud, and I intend to settle back in England permanently.' He looked thoughtful. 'It's plain to me that I need to consolidate my estates and there's a lot of work to be done putting them in order. First I had planned to see Tadcaster, my agent, and arrange for a new tenant here with a view to selling eventually. However, I am not so sure now that I wish to let the house, since I may need to keep it for my own use.' He sighed unconsciously. 'There is another complication in that, however.'

When he did not elaborate, Caroline glanced at her husband, then seized the bull by the horns in her usual blunt manner. 'You mean because of your proximity here to Alicia Carberry? But surely you would not be intending to spend a great deal of time here, James—it should be possible to avoid her if you try hard enough!'

James looked up, aware of an undercurrent in Caroline's voice that made her own feelings on the subject quite plain. He knew full well that Caroline and Alicia were still close friends, and until the previous week he had not seen why this should affect him at all. Now he realised that this had been naive—if he intended to avoid Alicia and the complicated effect she appeared to have on him, he needed to make a complete break with everyone and everything connected with her. He sighed. He had no desire to lose Caroline's friendship.

'It's not as simple as that, Caro. Bear with me and I shall explain in a moment. As for the rest of my future plans—in a few weeks I am travelling up to Worcestershire to see Louisa and her family, and finally—' he grimaced '—I plan to open Cardace House for the Season. My grandfather feels himself so improved that he wishes to come up to London for the first time in an age.'

'That'll cause a stir,' Marcus commented. He was happy to follow James's lead and not press him on the subject of Alicia Carberry, but he knew that James's hint had already led to Caroline being consumed with curiosity. 'You don't seem very enthusiastic at the prospect of the Season,' he added. 'Has middle age caught up with you already, James? You used to be so sociable!'

James shrugged. 'I don't know.' Once more a touch of constraint entered his manner. 'Perhaps I'm simply not looking forward to having all the old history raked up. In my heart I knew that I could not escape it, but now the prospect of having my past picked over by a bunch of quizzes is hard to bear!'

Caroline poured herself another cup of tea. 'You must confound them all by being a pattern-card of virtue!' she said, with a hint of malice. 'Perhaps you should take a wife! That should silence the gossips!'

Unbidden, infuriatingly, the image of Alicia Carberry rose in James's mind once more. Alicia, who had refused his proposal only last week. Alicia, whose memory was provoking, infuriating, tantalising... With a painful jolt of the heart he wondered if he would ever be free. He shook his head abruptly to dispel the image. Caroline was watching him over the rim of her cup with her steady, perceptive gaze and he was afraid that she might see too much, but she said nothing and a moment later an impish light had entered her eyes.

'We could help you in your search for a wife,' she suggested lightly. 'We know all the eligible debutantes who will be making their come-out this year.' She wriggled down comfortably in her seat. 'Let's see,' she mused.' Amanda Edgecot is pretty and biddable, but perhaps a little young for you at seventeen? Do you remember her? A skinny brat with pigtails? What would you prefer, James—a demure young thing, or perhaps someone slightly older, with a little more conversation?'

James winced. He had acknowledged to his grandfather that he needed to find himself a wife, but now the whole process sounded horribly commercial and—worse still—a dead bore. His thoughts turned once more with a predictable inevitability. Alicia... She was never boring or insipid...difficult, perhaps...challenging, even... Now he was starting to get really angry with himself for his preoccupation with her. He completely missed the conspiratorial glance which flashed between Marcus and Caroline Kilgaren, so profound was his combined distaste at an arranged match and his annoyance with himself.

'Well,' Marcus continued casually, when James had failed to answer, 'I don't doubt that you will be viewed as quite a matrimonial prize!' He met Caroline's eyes with a smile and they both studiously ignored James's look of disgust.

'If you do prefer someone older,' Marcus pursued, 'there are several sensible girls who have been out for a few seasons. They are up to snuff and would not expect too much from you!'

It said a lot for James's preoccupation that he completely failed to realise that they were teasing him. Caroline picked up the cue neatly.

'Yes,' she said thoughtfully, 'there is Maria Marston, although I hear she is a little...' she paused delicately '...well, stupid really, but ideal if you require an amenable wife! Or Georgiana Stapleford,' she added hopefully. 'Now, she is *very* beautiful!'

'But equally spoilt and selfish!' Marcus said roundly. 'No, my dear, I doubt we can foist Georgiana off on James even if he were not too particular in his requirements! Now, how about—?'

'When you two have quite finished!' James put his glass down with a snap indicative of irritation as much as amusement. 'I fail to see why my matrimonial plans cause such fascination! Not,' he added ironically, 'that I could not do with some assistance! Only last week I had a proposal of marriage rejected out of hand!'

The reaction to this deliberately provocative statement was all that James could have desired. Caroline gave a smothered squeak and clapped her hand to her mouth, the teacup in her other hand tilting at a dangerous angle. Even Marcus's habitual nonchalance suffered a severe blow. He ran his hand through his fair hair, adjusted his cravat and cleared his throat.

'Well, if that don't beat the Dutch! Dash it all, James, you can't just leave it at that!' A twinkle entered his blue eyes. 'Who is the lady who is discerning enough to reject your suit?'

James smiled sardonically. 'We have already mentioned her name. Five days ago, I offered my hand in marriage to Alicia Carberry!'

Caroline's eyes were the size of saucers. She stared, but could utter no sound. Marcus, showing no further visible sign of disturbance, carefully removed the cup from his wife's hand and put it down gently on the table. She did not even notice.

'Well, James,' Marcus said ruefully as the silence stretched out, 'you have achieved your object of silencing us both! Now you owe us an explanation! It is stretching credulity too far to expect us to believe that you have been nurturing a secret passion for seven years and have now come back to fulfil it—not after the terms of your parting from Alicia!'

James gave a reluctant laugh, lying back in his armchair and stretching his long legs towards the fire. 'True enough! But you are vastly behindhand in your knowledge of my reacquaintance with Lady Carberry!' A wicked twinkle came into his eyes. 'In the space of one week I have been involved in a carriage accident with her, spent a night in a lonely inn in her company, indulged in several heated arguments with her and had my proposal of marriage put to scorn!'

'James! Enough of this provocation!' Caroline held up a hand in mock surrender. 'If you do not instantly indulge my curiosity I will burst!'

James laughed aloud at that. 'Acquit me, Caro! I will try to make amends!' He paused to sort out his thoughts. 'Where shall I start?'

'The beginning would seem appropriate,' Caroline said, with asperity.

'Very well,' James agreed obligingly. He picked up the soft, sleepy puppy and settled him on his lap.

'On my way up from Cardace, my curricle was in collision with Lady Carberry's coach. No one was seriously hurt,' he added hastily, seeing Caroline's look of sudden alarm. 'I helped the ladies to the shelter of the inn at Ottery. It was a godforsaken place, but I had given up hope of being able to convey them to a better establishment as we had no useable vehicle. Then, fortuitously, Squire and Mrs Henley stopped, having seen Lady Carberry's carriage in the ditch. They offered hospitality at the Manor.' The hint of amusement left him and his tone took on a heavy irony. 'The Henleys had guests and could not take up both ladies at once, so Lady Carberry, for reasons best known to herself, sent Miss Frensham on ahead.'

'Oh, dear,' Caroline said faintly, sensing disaster.

James gave her a rueful grimace. 'The road was flooded,' he

said, with weary patience, 'the carriage could not return for her ladyship and thus we were marooned together overnight at the inn!'

'How uncomfortable for you both!' Marcus commented, with a twitch of the lips. 'Dare I ask how you felt about this meeting? And how you passed the time?'

James shot him a darkling look. 'My feelings could best be described as mixed! As for the rest, we spent most of our time together in argument! I accused Lady Carberry of a reckless disregard for the conventions and the conversation degenerated from there! She retired to her room and I did not see her for the rest of the evening. The following morning I mistakenly conceived it to be my duty as a gentleman to offer her the protection of my name. I was rejected.'

Marcus looked perplexed by this foreshortened tale. He frowned.

'Hold on a minute, James, you're not making sense here! By your own admission you have no very good opinion of Alicia Carberry, yet you could have come out of this encounter an affianced man! Doing it a bit too brown, old chap!'

James smiled reluctantly. 'I know! Misplaced chivalry...' He shrugged with an attempt at lightness. 'No doubt I should be grateful that Lady Carberry had the sense to refuse me!'

There was an inflection in James's voice that caused Marcus to look at him curiously. After all this time one might have expected there to be nothing but indifference between James Mullineaux and Alicia Carberry, but this was evidently not so. James had spoken lightly, but Marcus knew his old friend and sensed that James's feelings were neither detached nor clear-cut. His interest sharpened.

'So how did you find Alicia after all these years?' Marcus enquired, the casual nature of the question belied by the acute interest in his eyes.

A black frown descended on James's brow. 'I found her wilful, proud, selfish, spoiled and arrogant,' he said shortly. 'Perhaps she was always all of those things and I was simply too infatuated to notice!'

He saw the expression on Caroline's face change and felt instantly contrite. 'I am sorry, Caro. I realise that you have remained Alicia Carberry's friend.'

There was an awkward pause. Mullineaux picked up the poker and moodily stirred the fire up into a blaze again. Caroline was watching him with a thoughtful look in her blue eyes. She felt no need to justify her friendship with Alicia, but she did feel an obligation to her friend. For once she thought very carefully before rushing into speech. She met her husband's steady gaze in a look of complete understanding. He did not say a word.

'No doubt you find it odd that I should still be a friend to Alicia after all that happened,' Caroline began carefully, 'and if it is your wish, James, we shall not mention the matter again. However, I should like to explain.' She saw his discouraging look, hesitated, then ploughed doggedly on when he did not speak.

'I am still close to Alicia because I do not believe that she was ever a...' she searched for the right words '...a scheming adventuress who was out to marry for money or a title. Alicia did not change—she is still the same person we all knew, and we knew that she was not like that! She has never told me the circumstances of her marriage, but I *know* Bertram Broseley forced the match and I am willing to believe that he exerted a lot of pressure to do so. I cannot blame Alicia for a situation of which I feel she was as much a victim as you were!'

There was silence. James looked totally unconvinced by this undeniably heartfelt plea. After he had clearly thought about and discarded several potential replies, he merely said, 'I'm sorry, Caro. I know you are sincere and I admire your loyalty even whilst I think it misplaced, but I cannot feel the same way as you do.'

Something closed in Caroline's face. 'No, of course not.' She put her teacup down gently and rose to her feet. 'Well, if you gentlemen will excuse me, I think I shall have an early night.'

Her gaze met Marcus's and a powerful message passed between them. Both men rose politely to their feet as she went out, closing the door softly behind her. James hesitated, put the pup down then walked over to the desk, reaching for the brandy decanter this time. Nod raised his head from his paws and gave a sleepy snore.

There was the companionable quiet that often existed between old friends and Marcus yawned, stretching in the warmth of the fire. He had not been remotely disturbed by the conversation between Caroline and James Mullineaux. He had great respect for Caroline's judgement and for his own part he had always liked Alicia Carberry. Like Caroline and a great many of their immediate friends, Marcus was certain that Bertram Broseley had compelled Alicia to marry George Carberry by some very questionable means. The fact that Alicia had never spoken of this even to her closest friends suggested to Marcus that it must still be very painful for her to recall.

However, he felt it would be naive to expect James to hold the same opinion. Whatever the truth had been, the relationship between James and Alicia was smashed beyond repair.

'So what happened after Lady Carberry dented your self-esteem with her rejection?' Marcus enquired lazily, looking up as James passed him one of the balloon glasses of brandy. 'You mentioned arguments in the plural—have you met since Ottery, then?'

James looked rueful. 'You don't miss much, do you, Marcus? I have met Lady Carberry on two subsequent occasions and our antagonism has not waned! The rest of the time I have been obliged to hear all and sundry sing her praises! It's enough to try the patience of a saint!'

Marcus grinned. 'So you don't list yourself with her admirers, then, old chap!' He stole a quick look at James's face and added guilelessly, 'It seems you still hold her in complete dislike!'

Surprisingly, James did not immediately agree with this. He turned his empty port glass over absent-mindedly between his fingers a few times, then he looked up and smiled.

'Cut line, Marcus—you know you don't really believe that! I never could fool you, could I, not even when we were in short coats? Damn it, my feelings really don't bear examination at the moment, but, despite that, I think you had better tell me whatever it is both you and Caroline feel I should know about Alicia.'

Their eyes met in a split second of tension, then Marcus gave a nod of acknowledgement.

'Well, you don't miss much either, do you, James? I suppose it's only fair...I cannot speak for Caro, but for myself it's simply that I dislike injustice and I think Alicia has been misjudged. Like Caro, I believe that she was forced into marriage with Carberry. I can't prove it, of course,' he added quickly. 'Alicia is the only one who could tell you the truth, but it grates on me that she should be condemned without a hearing.'

James's gaze rested on him with acute intelligence. 'There's more to this than that, though. You both remain convinced of her innocence when all the evidence points to the contrary. You must have some basis for your belief in her integrity.'

Marcus shifted a little uncomfortably in his chair. 'Yes, there is something... But it's hardly my secret to tell. Can you not take my word for it?'

There was a silence, then James shook his head slightly. 'On anything else I would say yes without reservation, Marcus. But you are asking me to agree to something without letting me judge the evidence myself—something which has profoundly affected my own life! I can't do it.'

Marcus sighed resignedly. 'I take your point. Well, this is Caroline's tale rather than mine, but I do not suppose that she would grudge my telling you.' He paused, aware of the sudden tension in the room.

'Caroline was one of the few people who saw Alicia immediately after George Carberry had died. She had heard that Alicia was back at Stansfield House and went to see how she was. That was typical of Caro,' Marcus said, his pride showing in his voice. 'Everyone else was talking scandal, but all she was concerned about was Alicia's welfare.'

He looked up to see James's gaze fixed on him with grave intent.

'Anyway, at first Lady Stansfield refused point-blank to let Caro in, but you know how persistent she is! In the end Lady S. agreed that it might help Alicia to see a friend, but she warned Caroline that Alicia was very unwell.' Marcus looked sombre. 'I called to see Caroline later in the day and she was still very upset by the experience. She poured it all out to me—how Alicia was covered in disfiguring bruises and cuts and was so disorientated that she barely had any idea where she was—even who she was!' Marcus shrugged uncomfortably. 'It was profoundly distressing.'

James's eyes had narrowed in disbelief at the story he was hear-

ing. 'What are you saying, Marcus? That Carberry—or Broseley—
did this to her?'

Marcus met his eyes directly. 'Precisely, James.'

There was a silence whilst James struggled with what he had
been told. Then, suddenly, the enormity of it struck him. He looked
aghast. 'Marcus, I cannot believe... Why would Broseley do such
a thing?'

Marcus looked grim. 'Who can say for sure? It was in his interests to achieve a marriage between two mercantile empires and
this was a good way to seal such an arrangement. If Alicia cut up
rough at his plans, he would have to change her mind for her,
somehow. After all, persuading unwilling offspring into marriage
is hardly a new concept!'

'Last century, perhaps, but in this day and age...?' James ran
his hand through his hair. 'I'm sorry, Marcus, but I really can't
believe this...'

Marcus shrugged. 'That is your privilege, of course, and I would
not seek to change your mind. All I know is that Caro would not
lie.'

'No, of course not...' James was struggling to equate his own
view of events with this new evidence. 'But perhaps she misunderstood? Damn it, Broseley told me Alicia had chosen Carberry
of her own free will!' He slammed his fist down on the arm of
the chair as his feelings caught alight. 'Marcus, Alicia's letter
damned her more eloquently than I ever could! It was the most
blatant piece of self-seeking greed that I have ever come across!'

Marcus drained his glass. 'She never *told* you to your face, did
she, James?'

'No.' James was looking impatient. 'But—' He broke off. 'What
exactly are you suggesting? That Broseley contrived it all? That
he made her write something against her will?'

'Precisely,' Marcus said again. He waited for this to sink in and
watched the conflict of thought that was clearly displayed on
James's face.

'But—' James was really struggling now '—there were all those
stories circulating in the clubs that Alicia had always been up to
the highest bidder, that she had married Carberry for his money...'

Marcus looked at him a little pityingly. 'Come on, James! Any-

one can put a tale about—you should know that! Who do you
think started those rumours?'

James looked incapable of commenting. He was scowling into
the heart of the fire, but it was not the flames that he was seeing.
His imagination was quite capable of summoning up all kinds of
demons prompted by Marcus Kilgaren's words. It all sounded so
horribly plausible and yet he had never even imagined it. Wrapped
up in his own pride and disillusion, he had never questioned his
interpretation of events. He had swung from the extreme of love
to hatred and disenchantment, and had joined the chorus of those
who had condemned Alicia to social damnation.

James shook his head in disbelief. 'Why did she never say anything if it were true? Why didn't *you* ever say anything before?'

Marcus laughed at that. 'When would you have liked me to tell
you? If I'd written to you immediately after you'd left the country,
how much credence would you have given the story? We're talking about it seven years later, in cold blood, and you're still having
difficulty believing it. Besides, as I said before, it is Caro's story
about Alicia, not mine—I had no right to tell you things Alicia
might not wish you to know. Even now I only spoke because I
felt you were maligning her.'

'If what you say is true, everybody has maligned her,' James
observed sombrely. 'Why has she never told anyone the truth?'

'Would you?' Marcus asked bluntly. 'It's hardly an edifying
tale, is it? For a start, I imagine that it was too personal and painful
for Alicia to want to discuss it and, God knows, the scandal was
great enough as it was! Would anything Alicia said have had any
effect other than to fan the flames? Also, she was very ill after
this happened. Lady Stansfield took her away for a long time and
it was generally said that that was to allow the scandal to die down,
but I think it was because she was very ill indeed.' Marcus paused
reflectively. 'No, I think Lady Stansfield handled it in the only
way possible—by subtly hinting that Alicia had been the victim
of a forced marriage, and by reintroducing her into Society in as
slow and circumspect a way as possible.'

Marcus did not add that James's own defection had done im-
measurable damage to Alicia's reputation. His public denouncement of his betrothed could only add weight to the story that she

was an adventuress who should be drummed out of Society. James was, however, quite capable of working that out for himself. He reached almost blindly for the brandy decanter.

'Indulge me,' he said after a moment, 'and answer some more questions.'

'If I can.'

'Why do you suppose that Alicia has not remarried? Surely she could have added a better title to her fortune by now?'

Marcus laughed 'She has hardly been short of offers! They say that Peter Weston proposed to her six times before he settled for Maria Loseley, and Severn's heir was the latest to try his luck and end up nursing a bruised ego at her rejection! She does not covet a title,' Marcus added with certainty.

'Then what else is there? Money, property, status—she has them all,' James pursued.

'I suppose,' Marcus agreed, 'that there's very little anyone could offer her which she does not have already. Respectability she has won by hard work, which leaves only love, and I expect Alicia feels she has burned herself badly enough on that in the past! Now I can only imagine her choosing to marry for companionship.'

'Is there no one she might wish to marry?' James asked quizzically.

Marcus laughed. 'No one! Alicia lives like a nun, James! She has become such a figure of virtue that she is almost a caricature! She has a reputation for coldness to the point of frigidity.'

James slanted a look at him. 'Is that a rumour spread by those whose suit has not prospered?' he suggested with a smile. 'It's usually the way!'

Marcus smiled reminiscently. 'Well, those who have offered a carte blanche do not make the same mistake twice! Alicia has a temper to rival her grandmother's when she wishes to use it!'

'I know!' James said with feeling. He picked up one of the chess pawns, idly admiring the intricate carving. 'And Christopher Westwood?' he asked, with apparent casualness.

Marcus looked surprised. 'Oh, so you've heard about him, have you? Well, he is Lady Stansfield's great-nephew, and as such I suppose he has a legitimate reason for hanging on the family's coat-tails. I don't like him,' he admitted, 'but Alicia seems to enjoy, his company. There's no more to it than that, though, even though he moons about her like a lovesick puppy! She won't marry him,' Marcus concluded, with certainty. 'Alicia's reputation for coldness is well-founded. Whether to avoid fortune-hunters or the intimacies of marriage it would be difficult to ascertain, but, for whatever reason, it is true.'

Now it was James's turn to laugh. 'Coldness?' Involuntarily he remembered the intense physical awareness that had flared between himself and Alicia. 'Maybe on the surface she appears cold, but it is only skin-deep. The fire is banked down, not burned out.'

Marcus gave him a look of genuine curiosity. 'Is that so? Well, if you saw that much, old fellow, you must have had more of an effect on her than anyone else in the last seven years! But then, you did catch her at a disadvantage. Next time you meet her, I expect she will have resumed her habitual chilliness!'

James slanted a smile at him. 'So you think that there will be a next time, do you, Marcus?'

His friend gave him a very straight look. 'I would lay odds on it, James!' He yawned suddenly. 'Well...I must retire, or Caroline will come looking for me! We always keep early hours in the country. Goodnight, James!'

James stayed by the fire for a little while, finishing his brandy and stroking the somnolent puppy he had lifted back into his lap rather absent-mindedly.

There was something about the name Westwood that was nagging at the edge of his memory, although he could have sworn that he had never met the man. He moved the chess pieces thoughtfully back to the side of the board, deliberately avoiding any thought of Alicia. And then he remembered. He *had* met Westwood before, and the circumstances of it gave him pause.

It had been seven years previously, and play at White's had been high and drinking deep. It was only a couple of nights after Alicia's scandalous defection and James had been trying to drown his sorrows. He had been on a phenomenal winning streak, but even he knew that there had been an explosive element in his own behaviour, just waiting for release. Westwood had given him the opportunity, by being amongst the first to sling mud at Alicia's name.

James frowned, remembering with unpleasant clarity the real hatred on Westwood's white face as he had made those claims about Alicia, claims which had found their mark with James because he was vulnerable and in two minds about her innocence himself. The whole of White's cardroom had heard Westwood denounce her as a duplicitous adventuress who had the benefit of an innocent face hiding an amoral soul. James had raised his fist to hit him across the room, but Marcus had caught his arm in a grip of iron and persuaded him rather forcibly to let the matter drop. James, half inclined to agree with Westwood's assertions, had gone and got seriously drunk instead, after which he remembered nothing. Unfortunately there were plenty of kind souls who later reminded him that in his cups he had damned Alicia with more colourful invective than Westwood had ever used.

Remembering all this, James found it odd in the extreme that Westwood was now so close to both Alicia and her grandmother. In those days Westwood had not been a visitor at Stansfield House, but had pursued a far more rackety existence on the fringes of Society, always wagering more than he could afford and indulging in some very expensive habits. There were many such, living beyond their means and gaining membership to the exclusive clubs such as Whites' by extracting a favour from some luckless sprig of the nobility over whom they had some hold.

James wrinkled his nose with disgust. Something had evidently occurred to help Westwood overcome his loathing of his fair cousin to the extent that he now wished to marry her. Or perhaps, James pondered, he simply saw ingratiating himself with his Stansfield relatives as the best hope for the future. Either way, it left a rather unpleasant taste in the mouth. James wondered whether Lady Stansfield, normally sharp as a razor, had ever known that Westwood had been one of the first to denounce her beloved granddaughter. Still, it was none of his business, after all.

What had become his business was the truth about Alicia. For the first time in years he allowed himself to wonder if he had made a mistake, and to think of the Alicia Broseley he had once known, with her bright, indomitable spirit. To think of that life and brightness crushed and defaced by the likes of Bertram Broseley and George Carberry was almost intolerable.

He put down the pup and raked out the embers of the fire. He was determined to see Alicia again. He had to make her tell him the truth. Only then could he be free of the past. He paused, remembering the lovely, heart-shaped face, the flashing green eyes, the perfect, curved mouth...and felt a rush of desire that took him by surprise. He was hardly a callow youth to be enslaved by a pretty face and neat figure! If he was not careful, he could find himself in as deep as he had been seven years before.

James Mullineaux had always been a gambler, but he seldom took an uncalculated risk. It meant that he did not often make mistakes. But now he knew the course he had chosen was going to be dangerous. It made no difference. He had made his decision.

Chapter Five

Chartley Chase had changed since the days when a young James Mullineaux had been taken there as a protesting child to visit some indigent maiden aunt. In the pale sunlight of the late February morning its creamy stone gleamed warm. In his memory was the smell of camphor and sal volatile—now he noticed the mingled scent of beeswax and lavender in the air, and paused to appreciate the sparkling stained glass of the landing window as the sun scattered its colours over the graceful, curving stair. The whole house exuded an understated good taste and subtle, welcoming warmth that was a reflection of Alicia's hospitality.

Alicia was standing by the drawing-room window looking out over the garden to the moors beyond. She turned as the Marquis's name was announced and came forward unhurriedly as he started to cross the room towards her. She was wearing green, a colour which established a satisfyingly subtle contrast with that glorious auburn hair, today piled on the top of her head in an artfully contrived knot of curls. She looked every inch the Society hostess; no genuine emotion could be discerned in her manner or countenance. Her smile had exactly the right degree of warmth in it for one dealing with a surprise visit from a mere acquaintance, which put him in his place, James reflected ruefully. Marcus had been quite correct. There was a chilly composure about Alicia which suggested that her defences were firmly in place. Well, they would see.

Alicia, contrary to her outward calm, was shaking inside. When

Cheffings had announced that the Marquis of Mullineaux had called to see her she had been astounded, for she hardly considered that they were on calling terms. Her second reaction, following swiftly on the first, had been a cowardly instinct to avoid James by pretending to be out, but in the end the urge to see him again had proved too strong. She had put aside her book, pressed her palms together in a brief, nervous gesture, taken up her stance by the window, and sent Cheffings to show James in.

She watched him cross the room towards her, casually elegant and assured.

'Lord Mullineaux.' Alicia summoned up a faint, distant smile. She felt a little colour come into her cheeks as he took her hand in his, and took a deep breath to steady herself. 'How good of you to call, sir. Will you take a seat? May I offer you some refreshment?'

'Thank you, but no.' James inclined his head, as formal as she. 'I am to join Caroline and Marcus Kilgaren at Pilton Abbey shortly, so this is only a brief visit.' He took the chair that she indicated and returned his attention to his hostess, allowing his gaze to travel over her in a thoroughly disconcerting manner.

'Caroline and Marcus both send their best wishes. They are looking forward to seeing you later in the week. I called to enquire whether you had recovered from your accident,' James added, in an impersonal tone. 'The last time we met, I had no opportunity to enquire after your health.'

And whose fault was that? Alicia thought rebelliously. He had been too busy hurling accusations to indulge in polite conversation! She crushed down the prickles of resentment. Today he would *not* get under her guard. Today, her equilibrium restored, she could view him as a mere acquaintance. She knew she was lying to herself, but did not want to stop and think about it.

'How kind of you to ask,' she said coldly, drawing on the strength which had seen her through so many trials in the past. 'As you see, I am much recovered.'

She thought she saw James's lips twitch slightly at her formality.

'You are still a trifle pale, perhaps, but I see that you have had your wrist attended to properly,' he observed solemnly.

'Yes, indeed.' Alicia glanced down a little self-consciously at the bandage, its pristine whiteness reminding her of their last meeting. 'The doctor tells me that it is a slight sprain, nothing worse, but that I must rest it for a week or so more.'

'You were fortunate that your injuries were not more severe,' James commented.

The conversation lapsed. Alicia wished he had agreed to a glass of Madeira—at least it would have given them something to do to pass the time. She was aware of a feeling of resentment growing within her as she watched him marking time to the end of what must constitute for him a tedious, duty visit. He could not have made clearer that he had called only out of a sense of social obligation. She wished that he had not bothered. The nature of her feelings for him had inevitably led her to hope for more than the grudging consideration he was according her.

'And Miss Frensham?' James enquired, after a strained pause. 'Do you have any news from Ottery?'

Alicia fought down the sense of irritation that this superficial conversation was provoking in her. It seemed they could never be comfortable together, for they must always be either coming to blows or talking in trivialities. She pinned on a bright, insincere smile.

'I hear that Miss Frensham is recovering well from her ordeal,' she replied. 'She hopes to return here in a couple of weeks. Mrs Henley also mentioned in her letter that you had called to enquire after Miss Frensham's health before you left Ottery.' A shade of genuine warmth came into her tone. 'That was most kind of you, sir. I know that Miss Frensham deeply appreciated the help that you gave her that evening.'

James was also suffering from the artificiality of the conversation. Matters were not progressing as he had intended, but he seemed powerless to bridge the gap between them. Alicia's chilly welcome had set him at a distance and she had seemed disinclined to allow him any closer. He, in turn, had responded by taking his cue from her and talking at only the most shallow of levels. He was beginning to find their stilted words deeply frustrating.

Alicia was fidgeting with her dress, pleating and re-pleating the material between her fingers. James looked at her bent head and felt a sudden acute pang for what they had lost.

Alicia looked up abruptly and met his eyes. Just for a moment she surprised there an expression which she thought she recognised, before his face was wiped clean of all emotion. She must have imagined it. Once again, she summoned up a brilliant, superficial smile.

'I hope that you have found the house at Monks Dacorum to your liking, my lord.'

James shifted restlessly. 'Monks Dacorum is a fine house. I like it a great deal.'

'And the estate?' Alicia continued politely. 'You must have found much to interest you in the past week.'

'Yes, indeed.' James leant forward, a sudden flicker in his eyes. 'I have heard much spoken of your good works, Lady Carberry. Tell me, how do you equate your apparent determination to make a profit with the almshouses you have had built? And how much revenue does the village school generate for you?'

Alicia opened her mouth to deny all knowledge and met his quizzical gaze. She swallowed hard. Suddenly finding she could not prevaricate, she tried to make light of it. 'It is no great matter, my lord.'

'No?' James refused to smile and let it drop. 'I believe I owe you an apology, Lady Carberry. You misled me with your insistence that you always sought financial gain, but I believe I should not have been so quick to condemn. The facts do not bear out your words.'

Neither did the facts seven years ago, Alicia thought with sudden anguish, but you waited for no explanation then. She had to turn away from him, so acute was the sudden pain in her breast. It took a moment for her to regain her composure, but then she was able to turn back with a gracious, social smile.

'I repeat, my lord, it is of no great moment.'

'I think it is.' James was looking sombre. 'It is easy to make false assumptions.' He held her gaze very deliberately with his own. She could read there the one question he did not put into words: *Why did you lie to me?*

Alicia could not even begin to consider the implications of that question. She broke the contact between them with an effort.

James now found that he was the one in danger of losing his temper. He scrutinised the flawlessly perfect face before him, but Alicia was looking completely unmoved. James was suddenly determined to break through the polite triviality of the conversation. If she would not respond to his veiled comments on the past, he would try a different provocation.

'Lady Carberry, will you explain something to me?' He was looking at his most satirical, Alicia thought, with misgiving. Where was this line of questioning going?

'When I was at Ottery Manor it became apparent to me that Mrs Henley's guests were all aware of my ill-considered proposal to you, and your still more reckless refusal. Whatever possessed you to make them free of such information?'

Alicia felt the humiliating colour flame into her face. Her green eyes widened with a mixture of mortification and anger. She could feel her façade of bland courtesy wavering and it suffered another blow when she looked at James and saw that he had recognised her discomfiture. With all her strength she struggled to regain her composure, wipe all expression from her face and achieve an appropriate level of civility.

'I am very sorry that you should have been exposed to such speculation,' she commented, with constraint. 'I spoke to Mrs Henley in private and cannot believe that she would break a confidence. I can only assume that our conversation was overheard. I must offer you my apologies,' she finished stiffly.

James was appalled at the violence of the frustration that shot through him. When they had met at Ottery, Alicia had been at a severe disadvantage, hurt and distressed, unable to deploy her defences as she was doing now. But how much more attractive had been that more brittle, accessible Alicia—even at the height of their conflict he had preferred the real flesh-and-blood woman to this infuriating cipher.

'Pray do not apologise, Lady Carberry,' James said, a little grimly. 'All that I believe you owe me is an explanation for your wilful courting of Society's disapproval! To have become stranded with me was folly enough, but to let it be known that I had offered the protection of my name only to be rejected was madness!' His voice took on a reflective quality. 'I find a strange contradiction here. Over the past couple of days, more than one person has commented to me that you behave as a pattern-card of conformity. How is it, then, that in your dealings with me you appear to feel a compulsion to challenge the rules all the time?'

This was coming uncomfortably close to the mark, and he was pushing her very hard, far harder than good manners allowed. Alicia knew it, but could not imagine what was prompting his behaviour. She was not to know that it was James's sole intention to provoke her into losing her temper, for paradoxically he knew that he could get far closer to her if she dropped her guard. Their explosive encounter at Ottery had proved as much.

But not this time. Alicia stood up, a faint, wintry smile on her lips, indicating that their meeting was at an end.

'I do not believe that I have anything further to explain to you, sir,' she said sweetly. 'Do not let me keep you from your other engagements! I thank you for your consideration in calling on me. Please convey my best wishes to Caroline and Marcus. Good day to you!'

James gave her a long, level look, which she met with nothing but an impervious blankness in return. He got to his feet slowly. After a moment's hesitation he took her hand and bowed over it.

Alicia felt the tension uncurl within her a little. At last he was going to go away and leave her alone! She should have been more careful, knowing his complete unpredictability; it was only a momentary lack of vigilance on her part, but it was enough. With great deliberation, James turned her hand over and kissed the palm, watching with amusement as she snatched her hand away and took several hasty steps back. She knew that for a long moment her expressive face gave her confusion away, then, as movement returned to muscles which appeared temporarily frozen, she turned hastily aside to pull the bell for the butler, addressing him in arctic tones as the door opened. 'Cheffings, be so good as to escort the Marquis of Mullineaux out. He is leaving now.'

Despite the coldness of his dismissal, James was smiling as he sauntered down the steps and out into the crisp morning air.

* * *

'Well, miss, you must have windmills in your head if you think that I'm going to accept this latest piece of nonsense!'

The Dowager Countess of Stansfield descended from her ancient carriage onto the gravel in front of Chartley Chase and addressed her granddaughter in her usual pugnacious terms. Alicia repressed a smile.

'How lovely to see you again, Grandmama! But what can you mean?'

'Humph!' Lady Stansfield made a noise reminiscent of a camel snorting and looked Alicia over critically. The bright green eyes, exactly like her granddaughter's, were still as shrewd and sharp as ever. She was attired in vivid red, her favourite colour, and a hat adorned with many and varied feathers sat atop her white curls. She fixed Alicia with her ferocious gaze.

'This tale going the rounds concerning a secret rendezvous between yourself and the Marquis of Mullineaux! Barely is the man back in this country and you are running off to meet him alone in some country inn! What do you have to say for yourself, miss?'

Alicia remained calm beneath the interested gaze of the coachman, several footmen, her own butler, her grandmother and Christopher Westwood, who had assisted Lady Stansfield from the carriage and now stood on one side still waiting to greet her. This, it seemed, was only the start of the onslaught. Still, there was no point in retaliating with Lady Stansfield, who could give as good as she got anyway. Alicia gave her grandmother an unconcerned smile.

'How gossip does travel!' she marvelled innocently. 'Why, the only thing I have to say, ma'am, is that were I to arrange a secret meeting I would do so more efficiently and no one would know of it!' She turned to greet Westwood, signalling that the topic was at an end. 'Good day, Christopher, I hope that you had a comfortable journey!'

Lady Stansfield took this set-down in good part. Alicia had learned a long time ago that the only way to deal with her outspoken grandmother was to refuse to submit to her bullying. This had endeared her to the old lady rather than the reverse and Lady Stansfield's eyes now took on a distinct twinkle as she came forward to kiss her granddaughter.

'Well, well, that's as maybe, miss! Christopher is quite out of charity with you! It doesn't do to make him jealous!'

Lady Stansfield had always had a squirm-inducing habit of talking about people as though they weren't there, and Westwood was far too deferential to object. He merely stood looking sheepish and shifting uncomfortably from one foot to the other.

Alicia gritted her teeth. There was no point in telling her grandmother that Christopher Westwood had no right to question her behaviour—that would only give the old lady another opportunity to remark on the sense in the two of them marrying. It was no secret that Lady Stansfield wished to promote such a match and Westwood was more than willing. Only Alicia's stubbornness was opposing it.

'I am fagged to death after the journey,' Lady Stansfield continued, her gold-topped cane tapping across the gravel and up the steps. 'I wish to rest. We shall talk later, my dear. You—' Her beady gaze turned on Cheffings, who looked somewhat unnerved. 'You are not Fordyce! Where is he?'

'Fordyce is in London, opening up the house for the Season,' Alicia replied patiently. 'This is Cheffings, Grandmama, and I do beg you not to terrify him!'

'In London! So early in the year! And two butlers! How extravagant!' Lady Stansfield looked scandalised, as though Alicia had admitted to some perversion. Her accusing gaze swept over the hapless Cheffings as though it were all his fault. 'Well, Cheffings, I suppose you will have to do! Show me to my room!'

She swept regally up the staircase, trailed by the startled butler. Alicia was left with Christopher Westwood, who was looking positively miserable.

'She means no harm, you know,' he offered pacifically, his fair, good-humoured face troubled. 'We heard all the gossip and were only at pains to think how best to help you.'

Alicia reflected that that was exactly the sort of appeasing comment that put her out of humour with him. It might be unfair to blame him for being so eager to please, but she could not deny that it annoyed her. Ushering him into the library, she turned to order refreshments then closed the door thankfully on her grandmother's retreating back. She felt exhausted already, and the rest of her house party had not even arrived yet.

They talked on trivialities such as the weather and the state of the roads whilst the refreshments were being served, but it was clear that Westwood was somewhat preoccupied for his answers to Alicia's questions always seemed to be a little late on cue. He was a fair young man who was related to Lady Stansfield through her sister. Cultivated and refined, he affected dandyism in his style of dress, and his shirt points were high, his cravat a miracle of intricacy and his boots as highly polished as the library mirrors. Yet despite, or perhaps because of, his regard for fashion, he did not seem able to achieve the careless elegance of James Mullineaux. Nor did he have any of James's instinctive authority. Alicia found herself making the comparison and disliked herself for it, but she could find Westwood amiable, nothing more.

On this occasion he had a more than usually anxious look on his face and Alicia wondered what was distracting him. He knocked his glass over, set it to rights and cleared his throat, then sat forward and fixed her with an earnest look.

'Alicia, this business with Mullineaux—' He broke off immediately, clearly unsure how to proceed.

'Yes?' Alicia asked unencouragingly, determined to make him suffer. She was still out of charity with him and did not see why he had to pry into her personal affairs. And anyway, the last thing she wanted to do was talk about James Mullineaux.

'Well...I mean...surely it was an accident?'

'Certainly.' Alicia deliberately misunderstood him. 'A carriage accident.'

Westwood had the grace to look slightly ashamed of himself. The hot colour flooded his face. 'I hope,' he said constrainedly, 'that you came to no harm?'

'Fortunately not, thank you,' Alicia said, with composure. 'I injured my wrist in the accident, but it is only a slight sprain and already on the mend. However, Miss Frensham caught a chill from standing about in the rain and she is still at Ottery Manor with the Henleys.'

'I am sorry to hear it,' Westwood murmured, still abashed. He seemed to steel himself. 'No doubt it is unpleasant for her to have taken a chill, but surely it is worse for you, Alicia! To have spent a night alone in an inn with Mullineaux... Well, you can see how people will be talking!'

Alicia wondered briefly whether a scream of aggravation would put an end to this topic of conversation. It seemed likely, but rather an extreme measure to take. She smiled politely.

'I can understand perfectly. However, I rely on you to squash the rumours, of course.'

Westwood looked taken aback. Clearly whatever outpouring of regret or apology he had expected would simply not be forthcoming.

'Of course,' he agreed doubtfully. 'But, Alicia—'

Alicia cut across him decisively. 'Indeed, it's very unfortunate that Miss Frensham is still indisposed! We should not be so careless of the conventions as to meet like this without chaperonage, Christopher! Not everyone views our family connection in the same light as we do!'

Westwood swallowed hard. It seemed a little ironic to him that Alicia should choose to play propriety now, having spent a night alone in an inn, however innocently, with another man. He stole a glance at her charming profile, but learned nothing. Her expression was as calm and serene as usual, although he fancied he could detect a hint of determination in the set of her jaw. Westwood sighed unconsciously. He knew Alicia could tie him in knots should she choose, but it made little difference to his main aim, which was to marry both her and her fabulous fortune.

He had been finding it more and more difficult to get Alicia on her own in recent weeks, and suspected that this was because she deliberately avoided this. Now he had his opportunity and he intended to make the most of it. Although he had not planned to speak so soon after his arrival, he was in such a state of pent-up nervousness and anticipation that he could not help himself.

'I am glad Miss Frensham is not with us,' Westwood said desperately, 'for there is something I particularly wished to say to you, Alicia.'

Alicia was aware of a sinking feeling in the region of her heart. She could hardly be unaware of what was coming. Westwood's attentions had been becoming so marked over the past few months that she had known it could only be a matter of time before he made her a declaration. With vague amazement she realised that a week ago she might have even considered his suit. Now, as her thoughts slid imperceptibly but inevitably towards James, she knew that she could never marry Christopher Westwood.

It was evident that Westwood, having announced his intentions, was unsure of exactly how to begin. He cleared his throat a couple of times, leapt restlessly to his feet and finally burst into speech.

'Confound it, Alicia, I have been trying to show you for months—no, years!—how I feel about you!' he went down on one knee before her, and seized her hand. 'Marry me! Give me the right to protect you! I know it is presumptuous of me even to think of proposing to you, but we would deal well together, I know it! We enjoy each other's company, and—' he seized on another advantage to strengthen his suit '—your grandmother would be delighted!'

His intense grey eyes were fixed unwaveringly on her face and he raised her hand to press a feverish kiss on the back of it.

At this passionate and highly inconvenient moment, the door opened to admit a footman with a message from Lady Stansfield. Alicia had never been so glad to see anyone. Westwood dropped her hand as though he had been burned and scrambled to his feet, his countenance flushed with mortification. The footman, equally scarlet, hovered hopelessly in the doorway, his tray tilted at such an alarming angle that the missive slid off it onto the floor.

'Please come in, Liddell,' Alicia instructed coolly, quite as though nothing untoward had occurred. She retrieved the note, read it and waved him away without a reply. The door shut behind him with indecent haste as he shot downstairs to regale the servants' hall with the news that Mr Westwood was proposing.

Westwood himself was clearly furious at the interruption but could not see any way of resuming his declaration without appearing even more foolish.

Alicia seized her chance. 'Dear Christopher,' she said gently, 'I am very flattered that you wish me to become your wife, but I really must decline. You know that I esteem you as a friend, but I do not believe that we should suit.'

The hot colour rushed back into Westwood's face. Already humiliated by the tactless entrance of the footman, he was in danger of losing his self-control.

'Why not?' he demanded, with more indignation than manners.

Alicia bit her lip. This was difficult, as she was well aware that she had given him every indication that she enjoyed his company, whilst not having the least desire to marry him. Worse, she realised with a guilty pang that she had used him to keep other admirers at a distance, even whilst she had been aware of his growing regard for her.

'I am too used to having my own independence now to comfortably adapt to another arrangement,' she temporised. 'I am used to running my own estates and ordering my life, and all that would have to change were I to marry.'

'If you wanted to remarry, none of that would be of the least consequence,' Westwood retorted, unanswerably.

Alicia sighed. She could hardly tell him that she found him dull, and that life with him would be lacklustre. When he had touched her she had felt none of the explosive chemistry which was between herself and James Mullineaux. What a trying week it had been! Three marriage proposals, albeit one was by proxy, and none of them acceptable!

Westwood was still gazing down at her with a dogged determination. How could she finish this? Briefly she toyed with the idea of bursting into tears, thus putting him firmly in the wrong. After all, no gentleman should persist in an unwanted suit. A moment later, however, she rejected such a shabby idea. She had treated him badly enough as it was.

'Please come and sit down, Christopher,' she urged, patting the seat beside her. 'We have been good friends—must it all be at an end?'

Some of the sulky, mulish expression left Westwood's face, and he sat down beside her with an ill grace. He gave a despondent sigh.

'Suppose I never really thought you'd accept,' he admitted ruefully. 'After all, you turn fellows away by the barrowload, and why should I be different?' He was already looking more cheerful, as he had a disposition which could not sulk for long. 'Still, can't blame me for trying!'

He looked at Alicia thoughtfully, then added, 'I don't suppose it's anything to do with Mullineaux, is it?'

Alicia jumped involuntarily. 'What do you mean?'

Westwood looked a little confused. 'Well, you're forever turning away proposals from eligible men. I wondered if you were comparing them with some ideal? And as you have just met him again...'

This was surprisingly perceptive of Westwood, who was not known for his sensitivity to others' feelings. Alicia, who had no inclination to examine her own feelings on this point, ignored the difficult part of his question to concentrate on the bit she could deny.

'Well, disabuse yourself of the notion that Mullineaux was—or is—some kind of ideal!' It came out more fiercely than she had intended. Remembering their disastrous encounters and the even more dangerous feelings which James could arouse in her, Alicia felt tormented beyond bearing.

'When he was younger,' she said coldly, 'James Mullineaux was arrogant and conceited, and time has improved him into a man overbearing beyond toleration and downright rude! We met by complete chance and it was undoubtedly the worst piece of luck I could have had!'

'You don't like him, then,' Westwood said, without irony and with complete satisfaction.

Annabella Broseley's wedding took place on a bright afternoon in early March with the first blossom bursting out on the trees and the breeze setting the daffodils dancing on the green before Taunton Castle. That the wedding was being held in Taunton had been the first bone of contention between the St Auby family and Bertram Broseley—he had wanted to hold the ceremony in St Mary Redcliffe in Bristol, at the heart of his mercantile empire. The St Aubys had thrown up their hands in horror. No smell of the shop was going to infect the wedding of their only son, no matter how much he was going to benefit from the profits of trade after the event. So the wedding was held in Taunton and the St Aubys invited half the county in the hope that some of them would actually attend.

Alicia had agonised over her invitation for what felt like an age. It had arrived shortly after her return from Greyrigg and she had hidden it behind the clock on her mantelpiece, unwilling to see her father ever again. She felt very little kinship with Annabella either, and acknowledged to herself that this was a great shame. It seemed that she had made her choice and that her grandmother could be her only family now. Nevertheless, a niggling sense of guilt had caught her every so often and in the end she had found herself at her escritoire, penning a stilted little note to her father to the effect that Lady Carberry would be very happy to attend the marriage.

So here she was. The church was as flower-bedecked as Annabella herself, whose huge organza frills resembled nothing so much as a large meringue dessert, to Alicia's mind. She was clearly very pleased with herself, casting languishing looks at her young husband throughout the service and tossing her golden curls as she trilled with excited laughter. Alicia found it all vaguely sickening, particularly as before the service had started she had also spotted Francis St Auby exchanging looks of an intimate nature with a fast-looking matron in stripes. Worse, from Alicia's point of view, Bertram Broseley had made sure she was installed very ostentatiously beside him on the front pew and had joined her, beaming, after he had given away the bride.

Relations between them had been superficially pleasant so far. Shortly after her arrival at the St Aubys' house, Alicia had rather tartly enquired whether her father had invited his mysterious business associate to be amongst his guests, sure that he would not miss this opportunity to try to promote the match he had mooted to her before. Rather to her surprise, Broseley had appeared to find this highly amusing, relating that Mr Wood, as he referred to him, had a previous engagement in the county and could not attend. A little later, Alicia had caught her father's eye resting upon her roguishly, as though he was enjoying a good joke, and she had even thought she saw his shoulders shake slightly. Vaguely irritated, she had dismissed it as of no importance.

Also absent from the nuptials was Josiah, whom Alicia had expected to see at an occasion where he could have played the gentleman. Again, her father had seemed amused by her enquiry after her cousin, telling her Josiah was indisposed and could not attend. Alicia, concerned, had asked if his illness was serious, at which Broseley had looked as though he was about to burst out laughing. It was all rather odd and, Alicia thought, rather childish of him.

Alicia sighed. The St Auby family were Catholic and had insisted on a wedding mass, and the service was lasting some considerable time. Annabella appeared not to mind, no doubt caring little about the religious denomination of her husband as long as she could hang upon his arm in front of the assembled throng. Francis was a slender youth whose delicate fair looks might well appeal to some women, but whose nature could be described as neither delicate nor fair. Alicia did not like him at all. From her vantage point she could see him shifting from one foot to the other and trying to catch the eye of the stripy lady whilst Annabella's attention was distracted. Beside her, Broseley exuded all the confidence and complacency of the self-made man.

Alicia could feel her own attention wandering as the priest's voice droned on. She turned her head, idly scanning the rows of guests in the side aisles, mostly the local gentry who had decided for whatever reason to grace the occasion with their presence. Lady St Auby had managed quite a creditable turnout, Alicia thought with surprise. She had expected most of the gentry to spurn the invitation on the grounds that Broseley was a jumped-up nobody, but evidently curiosity had done the trick... Her train of thought came to an abrupt end as she recognised a familiar dark head across the other side of the church, at the front of the congregation. Surely it could not be! Whatever could he be doing here? Alicia stared harder to make quite sure. And at that moment the Marquis of Mullineaux turned his head and met her startled gaze with the very faintest sardonic glint in his own eyes. He inclined his head in acknowledgement.

Alicia removed her gaze hastily, blushing furiously and flustered at having been caught staring. What on earth was Mullineaux doing there and how could she possibly have missed his arrival? He must have already been in the church when she went in, for Alicia had arrived deliberately late and some of Bertram Broseley's acquaintances had kept her talking until just before Annabella had arrived.

Alicia was utterly dumbfounded by Mullineaux's presence. She realised that she was breathless, gripping her dainty reticule between clenched fingers, brought close to panic by the sudden and unexpected nature of his appearance. She took a deep breath in an attempt to calm down. The congregation was standing up, indicating that the service was almost over. Annabella and her new husband were walking slowly down the aisle and Bertram Broseley was offering his arm to her as the St Aubys swept out in front of them. Alicia took the proffered arm numbly, all her thoughts suddenly centred on Mullineaux and the necessity of trying to avoid him during the rest of the celebrations.

This proved relatively easy to begin with. The wedding breakfast was being held at the St Aubys' town house in Fore Street and Alicia was relieved to find that her place at table sandwiched her between Sir Frederick St Auby and his elder daughter, Lady Grey. James Mullineaux was out of Alicia's sight, as Lady St Auby had claimed the hostess's privilege and put him on her right hand as an honoured guest. Although Alicia could not see James, her senses seemed intensely aware of him. She knew, for instance, what a commotion his presence at the wedding was still creating, as guests clamoured to greet him and speculate over his motives in accepting Lady St Auby's invitation. In her mind's eye, Alicia could see the friendly greetings of the men and the fawning of the women, and could imagine the tilt of Mullineaux's head, that slow, devastating smile, the sleepy look in those dark eyes which masked the shrewd appraisal as he summed up his fellow guests.

Alicia was no less perplexed than they about his presence, though perhaps for different reasons. It was natural for Lady St Auby to have invited him, she supposed. Together with the Piltons and Cavanaghs, the Mullineauxs must be considered one of the premier families in the county whose appearance at the wedding could not but add cachet. To leave Mullineaux off the guest list could have been interpreted as a monstrous snub. On the other hand, Alicia, not normally prone to gambling, was willing to bet that Lady St Auby had never expected Mullineaux to accept and had probably had a fit of the vapours when he had done so.

And why had he done so? Alicia could not puzzle it out. Surely any event involving her family would naturally lead him to cry off? He was certainly making no attempt to seek her out, and whilst this relieved her she also found to her annoyance that it piqued her as well.

The banquet over, the guests began to mingle and chat. Alicia was immediately pounced upon by Richard, Viscount Pilton, the youthful heir to a local earldom, who made a beeline for her side and stuck fast.

'Splendid wedding, Lady Carberry, quite splendid!' His fair, cheerful face beamed with good humour and good claret. 'Such a shame Lady Stansfield could not be here!'

Alicia did not enlighten him. Her grandmother had not been invited.

'Splendid to see James Mullineaux back amongst us,' Pilton continued, oblivious of the tactlessness of his observation. 'Always said he had been away too long!' He looked across the room to where Mullineaux lounged at ease, one shoulder resting against a pillar, a faint smile on his lips as Francis St Auby's inamorata plied him with wine and conversation. 'Taken up where he left off,' Pilton said enviously. 'God, I wish I had his style! Francis won't be pleased—' He broke off, flushing as he encountered Alicia's quelling gaze, and realised that such a comment was hardly appropriate to the sister of the bride. But a moment later Alicia smiled charmingly at him and he instantly forgot his tactlessness and smiled back, completely enraptured.

A hand fell on his shoulder.

'Richard,' the Marquis of Mullineaux said in his distinctive drawl, 'your aunt Marion is looking neglected. Go and fetch her a glass of lemonade, there's a good fellow!'

Pilton was already halfway across the room before he stopped to wonder how Mullineaux, who a moment before had appeared engrossed in flirtation, could possibly know of his aunt's need for refreshments. He scowled, but it was too late.

Mullineaux watched him go with a slightly pitying smile on his face.

'So easy to mislead,' he mused, with mock sadness. 'Modern youth has much to learn!'

'Doubtless he has not your wealth of experience,' Alicia said sarcastically, and saw him smile with appreciation.

'True enough, I suppose! And by the same token he is out of his depth with you, Lady Carberry!' Mullineaux's frankly admiring gaze approved her dress of aquamarine velvet, lingering on its fichu of almost transparently fine lace. 'I was merely saving our young friend the inevitable humiliation of falling prey to unrequited love!'

'Not a misfortune ever likely to afflict you, sir,' Alicia snapped, before she had time to bite her tongue. His comment had caught her on the raw for she already seemed to have fallen prey to that undesirable condition herself. Her hypnotised gaze travelled over him. His coat of darkest blue, worn with pale buff pantaloons and a cravat immaculately tied in the Mathematical, gave him the same indefinable elegance that she had noted at Ottery. His black hair was carefully disordered and as her eyes met his she saw that he was watching her with interest and not a little amusement. Alicia felt her colour rising and cursed the perfect, pale complexion which betrayed her so easily.

'Oh, I do not know about that,' Mullineaux said thoughtfully, his disturbing dark gaze never leaving her face. 'And you, Lady Carberry—do you have any experience of that melancholy state yourself?'

Drat the man! He was too perceptive! Alicia was certain that some degree of her discomfort must be showing in her face. She said the first thing that came into her head in order to distract his attention.

'Whatever are you doing here, anyway, Lord Mullineaux? I would scarce have expected to meet you at my sister's wedding!'

'Nor I you perhaps, Lady Carberry,' James Mullineaux said, somewhat obscurely. His wicked grin lightened his expression suddenly in a way that always made her heart turn over. 'We really must make an attempt to greet each other with more originality! This must be the second or third occasion on which one or other of us has uttered those words! But I suppose I should be grateful, for at least they have helped me place your mood.' He gave her a sideways look. 'And now I perceive that you intend to be eccentric. How am I to answer such a blunt question? I could be courteous and claim a close friendship with the St Auby family, or flattering and claim I wished to see your beautiful sister wed...'

They both looked over to where Annabella stood in a group of admiring young bucks, tossing her fair curls and giggling girlishly. Mullineaux grimaced.

'But then, alas, I would be lying!' His dark eyes moved over Alicia's face feature by feature, with a grave consideration. 'In some ways you look very alike,' he said thoughtfully, then added softly, 'But you are very different in character, are you not? And she cannot hold a candle to you, Alicia.'

Alicia's breath caught in her throat. The expression in his eyes was making her feel both hot and dizzy at the same time. There was a dangerous intimacy in that dark gaze, a disturbing power which held sway over her senses. For a moment she saw the white heat of a remembered passion flare in his eyes, then it was replaced by his customary cool detachment.

'Or,' Mullineaux finished lightly, as though the intervening moment had never occurred, 'I could just admit that I was bored and succumbed to the impulse to discompose your father by appearing at a public function where I knew he could not cut me dead!'

Alicia, still trying to recover her poise, barely took in his words at first. Had she been concentrating she might well have chosen not to take him up on a comment which might well lead to trouble. But now she regarded him with some puzzlement.

'Why should you wish to do that, my lord? I was not aware that you had ever met my father!'

Mullineaux viewed her with weary cynicism. 'Oh, come, come, Lady Carberry, you can do better than that! It may be old history, but let us not pretend that it never happened!'

Alicia raised her chin stubbornly at this reference to what she could only assume was their previous, unhappily concluded relationship. 'I have no wish to pretend anything, my lord,' she observed frigidly. 'However, I do not understand you. I did not know that you had ever met my father.'

Mullineaux looked exasperated, both with himself for raising the subject in the first place and with her for pursuing it.

'It seems, then, that we must be very frank, you and I,' he said dryly. 'You must know—none better!—that your father and I are old adversaries! We met on the fateful occasion when I called in at Bruton Street to question your sudden betrothal to George Carberry and he had me thrown out into the street on your—'

He broke off as all the pretty colour fled from Alicia's face, leaving her chalk-white and her eyes huge and stricken pools of green. She opened her mouth, but no sound came. Mullineaux instinctively took her arm, fearing she would faint. Then her attention was claimed by Broseley himself, insinuating his large bulk between the two of them with the superficial social smile reserved for such occasions.

'Alicia, my dear! May I make you known to some friends of mine?' His glacial gaze touched Mullineaux briefly and slid away. 'Excuse us, Lord Mullineaux.' He shepherded his daughter away with a possessive arm around her waist.

Alicia looked back at Mullineaux over her shoulder as she walked away. She looked completely shattered, the lovely, heart-breaking innocence he remembered showing clearly in her eyes, overlaid with disbelief and puzzlement. The truth burst over him with the power of a tidal wave. She had never known. Broseley had never told her.

Mullineaux put down his drink gently and turned to answer some casual question put to him by an old acquaintance. But his mind was elsewhere. He had had enough of rumour, half-truth and equivocation. There and then, he resolved that he would make Alicia tell him what had really happened, if it was the last thing that he did.

Monks Dacorum Hall was very quiet. Caroline and Marcus Kilgaren had left the previous day to join Alicia's guests at Chartley. James was alone in his study, attempting to formulate a reply to his sister Louisa, who had written to ask him to postpone his visit to Worcestershire. Two of the children had developed chickenpox, she wrote, and the house was all at sixes and sevens. If he could delay for a week or two, they could give him a better welcome.

With surprise, James realised that it would be no hardship to stay at Monks Dacorum for another week. He put the letter down on his desk and stared out of the window into the dark. Before he had gone abroad he had considered the country to be good only for hunting and a dead bore otherwise. He had had no desire to live on any of his country estates, finding amusement and company only in London. The West Country was particularly alien to him with its mixture of wild, heather-clad uplands and its flat, water-logged levels. Yet now...

He picked up his pen again, and it was then that he heard the music. High, sweet and piercing, it was the sound of a single violin. Intrigued, James leant on the desk in order to peer out of the mullioned window. The ivy grew close, but he could just distinguish the dark outlines of the garden and the retaining wall which bordered the road.

The moon was a silver disc, high and bright, in a cold black sky studded with stars. By its light, he could just discern a procession of shadowy figures moving along the road. At first he wondered if it was the fabled free-traders who were particularly active in the Bristol Channel, but they would hardly herald their approach with music. James turned back to the lamplit room and rang the bell.

'Russell, what is going on outside?'

The butler was a local man and for a moment it seemed that he had caught some of the excitement in the atmosphere outside. He struggled to regain a suitable gravity.

'It's the annual cider wassail, my lord.'

'Cider wassail?' James raised his eyebrows. 'What sort of festival is that?'

The butler scratched his head. 'Every spring, folk from all the surrounding villages come to the orchards to celebrate the previous year's crop and drink a toast to the next harvest, my lord,' he explained. 'There have been cider wassails for generations in these parts. Why not go along and see for yourself, sir?'

James almost dismissed the idea out of hand. It sounded to him like an excuse for excessive drinking and precious little else, but something gave him pause. He had nothing else to do that evening—why not experience a little local colour?

'Where is it being held, Russell?' he enquired casually.

'On Chartley land, sir,' the butler replied. 'Lady Carberry provides the food and drink, and a barn for the dancing. There's no side to her ladyship! Why, sometimes she even attends herself!'

'Does she, indeed?' James murmured, and as he made for the door the butler could have sworn that his master was smiling.

It proved very easy to find the revels. The sound of the fiddle was still faintly audible above the soughing of the wind in the trees as James set off on foot down the track to Chartley. He felt a sudden lifting of spirits to be out in the fresh air after a day spent poring over the estate books. And there seemed to be something in the air that night—something of magic, excitement and anticipation. James shrugged the feeling off as fanciful, but it persisted.

There were many orchards thereabouts which stretched from the fertile east of Chartley village towards Monks Dacorum, but only one barn large enough to house the celebrations. As he drew near, James observed that the wassail was already well advanced. Figures were milling around the wizened trunks of the apple trees, torches flared, and the cider flowed freely from a multitude of casks. Someone at the front of the crowd was making a speech— there was much laughter and shouts of encouragement—and as James drew close the crowd burst into spontaneous applause before breaking up and streaming towards the open doors of the huge tithe barn.

Torchlight and firelight spilled out from its doors. There was a delicious smell of roasting meat and James, anonymous on the edge of the crowd, could just see inside, where wicker baskets spilled their contents of fruit over the cobbled floor and the village children picked them up with cries of excitement. Oranges and lemons were expensive commodities—no doubt these had also been provided by the philanthropic Lady Carberry. James smiled to himself. There really was no stopping her.

The press of people about the barn was so great that not everyone could get inside. Trenchers of food and huge, overflowing tankards of cider were passed good-humouredly out to those in the cold. James glimpsed bottles of liquid other than cider being passed surreptitiously from hand to hand, and wondered fleetingly how many of the locals augmented their wages with free-trading. It was an accepted fact that smuggling was rife in the Bristol

Channel—perhaps the charitable lady of the manor also bought her brandy without paying duty?

James stayed at the back of the crowd, preferring to remain unrecognised. He felt almost like an interloper in this merry throng. All around him the conversation buzzed and the laughter grew raucous as the cider made the rounds again. People were beginning to disperse a little now. Some amorous couples, oblivious of the cold night air, drifted off between the trees, absorbed in each other. An area was cleared at the front of the barn and the fiddles struck up again, several of them in haunting melody. It was time for the dancing. James was about to slip away when he received a surprise.

A small party of people were coming forward from inside the barn where they had been out of his line of vision. With a slight shock he recognised Caroline Kilgaren, her piquant face upturned to Marcus's, her eyes bright with excitement. A fur-lined cloak framed her fair curls. Marcus's head was bent towards her and in a moment he grinned, took both her hands, and whirled her into the dance. A small ripple of applause went through the throng of watchers and some of them came forward to join in.

There was another girl there whom James did not recognise, but whose identity he could guess. Caroline had mentioned that the Stapleford family would be joining them at Chartley—this, then, must be the celestially fair but unfortunately rather spiteful Georgiana, whom they had maliciously put forward as a potential bride for him. She was indeed very beautiful, James thought dispassionately, but her beauty was marred by her expression, which at the moment mirrored her shock and disgust that members of her party should condescend to join in the festivities with the local peasants. Clearly she felt that it was all very well to be seen to patronise the event, but a suitable distance should be maintained.

The reel finished and one violin immediately took up an air for a jig. Caroline and Marcus showed no inclination to stop dancing. Georgiana Stapleford turned to look for the rest of her party. Evidently her parents and Lady Stansfield had considered themselves too staid and ancient for such revelry, particularly on a cold spring night. Which only left...

Then he saw them. The torchlight burnished Alicia's hair with a dark copper glow and shadowed the brilliant green eyes with a deep mystery. She had her hand on Christopher Westwood's arm and was speaking urgently to him. Westwood's expression was unencouraging; in fact, it was a close match with Georgiana's. Apparently he would not be obliging her by dancing, no matter how much Alicia wanted him to.

James was not aware of having moved until he had almost reached them. The crowd parted silently to allow him through and then he was bowing before Alicia and looking down into her wide, startled eyes.

'Would my lady care to dance?'

He felt, rather than saw, Westwood stiffen beside him, as though he was about to object. But it was Alicia he was looking at and only her. She absorbed his whole attention and the look she gave him was one of pure, uncomplicated pleasure.

'Gladly, my lord.'

He took her hand and drew her into the dance. A murmur ran through the crowd, but James barely noticed. His awareness of Alicia was intense. The firelight gave her skin a golden glow and lit her eyes with luminous brightness. She burned with an excitement he could feel emanating from her whole body. Around them the other dancers dipped and whirled, but it was as though the two of them were alone, absorbed in the same magic that had touched James earlier. The wind whipped back the hood of Alicia's cloak and she laughed aloud in pure enjoyment. Despite their large and very interested audience, James could simply have picked her up and carried her off there and then. He wanted her more than any woman he had known.

But all dreams must end. The musicians had already played one extra chorus and now the dance drew to a close. Alicia was rosy and breathless but the magic was draining away. The violins finished with a flourish and a moment later Marcus and Caroline Kilgaren were at James's shoulder.

'You never told us you intended to be here tonight, James! We could have made up a party!' Caroline's speculative gaze slid from him to Alicia with puzzlement.

Some element of restraint had entered Alicia's manner, as though she could not believe what she had just done. James knew that during the dance she had felt exactly the same as he had done but now her glance was suddenly shy as it met his. 'We should be glad if you would come back to Chartley with us for refreshments, Lord Mullineaux,' she said, with constraint.

Christopher Westwood was lurking behind her with a face like thunder, whilst Georgiana Stapleford's avid blue gaze moved from one face to another ceaselessly. For James, too, the descent to reality had happened too quickly and he bowed abruptly.

'Thank you, Lady Carberry, but I must decline. Your servant, ma'am, Lady Kilgaren...'

He turned on his heel and walked away without a backward glance. The murmur of the crowd rose to a crescendo behind him and over it could be heard Georgiana Stapleford, in a voice as sharp as daggers. 'So *that* is the dangerous Marquis of Mullineaux! *What* an attractive man!'

'All I am saying, Alicia, is that such behaviour cannot help but fuel the rumours that there is some kind of illicit relationship between yourself and Mullineaux!'

The entire household could hear Christopher Westwood's complaints on the subject, for he was standing stubbornly in the entrance hall at Chartley Chase and would not move. He was white with anger and determined to have his say.

Alicia strove to keep her own temper and to keep her voice level. She knew that Westwood was right and that her actions had been ill-considered. But how could she explain to anyone, least of all Christopher Westwood, the spell which had held her captive from the moment she had seen James Mullineaux stepping forward to take her hand? At that moment nothing on earth would have prevented her from dancing with him. Now, it seemed, she must bear the consequences.

'Since you know such rumours to be false, Christopher, I can only suggest that you disregard them!'

'But you are encouraging them! Why dance with the man if you wish to quash the speculation?'

'What would you have me do?' Alicia snapped. 'Must I refuse to even speak to him just to satisfy you? I am not so poor-spirited as to regard this gossip, and neither should you be!'

'But you should have seen yourself! The look on your face alone—'

Alicia turned on him, eyes flashing. All enjoyment she had derived from the evening, and in particular her dance with James, had long fled.

'I was simply enjoying myself! Really, Christopher, you are becoming the most complete puritan!'

'Dash it, Alicia, will you not take this seriously? Your reputation is hardly such that it can afford another scandal!'

Westwood regretted the words as soon as they were said, for Alicia was looking at him with a glacial expression very reminiscent of her grandmother. The fact that he had spoken nothing but the truth did not really help.

'Thank you for your consideration, Christopher. I do not believe that I have given you the right to judge such matters, however.'

Westwood winced. For someone who looked so sweet, Alicia had a damned unpleasant way with her sometimes! He stood his ground.

'Nevertheless, as your friend I feel I must say something!'

'But not in front of the servants, Christopher! Very bad *ton*!'

Lady Stansfield's voice carried with the clarity of a bell from the first landing, where she was standing dressed in a silk kimono of dashing but unorthodox design. It was clear that she had been roused from her slumbers by the altercation and was in a very bad mood. She had no difficulty with criticising others for faults which she had herself, and addressed herself to both of them, oblivious of the embarrassed footman standing by the front door.

'You, Christopher, will hold your tongue and show a little more self-control! Alicia, you will come up and talk to me! At once!'

Westwood flushed to the roots of his fair hair and slammed off into the library in search of a drink. Alicia sighed and started up the staircase. It was useless to argue with Lady Stansfield in such a mood. She followed her grandmother into her bedroom, which smelt strongly of snuff, and took a seat in one of the armchairs disposed beside the fire. The room was dimly lit, the embers of the fire glowing hot in the grate. An abandoned piece of embroidery lay on the table, and Alicia's heart sank further. Lady Stansfield only ever resorted to what she termed 'frippery, female pursuits' when she was very bored and it inevitably put her in an even worse mood. Her evening with the Staplefords must have been a tedious one.

Lady Stansfield eased herself into the other chair and turned her sharp gaze immediately on Alicia.

'Well, miss! Here's a fine to-do!' Her expression was at its most autocratic. 'I've been wanting to talk to you! I think it's best for you to tell me the whole—what is the relationship between yourself and James Mullineaux?'

'Our relationship is mainly categorised by ill-temper and conflict,' Alicia said, with a touch of bitterness.

She hesitated, but knew better than to try to argue with her grandmother in her current mood. She related the carriage accident and her subsequent rescue by James, how it had come about that she had compromised them both by sending Miss Frensham away, their quarrel, their subsequent meetings, and finally her dance with him that night. She left nothing out of her factual account, but made no reference to her feelings. Let Lady Stansfield make of that what she would.

When she had finished, Lady Stansfield stirred a little in her chair. Throughout Alicia's account her attention had not wavered.

'So Mullineaux is not in fact your lover,' she observed thoughtfully.

'I fear I cannot claim that privilege,' Alicia said, very dryly. 'The terms of our relationship could scarcely be described in such a cordial way!'

'Humph! A pity!' Lady Stansfield looked her over comprehensively. 'Still, I am hardly surprised. I would have expected you to look much more cheerful if he were!'

'Grandmama!' Alicia had never grown out of being scandalised by her grandmother's plain speaking. 'Do I understand you to be encouraging me to indulge in a love affair?'

'I should think so!' Lady Stansfield said energetically. 'You are too strait-laced, Alicia, and I have given up all hope of you ever losing your puritan streak! Lord, a man wants a cosy armful in bed, not a block of ice! I know that your marriage gave you a disgust of a physical relationship, but that is all in the past now. You should allow yourself a little amusement!'

Despite herself, Alicia's wayward mind presented her with a series of images which all too graphically suggested what it might be like to take James Mullineaux as a lover. Carberry had been gross and grotesque, but James's lithe body would be quite a different matter. With an effort she tore her mind away and found her grandmother watching her with amused comprehension.

'Exactly! In my day we were not so shy to follow our inclinations! Why, I remember—'

'Grandmama!'

Lady Stansfield subsided with a sniff. 'Oh, very well, very well, I can see that you mean to be odiously strict! But it's no good you denying that you still care for Mullineaux, for I can see it as plain as a pikestaff!'

Her assertion made Alicia face squarely up to the facts that she had been trying to ignore since meeting James again; not only did she find him intensely attractive but she also still cared deeply for him. It did not seem to matter that he held her in contempt and that they always seemed to end up quarrelling. She had loved him for over seven years and his return had only served to stir up all the old emotions which had never really left her. He is arrogant and high-handed, she told herself severely, but it made no difference to her feelings.

Alicia was aware that her grandmother was still watching her like an inquisitive sparrow with its head on one side. She shrugged uncomfortably.

'I cannot deny it, Grandmama! Oh, I have tried to tell myself that what is in the past is over, but my feelings are not so easily dismissed. And at least you should now see why I am not able to marry Christopher!'

Her look dared her grandmother to contradict her, but the old lady was silent. She knew that a man like Christopher Westwood was no substitute for James Mullineaux.

'I thought Mullineaux had never met my father,' Alicia said suddenly, 'but at Annabella's wedding he told me he had been to Bruton Street all those years ago to demand to be told what was happening. I always thought...I never believed...' Her anguished gaze met that of Lady Stansfield. 'He had no reason to lie to me, did he?' she appealed.

Lady Stansfield smoothed the silk of her kimono. 'None at all,' she said, a little gruffly. 'It don't surprise me—the last time I ever saw James Mullineaux he swore he would visit your father to demand the truth. I always liked Mullineaux,' she added, with a smile. 'Oh, he was impetuous, but he was generous with it and he could charm the birds off the trees. And he loved you, Alicia. Really loved you.'

She looked at her granddaughter's downbent head. 'You always believed he had deserted you, didn't you, Alicia? And now you know it is not true you have very little left to reproach him for—'

'Except pride,' Alicia snapped. 'I don't forgive him for being so quick to condemn! The arrogant conceit of the man! That is one thing about him that has not changed!'

Lady Stansfield hid her smile. 'Whereas he,' she continued, 'has rather more to forgive—or so he thinks.'

'For Mullineaux it is not a matter of forgiveness,' Alicia said bleakly. 'He has made his judgement. Why should he wish to change it?'

Lady Stansfield shifted slightly in her chair. 'Those encounters you describe hardly suggest a disinterested man... If he holds you in such dislike, surely he would never have offered you his help at Ottery!'

Alicia smiled. 'I can only assume that, being a gentleman, he came to the rescue of Miss Frensham only to discover that he was faced with the unpleasant task of rescuing me as well!'

'True.' Lady Stansfield had her head on one side once more. 'But he need not have made you a declaration the following morning, particularly as it was all a bumblebath of your own making!'

'Thank you! I am well aware that I was to blame! But I can offer no explanation, I fear, Grandmama, other than the prosaic one which is that Mullineaux conceived it to be his duty!'

Lady Stansfield looked unconvinced. 'Stuff!' she said, with finality. 'There is more to this than you think, Alicia. And, leaving that aside, why did he seek you out here, let alone go to the wassail and draw such attention to the pair of you by asking you to dance?'

Alicia did not reply. She hardly understood herself the impulse which had prompted James to ask her to dance and her to accept. It had been unreal, a moment out of time. But she was not foolish enough to build any hopes upon it. To do so would only leave her more distressed and disappointed in the end. She made a slight, dispirited gesture.

'Do not refine upon it too much, Grandmama. I do not! As we are alone, I will admit that it was foolish of me to encourage the gossip by dancing with Mullineaux tonight, but there is no real cause for speculation. The meeting at Ottery was the merest chance, what followed was bad luck, and how I feel is really irrelevant given that Mullineaux will never think of me as anything but a fortune-hunting adventuress who jilted him to marry a richer man!'

Lady Stansfield snorted with disgust. 'The facts don't fit the case, my love, but by all means believe them if you must! How did you find your father after all these years?' she added, changing the subject as she saw Alicia's instinctive rejection of her words.

Alicia looked up and met her eyes squarely. 'Oh, he was just the same! He scares me, Grandmama. I feel as though I can never be free of him.' A darker shadow touched the shadowed room. Alicia shivered convulsively. 'All the time his presence is there, even when he is not!'

She did not add that she had already received a letter from Bertram Broseley inviting her to stay at Greyrigg. Annabella was still on her wedding journey in the Lake District and Broseley was claiming to be lonely without the company of either daughter to comfort him. Alicia had crumpled the letter up in disgust, but it had brought back all her feelings of disquiet.

'Bertram Broseley, faugh!' Lady Stansfield wrinkled her nose as though there was a vile smell beneath it. 'The man was always an out-and-out bounder, for all he is your father!' A faraway look came into her eyes. 'He was a cit trying to buy his way into good company when he met your mother. We knew Julia was taken with him—looked like a god, did Broseley in those days, with his fair hair and finicky gold waistcoats!' Lady Stansfield snorted in disgust.

'I never spoke to him,' she continued, with the unconscious aristocratic arrogance which had led her son-in-law to detest her, 'but I could see how he turned heads and Julia always was a silly piece.'

Alicia sighed. She did not remember her mother very well, for Julia Broseley had died at Annabella's birth, but she did recall a gentle, soft-voiced creature with an anxious face framed by soft brown ringlets. Julia had inherited none of her mother's acerbic wit or hot temper. Such strength might have protected her from Broseley's casual cruelty. As it was, the runaway match had been an unmitigated disaster. The Earl of Stansfield had refused to accept Broseley as his son-in-law and since Bertram had only married Julia to increase his social stature he had viewed the alliance as worthless. It was only after the Earl's death that Lady Stansfield had been able to make contact with her granddaughter, and by then Broseley himself had been deeply embittered and the breach could not be healed.

Lady Stansfield patted Alicia's hand comfortingly with her own be-ringed one. 'But your father cannot touch you now, Alicia. You are quite safe.'

Alicia shook her head. She did not believe Bertram Broseley could be dismissed so easily. She got to her feet.

'If you will excuse me, Grandmama, I am very tired. I must seek my bed now.'

She kissed her grandmother's cheek and straightened up.

'Alicia.' Her grandmother's voice halted her as she had her hand on the doorknob. 'Just one small piece of advice. Think twice before you play off any tricks on Mullineaux again. He is hardly the man to tolerate them for long! I predict that you will find it more difficult to avoid him than you think.'

Alicia smiled a little sadly but did not reply and the door closed softly behind her. After a moment Lady Stansfield sighed. The fire had gone out and she was cold. With an old lady's stiffness she rose and went to bed.

Chapter Six

Alicia reined in her horse on the top of the moor, her cheeks becomingly flushed with the sting of the cold afternoon air. The ride up from Chartley Chase had been exhilarating for she had given Savannah her head, the mare's inclination for a gallop coinciding with Alicia's own inclination to escape.

The spirits of the Chartley house-party had not managed to reassert themselves in the days following the cider wassail. Christopher Westwood was still nursing a fine sense of grievance and was displaying his disapproval of Alicia by sulking. Georgiana Stapleford was making life a misery with her sharp looks and sharper comments, Lady Stansfield was suffering from rheumatism and was inclined to snap, and Alicia herself was unable to throw off the depression which had possessed her after that evening. Despite the visits, card parties and impromptu theatricals, it had somehow proved impossible to please people and it had been very tiring for Alicia in trying.

One look at the sullen faces around the breakfast table that morning had prompted Marcus Kilgaren to suggest a trip out, in the hope that the fine day might dispel the bad humours. After some discussion it was agreed that the whole party should drive over to Pilton Abbey for the day, both to admire the fine house and to take Countess Pilton up on the hospitable invitation she had issued the week before. There had been general agreement to the plan, but Lady Stansfield had declined to go, saying that Hermione Pilton bored her to death, and Alicia had pleaded a headache in order to be excused. She was desperate for a little solitude.

A false air of calm had settled on Chartley Chase as the carriage and the riders had clattered away through the village in the early afternoon. In the blue saloon Lady Stansfield had snored over her post-prandial cup of chocolate and, peeping around the door, Alicia had seen that she was dead to the world. She'd needed no further encouragement, for she had never had any real intention of resting that afternoon. In her room she'd hastily donned a riding habit of apple-green, severely styled and most becoming, and braided her hair into one fat plait beneath her round-brimmed hat.

There had been a little more activity in the stableyard where Alicia's groom, Jem, had willingly led out Savannah for her. The mare's coat was gleaming with good health and it seemed that she was as keen for exercise as Alicia herself. Jem had smiled as he'd looked up at them. They seemed very well matched.

'Reckon you shouldn't be riding out without a groom, ma'am,' he'd offered thoughtfully, knowing full well his advice would be rejected.

Alicia had laughed, already impatient to be off. 'In the country! I assure you I am quite safe, Jem!'

She had wheeled the horse round and made for the moor before Jem could reply and he had only smiled and scratched his head as he made his way back into the tackroom. Her ladyship was a law unto herself like the old Countess, and no one could gainsay her, least of all Mr Westwood. In company with the other servants, Jem had heard of the failure of Christopher Westwood's suit and he'd smiled to himself again. It would take more than that tailor's dummy to appeal to Alicia Carberry.

From the top of the hill there was a spectacular view across the patchwork countryside to the Bristol Channel, gleaming like a silver ribbon in the sun. Chartley Chase was a tiny dolls' house below her, with the village scattered beyond it. A light breeze fanned Alicia's face and stirred the tendrils of hair beneath her hat. Savannah snorted softly and turned away from Chartley, picking her way over the hillside in the direction of Monks Dacorum. Alicia made no effort to change direction.

The mare had picked up one of the old drover's tracks across the moor and was now trotting briskly along, her chestnut ears pricked. The heather and bracken were springing back after the winter and the peat track was firm beneath the horse's hooves for there had been no rain for several weeks. The air had a keen, pure feel and there was not a single person in sight. Alicia, feeling her tensions slipping away with a rush of relief that was almost too euphoric, urged Savannah to a gallop.

They slowed to a reluctant trot when the heathland gave way to cultivated fields again, and took a road that wended between drystone walls and high hedges. Alicia had lost her sense of direction completely but had no worries for she knew that she would eventually find a village where she could take directions back to Chartley. For now, just the sense of escape was enough. She had not realised how oppressed she had become by both the talk of scandal and the pressure of constantly having to put on a public face. But for now she need think of nothing but the sting of the cold wind, the scent of leather and her pleasure in being out of doors.

The road ran on between the fields, then into a small, coppiced woodland through which the distant, rhythmic thud of the forester's axe could be heard. Savannah splashed through a ford and the narrow track began to climb again. Pallid blue sky stretched overhead and the breeze had a cutting edge to it. Alicia's spirits lifted with every step away from Chartley Chase.

They had gone perhaps a couple of miles along the track when the trees fell back suddenly to reveal a sinister huddle of cottages. They were all empty, walls crumbling and once neat gardens overrun with weeds. An old estate wall on both sides culminated in a pair of iron gates swinging on rusty hinges. Alicia allowed the mare to walk forward slowly, almost afraid to disturb the stillness. The track was grassed over now and the horse's hoofbeats were muffled. She picked her way with dainty care between the half-open gates.

So this must be one of the neglected entrances to Monks Dacorum. Alicia had never seen the house, for old Mr Rowley, the previous tenant, had been a recluse who never entertained. Those of her neighbours who could remember the days of the previous Marquis had told her that the house was vastly pretty and charmingly modernised. Caroline, too, had declared it to be a delightful house, if somewhat neglected in recent years.

The obvious course of action now was to turn back. The house would be empty, of course, for James Mullineaux would have left a week ago to visit his sister and the servants would have been laid off until a new tenant could be found. However, that hardly gave Alicia the excuse to indulge her curiosity and go further. But still she hesitated and Savannah, who clearly had different ideas, set off down the drive at a lively pace.

They passed a lodge where a family of blackbirds flew off with shrill cries of alarm at their approach. The house was empty, its windows dark and unfriendly. The track was descending quite steeply now under a thick canopy of trees whose bare branches knitted together overhead. The pale winter sun could not penetrate here. Rhododendrons grew close to the track and weeds smothered it. There was one more sharp bend to the left and the trees ended suddenly, revealing to Alicia's fascinated gaze the scene which lay before her.

In the distance she could see a village nestling amongst the fields. Curls of smoke plumed into the winter air and a church spire cut the pale sky. In the foreground, cradled in the hollow of the hill, was the most perfect house Alicia had ever seen. It was small, half-timbered, and built around a central courtyard. There was a medley of decorative chimneys and a show of gables, orioles and leaded casement windows.

The whole house and garden were surrounded by a moat of glassily green water on which she could see an assortment of swans and ducks preening and swimming. The moat was fed by a narrow river which wended its way towards the village in a series of lazy curves, and in one of these lay the ruins of the abbey church that had originally given the house its name. The pattern of gardens was fascinating—Alicia recognised an overgrown maze and the outlines of a knot garden, both almost choked with weeds. The blank, mullioned windows of the house stared back at her solemnly.

Alicia dug her heels into Savannah's sides and the mare trotted obediently down the drive, passing the unkempt lawns carpeted with wild daffodil and narcissus, and over the moat bridge into the stableyard. At close quarters the house was eerily quiet, its windows shuttered with ivy. Alicia, held as she was in the grip of some powerful enchantment, dismounted and tied the mare to the block by the stables. Her footsteps sounded loud on the gravel as she made a circuit of the courtyard and peered beyond the stable doors into the musty and disused interiors. The house and the stables themselves appeared in good condition, unlike the neglected gardens, but there was an air of emptiness about the place.

The house was built in an L-shape around two sides of the courtyard, with the stables in front of Alicia and on her left a high wall dividing the courtyard from the gardens. There was a door in the wall and it was open a few inches. The temptation was too strong. She pushed the door tentatively and it yielded with only a squeak of hinges.

Alicia found herself standing in a walled garden—a mellow, secret garden set between the moat and the high courtyard wall. She stared about her, entranced, all sorts of ideas coming into her head. In the summer the sun-warmed stone would be covered with sweet-scented honeysuckle and ancient, fragrant roses. The flowerbeds would hold columbine, speedwell and flax, mingling profusely with cornflowers and valerian. She could imagine tall Canterbury bells nodding at the back of the borders and bees lurching intoxicated from flower to flower.

There was an old rustic bench under the gnarled branches of an apple tree and Alicia sat down and let her thoughts drift over the warm, hazy days of summer. If only she were able to buy Monks Dacorum she could re-create the gardens just as they would have been in Elizabethan times. But James Mullineaux would never sell to her...

Alicia sat there until the March chill began to seep into her bones and made her shiver. The colour fading from the sky warned her that evening was already closing in and it was time for her to return home. She got to her feet and shook out the skirts of her riding habit. The feeling of enchantment had begun to fade as she grew colder, and almost immediately the extreme impropriety of her actions became apparent. Though the house was empty, that was no excuse to indulge her curiosity and trespass in this shameless way! The light was fading and there was suddenly something sinister about the neglected gardens and shuttered windows. A feeling akin to panic rose in Alicia and she almost ran down the path to the old door in the wall.

Grasping stems of wild roses caught at the skirts of her riding habit, detaining her. She wrenched the material free of their thorns and fled precipitately to the doorway.

A mere five steps brought her to the door, which still stood open, and to confront the man who stood with his shoulders propped negligently against the frame, blocking her path. And this time there was no moonlight, and no enchantment, and she was looking up into eyes which were as dark and cold as the chill of a winter's night.

Alicia felt herself to be at a distinct disadvantage. To have been caught trespassing could only be proof of a most vulgar curiosity. Worse, she had now provoked a confrontation with the one man she would have chosen at all costs to avoid. They had not met since the night of the cider wassail, an occasion which brought her to the blush when she remembered the abandonment of her behaviour. She felt paralysed with embarrassment.

No such problem appeared to afflict the Marquis of Mullineaux, however. His dark, direct gaze was unflinching, quizzical and slightly mocking.

'Good afternoon, Lady Carberry. What a pleasure to see you again!'

'Whatever are you doing here?' Alicia could have bitten off her tongue as soon as she had asked such a naive question. Caroline and Marcus had said that he would be away, but they had obviously made a mistake—a mistake which was proving costly to her. Flustered, she could feel herself blushing and was even more annoyed.

James Mullineaux raised an eyebrow and straightened up, driving his hands into his jacket pockets.

'It *is* my house! Surely it is more appropriate for me to make that enquiry of you? If only I had known that you planned to visit Monks Dacorum, Lady Carberry, I would have been at pains to show you round myself!'

The words were smooth, but Alicia did not miss their sarcastic undertone and it brought more blood up into her face. She gritted her teeth.

Odious, odious man! Still, she was forced to admit that she was firmly in the wrong. What could have possessed her to come here in the first place? She was utterly mortified. Worse, James was still blocking the doorway and seemed completely at ease and in no hurry to move. Alicia was seized with panic. She simply had to get away. With a great effort of will she overcame her embarrassment sufficiently to look at him. She could not quite meet his eyes—almost, but not quite.

'Lord Mullineaux.' Alicia's voice still sounded annoyingly squeaky with emotion. 'I must apologise for my presence here. You are quite right to view it as an unwarrantable intrusion and I have no wish to prolong a meeting which must be so mutually disagreeable.' She tried to gather up her skirts into her hand. 'I shall take my leave.'

It was a creditable speech, only marred by the fact that Alicia could feel her hat slipping backwards and could see that her skirt was already tangled again with the treacherous roses. She was quite prepared to push James Mullineaux aside, so single-minded was her desire to escape the turmoil of her emotions and that unremittingly quizzical gaze.

James allowed her to wrench her skirts free of the thorns again without comment, but when it appeared that Alicia was about to flee past him he laid a restraining hand on her arm.

'Just a moment, Lady Carberry. Surely you do not expect me to let you go as easily as that? We need to talk, you and I. You cannot just walk away as though you had not met me!'

There was a silence which felt to Alicia as though it lasted several hours. Her mind seemed incapable of understanding the implication of his words. She had focused so completely on getting herself away from him and the embarrassment of the situation that she had not contemplated an alternative. And why should James wish to talk to her anyway? He had never given any indication that they should be anything other than mere acquaintances.

All this went through her mind as she stepped through the doorway into the courtyard, and James tightened his grip on her arm and drew her towards the main door of the house.

One of the stable doors was open and a groom was leading a docile Savannah towards it. The mare was still within reach, but Alicia had barely half formulated the idea of grabbing her reins and riding off when James disconcertingly read her thoughts.

'I wouldn't even think about it if I were you,' he said, pleasantly but definitely. 'It's only in stories that a lady encumbered by a side saddle and long skirt is still able to make some dashing escape. You would merely look foolish, and I would be put to the trouble of bringing you back!'

Alicia fumed, resolving that he was quite the most unpleasant man she had ever met. On the principle that attack was her best form of defence, she stopped dead on the cobblestones and rounded on him.

'So you intend to keep me here by duress? Might I enquire to what purpose?'

James did not appear disconcerted. 'But you came here of your own free will, my lady! I could ask what you are doing here at all!'

'I wish to buy Monks Dacorum,' Alicia snapped, half-truthfully. 'I thought that you had left for Worcestershire, and I came over from Chartley to inspect the property.'

'How very unorthodox,' James observed mildly, with a smile that made Alicia's blood boil. 'Most prospective purchasers would surely contact my agent first! But you, Lady Carberry—' it was said with exaggerated politeness '—you are always different!'

Alicia's understandable humiliation at being caught on the property was fading fast before this mockery.

'You still have not answered my question, my lord,' she pointed out frigidly. 'Do you intend to hold me here by force?'

The corners of James's firm mouth twitched in a smile. 'How very melodramatic! If you insist on expressing it in those terms, then yes, I intend to keep you here for a while!'

A breeze rippled along the surface of the moat and shivered down Alicia's spine. Savannah had now gone into her stall and Alicia could hear the groom talking softly to her as he rubbed her down. The shadows were lengthening in the courtyard and the air was cold. In the slowly gathering dusk the ancient house looked less approachable.

So there it was. James wished to speak with her and was prepared to follow the unconventional route of holding her against
her will in order to achieve his aim. This was presumably the cue
for any gently bred lady to faint or have hysterics, Alicia reflected.
Being held hostage might seem appalling to some and romantic to
others, but Alicia was not a reader of Mrs Radcliffe's gothic novels
and doubted prosaically that she was in any serious danger.
Clearly, all James wanted was information, not to force his attentions upon her.

Alicia abandoned the idea of creating an awkward scene. On a
practical note, she was fairly certain that James would only throw
cold water over her if she had a fit of the vapours.

She stole a glance at his profile and sighed inwardly. Beneath
the tan his face was set in hard, uncompromising lines which did
little to reassure her that the coming interview would be a pleasant
one. She took a deep breath. She might as well make one last
attempt to persuade him of the impropriety of his actions. They
were crossing the gravel towards the oaken front door now, and
Alicia stopped again. James slanted a look down at her, but did
not release her arm.

'Whenever we have met, my lord, you have made me well
aware that you disapprove of my flouting of convention,' Alicia
observed quietly, tilting her head to look up at him properly. 'It
therefore seems strange that you should be breaking with propriety
yourself in behaving like this.'

'That's true.' James appeared to give the statement serious consideration and now sounded infuriatingly reasonable. 'I accept that
word of any meeting between the two of us here would damn forever your hopes of overriding the previous scandal. However, I
want to talk to you, so you will stay and hear me out.' He gave
her a thoroughly unnerving smile. 'You think me high-handed, no
doubt. Well, so I am, but there is not a great deal that you can do
about it. A novel situation for the self-sufficient Lady Carberry, I
suspect.'

Alicia gave up. She was not going to give him the satisfaction
of retaliating in any way. She made the tacit admission to herself
that she was as much his prisoner as his guest, and steadfastly
refused to think about what her grandmother might say if news of

this latest escapade reached her ears. She would worry about that later; just now she needed her wits about her to deal with whatever it was James intended to say to her.

James was waiting with scrupulous courtesy to allow Alicia to precede him into the house, and after a moment she stepped over the threshold and found herself in a dark, stone-flagged hallway. The ceilings were low above walls of beautifully moulded plaster, with heraldic devices entwined with flower designs and mythical beasts. There were fresh flowers on the highly polished table and the scent of beeswax in the air. It was both charming and welcoming. Alicia forgot both her hostility and her embarrassment, and gazed about her, captivated. James gestured to a door at the end of the passage.

'Will you step into the Hall?'

The Great Hall, with its huge, dominating stone fireplace and minstrel's gallery, appeared little altered from its original style. It was a coldly impressive, baronial room, the only concession to modernity being the long windows which looked out across a terrace to the moat and the woodland beyond. A suitably large fire was burning in the grate, but made little impression on the chill air. Alicia shivered. Even the pools of light cast by the multitude of candles appeared cold, and the shadows beyond the light were deep. There was something awesome about such splendour, but it was chilling too.

In such a setting James Mullineaux seemed peculiarly at home. On the walls were the pictures of his ancestors—Sir James Mullineaux, who had been an Elizabethan privateer and had bought Monks Dacorum and a peerage from the Crown with the ill-gotten gains of piracy; the fourth Baron Mullineaux, who had been a rake and a gambler, and a close friend of Charles II; the sixth Baron, an astute politician who had been granted the Marquisate for services to the Crown, followed later by the Dukedom of Cardace to crown his glittering career. The dark, patrician countenances all showed the same elements of danger and excitement; the watchful eyes held a gleam both wild and calculating. James, in the casual hunting jacket that so became his lithe physique, was the epitome of the reckless attraction that had been the hallmark of the Mullineaux family down the centuries.

Alicia allowed her gaze to travel to the opposite wall, where the ladies who had married into the Mullineaux dynasty looked down with a painted disdain that matched that of their menfolk. There was more variety here in terms of appearance and expression, but all had one characteristic in common, and that was a determined look which suggested that they had no intention of letting this parade of charismatic manhood overawe them. Alicia smiled despite herself. The Lady Henrietta, who had almost single-handedly defended the Oxfordshire estates against Cromwell's men, looked to have been a fearsome battleaxe, and even Lady Rose, James's famously sweet and beautiful mother, had a set to her chin which suggested that she would take no nonsense no matter how amiable her reputation.

Alicia turned impulsively to James, whose unreadable gaze had never left her face as she'd assimilated her surroundings.

'In truth, it is very imposing, my lord, but rather cold! Surely you must find such grandeur a little lonely on a day-to-day basis?'

James smiled, and the change was remarkable. For a moment the bitter lines were smoothed away and it was like coming face to face with the young James Mullineaux, beloved of the match-making mamas. Alicia's heart did not simply skip a beat, it did a somersault. The illusion lasted only a moment, however, before the shutters came down again.

'Indeed I do,' James was saying, 'but it seems peculiarly appropriate for this evening. You will, I hope, honour me by staying to dine?'

His tone was wholly courteous, but it was hardly a question, more a statement. Alicia hesitated. She could scarcely send a messenger to Chartley with the news that she was dining alone with the Marquis of Mullineaux; that would fan the flames of gossip to a positive bonfire. On the other hand, if she did not send word, her grandmother for one might be unnecessarily worried. She bit her lip.

'Thank you, Lord Mullineaux, but I must return to Chartley soon. I have guests, and they will become concerned if I am missing for any length of time...'

Her voice trailed away as she saw his ironic smile.

'No doubt you thought of that before you chose to go riding

alone? Tell me, Lady Carberry, do you always do exactly as you please?'

Alicia's eyes widened. Here he was again, watching her with the critical amusement one might show to a spoiled child! She felt her simmering resentment rising, but before she had framed a suitably crushing reply he had turned away.

'Never fear, I will arrange for Lady Stansfield to be sent an appropriately reassuring message! And I will see you safely escorted back to Chartley—after dinner. Now, will you not take a seat?'

Rude, arrogant, high-handed... Alicia ran out of mental epithets, and, rather to her surprise, found herself already installed in a high-backed chair before the huge fireplace. James poured two glasses of wine and passed one to her gravely. Their fingers touched and Alicia felt her pulse rate increase. Tearing her gaze away from him, she chided herself for being a fool. It was intolerable to want to be free of the spell he had cast on her, but to find herself welcoming his touch with a shiver that owed nothing at all to revulsion. She had no control at all over her wayward response to him.

'So you did not know that I was still here?' James asked. Sitting opposite her with his long legs crossed negligently at the ankle, he looked both relaxed and watchful at the same time.

'No, I did not!' Alicia blushed at the possibility of him thinking she had intended to meet him. 'It was not my intention to seek you out, my lord!' Her tone implied that nothing on earth would have induced her to go to Monks Dacorum knowing he was at home, and she saw him smile as the point went home. 'I set out for a ride with no fixed intent, and when I reached the gates here I thought to take a look at the house. I know it was an unpardonable intrusion, but I scarcely expected—'

'That the price of curiosity would be so high?' James finished for her, very dryly.

Alicia kept a tight grip on her temper. Her well-known cool serenity was under severe attack and was all but lost. 'You are severe, sir. I have already apologised *several times!*'

James smiled slightly. 'Yes, I suppose it was unhandsome of me. And in fact your coming here is very convenient—I had been hoping for the opportunity to speak with you privately and could not have contrived a better one than this.'

Alicia's nerves tightened. She did not speak, not wanting to pre-empt anything he might say. She waited for him to explain, but James did not continue immediately; he got to his feet and placed another couple of oak logs on the fire, settling the remaining wood with his booted foot. The logs split apart, the fire jetting up to illuminate his intent features, the dark eyes which held no warmth for her any more. His expression was sombre.

'When we met last month at Ottery, I thought myself the un-luckiest man alive to have been obliged to meet with you so soon after returning to this country. I had wanted to put the past behind me and think on it no more. I certainly thought that we two had no more to say to each other.' He drove his hands deep into his pockets. 'Yet now I find that I cannot simply forget it. In order to be free of the past I must know the truth of what happened and I think that at the very least you owe me an explanation.'

He finished and simply stood looking at her.

Alicia found herself to be struggling with a cocktail of emotions. Part of her was not surprised by the sudden demand, since she had suspected that that might be what he wished to discuss with her. However, she was shocked and resentful at the abrupt way in which he had spoken, and beneath her anger ran the undercurrent of pain which was always there when she remembered the events leading up to their separation. He had implied that she owed him an apology, and, whereas before she would have given anything for the chance to explain it all to him, now she felt that she could not bear to expose so harrowing a tale to his critical analysis. Instinct and reality were at war again; intuition was telling her that this was the same man she had loved so much before, but reality was showing him to be a stranger to her. She found that she was shaking her head, retreating for defence behind a determination to say nothing.

'I regret, Lord Mullineaux, that I cannot offer you the expla-nation you seek.'

James's voice was expressionless. 'Caroline and Marcus both spoke for you. They implied that I had misjudged you in thinking you a common jilt or, if you prefer, a fortune-hunter. I was prepared to be persuaded, but only you could tell me the truth. As you are declining to do so, I can only assume that my original assumption was correct.'

'You have no right to ask for an explanation now, Lord Mullineaux.' It was only when Alicia tried to speak that she realised how upset she was, for it was almost impossible to frame the words without crying. 'The time for explanations was seven years ago, but you had so little faith that you did not wait for one. You have made some unforgivable, arrogant assumptions and I will not correct them just for your gratification!'

James's gaze had narrowed on her in disbelief. Alicia's green eyes were very bright with both defiance and tears, but he was in no mood to compromise or defer to her feelings. He had become obsessed with knowing the truth. Each time he saw Alicia his obsession worsened because he could not equate his opinion of her with what was before his eyes. The doubts which Marcus had planted in his mind nagged him and gave him no peace. Everywhere he went people spoke of Alicia in terms of the highest regard. She was the only person who could tell him the truth about the past and she was refusing to do so.

He crossed to her side in two strides and stood towering over her. Once again, as at Ottery, fury and frustration consumed him. She was so stubborn he could have shaken her. His fingers closed hard around her wrist and jerked her to her feet. The small table at Alicia's side toppled over with a clatter, cascading the glass of wine onto the flagstone floor in a ruby waterfall. The glass miraculously did not break, but rolled away to hit the hearth with a gentle click. Neither of them paid the slightest attention.

'So you think that I misjudged you seven years ago,' James ground out, 'and as a result you will behave like the spoilt child you are! Well, I thank you for your good opinion, madam! It's fortunate we were spared the chance of ever marrying—no doubt time would have proved it to be a disastrous mistake!'

Alicia itched to slap his face, but he was holding her too tightly and too close to him. It was impossible to speak with any dignity, but at least she was now wholly angry where before she had been upset. She glared up into the furious dark eyes only inches from her own.

'Oh, no, my lord, it is you who are spoilt and selfish! Just because you wish to know a thing, you care not how much pain you occasion others! This is hardly the first time I have had to endure your strictures on my character—from allegations of wilfulness to the indictment that I married for a fortune! You have insulted me in every way conceivable and now I can only suggest you let me go!'

She barely had time to draw breath before he wrenched her into his arms. It bore no resemblance to any embrace Alicia had experienced before; not even the most ardent of her admirers had treated her so, and James himself had always exercised considerable restraint in his dealings with her as an inexperienced girl of nineteen. But now he held her ruthlessly whilst his mouth moved over hers, the pressure forcing her lips to part. The intensity of the kiss did not ease even for a moment and Alicia was lost almost from the start. Even had she wished to escape, she could not have done so. The arms which held her seemed made of steel. Though she knew he had only kissed her out of anger and frustration, she found herself adrift on a sea of sensation, careless of thought, responding to him with a lack of restraint which she was powerless to prevent. Her senses had been starved of emotion for so long that her nerve-endings felt as though they were on fire. His mouth became more insistent, deepening the kiss still further, and she was achingly aware of every taut line of his body against hers. Then, as she was about to abandon thought completely, a small corner of her mind whispered that he did not care about her, did not trust her, and certainly did not love her as she still loved him.

It was like being doused by a bucket of cold water. Alicia tore herself from his grip and would have fallen had James not caught her elbow to steady her. She did not stop to think, but turned on her heel and made straight for the door with no clear idea of where she was going. James caught up with her as she reached for the latch and put his hand over hers to stop her.

'Please, Alicia...' His breathing was still uneven, but there was an urgent note in his voice. 'Please don't run away. I'm sorry. I know I've treated you unforgivably, but please give me a chance to explain.'

The heavy iron latch was cool under Alicia's fingers, but some-

how it seemed too much of an effort to lift it. She felt dizzy and
confused, hearing her own voice as though from a great distance.

'But I don't think I want to talk to you any more, Lord Mullineaux...I think it's a little too late for that...'

Alicia could feel the tears slipping down her cheeks and made
no effort to stop them. She tried to dash them away with her hand,
but they just fell all the faster. The room was blurring at the edges,
and suddenly she was grateful for the dark because she was so
tired. So tired, but there was no need to think any more—no need
to do anything at all. She closed her eyes.

James caught her before she fainted, and carried her over to the
chaise longue in an alcove by the side of the fire. Alicia had
already started to stir by the time he put her down and for a
moment she lay quite still, obscurely at peace. The only sound
was the crackle of the fire, and the distant clatter of pans in the
kitchen. Her eyes were closed, but her other senses seemed heightened. She could feel the thick velvet of the chair beneath her
fingers, the softness of the cushion beneath her head, and she could
smell the most wonderful aroma of food cooking.

Alicia turned her head slowly and opened her eyes with extreme
reluctance. It was dark outside now, and the Hall looked even more
austere with its stone-flagged floor and high ceiling wreathed in
shadow. There was a step beside her, and James appeared, a glass
of water in his hand. He helped her to sit upright and passed her
the glass without comment, but when he saw that she was still
shaking his hand closed around hers to steady it and raise the glass
to her lips.

'Dinner is ready,' he observed quietly. 'You will feel much
better once you have had something to eat.'

At that moment a maid appeared and started to set the long
trencher table with silver and sparkling glass. James helped Alicia
to her feet and escorted her over to the table with grave courtesy.
She felt as though she was floating, too tired to resist or even
think. Nor did James himself appear inclined to break the silence
between them. Alicia could feel his reflective gaze resting on her,
but she did not look at him, or speak.

The food was simple, consisting of a delicious home-made soup
of winter vegetables, followed by a side of beef and finally apple

pie and cream. However, it tasted as good as anything Alicia had ever eaten and she was surprised to find that she was ravenously hungry. After a while, her composure returning, she became more and more sharply aware of the man opposite her.

James looked up and met her gaze, and her heart jolted once, uncomfortably, as she saw the unhappiness reflected in those dark eyes. At once, as though avoiding any subject which might prove too emotive, he began to speak of his growing interest in the estate and to ask Alicia's opinion on several local issues. She answered his questions on everything from cider production to the village school with a clear interest and knowledge that intrigued and amused him.

'You evidently spend a great deal of your time at Chartley,' James observed casually, refilling their wineglasses. 'Do you prefer it to London? And do you have time to visit your other properties at all?'

Alicia considered. 'I usually spend the Season in London, and that's quite enjoyable. But—' she met his eyes squarely '—I love Chartley and the peace I find here. I have a house by the sea at Scarborough which I'll visit sometimes in the summer, but most of the other properties are let on a long-term basis.'

'To orphanages and other charitable institutions, often at a peppercorn rent, so I have heard.' James raised one black eyebrow. 'You may undertake your transactions through paid agents, my lady, but it is not so difficult to trace them back to you if one tries.'

Alicia looked at him reflectively. It was odd, she thought, how all constraint between them seemed suddenly to have vanished. It was as though they had passed the restrictions usually imposed by convention and could say anything to each other. So she had felt at nineteen, discovering with James Mullineaux an affinity that had been both comforting and exciting. They had been kindred spirits and had immediately recognised each other as such. Now, suddenly, that bond had reasserted itself, regardless of what lay between them, drawing them as close as they had been seven years before. It felt both stimulating and dangerous.

The candlelit room had an odd intimacy about it for so large a space and despite all that had happened Alicia knew suddenly that she would never be able to escape this feeling. She could refuse to discuss the past, she could claim never to want to see him again, but she would be lying and the awareness between them, which had flared into such explosive life earlier in the evening, could never be denied.

'You seem very well acquainted with my business, sir,' Alicia commented mildly. 'What else do you know? And why should you have troubled to discover so much?'

James smiled straight into her eyes. 'Because I wanted to know the truth about you,' he said, with shattering directness. 'You wrote me a letter in which you condemned yourself as an adventuress and at the time I was prepared to believe in your duplicity. I was young and very proud, after all.' He tilted the liquid in his glass, watching the firelight warm the rich ruby wine. 'What I said earlier was also true. I had considered the matter closed until I came back and met you again. Then I realised that you were not the caricature fortune-hunter I had built up in my mind, but I refused to accept the evidence of my own intuition. I spoke to Caroline and Marcus, and to the people here at Monks Dacorum, and they all spoke of your warmth and your kindness and your generosity—and I could not make the picture fit with my opinion of you.'

Alicia's gaze dropped before that intense regard, and after a moment James resumed.

'So the only thing I could do was to ask you directly. But, of course, I did it all wrong, because the gulf between the two of us was still so great that I could not bridge it. Now I will not press you for an explanation if you do not wish to give one.

'But, to answer your first question, I know that you have vast quantities of money tied up in charitable trusts, making more money for your beneficiaries. I know that you have invested heavily in local commerce and have opened schools and hospitals. And I must thank you for your care of my tenants while I have been away.'

Alicia had regained a measure of composure by now, and raised a hand in laughing protest. 'Enough, sir! You make me sound like a philanthropist!'

'Why, so you are!' James looked solemn. 'Why deny it?'

'Because I have a horror of being given credit for what I have done,' Alicia answered seriously. 'Unfortunately,' she added, a little sadly, 'the more schemes I think up to get rid of the money usefully, the more money it seems to generate!'

James burst out laughing. 'Vast fortunes have a habit of doing that, so I have heard! But why do you not wish to be thanked for the uses to which you have put your money?'

There was a silence. 'George Carberry's fortune was made by various dubious means, few of them legal,' Alicia observed at length, staring beyond James into the shadows. 'I wanted nothing to do with it and it should never have been mine. The only thing I could think of was to turn it to good—which I have tried to do.'

Their eyes met for a moment of tension. James sat forward, his gaze suddenly intent.

'Alicia, I know I said I would not press you for an explanation, but will you tell me what happened?'

Alicia looked at him for what seemed for ever, then she gave him a shaky smile.

'Very well, my lord. You will have your story.'

Chapter Seven

The study where previously James had entertained Caroline and Marcus Kilgaren was a small oasis of warmth and quiet, more intimate than the Great Hall, a place designed for confidences. It was lined on three sides with the bookshelves where reposed dusty tomes collected by generations of the Mullineaux family, some pristine and uncut, others whose well-worn covers bore testimony to their popularity. Once again, Alicia looked around her with interest. The furnishings were old and tattered, but had a comfortable quality that more than compensated for their threadbare appearance. It was a friendly house, Alicia thought, still showing the touch of Lady Rose, who had had the decorating of it thirty-five years ago when she had been a bride. Yet it was not just the outward appearance that was so welcoming; deeper than that was an atmosphere of warmth, of reassurance. Alicia shivered. She would need all that and more to help her tell her story.

Another exquisite plaster ceiling displayed the arms and devices of the Mullineaux family and those with whom they had inter-married. The only light came from the fire, which the servants had built up during dinner, and from one lamp which cast a golden glow in a corner of the room. In front of the fire was sprawled a very small black and white puppy. Alicia, recognising one of the Monks Farm litter, smiled to herself. The room was very quiet. The servants had seen to it that James and his guest had everything they needed, then they had slipped discreetly away, leaving the two in silence.

James could sense Alicia's tension as she sat uncomfortably on the edge of the chair Caroline had occupied the previous week. The food and wine had revived her colour and animation, but there was a wary look in her eyes as though she had already regressed some way into the past and was thinking on the events of seven years previously. She watched silently as he poured himself a glass of port and took the seat opposite her. She had declined any more wine, requesting a dish of tea, which sat prosaically on the table in front of her.

After a moment Alicia made a little gesture, almost of defeat.

'Well, I promised you the story, my lord, so I shall keep my word. First, however, I should tell you that no one else knows this, except my grandmother. I can only beg you to repay me by relating it to no one.'

James inclined his head. 'You have my word. But may I also know why you chose never to tell anybody else?'

Alicia smiled, a little grimly. 'When you hear the tale, sir, I doubt you will need an answer to that. Firstly, it was too...' she paused, searching for the right word '...too personal for me to tell. I did not wish to make an avid Society free with the details. And the scandal at the time was dreadful enough without my fuelling it further. I suspect—no, I know—that it would have been even worse had I chosen to make people aware of the true facts.'

She took a sip of tea, welcoming the comforting warmth.

'From something you said earlier, my lord, I imagine that Caroline and Marcus must have guessed at a version of events which may be close to the truth, but few people ever realised... Most drew their own conclusions—the most shocking, the most scandalous ones they could think of.'

James did not comment. He had, after all, been one of those very people. Now he had the opportunity to judge for himself. He never doubted for a moment that Alicia would tell him the truth—there was a brittle tautness about her which demonstrated all too clearly the profound effect that the subject still had on her. No, she would be telling him the truth and it would be at great personal cost. He watched her try to settle herself more comfortably in the chair. Her stress and reluctance to speak were almost a tangible thing, and James felt his own tension growing as a result.

'I suppose I must start with the day my father came up to Town,' Alicia said reflectively. 'You may recall that I had not mentioned beforehand that he was visiting, for I was unaware he even planned to open up the house in Bruton Street. I was very surprised to receive a message from him, but I was not suspicious in any way.' She shrugged. 'Why should I have been, after all? He asked me to call there, so, of course, I went.'

She looked thoughtfully. 'We had never been close, he and I— you may remember that I once told you how distant he had been as a father, wrapped up in his business affairs. Even so, I was a dutiful daughter. God help me, I even imagined that his arrival might herald a reconciliation between himself and my grand-mother, and that the family might be whole once again.'

A log fell in the grate with a soft hiss and Alicia looked up to meet James's absorbed gaze.

'It was not as I had presumed,' she said shortly. 'Naturally not. The butler showed me into my father's study and there I was acquainted with his plans for my future.'

Alicia shivered as she remembered the obsequious Castle with his black button eyes. Pausing, she took another drink of tea and put both hands around the cup for reassurance. James had still not said a word but his gaze did not once falter from her face.

'He told me that he had arranged a match for me with George Carberry,' Alicia resumed. 'Carberry himself was there, in fact, and the pair of them were in fine fig with all their plans. I was slow to understand what they were trying to tell me, for first I had to appreciate the enormity of my father's scheming. Once I had grasped that, though, I put up strong resistance. I told them that a marriage between myself and Carberry was out of the question for I was already promised to you, and you would be asking my father for permission to marry me as soon as you knew he was in Town.'

Her voice was colourless. 'They both seemed to find that most amusing. My father asked scornfully what possible benefit such a match could bring him. He was adamant. And when I refused again Castle, the butler, came in and hustled me upstairs in less time than it takes to relate. I was locked in a bedroom for two days without food before they tried to persuade me again.'

There was a distant, inward-looking expression on Alicia's face, for she had become completely wrapped up in the past. She did not even look at James—it was as if he were only there by coincidence rather than as the reason for her to be telling the tale. She stared past him into the shadows, and her face was as remote and beautiful as a porcelain sculpture, but equally cold.

'When they chose, I was taken back downstairs and once again both of them were there with their proposals. Carberry called me a foolish child for still obstinately holding out against them. He said that you had repudiated me and that stories were flying round the clubs that I was nothing more than a jilt and a fortune-hunter. He told me all the names they were calling me. My father said that Society had finished with me and that I had best just accept it.'

Alicia stopped. She had said nothing of her confusion and loneliness, the feeling of terrible isolation, the despair of being hopelessly trapped, but it was all there in the tone of her voice. James could hear it all, see her expression as she remembered how she had felt, and imagine the feelings of a girl whose sheltered and privileged upbringing had scarcely prepared her for coping with such a shock. Alicia had been strong, or she would have capitulated long before; perhaps it would have been better for her if she had done so.

Alicia looked up suddenly at James, and her gaze refocused on him abruptly. He was sitting, head bent, watching the liquid swirling in his glass, and the increasingly grim set to his mouth was the only outward sign that he had heard her words. His very stillness was frightening to her for she could not interpret it. She hurried on.

'I still refused to accept Carberry's proposal. My father tried very hard to persuade me, but to me it would have been betraying you to agree. He blustered and threatened me, and finally he had me beaten for my disobedience.'

James drained his glass in one mouthful and reached for the decanter. 'Go on,' he said curtly.

'That night...' Alicia paused. Her green eyes mirrored shocking disillusion and pain. 'Forgive me, my lord; some things are not easy to tell. That night my father hosted a party for his cronies. I will spare you the details, but there was much heavy drinking and ''entertainment'', and towards the end of the evening George Carberry decided that he would like to take a look at his latest business acquisition—myself. I was dragged from my bed and taken downstairs.'

James got to his feet, as though better to bear whatever she was about to say. Looking at Alicia, he saw that her expression was once again quite blank. She had laced her fingers together to prevent them from shaking and the knuckles showed white with the pressure.

'It was not so bad, I suppose,' she said deliberately, meeting his gaze directly. 'Now I realise how much worse it could have been, but for a girl brought up as I had been, in so sheltered an environment, the humiliation of being paraded half-naked before such a drunken company, the humiliating looks and comments... Well, the shock was terrible for me. I imagine that my father believed that the shame and horror of it all would convince me that I was ruined and had no choice but to marry. But still he took no risks.

'The following morning, a maid brought me the first proper food and drink I had had for a week. Like a fool, I ate it all. I remember nothing of the next day—I do not even know how the day—or days—passed. The food must have been laced with a sleeping-draught, but I never imagined... Anyway, when I awoke, my father produced his final ultimatum.'

Her voice was now so quiet that James had to strain to hear her words, but when she looked up her gaze was full of emotion.

'He told me that if I did not agree to marry Carberry he would ruin you, destroy you.' She shrugged dismissively. 'In retrospect I wonder if he could have carried out such a threat. Perhaps so; perhaps not. At the time I was hardly in a fit state to think at all, but I would not have taken that risk anyway. So I agreed. God help me, of course I agreed.'

It was all far worse than James had even imagined. Although close to Marcus's version of events, told by Alicia in such factual terms it somehow became even more chilling. She had not tried to invest the words with any particular feeling, but her sense of desperation and hopelessness had come over strongly. James found that his anger and pity were so great that he could not speak and had to clear his throat first.

'I did not know...I had no idea.' He tried to think about it rationally, but found that he could not even begin to do so. It was too sudden and involved too much reappraisal to be dealt with easily. His mind was spinning, but overriding all else was an intense, impotent anger at what they had done to her—and a disgust with himself for believing her false when she had suffered all this for him.

'How could anyone do such a thing?' he finally burst out, with all the suppressed violence he would have liked to wreak out on Broseley himself. 'God damn him to hell, I could kill him myself.'

Alicia almost laughed. 'Locking up recalcitrant daughters to encourage them to marry their parents' choice is hardly a new concept,' she pointed out, in another unconscious echo of Marcus Kilgaren's observations. 'Many a young lady has changed her mind about a prospective suitor when under duress! In my case the duress was particularly severe and the suitor particularly unpleasant, but that is the only real difference!'

James was shaking his head in disbelief. 'You can say that? After everything that they did...! And so you married him. Of course you did! What choice did you have?' He brought his fist down on the mantelpiece with a violence that made the whole structure shiver. 'I wish...I just wish that I had known the truth!'

Alicia said nothing. No platitudes would make it any better. James was experiencing one small part of the anger, misery and shock that had been hers so long ago. After a moment he turned back to her, a question in his eyes.

'Did he tell you—did your father ever tell you that I went to Bruton Street to find out what had happened to you?' he demanded.

Alicia did not look surprised. A smile that could have been ironic touched her mouth fleetingly and was gone. 'No, he did not. But at Annabella's wedding, when you said you had met him, I realised... What did he say to you?'

James drove his hands forcibly into his pockets as though to restrain them from violence. 'For several days he would not receive me, although that thug of a butler gave me a message to the effect that you had gone to your father of your own free will. He implied that you had no wish to marry me and felt forced into it by Lady Stansfield. I flatly refused to believe him and went back every day demanding to see your father. The stories to which you referred earlier started to circulate in the clubs, but I tried to ignore them and finally Broseley granted me an interview—' He broke off, staring into the fire with a black frown on his forehead.

'I was almost demented with worry by that time. But if I had known—' He broke off again, then resumed. 'Anyway, when I saw him, your father confirmed that the stories were true and that you were marrying George Carberry. He said some terrible things.' James's dark gaze rested on Alicia thoughtfully. 'He implied that you were marrying for money, a course of action of which he thoroughly approved. Finally, he gave me the letter you had signed. You did sign it, didn't you, Alicia?'

'Yes.' Once again Alicia's voice was devoid of all expression. 'It was when he threatened to ruin you that he gave me the letter to sign. I did not even read it, I'm afraid. I just...put my name to it, whatever it might have said. Was it very bad?'

'Just bad enough to convince me that you meant it,' James said grimly. 'I realise now that my judgement was seriously flawed, but I was in such a state of tension that it seems understandable, if not forgivable, that I misjudged you so. I am so very sorry that I ever believed it, Alicia...'

He could read nothing but sadness in her face. 'I am sorry too,' she said slowly. 'For all that happened. But it is done with now.'

'But what of the rest?' James ran a hand through his hair. He paced over to the French window as though he was unable to keep still. 'You must finish the story.'

'There is little more to tell.' Alicia sighed. 'I married Carberry and we returned to my father's house. There was much carousing on the part of my father's friends and creative suggestions for the wedding night... Carberry died that night,' Alicia said deliberately. 'He was puce with drink, excitement and excess, and he died before my eyes. Better for me, perhaps, that he had been drunk— too drunk at any rate to consummate his marriage!

'I roused a servant to go for a physician—a reputable doctor who had attended my grandmother. He almost refused to come to such a house, but in the end he agreed, though there was nothing that could be done for Carberry anyway. My father was drunk in the arms of a maidservant, and so I took my chance and ran away. I ran all the way back to my grandmother's house, desperately hoping that she would take me in.' She paused, remembering with what trepidation she had hammered on the door of the darkened house. 'And when I arrived she was there, and I was safe at last. I think I must have lost consciousness—I believe Caroline came to see me, but I remember nothing of it, and it was a long time before I recovered enough to ask about you, and then my grand-mother told me that you had gone abroad. I remember little after that, but I think I was ill for a very long time...'

A stray breath of wind set the candle flames dancing. James watched as the tears gathered with dazzling brilliance in Alicia's eyes. She cried soundlessly, but all the more poignantly for that, finding to her horror that once she had started she seemed unable to stop. It was relief, not misery that prompted her tears, for after so long a silence she could hardly believe that she had been able to tell James the truth. The relief of knowing that he believed her was overwhelming, and he had not turned from her in disgust—not yet...

It was only when the storm of her tears had begun to subside that Alicia realised that James had crossed the room to her side and had gathered her into his arms without a word. Her head was resting most comfortably on his shoulder and he was stroking her hair gently as he murmured soothing endearments. She felt warm and secure, and it was entirely delightful. This discovery was such a surprise that she stopped crying in order to think about it, then immediately realised the impropriety of their situation. She drew back with a small hiccuping laugh, for was it not a little late to be considering propriety?

James let her go without haste and handed her his handkerchief.

'I do apologise,' Alicia said unsteadily. 'I have ruined your jacket, my lord.'

'It does not matter.' She could hear the warmth in his voice although she found she could not look at him. 'I am not such a slave to my tailor as I used to be!'

His face was in shadow. 'I am only so very sorry that I ever believed ill of you, Alicia,' he said sombrely. 'I have treated you with the most appalling discourtesy and can only beg your pardon. When I think what you had to endure... The whole experience must have been quite dreadful for you, and then I had the insufferable arrogance to consider myself the injured party!'

He turned away, still driven by the oppressive fury he wanted to unleash on Broseley and Carberry. Well, Carberry was beyond his reach now, but Broseley... He would make him pay for everything that Alicia had suffered, but even then it would not be enough to compensate—it could never put things right for her. He tried to imagine how a young and gently bred girl would feel when confronted with the unbridled lust of a gross libertine such as George Carberry, and groaned aloud with despair. Such things were beyond his imagination. A moment later he was overcome with the most hopeless guilt at his failure to save her and was so ashamed that he could hardly look at her.

Alicia was trying to regain a little composure. She felt completely incapable of talking any more, or even thinking beyond the superficial, but seeing James's agony she managed a watery smile. 'You were not to know, my lord! And even if you had done, how could you have helped me? No one could intervene—not you, not my grandmother, nobody! It is best forgotten now for, believe me, I have learned to live with it in the intervening years. I am just grateful that we have had the opportunity to put matters to rights between us, even if it is a little late in the day.'

She tried for a lighter note. 'At least I shall now have no fear that we shall spend the Season avoiding each other—or cutting each other dead! No, we may be comfortable, you and I, knowing that the past is laid to rest and we are free of it.'

It was only what James himself had said earlier, but now it rang a little hollow. Now that she had got over her immediate relief at telling him the truth, Alicia found the prospect of a future of mild friendship with James almost as intolerable as their previous antipathy had been. The relationship between them had always been characterised by intense emotion—first love then hatred—but it had never been one of bland insipidity and she could not bear to think of it degenerating into that now. However, she had no way of knowing how James would feel once he had had time to assimilate her story. It was hardly an edifying tale, and she could not blame him if he never wanted to think of it again.

Neither did James himself seem much taken by her words for he did not smile. Watching her in the glow from the firelight, he was suddenly aware of an extraordinary shift in perspective. It was as if for the previous seven years he had lived with all his beliefs and values displaced. Now, suddenly and shockingly, they had shifted back like the changing colours of a kaleidoscope, abruptly forming the most perfect and brilliant pattern. The thread of affinity stretched between them once more, both precious and amazingly strong. He could not tear his gaze away from her.

The intensity of his regard disturbed Alicia. She felt completely exhausted from the effort of reliving the experience and suddenly ill-equipped to deal with her thoughts on the future. She was glad when the clock on the mantelpiece chimed the hour and broke the moment.

'Eight o'clock! I really must go before my grandmother has roused the whole county to look for me!'

'I sent a message before dinner,' James replied, with a smile. 'Your mare has thrown a shoe and you have been staying at the blacksmith's whilst the damage is repaired. They have given you some supper and you will be on your way home shortly!'

'I see!' Alicia smiled mischievously. 'He will gain a reputation as a remarkably slow worker! It can only have been three o'clock when I set out!'

'Yes, indeed... Alicia, before you go, there is something I should like to show you...'

James had moved back to the French windows which, like those of the Great Hall, gave onto the terrace at the back of the house. The latch was stiff and squeaky from disuse, but it lifted with only slight resistance and the door opened silently. The fire guttered and roared as the cold night air flooded in, then James stood aside to let Alicia pass and they were outside with the door closed behind them.

Alicia shivered in the cold air, but after the emotional scene in the study it acted like a tonic and helped to clear her head. Here at the back of the house the ivy grew thickly over the mellow stonework and tumbled down over the lichened terrace towards the sweep of grass above the moat. The air was filled with the scent of cypress and the sky was clear. The lamplit room behind them seemed suddenly distant. Alicia turned questioningly to James.

'Wait...' His voice was barely above a murmur. 'The moon is rising behind the hill. In a moment—'

He broke off as the moon topped the hill, pouring its light pure and clear along the water of the moat and turning its path to rippling silver. The night was suddenly alive, the shapes of the trees cut as sharply as sentinels, the gardens mercilessly exposed in the bright white light. As though on cue, a barn owl slid like a shadow from the trees, hunting along the edge of the moat before disappearing into the dark.

It had been a mistake to go out into the darkness. As Alicia moved forward to the balustrade at the front of the terrace, James put his hand on the parapet, barring her way. It was too dark to see his face, but she was acutely aware of his tall figure beside her, his proximity infinitely disturbing to her senses.

'Alicia...' She read the warning note in his voice a second too late, for he was already drawing her gently into his arms. This time was very different from before: his mouth moved softly, persuasively, over hers, keeping a tight control as the kiss became more searching. It teased and provoked her until the slow-burning in Alicia's blood threatened to overwhelm her defences completely.

She arched her body against his, running her fingers into the thick black hair so that she could pull his mouth back down to hers when he would have drawn back. She wanted more, much more. James groaned. He could not resist.

He knew he ought to stop, that the onus had to be on him because Alicia was too inexperienced to understand what she was doing to him with her breathless endearments and soft gasps of pleasure. The trouble was that his inclination and his duty were diametrically opposed—and duty had never appealed to him very much as a concept anyway. He kissed her again lightly, first one corner of her mouth, then the opposite one, waiting until she caught her breath on a moan before he captured her lips fully once more and resumed the slow, exquisite exploration of a moment before.

Alicia did not care about anything at all, other than that James should carry on kissing her. She slid her hands beneath his jacket, luxuriating in the warmth she could feel emanating from the skin beneath his linen shirt. Her caress wrung a groan from him and he savagely forced her lips further apart, the skilful, sensuous demand of his tongue causing a flaming heat to wash through her in response. For a long, mindless interval they surrendered to their mutual need, locked in each other's arms.

When James's mouth finally, reluctantly, left Alicia's, it was only to renew its torment, tracing a burning line from the point of her jaw to the delicate curve above her collarbone. Alicia's head fell back in pleasure, the auburn hair spilling over his arm as James lowered his lips to the tantalising swell of her breasts which were barely revealed by the severely cut riding jacket.

Fortunately, from James's point of view, the drawback of the high neck was more than amply compensated for by the row of tiny buttons down the front of the jacket. These proved no hindrance to his experienced fingers, and in very little time he had undone enough to lay bare much more of the deliciously creamy skin beneath. He let his mouth drift teasingly over the curves he had exposed until Alicia dug her fingers into his back in an agony of wanting.

To play with fire... They were engulfed once again in the same searing tide of emotion that had threatened them earlier in the evening, only this time it was a thousand times more potent, releasing all tension between the two of them.

James found himself perilously close to losing all self-control. He made a desperate grasp for his sanity, turning his face against Alicia's hair and breathing hard. The faint, flowery perfume that clung to her skin was almost his undoing, and when she instinctively pressed closer to him he gave a groan and put her forcibly from him. He had miscalculated in thinking that he could dictate the situation. He wanted her so badly that the physical ache was almost intolerable and the inclination to abandon all rational thought was almost as strong. They could blot out all of the past seven years in an ecstasy that would bind them closer than ever...

And yet James knew that he could not do it. Alicia was in such a vulnerable state now that whatever happened between them at such a time might be bitterly regretted by her later. He suspected that he would be able to seduce her very easily now because the chemistry between the two of them was in danger of carrying them beyond the point of coherent thought. But it would be a mistake. Alicia had suffered enough as a result of the careless whims of men who had used her for advantage—he would not add himself to their number. Nor did he simply want to take her and dismiss her casually when the moment had passed. She affected him too profoundly for that.

Acting in such a responsible way was hardly his specialty, James reflected sardonically to himself as he leant both hands on the parapet and attempted to bring his wayward impulses firmly under control. Under normal circumstances there could only be one outcome to an encounter between himself and a young and beautiful widow—particularly when she was alone with him at one of his establishments. But Alicia had always been different. Cursing under his breath, he admitted to himself that, whilst his feelings for her were all too obvious on one level, they ran very deep on others.

He took her very firmly by the arm and steered her straight back into the house.

'One thing I cannot have on my conscience is the responsibility for you catching a chill!' There was an undertone of laughter in James's voice, though he still sounded shaken. 'And you were right, Alicia—you had better go now! I can't deny that I want you to stay with me, but it would not serve. God knows, I must be getting old! I never thought to find myself acting so much against my own inclinations!'

He scanned Alicia's face, upturned to his, and his gaze softened as he smiled. 'Damn it, Alicia, don't make it any more difficult for me! I'm hardly a candidate for sainthood as it is!'

It was a mild evening for March and Alicia had not felt the cold at all until James had let her go. Then, slowly, sanity had reasserted itself and with it a bereft chill that had made her shiver. More than anything in the world she wanted James to take her back in his arms and blot out the cold for ever. She stared up at him, watching as desire for her darkened his eyes again, and the moment hung in the balance. She knew she could make him change his mind, wanted to do it... Then she pulled herself together, picked up her cloak and turned towards the door.

She was still shaking with the effect James had on her as she walked out into the central courtyard. It would be easy now to forget everything, to persuade James to let her stay with him and damn the consequences. She knew instinctively that it would take very little coercion on her part to accomplish her own seduction, for she could feel the tension in him as tight as a coiled spring and knew he had only a perilously slender grip on his self-control. Alicia also knew that she should be shocked with herself for even contemplating such a course of action but there was no point in self-deception. If James had tried to seduce her she would not have resisted; she would have been glad. But then, what would have happened next?

Alicia gave up the unhappy tussle with her emotions and drew on all the cold practicality she could muster. Whatever happened between them in the future, for now she had to return to Chartley and dissemble her feelings for the benefit of her guests.

They reached the stables, where Ned was saddling up Savannah. James's own raking grey hunter was already saddled and chafing impatiently at the delay. Alicia turned to James with a smile.

'For the sake of my reputation, I think you must let Ned escort me back to Chartley and not do so yourself!'

She saw James frown and hesitate visibly before he nodded in reluctant agreement. He had to admit that any story that Alicia had spent her missing hours visiting innocuously in the village would be immediately discounted if he were seen in her company.

'Very well. It's not what I would choose, but you will be safe enough, and Ned will bring word when you are home.'

Savannah's hooves rang out on the cobbles and Ned swung himself up onto the other horse. James raised an eyebrow.

'Tempting fate, Ned? That horse is as recognisable as I am!'

Ned grinned. 'I won't let anyone see me, my lord! And he does need the exercise.'

James held Alicia's stirrup for her and straightened up, smiling at her.

'So it is farewell, then.' He touched her cheek, a fleeting contact which nevertheless felt as though it burned her. His gaze was serious though his eyes still had a smile in their depths.

'Take care, Alicia. I cannot begin to thank you...'

Alicia wheeled Savannah round and trotted briskly out of the courtyard, Ned at her side.

Back at Chartley Chase, her excuses and apologies were received with little curiosity. The expedition to Pilton had been a success and the visitors had returned only shortly before Alicia, having stayed to dine. Georgiana Stapleford in particular was in high spirits for a change, for she had enjoyed the undivided attentions of both Richard Pilton and Christopher Westwood. Only Caroline Kilgaren gave her friend a particularly piercing look as Alicia guilelessly related the tale of her fictitious, unscheduled stop at the blacksmith's.

It was old Amos, the head groom, who was the only one to know that the story was not true, and he would never say a word. In the first place, he had glimpsed briefly the prime piece of horseflesh which Ned had been riding as he had bidden goodbye to Alicia at the gates. Amos had worked at Monks Dacorum in the days of the old Marquis, knew James Mullineaux well, and also knew his excellent taste in horses.

In the second place, Savannah had been rubbed down and fed with a care that Amos respected. And she had not had a shoe replaced that day, or recently.

Amos grinned a little to himself as he put Savannah back in her stall. All the servants had heard of Lady Carberry's meeting with the Marquis of Mullineaux at Ottery and it had given rise to much speculation. Most of them had been present at the wassail and had wagered it would only be a matter of time before the Marquis and the lady met again. Then there was Christopher Westwood, whose suit had not prospered. Hardly surprising, Amos thought, when contrasted with such a man as James Mullineaux. For certainly Alicia Carberry had been at Monks Dacorum that evening, and the dreamy expression on her face when she had returned owed nothing to a visit to the blacksmith!

* * *

They met unexpectedly at church the following Sunday. Chartley Church still had a Mullineaux family pew from the time that the Chase had been part of the estate, but in recent years it had never been occupied. The sight of James Mullineaux in that pew for the morning service riveted the entire congregation to the extent that the finer points of the sermon were completely lost on them, and the vicar would have been furious had his unexpected parishioner been someone less august.

Alicia also found James's presence most distracting. She had not expected to see him again until the Season started and had tried to come to terms with the flat feeling which the thought had engendered. Despite the demands of her guests, she seemed to have spent a great deal of time thinking about the meeting at Monks Dacorum, and found that her feelings were in even more of a turmoil after the meeting than they had been before. Before, she had had nothing to hope for, and although this had been depressing it had at least been certain. Now she could not help the great number of unspecified thoughts and dreams which always centred in some way on James rediscovering the feelings he had previously held for her.

She stole a sideways look at him through her lashes and wondered what on earth he was doing there. There was something about his clear-cut silhouette which set her in mind of the alabaster profiles on the tombs of his ancestors, which decorated both this church and the one at Monks. Whilst many of the Mullineaux family had chosen to be buried at their main seat in Oxfordshire, there was plenty of evidence to suggest that earlier generations had liked Monks Dacorum sufficiently to live and die there.

Well, Alicia thought, she supposed that James could attend church wherever he wished and scolded herself for the presumption that he might have chosen to come to Chartley in order to see her. Certainly there was nothing in his bearing towards her that suggested it. They had exchanged the briefest of greetings when he had taken his seat, and he had not looked at her once since. She imagined that it was just his way of behaving as though nothing untoward had ever happened between them. Perhaps, she thought, he was already regretting what had happened.

The service over, James spent a considerable time chatting to the vicar at the church door whilst the more forward members of the congregation stood about with ill-concealed interest and waited to greet him. As soon as he was free, Caroline hailed him in her usual blunt manner.

'James! We thought you had already gone to Worcestershire!'

'I travel tomorrow.' James smiled impartially around the group, and Alicia stepped forward with slightly more alacrity than she had shown at Ottery to smooth over his greetings to the Staplefords and Lady Stansfield, whom he had not seen for a very long time.

'Ha! Mullineaux!' Lady Stansfield raised her lorgnette and viewed him critically. She smiled suddenly. 'Good to see you again, boy! Do you go up to London for the Season?'

'I do.' He returned her smile. 'No doubt we shall all meet up then. You must excuse me—I have a hundred and one matters to attend to before I leave tomorrow. It was a pleasure to see you all again. Your servant, ladies and gentlemen.' He bowed to them all, caught Georgiana Stapleford fluttering her eyelashes at him, and gave her an appreciative smile.

As an exercise in discretion, it had been admirable. All fences had been effortlessly mended and a basis for future meetings established. Alicia had been in no way singled out, but had been treated with exactly the same degree of impartial warmth as everyone else. There was nothing left to gossip about. Alicia understood this and could admire James Mullineaux for his strategy even whilst she resented it. It made the heated passion of that night at Monks Dacorum seem a mere figment of her imagination.

They watched as he walked off to the lych-gate, exchanging greetings with those members of the congregation who still lingered.

'Charming man,' Lady Stansfield opined. 'Come along, Honoria! Got to get out of this demmed cold wind!' She slipped her arm through Lady Stapleford's and the party from Chartley Chase turned for home. Caroline caught Alicia's arm.

'Alicia, while we're here I'd just like to take a closer look at the church. No, it's all right, Marcus.' She smiled at her husband. 'I know you don't rate church architecture high on your list of entertainments, so please go on ahead! If Alicia doesn't mind waiting, we can have a little chat on the way back. I won't be long—'

So saying, she dived back inside the doors and left Alicia standing in the porch.

Despite the cold breeze it was a beautiful day, and Alicia sat for a little while admiring the view across to the sparkling sea. After a few minutes, however, she realised she was becoming chilled and resolved to take a quick turn around the churchyard whilst she waited. Caroline had always been interested in history, and her minutes could stretch to an hour without too much difficulty whilst she wandered around an ancient building in enraptured silence. It was perhaps an unusual pastime for a Society matron, but Alicia liked Caroline for it. She never felt the need to apologise for her lack of conformity.

The cypress-lined path wended its way around the ancient graveyard. It was very quiet now that all the churchgoers had left and the bells had ceased their ringing. Alicia made one circuit, relishing her solitude, then another, appreciating the view over the hills. When she had almost reached the church door again, she decided she would really have to go in soon and prise Caroline away from the glories of the past.

Her hand was on the church door when she felt a touch on her arm and turned, startled. She had heard no one approach up the stone-flagged path and in the shadows of the porch it was a moment before she recognised James Mullineaux. She never had a chance to greet him. He slid an arm around her waist and pulled her against him, stifling her instinctive exclamation with his mouth on hers. One hand was in the small of her back, holding her hard against him, whilst the other dispensed ruthlessly with her bonnet in order to entangle itself in her hair and draw her even closer.

Had Alicia been able to think at all, she might have reflected that all she had heard of James Mullineaux's reputation had unexpectedly proved itself to be true—this was not the man who had tried very hard not to seduce her two nights before, but the predatory rake of all the stories, a man accustomed to take the opportunities which presented themselves to him.

His devastating expertise swept her beyond coherent thought. His mouth plundered the sweetness of hers, shamelessly insistent, and the response it provoked in Alicia was equally abandoned. She felt as though every inch of her skin was on fire, burning for his touch. She wanted to dispense with the heavy layers of clothing which separated them, and feel his naked skin against hers.

He let her go at last, dropping one final kiss on her parted lips.

'And that, Alicia, my sweet,' he said very softly, 'was in case you were tempted to forget. Be assured I shall remind you again, when the time does serve.'

Alicia sank down onto the stone seat, one hand to her bruised lips, the other steadying herself as she took a very deep breath. She watched for a second time as James walked down the path to the gate and disappeared down the lane towards Monks Dacorum. Conceited, presumptuous... She gave up. Once again she was becoming repetitious and none of those words came anywhere near describing the boundless audacity that characterised James Mullineaux's behaviour. At that moment Alicia could not even begin to work out how she really felt.

She had completely forgotten Caroline Kilgaren. She turned her head slowly, to see her friend standing in the church door, the expression of comical consternation on her piquant face stating clearer than any words that she had seen exactly what had happened.

It was either very good or very bad luck that Christopher Westwood arrived at the church gate approximately two minutes later. Had he arrived sooner, and seen her with Mullineaux, Alicia realised it would have been disastrous. On the other hand, Caroline had only got as far as saying, 'Alicia, what—?' when she broke off, and set her lips in a very tight line as Westwood came up the path.

The friends had no chance for a tête-à-tête that day, for the demands of her guests kept Alicia fully occupied and she was never alone. On the following day, a number of visitors came to Chartley Chase. Mrs Henley delivered Miss Frensham home from Ottery on her way to Bath and a visit to her married daughter. The other occupants of the Henley coach were none other than Mrs Eddington-Buck and her daughter, who were also set to devastate that unsuspecting city. Good manners obliged Alicia to offer them refreshment on their journey, but she was profoundly grateful when the Henleys' coach lumbered off out of Chartley, weighed down with the Eddington-Bucks' monstrous amount of baggage.

'That woman is an ill-bred toad,' Caroline Kilgaren observed roundly if inelegantly, when all the visitors had gone and she and Alicia were alone. 'Did you hear her telling Lady Stapleford that her elder daughter Jane had had her heart broken by Peter Weston, of all people, and had thrown herself away on a half-pay officer when Peter did not return her love? What utter nonsense! Why, everyone knows that Jane Townley is the only woman of sense in that family, and she and Townley determined to wed from the moment they first met! Oh, it puts me out of all patience!'

Alicia smiled slightly. 'Now we have seen for ourselves how gossip starts, Caro!' She had been playing Scarlatti very quietly, so that the bright breeziness of the music was muted, but now she broke off and lowered the piano lid. 'I did hear her telling my grandmother that she intended to catch Mullineaux for her younger daughter, now that he no longer had a penchant for auburn hair!'

'It is blondes, not brunettes, that are all the rage,' Caroline observed without inflection.

'Very true.' Alicia smiled mischievously. 'And it was a foolish thing to say to Lady Stansfield, who told her that if she wanted to risk her daughter's reputation with so dangerous a man she should not regret it were he to ruin her!' She looked up and met her friend's blue eyes with a challenge in her own. 'There now, Caro, I have made it as easy for you as I can... Now, ask me what you want to know!'

There was a pregnant pause, then Caroline took a deep breath.

'I collect you mean about James Mullineaux...' She gave Alicia a frank look. 'I would do so if I dared! You must know I am expiring with a most ill-mannered curiosity!' She looked so uncharacteristically confused that Alicia felt quite sorry for her. 'I mean, I never thought that you and James had really—' She broke off and started again. 'When you met at Ottery, I thought it was an accident... James never suggested... Well, I suppose he wouldn't—' She broke off again, caught Alicia's amused look and met her eyes accusingly.

'Damnation!' she said abruptly. 'What I am trying to say, Alicia, is that it makes no odds to me whether you and James are lovers! I just thought that you would both have been honest with us!'

Alicia realised that the intimate embrace she had shared with James at Chartley Church must have looked particularly incriminating. If she had been Caroline, how would she have interpreted finding Alicia locked in James's arms in what appeared to be a pre-arranged secret assignation?

'I suppose I should have slapped his face,' she said casually, shuffling the sheets of music together. 'Unfortunately, he took me completely by surprise! I realise how it must have appeared to you.'

There was a pause. Caroline was looking even more thunderstruck as she took Alicia's meaning. 'You mean that you did not arrange to meet? That you had not intended—? But Alicia—'

Alicia made an expressive grimace. 'You know James's reputation as well as I do, Caroline! It would be difficult to judge which of the two of us was more shocked—you at witnessing the scene, or myself at being the unsuspecting recipient of James's attentions!'

Caroline swelled with indignation. 'Well, upon my word! The presumption of the man!'

'Indeed!' Alicia said, very dryly.

Caroline eyed her closely. 'You do not appear much offended, Alicia! Are you sure that there is not more to this than meets the eye?'

Alicia burst out laughing at that. 'You're very shrewd, Caro! Come on, let's go for a walk in the gardens—and I will tell you everything!'

Donning warm pelisses and stout boots, the two friends slipped out of the garden door and began to wend their way by common consent through the maze of garden paths. The gardens at Chartley were small by the standards of the major local estates, but Alicia had not lied when she'd claimed gardening as her passion, and they demonstrated a range of styles and plants carefully and lovingly cultivated. Now that spring was upon them, the Chartley grounds were beginning to show all their promise.

'So what's to tell?' Caroline asked bluntly, seeing Alicia was preoccupied with her thoughts. 'How about your meeting with

James at Ottery? I have heard a little from other sources—indeed, James himself mentioned the encounter to us. I imagine,' Caroline said with a slight smile, 'that it must have been quite eventful!'

'Yes,' Alicia agreed reminiscently, 'but perhaps not so eventful as the scene at the church might have led you to believe!' Her smile faded. 'It was an uncomfortable meeting, to tell the truth. I was ill-prepared to meet James again after all that time, and he...well, he made his low opinion of me very plain! I accept that I was much to blame for sending Miss Frensham away, but at the time she was cold and ill, and I thought I was doing the right thing! Anyway, James was very angry—I expect he told you— and we quarrelled very badly. As I said, it was an uncomfortable meeting!'

They turned into the herb garden, where the air was lightly scented with thyme. Caroline drove her hands more deeply into her fur muff—though there was a sun, the air was still cold.

'It seems even more surprising, then, that James proposed to you the following morning,' Caroline ventured, and watched with interest as the colour flooded into Alicia's face.

'As a gentleman, I suppose—'

'Oh, stuff and nonsense, Alicia!' Caroline reverted to type and forgot her gentle line of questioning. 'James never behaves as a gentleman ought; you should know that!' Their eyes met, and they both burst out laughing.

'No, Caro, that is too harsh!' Alicia protested, through her laughter. 'I can think of at least one occasion—'

'Just how many times have the two of you met?' Caroline demanded. 'James mentioned several heated arguments, but failed to elaborate on where they took place!'

Alicia counted on her fingers. 'Two at Ottery, one at Theo's vicarage, one at Monks Farm...I think that's all, for we were very civil on the other occasions!'

'More than civil,' Caroline said dryly.

'Oh, and, of course, we quarrelled at Monks Dacorum,' Alicia said, with a wicked twinkle in her eye. 'But that was before we had the chance to talk properly and sort matters out between us!'

Caroline gave an infuriated squeak. 'Alicia Carberry, I shall shake you in a moment! So you *were* at Monks Dacorum last week! Marcus and I thought so! Now how did that come about?'

They were walking through the orchard now, between the laden branches of the fruit trees, towards the greenhouses where some of Alicia's most prized vegetables were growing.

Alicia was looking amused. 'I met James by chance when I was out riding,' she said, quite truthfully, but with a little, secret smile which Caroline did not miss. 'He...persuaded me to dine with him and after dinner I told him what he wanted to know, which was the truth of my marriage to Carberry.' Her green eyes met Caroline's blue ones quite frankly. 'The past is now all explained and can be put behind us.'

'And what of the present and future?' Caroline demanded. A flush rose in her cheeks. 'Alicia, you can be the most vexatious creature at times! You tell me the merest outline of what must have been a very interesting meeting indeed and then you glibly gloss over the rest! Tell me properly!'

A rueful smile lit Alicia's face. 'I'm sorry, Caro! What do you want to know? I suspect that you and Marcus had already been instrumental in encouraging James to seek a meeting with me, and for that I must thank you. As for the rest, it is as I said; it seems that James did not desert me as I had imagined, and he now no longer believes that I jilted him to marry Carberry for money, so now we may all be comfortable, and act as though it never happened!'

'Pshaw!' Caroline gave a snort of disgust. 'You can hardly have forgotten that you were in love with each other once and pretend that that never happened! And, good God, Alicia, if you had seen the pair of you yesterday, you would have drawn the same conclusions as I, and have thought that the two of you were lovers!'

They had reached the gate in the wall which led through into the quiet churchyard. Alicia put out her hand and pushed it open. All amusement had fled from her face, and her voice.

'Love?' she said, a little bitterly. 'No, I do not forget that, Caro. But that was seven years ago, and people change. And are you not confusing two quite different matters? What you saw yesterday was nothing more than James indulging a whim! He had the opportunity—'

'And the inclination,' Caroline said dryly. 'This is all becoming a little sophisticated for me! Are you sure you do not mistake James's feelings? And what of your own?'

Alicia's pain showed in her eyes. 'I have had plenty of time to think about this,' she said, very quietly. 'For my part, my feelings have not changed in all the time I have known James, but I cannot expect him to feel the same. Since we cannot go back to how matters were before, we can only go forward as friends. Things will be more comfortable now—only imagine how intolerable the Season would have been if we were constantly avoiding or ignoring each other!'

Caroline looked unconvinced. 'My dear Alicia, the feelings between yourself and James were never *comfortable*—' she stressed the word with heavy irony '—either before or after you quarrelled! You can hardly expect them to be so now!'

They were walking along the cypress-lined path around the church. The air was a dim green beneath the trees. There was a rustic bench placed to allow visitors to take the view, and they sat down, looking out across the moors in much the same way as Alicia had done the previous day. For a while there was silence between them, then Alicia sighed.

'You are right, of course,' she admitted quietly. 'I am still in love with James, and though I am glad that the past is now settled between us I cannot see that it will make matters easier for me in the future. I shall always be wanting more than he is prepared to give!'

A blackbird squawked off overhead.

'Look, Alicia.' Caroline spoke energetically. 'Marcus had a long talk with James when we were at Monks Dacorum and he thinks that James is still in love with you, too. He may not necessarily realise it, or even want it to be so, but in the end he will have to accept it. He was very angry with you. That was getting in the way, but now, as you say, it is resolved.' She looked at her friend appraisingly. 'James evidently still finds you exceedingly attractive,' she said, with a hint of a smile. 'Who knows? Perhaps in time—'

But Alicia was shaking her head, smiling a tight little smile which did little to conceal her hurt.

'No, Caro,' she said, with finality. 'I will not allow myself false hope. I admit that, at Monks Dacorum, I thought there might be a chance—' She broke off, and resumed. 'But it only took me a little time to see that what happened that night was in the heat of the moment. It is better this way.'

Caroline was looking almost as shocked as she had done earlier. 'Alicia, are you telling me that James seduced you that night?'

'No,' Alicia said again, this time with the same small, secret smile which Caroline had seen earlier. 'In point of fact he did not. He could have done, but he was very careful not to!' The smile faded. 'So you see—' she shrugged '—even then, he was thinking far more clearly than I!'

'He has had more experience,' Caroline observed coolly. 'I'll say this for James—he works very fast!' She looked at Alicia thoughtfully. 'And if he were to offer you carte blanche, what then?'

'No,' Alicia said, for a third time. 'I won't deny I've thought about it, Caro.' The colour came into her cheeks. 'Oh, I dare say it was immodest of me even to consider...but anyway it wouldn't do! In the end it would only make me more unhappy. For me, it has to be all or nothing!'

She shivered suddenly, and rose abruptly to her feet. 'Enough of this! I feel a fit of the megrims coming on! Shall we take a turn around the village? I wanted to tell you of my visit to Greyrigg and the interview with my father, not to mention other matters.'

They walked to the lych-gate and went out onto the village green, circled the duck pond, and made a detour down the lane which ran along the garden wall of Chartley Chase. Once again, Caroline turned her enquiring blue gaze upon her friend.

'So what of those other matters that are on your mind? Is one of them Christopher Westwood—he has made you an offer, hasn't he?'

Alicia nodded, glancing sideways at her friend. 'Yes, and I have refused him.'

'I should think so!' Caroline had no very high opinion of Westwood. 'If you had agreed I should have disowned you! You could do much better than that, leaving aside your feelings for James!'

Alicia looked amused. 'I did think about accepting,' she admitted, 'before I met James again. I knew Christopher was going to make me an offer and I wondered if I should accept for the sake of companionship.'

'What fustian you do talk sometimes!' Caroline looked totally disgusted. 'Next you will be telling me that you should marry him because your grandmother likes him!'

'Well, and so she does—' Alicia began, caught her friend's eye and they both burst out laughing.

They walked on for a few moments in silence. Alicia knew that Caroline was quite right—none of the reasons she had thought of for marrying Christopher were compelling enough and compared to her feelings for James Mullineaux they paled into insignificance.

'I did not tell you,' she added presently, 'that my father had also proposed that I enter the married state again. His was a proxy proposal, on behalf of a business acquaintance, but it was even less tempting than marrying Christopher!'

Caroline stopped dead and stared at her. 'We thought it odd that Annabella had married and settled in Somerset when you were supposed to be giving her a Season,' she commented. 'Was it all a ruse, then?'

Alicia nodded sombrely. 'Yes, I think it was just an excuse to get me to Greyrigg.' She shivered suddenly. 'I had not thought of it much, my visit there having been overshadowed by other events lately, but it was a most unpleasant interview, Caro. I always feel that no matter what distance I put between myself and my father he is always there. I can't explain it...' she finished lamely.

Caroline was frowning, her hands deep in the pockets of her pelisse. 'This match... Did your father say who his business associate was?'

Alicia looked surprised. 'No, I never thought to ask his name... Why do you ask?'

Caroline shrugged. 'I'm not sure, really... It just seems an odd coincidence that you should be the recipient of so many proposals at once!' She gave her friend a look of amused raillery. 'I know you reject them by the dozen, Alicia, but three in one month!'

Now it was Alicia's turn to frown. 'It does seem a little excessive, I know... But surely there can be no connection between the three! The idea's absurd!'

Caroline agreed, but she continued to frown. 'You do know that
Christopher is in debt, don't you, Alicia? I'm not wishing to suggest that his affection for you is insincere, but...' Her voice trailed
away unhappily.

Alicia had not known, and felt vaguely surprised. There was
nothing in Westwood's demeanour or dress which suggested straitened circumstances, but that in itself was hardly unexpected. Often
those with the smallest means put on the greatest show in the
society in which they lived. She wondered suddenly whether a
man like Westwood would borrow from the same sources as her
cousin Josiah, for example. It was an odd thought, for there was
such a fastidious, finicky element to Westwood's nature that she
could not imagine him seeking out a money-lender in the back-
streets of London...

Yet when she considered it there *were* similarities between her
cousin's case and that of Christopher Westwood: the lack of visible
means of financial support, the enjoyment of expensive living and
the love of deep play... At the back of her mind a thought stirred
briefly, but Caroline was pulling her arm, drawing her attention to
the light, grey drizzle and the mist that was descending again on
the moorland behind the house. Alicia forgot her thoughts as the
two girls slipped in at the back gate of Chartley Chase and made
their way up the damp path. Marcus Kilgaren and Christopher
Westwood could be seen through the games-room window playing
at billiards, and Alicia sighed unconsciously at the thought of returning to the drawing-room and the barbed observations of Georgiana Stapleford. Caroline gave her arm a comforting squeeze.

'Only a few days until we all leave you in peace!' she whispered
irrepressibly. 'Then all we need to worry about is the Season, and
how on earth we engineer your first public meeting with James!'

Chapter Eight

It was the most perfect dress that Alicia had ever seen. Her maid, Gibley, brought it forward into the light almost reverently and the dress fell like a golden waterfall over her arm, rustling softly as she moved.

The first major social event of the new Season—a ball at the home of fashionable hostess Mrs Laetitia Bingley—was taking place that evening. It was also to be the first meeting of Alicia and James before the *ton*. Dealing with a handful of former acquaintances in a Somerset churchyard was one thing, Alicia reflected; could James achieve a similar success under the critical, fickle gaze of his peers? Alicia knew that the two of them would be a cynosure for all eyes and the thought was a daunting one, even to one as accustomed as she to the whims and ways of Society. In addition, she had had to cope with her own rising sense of anticipation at the thought of seeing James again. Hence the gold dress—she needed to give herself confidence. Such an outrageous gown, she thought comfortingly, could not fail.

Like all of Alicia's clothes it was very simple and elegant. Slashed low across her breasts, it revealed a dizzying amount of bare skin and hinted at other delights only just concealed beneath its sinuous, flowing silk. To match the style, Gibley painstakingly swept Alicia's hair back in a simple Grecian knot, restraining the copper curls with a small gold circlet that added a regal touch.

Alicia studied her reflection thoughtfully. She looked cool, untouchable, and almost impossibly tantalising, a far cry from the nervous turmoil that shook her inside. You're a fool to yourself, Alicia Carberry, she told her mirror image astringently. You have had any number of offers from the most eligible *partis* in Town, and yet you persist in pining for the love of the one man who is beyond your reach. The girl in the mirror looked back at her with the faintest hint of a compassionate smile on her lips. No matter. Tonight her feelings would not be on view for public consumption. She intended to dazzle and deflect the barbs of the curious. And as an additional aim she would show the Marquis of Mullineaux that she was not about to fall into his arms again. The memory of the scene at Chartley Church was with her still. She raised her chin. Damn his impertinence!

Gibley smiled slightly, standing back like her mistress to admire her handiwork.

'You'll set the Town by the ears tonight, my lady,' she opined. 'Do you wish to wear any jewellery?'

Alicia's eyes met hers in the mirror. 'Just the green star,' she said softly.

Gibley was surprised and showed it. In her opinion, Lady Carberry had many pieces of beautiful jewellery and the fact that she seldom chose to wear any of them was a great pity. The green star, an enormous emerald, had been brought back from India by George Carberry and set for him in a barbaric and vulgar gold necklace. Alicia had immediately had the emerald reset when she had inherited it, but she had never shown any inclination to wear it—until now.

Gibley unlocked the case and brought the necklace across gingerly, almost as though she expected it to bite her. There was no denying that the single jewel was very effective, set as it was now on a plain gold chain. Around Alicia's neck, it suddenly took fire from her eyes and reflected the intense green light back again. Under any circumstances it would have drawn all eyes, but Gibley could not even begin to imagine what effect it would have that night in combination with the dress and Lady Carberry's luminous beauty.

Alicia moved slightly and the light struck the carved surfaces of the emerald, scintillating deep within its depths. A faint, satisfied smile touched her lips, and Gibley watched her curiously. Lord

Charles Oxley was her ladyship's escort to the ball that night, but Gibley doubted profoundly that all this finery was for Lord Charles's benefit. He and Alicia had been friends for many years without her betraying even the slightest *tendre* for him. Whereas the Marquis of Mullineaux would also be at the ball, and Gibley rather suspected that Lady Carberry's feelings for him were another matter. There was no doubt that her ladyship was playing a deep game—a game designed to fool the *ton*, but possibly to deceive the Marquis as well.

Alicia stood up and the pale gold skirts shimmered around her. Lost in admiration, Gibley passed her the matching gold reticule and fan, and the gossamer-light scarf for her shoulders.

It was as Alicia was about to go downstairs to join Lord Charles and Miss Frensham that Gibley suddenly realised what was missing.

'Your bracelet, madam! Are you not wearing it tonight?'

Alicia paused in the doorway and smiled. 'Not tonight, thank you, Gibley. It does not suit the occasion.'

There was a whisper of silk, and she was gone.

When Charles Oxley saw Alicia he experienced serious misgivings about the decision he had made only the previous day to propose marriage to the debutante daughter of Lord and Lady Mountjoy. Compared with the wanton beauty before him, the youthful charms of Sarah Mountjoy paled into insignificance. A moment later, he recalled that he had already asked Alicia to marry him twice in the past, and she had turned him down and always would. He suddenly realised that he had been gaping like a fish ever since she had entered the room and tried to pull himself together.

'I say, you do look splendid tonight, Alicia!' Lord Charles considered the gold dress in more detail and felt his collar become rather constricting. He was almost certain that he had turned bright red. 'Splendid!' he repeated, finding it almost impossible to drag his gaze away from the green star, where it shone so seductively in the hollow between Alicia's breasts.

Miss Frensham, conservative in her usual lavender muslin, was also struck by the dress, but in a rather different way.

'Lady Carberry! Why, you *never* wear that style!'

'No. Does it not make a delightful change?' Alicia seemed blissfully unaware of her disapproval. 'I like it so much that I think I will place an order for several more with Madame Celeste!'

Miss Frensham murmured something fortunately inaudible, although Charles Oxley thought that he had heard the word '*demimonde*' mentioned. He hurried forward with Alicia's velvet cloak, clumsy in his efforts to get something more substantial around her body. Alicia gave him a melting smile over her shoulder which raised his blood pressure even higher. He had always agreed with those who had categorised the lovely Lady Carberry as sexually cold, but it seemed he had been in grave error. Either that, or something extraordinary had happened to her since the last time they had met.

Miss Frensham was tutting in a worried sort of a way. The guardian of Alicia's reputation ever since her unfortunate marriage, Miss Frensham had a lowering feeling that matters were slipping from her rather tenuous grasp. First there had been that distressing episode at Ottery, although Lady Carberry had been all that was proper in quashing *that* scandal! Now, however, it seemed she was set on creating a whole new set of rumours of her own accord! Never had Miss Frensham seen her ladyship in so—she boggled at the word, but it was applicable—wanton a mood. It did not augur well for the rest of the evening.

The road outside the Bingleys' town house was already crowded with carriages as they arrived. Flaring torches lit the steps to the door and a multitude of people appeared to be going in. It was very early in the evening for such a crush and Miss Frensham could not help but wonder whether Alicia's meeting with Lord Mullineaux was the sole reason for all this interest. To judge by the avid glances cast their way, this was very much the case. Miss Frensham's timid heart sank even further, particularly as she caught sight of the wicked sparkle in Alicia's green eyes, a look which her long-suffering companion could not help but mistrust. With a slight moan, Miss Frensham excused herself and dashed into a side room where she administered herself a large dose of sal volatile and waited for her nerves to calm a little.

Fortunately, Miss Frensham played no more than a peripheral

part in the encounter which Caroline Kilgaren had orchestrated so carefully for her friends. According to plan, Alicia and Charles Oxley now progressed into the ballroom, which Mrs Bingley had decorated with an oriental theme. Oxley, a simple soul, was inclined to disparage the opulent draperies and colourful Chinese lanterns, and he shuddered visibly at the murals of rampaging elephants. Alicia, who was feeling ever more nervous beneath her confident façade, thought that Mrs Bingley had perhaps overdone the theme a little, and was assailed by a fit of the giggles. Ever since some ambitious hostess had held a ball complete with a troutstream running through the ballroom, the fashionable had outdone themselves and each other to come up with new and original ideas.

The ballroom was filling rapidly and Alicia was soon surrounded by her usual court of admirers who found to their annoyance that it was impossible to prise her away from Lord Charles. Since Caroline had specifically told her brother to stay with Alicia until after James Mullineaux had arrived this was not surprising, and Charles was sticking doggedly to his duty. Not even the twinkling smile of Sarah Mountjoy could draw him across the ballroom, although he would have felt more comfortable next to her than in the orbit of Alicia's bright, particular star. She was dazzling in a way which made him feel quite ill at ease that evening, and he did little other than watch her silently as she automatically parried the compliments of others more articulate than himself.

It was strange, Charles reflected, what a change could be wrought in a person, and it was not simply the dress which had effected the transformation. Alicia had always represented all that stood for restrained good taste, with the emphasis very much on the restraint. Her clothes were faultlessly elegant, but seldom so provocative, and she never wore jewellery. Not simply that, but there was something in her manner, some suppressed air of excitement, that was positively sensual. Watching her flashing smile, Charles once again tried to ease the tightness of his collar. How could he ever have imagined her to be cold? She was giving off so much heat that he was afraid of burning up. And he was not the only one who was looking at her with a mixture of fascination and puzzlement. Several of her oldest admirers, who flattered themselves that they knew Alicia extremely well, were looking completely confused.

The noise level in the room was growing, as was the excitement in the air. Alicia's own tension levels were well ahead of the rest, however. She was barely able to prevent herself shaking visibly and found it incredibly difficult to concentrate on what anyone said to her. Lady Stansfield came in, fixed her granddaughter with a shrewd eye, and crossed the room to bestow on her a very public kiss of approval. Her arrival had the fortunate effect of removing some of the less respectable of Alicia's admirers and making space for Caroline's cousin Charlotte and her husband Perry Renwick.

Everything was happening at once now. Lady Stansfield drifted off to join the Staplefords and Christopher Westwood, then there was a ripple of excitement, and Alicia, turning with everyone else, saw that Caroline and Marcus had come in, accompanied by James Mullineaux.

'The Earl and Countess of Kilgaren. The Marquis of Mullineaux.'

The stentorian tones of the Bingleys' butler floated across the room, putting a stop to all conversations. Caroline and Marcus greeted their hostess and came down the steps into the ballroom first, Marcus resplendent in evening dress and Caroline ethereal in silver gauze. Meanwhile, Mrs Bingley was greeting James Mullineaux very warmly. To her natural pleasure at seeing him again was added the fact that his presence had just about guaranteed the success of her ball. And he was, after all, a very attractive man. She let him go with obvious reluctance as another flurry of guests arrived and he joined Caroline and Marcus, who were chatting with Peter and Maria Weston. Peter seemed very pleased to see his old friend again and from Maria James got a shy smile, and a kiss on the cheek. All was going according to Caroline's plan. She took James's arm, and the whole group turned towards Alicia and Charles.

The years rolled back and Alicia could suddenly see the tall figure of James Mullineaux crossing the Stansfield House ballroom towards her, moving with that lithe grace which was peculiarly his own. Tonight he was dressed with elegant simplicity in black and white evening dress and in many ways he looked the same as he had done seven years before; the same tanned, classically hand-some features, the same intensely dark and disturbing gaze, the same lazy assurance in his manner...

The murmur in the room died to almost total silence. Only the music of the string quartet still tinkled in the distance. Caroline, performing the introductions, did not bat an eyelid at finding her-self the centre of attention. She had always had a flair for drama.

'You remember my cousin Charlotte, don't you, James? And this is her husband, Peregrine Renwick. Perry, may I make you known to James Mullineaux?'

The two men exchanged bows. Renwick was a spare, sandy-haired, humorous man, who had heard plenty about James Mul-lineaux even though he had never met him. He gave the Marquis a penetrating look, quite disposed to like what he saw. Charlotte was blushing in much the same way she had when James had greeted her at Stansfield House seven years ago. She had never quite grown out of her admiration for him, although she had equally never felt quite comfortable with him—there was some-thing about such blatant masculinity that was too dangerously at-tractive. She murmured a few words of greeting, moving instinc-tively closer to Perry's side, and James smiled at her and turned to Alicia.

'Lady Carberry you know already, of course.' Caroline's voice held only the faintest hint of mischief as she looked from one to the other, although she could sense as well as everyone else the peculiar tension emanating from the two figures before her.

James was not smiling any more. There was a pause—the entire room appeared to be holding its breath. On the one side were those who waited hopefully for James to administer the cut direct, a cruel snub to the woman he had once loved. On the other were those equally avid watchers who wanted confirmation of the ru-mours they had heard about a clandestine love affair between these two. There were very few uninterested observers.

James had intended to follow the same strategy as at Chartley, and acknowledge Alicia coolly and civilly before moving on. That would have squashed speculation on both sides and left the gossips with nothing to talk about. He had no intention of showing her any particular regard, despite his feelings, which could have been described as more than warm. Yet when it came to the point he could not do it.

He had been aware of Alicia from the moment he had stepped into the room. Leaving aside the effects of the outrageously provocative dress and the sheer ostentation of the green star, all his senses were conscious of her presence. Had he not exerted the most supreme self-control, he would have been drawn irresistibly to her side from the first moment. He had not seen Alicia for several weeks and had been astonished, chagrined and finally resignedly amused to discover how she had haunted his thoughts.

Now she was here before him and, sensitive to her every feeling, James realised that she was very nervous. He took her hand and smiled straight into her eyes. It was a smile for her alone, conspiratorial and full of shared amusement. The room took a collective breath.

'You dim the candlelight, Lady Carberry.' His voice was low, but not too low for those about them to miss his words. 'It is a great pleasure to see you again. May I beg the honour of a dance with you later?'

In silence Alicia handed him her dance card. Their fingers touched, and a quiver of awareness shot right through her. Her heart was beating suffocatingly in her throat. James scribbled his monogram against one of the dances and handed the card back to her. Their audience watched. Alicia made an effort to speak. She knew she had to do it, but found it was one of the most difficult things ever to confront her.

'Lord Mullineaux.' It came out a little huskily, but better than she had hoped. 'Welcome back to London.'

He gave her another smile which increased her pulse rate several notches further, then Charles Oxley was stepping forward to shake his hand and second Alicia's welcome. The noise level rose again as several people who had been holding back now came forward to greet James. Soon he was at the centre of a circle of well-wishers and Alicia was able to slip away unnoticed.

She found that she was shaking. The whole encounter had been so short, but had affected her so profoundly. Aware that there were still plenty of people watching her, she turned round and found Christopher Westwood at her elbow. He was looking absolutely furious. He took Alicia's arm in an iron grip and practically dragged her behind a nearby group of statuary.

'Well, I don't suppose many people can be in any doubt about your relationship with Mullineaux now, Alicia!'

Alicia shook him off, careless of the watchers. 'Oh, don't be absurd, Christopher! Would you have had him cut me dead? Mullineaux always was outrageous in his compliments. I am sure nobody but you thought it odd.'

Westwood was flushed with anger. 'Really? I can assure you that everyone thought it most particular! No one has any doubts now that you are Mullineaux's mistress! I suppose it was beyond either of you to try for a little discretion!'

There was a frozen silence, more effective than any words would have been. Westwood realised he had gone far too far. He started to splutter an apology, but Alicia cut him off.

'Would you escort me back to the Countess of Kilgaren, please, Christopher? I feel sure that I shall find more congenial company elsewhere. Leaving aside my own feelings on what you have said, you have now single-handedly given the gossip-mongers plenty more food for thought. I congratulate you!'

She set off across the ballroom without waiting for a reply so that Westwood was forced to hurry to catch up with her. Once out on the floor in full view of the assembled throng, he was prevented from saying anything further by the risk of drawing even more attention to them, and spent the journey to Caroline's side in red-faced, tight-lipped confusion.

Around the room the fans were waving and feathers nodding as the matrons exchanged opinions. The evening was far exceeding expectation, and it had only just started. There was the Marquis of Mullineaux, as arrogantly attractive as ever. There was Alicia Carberry, extravagantly beautiful, who seemed to have overcome the dreadful scandal of their parting and been reinstated in his affections. There was the conspicuous opulence of the huge emerald at Alicia's throat—vulgar, some said, but enough to draw the fortune-hunters in droves. Finally there was Christopher Westwood, deep in the throes of a jealous passion and unable to hide it. What an entertainment!

The music was striking up. The crowd around James had hardly diminished at all, although some were now drifting away as the dancing started. As well as old acquaintances, he was now surrounded by people he had never met before who were taking advantage of the informality of the occasion to introduce themselves. Chief amongst these was Lady Corinna Dawe, a dark beauty married to a complaisant husband, whose love affairs since her marriage had titillated the whole Town. She was standing very close to James, one little white hand on his arm to claim his attention, all melting doe eyes and lustrous black hair. Lady Dawe leant closer to give him the full benefit of her voluptuous figure, and Alicia, watching from across the floor, suddenly decided that she disliked her very much indeed.

Charles Oxley came up to claim Alicia for the first dance and Westwood, who had been dithering beside her in agonised silence, went off in a huff.

'I say, Alicia, I'd almost forgotten what a capital fellow James Mullineaux is!' Oxley was full of the enthusiasm of relief that all had gone so well. 'Corinna Dawe certainly finds him to her taste!'

He chuckled, watching as Lady Corinna artfully inveigled James into the set that was forming. 'I'll wager that it won't be long before those two come to some mutually agreeable arrangement! Lady Corinna is not one to let the grass grow under her feet when she sees something she wants, and James always did have an eye for the prettiest faces!'

Alicia felt sick. James certainly appeared to be enjoying Lady Corinna's company, his dark head bent attentively to hers, a smile of genuine amusement on his lips. Well, the scandal-mongers had plenty to muse on now! It would be most piquant to imagine that a current and potential mistress of the Marquis of Mullineaux were both at the same ball!

'I don't think I will take your bet, Charles,' Alicia said, trying hard to keep all evidence of her true feelings from her voice. 'Lady Corinna is said to be irresistible when she decides she wants something—or someone—and Lord Mullineaux, as you say, has hardly been known for his inclination to resist beautiful women in the past! They deserve each other!'

Oxley was not a sensitive soul, but the waspishness of this reply penetrated even his slow brain. Giving Alicia a thoughtful look, he realised that this was perhaps not the most tactful of topics to broach with her and turned the subject to less controversial matters.

Alicia was glad when the dance came to an end. The initial purpose of the evening achieved, she realised that she was not enjoying herself at all and would have given much to retire from the ball. Knowing the speculation this would inevitably engender, however, she also realised with resignation that she was forced to carry on as though she were having a good time. The prospect of the whole Season suddenly opened up before her. Having got over the difficulty of meeting her again, James could now ignore her and concentrate on pursuing Lady Corinna, or indeed a whole succession of willing partners. At the same time he could be weighing up the merits of some youthful bride, and then what price the confidences of Monks Dacorum? It was as though it had never been. And Christopher Westwood would be pestering her with unwanted attentions—the whole thing would be intolerably tiresome.

Marcus Kilgaren came up to claim the next dance and needed only one look at Alicia's face to realise which topics of conversation were out of bounds. At the end of the dance he steered her unobtrusively towards Caroline, who was conversing with Perry Renwick, and for a while at least Alicia had the balm of their companionship. Her dance card was full, however, and she could not hide away for long. Peter Weston was her partner for the following set of country dances and by the end of that her usual coterie of admirers was re-forming, its ranks swelled by several gazetted fortune-hunters drawn by the dazzling lure of the green star.

James, meanwhile, had temporarily shaken off the attentions of the predatory Lady Dawe and was confusing the gossips even more by blamelessly leading out a series of starry-eyed debutantes. Returning the latest of these, the youthfully pretty Miss Osborne, to her beaming mama, James handed her over with a charming word of thanks and turned to scan the ballroom. A moment later, Marcus Kilgaren, his hands full of refreshments, collided with his old friend as James stopped dead in front of him.

'How well does Alicia know that fellow?' James demanded without preamble, a heavy frown marring his brow. Marcus followed his gaze to where Alicia was waltzing in the arms of a man in striking scarlet regimentals—a man whose very attitude and manner towards her indicated intimacy.

'Patrick Wickford? He's been paying half-hearted court to Alicia for years and getting nowhere,' Marcus observed. 'No doubt the sight of the green star made him feel it was worth his while to try again,' he added, with customary cynicism.

James was looking grim. 'I came across him in Dublin. He's got a very unsavoury reputation. His pockets are to let and he's been hanging out for a rich wife, but he's quite prepared to pass the waiting time in the pursuit of other women.'

'Well, perhaps Wickford has cast Alicia in the role of rich wife,' Marcus commented thoughtfully, 'although Alicia's no fool and I should say that she can take care of herself! Anyway,' he added pointedly, 'what business is it of yours, James?' He looked down at the disintegrating ice cream in his hands. 'I must get this ice to Caro before it melts completely! I'll settle for lemonade next time, in case you delay me again!'

So saying, he left James still glaring in the direction of Alicia and the dashing Captain.

Alicia, much to her own surprise, was finding solace in Captain Wickford's attentions. He was very handsome in a rugged way and the piercing blue of those eyes rested on her in a manner so blatantly admiring that it was difficult to resist. Soon after she had been widowed he had paid her very marked attention, but she had never deluded herself that his feelings ran any deeper than the bottom of her purse. She had repelled him then with the cool charm that had thwarted so many potential suitors and he had taken his dismissal with good humour. He had been surprised to find her so receptive to his advances now, but had been quick to define the cause. No matter if it was James Mullineaux's presence which caused her to smile so sweetly on him—he might be able to benefit from it.

Since James was leading Lady Corinna into supper, Alicia graciously accepted Captain Wickford's invitation to join him and shortly found herself seated with him in an intimate corner tucked away from the crowds. Her attention was drawn repeatedly across the room, where Lady Corinna's tinkling laugh rang out often and she could be seen hanging on James's every word. Two impressionable young ladies, hidden from Alicia by an intervening pillar, were also discussing the Marquis and his fair companion, and Alicia found herself eavesdropping shamelessly.

'Is he not so handsome you could swoon?' sighed one, whose languishing looks in James's direction had so far been ignored. 'Louisa Osborne danced with him, and says that he is *devastating*, but disappointingly quite proper in his behaviour. Although,' she added, with a touch of anxiety, 'Mama did warn me that he has a shocking reputation!'

'Oh, he has!' murmured her friend, with a fair attempt at sophistication. 'He is rumoured to be very dangerous! But I doubt that that will deter Lady Dawe—she has quite a reputation herself!'

'Camilla! Don't let your mama hear you say so! You know how she dislikes us even referring to ladies of that type! Lady Dawe is very beautiful, though, isn't she?' the first young lady added, with a wistful note in her voice.

Camilla was evidently more discerning. 'I consider her to be rather overblown,' was her damning response. 'All very well if one cares for that sort of thing, I suppose, but I would have had more respect for Mullineaux's taste had he fixed his affection with Lady Carberry. She is truly beautiful.'

'Oh, yes, but so cold! They say she has broken many hearts and cares not for anyone! Though in that dress,' the first young lady said hesitantly, 'well, perhaps she has decided to change her style! At any rate, you know there can be no affection between the two of them after what she did! It was the most appalling scandal at the time, so my mama tells me! Why, did you know...?' Her voice sank confidingly low, and Alicia, losing the thread of her eavesdropping, realised that Patrick Wickford was watching her with some amusement.

Captain Wickford had also been looking in the direction of Lady Dawe and the Marquis. He had been Corinna Dawe's lover a couple of years before and admired her very much, but she could never give him what Alicia could. He leant forward until his breath stirred the copper tendrils of hair by Alicia's ear.

'Camilla Bennett is surely in the right of it, Lady Carberry! Corinna Dawe's a very attractive woman, but she cannot compare to you. For you are truly beautiful…all ice where she is fire, maybe—but underneath the ice I think there lurks the passion they all believe you lack.'

His hand moved to cover hers on the table. Alicia looked at him. He was very close, those brilliant blue eyes holding an expression which Alicia recognised quite easily as genuine desire. The Captain might covet her fortune, but he also had no objection to her personally. But he was taking a grave risk—Alicia had always behaved with such unimpeachable virtue that she might not be very receptive to such flagrant flattery. Yet tonight, in that incredible dress, she seemed quite different. Intrigued, Wickford waited for her reaction.

Alicia smiled at him. It was exciting to allow herself the luxury of a flirtation just for once. At first she had been obliged to behave with propriety to regain Society's good opinion; then it had become a habit, and no one had ruffled the surface of her calm. Now the Marquis of Mullineaux had thrown a stone into that serene pool and stirred up old emotions and feelings. Looking at her with renewed interest, Patrick Wickford realised that his words had been closer to the mark than he had imagined. Lady Carberry's serenely cool exterior concealed enough passion to burn a man down.

Neither of them noticed the presence of the Marquis of Mullineaux himself, who had come across to claim Alicia for the first dance after supper. His shadow fell across them, and both looked up from their preoccupation, the Captain's eyes bright with challenge and amusement. James gave him a nod that was barely civil and Wickford pressed a leisurely kiss on Alicia's hand before letting it go.

James was looking very forbidding. 'I believe that this is my waltz, madam.'

Alicia got to her feet with every appearance of surprise and reluctance. 'Good gracious, has the dancing started again already? I had not even noticed!'

James's gaze moved from her innocent face to Patrick Wickford and back again. 'No, indeed, I can well believe that you were too engrossed to realise!' He stood back to let her pass and Alicia, with a sudden frisson of anticipation, allowed him to escort her out of the supper-room.

It would have had to be the waltz, Alicia thought savagely, feeling her treacherous body respond immediately to James's proximity as he took her in his arms. Compared to the earthquake that shook her now, flirtation with Wickford was shallow and empty, exciting in a certain way, but superficial in its effects. This was real and therefore infinitely more disturbing to the senses. But he need not think that she was willing to join the ranks of his conquests, Alicia thought resentfully. Let him practise his charms on Lady Dawe—she was made of sterner stuff!

The struggle Alicia had to master her feelings against the unsettling attraction James held for her was quite enough to keep her silent for two circuits of the floor and it was eventually James who spoke first, slanting a glance down at her face.

'I see that you are determined to be displeased with me, Lady Carberry, for you have not said a word! May I enquire what I have done to incur your wrath?'

Alicia tried to give him a repressive look, which was difficult when she was so distracted by her awareness of him. Knowing him well enough to guess that he was perfectly capable of referring to their last, incendiary encounter at Chartley Church, she made haste to deny him the opportunity.

'You mistake me, Lord Mullineaux! I am simply at pains to quell any gossip by conducting our dance with decorum!'

'Indeed!' James raised a mocking eyebrow. 'You were not so scrupulous a little while ago when you gave such blatant encouragement to your military admirer!'

'I!' Alicia had risen to that before she had time to subdue her temper. 'It is you, my lord, who has been setting the tongues wagging with your attentions to Lady Corinna! Not,' she added hastily, reading his look of amused comprehension, 'that it is of the least consequence to me if you choose such company!'

James absorbed this evidently untruthful set-down without the smile leaving his eyes.

'I see. But are we not both just amusing ourselves—I with the delightful Lady Corinna and you with the gallant Captain?'

Alicia had herself back in hand now and refused to be provoked by that. 'Certainly I find Captain Wickford to be charming company,' she said coolly.

'He is most accomplished in his gallantry,' James agreed with a smooth sarcasm. 'I see that he even manages to remove his gaze from your necklace long enough to look meaningfully into your eyes!'

Alicia gritted her teeth, all too aware that surrounding couples were straining to hear their conversation and that she could not afford to let her mask slip. She smiled at him sweetly.

'You seem quite certain that you have discerned Captain Wickford's motives, my lord! I should say that yours towards Lady Corinna are equally transparent!'

James gave a genuine smile at that. '*Touché*, my lady! But do you not mean Lady Corinna's intentions towards me rather than the reverse? She seems to be a lady who knows her own mind!'

'Oh, I am sure I shall see you fighting her off!' Alicia snapped, abandoning restraint. 'And at least you may be flattered by the knowledge that she is not seeking you out for your fortune!'

Their dancing feet moved on smoothly enough, but neither of them was paying any attention to the music any more.

'Oh, I did not mean to imply that Wickford is attracted by your fortune alone,' James said affably. 'This evening—and in that dress particularly—you seem to have forsaken your severe image in favour of something entirely more exciting. I am disposed to test whether it is genuine or just for show!'

Alicia gasped and tried to pull away from him, but he was holding her far closer than convention dictated and she could not move. The heat of his touch seared through the clinging silk of the gold dress. She might have been naked for all the protection it afforded her. She could feel the hard length of his body against hers and shivered convulsively at the undeniable reaction between them. Once again, the memory of his kiss invaded her thoughts and she felt herself tremble in response.

'You are the most insufferable man—' Alicia began hotly, aware that her cheeks were suddenly suffused with colour and that many interested observers were watching avidly.

James only laughed. 'Admit that you were playing up to Wickford only to provoke me and I may consider letting you go,' he said softly in her ear.

Alicia shot him a furious glance. How dared James assume that she would pay attention to Wickford only in order to engage his interest? 'I shall do no such thing! Your arrogance, my lord, is beyond belief!'

'Then I shall have to prove it to you,' James observed, still very quietly. He glanced about them. 'Not here, perhaps, although it's tempting to do so! Are you prepared to accept that challenge, my lady?'

'No, I am not!' Alicia struggled to free herself as unobtrusively as possible and was completely unsuccessful. 'Your behaviour is intolerable, sir—'

'Ah, there speaks the virtuous and respectable widow, not the provocative seductress who chose that dress and whom I held in my arms not so very long ago! Do you remember, Alicia?' His voice had dropped several tones. 'You were not so cold to me then. In fact, I could have sworn that you wanted me as much as I wanted you!' He spoke in her ear, so softly she could scarcely hear, so sensuously that she felt she might melt on the spot. She could not believe that he was doing this in the Bingleys' ballroom, with a very interested audience only a few feet away.

'You were very soft and sweet in my arms that day at Chartley,' James's voice continued, barely above a whisper, 'and your mouth tasted like honey. I wanted to take so very much more, Alicia...'

She felt his lips graze her neck with the lightest of touches and she thought that she would gasp aloud. At some point she had closed her eyes, and only the fact that James held her had enabled her to carry on moving to the music whilst her mind was a million miles away. Alicia, whatever are you doing? her inner voice prompted her. She knew the answer. She was permitting James Mullineaux to make love to her in front of three hundred people. She had broken all her resolutions.

Alicia opened her eyes and interrupted firmly before it was too late. 'Have a care, sir! Do you forget that you are indeed addressing a virtuous and respectable widow? Such comments may well do for Lady Corinna, but not for me!'

She looked up into his face and saw the derisive glint in his eyes.

'Oh, I have heard tell that you are a model of virtue, madam, and I do not doubt the truth of it! What I do doubt is the universal belief that the lovely Lady Carberry is as cold as the driven snow, which I have just proved to you is false, have I not? Be honest and admit that there is enough intensity of feeling between us to outrage these good matrons if they only suspected one tenth of it!'

James had spoken more fiercely than he had intended. Tonight, when he had seen Alicia with Wickford, he could gladly have run the man through on the spot, fortune-hunter that he was. It had made matters infinitely worse that Alicia was not indifferent to him and clearly relished his admiration. For once James was on the defensive, suddenly aware that any intentions *he* might have towards Alicia could also be construed as seeking fortune on the part of one whose estates needed an injection of hard cash. The irony of it, when he had once accused her of jilting him for a fortune!

And that was not all. Alicia might well be almost overwhelmed by the onslaught on her senses, but she had just demonstrated that she did not intend to succumb if she could help it. She was not going to make matters easy for him. Clearly the situation called for tact and patience, and James smiled to himself. He would win the game in the long run and enjoy the challenge in the meantime. For now, though, his current strategy had succeeded only in infuriating her ladyship, who, now that she had regained her composure, looked as though she would like to drill the heel of her dainty slippers into his foot.

Alicia, fortunately unaware of his thoughts, gave him a cool smile. 'Your observations on my character and our relationship, whilst fascinating, my lord, are scarcely appropriate for such a public place!'

'Then grant me leave to address them to you in private!' James said promptly, and encountered such a glare that he almost burst out laughing. Yes, he would enjoy this battle of wills.

'If you do not wish to have the distinction of being left standing alone on the dance floor, I suggest that you pursue a different line of conversation!' Alicia somehow managed to get the words out through gritted teeth whilst preserving a spurious social smile for the benefit of Mrs Eddington-Buck who was deliberately circling near them.

There was a flash of amused admiration in James's eyes. 'Egad, and you would do it too, wouldn't you? I beg your pardon, Lady Carberry.' There was no trace of apology in his tone. 'I will leave this discussion to a more suitable occasion!'

There were plenty who had viewed this encounter with varying degrees of interest, cynicism and jealousy. Patrick Wickford, watching with a smile of amused regret, turned his attention away from the dancing couple as a voice he recognised purred in his ear.

'Patrick, darling! I need you to do me some small...service...'

Wickford's lips twitched as he looked down into the entirely enchanting face of Lady Corinna Dawe. These days he was all but immune to her charms, but could still appreciate that she was a lusciously attractive woman. He gave her a smile and allowed her to draw him away from the throng to a quiet alcove. He already knew what she was going to ask him.

Lady Corinna was watching the dancers, a petulant frown on her pretty face. 'I need you to keep that little milksop, Alicia Carberry, occupied for a few weeks,' she began, without preamble. 'I don't want her getting in my way! Judging by the manner in which you were panting over her tonight, you shouldn't find the task too difficult. Do it for me, Patrick, please!'

Captain Wickford's smile grew. How interesting! He had once believed Lady Corinna far too clever in her pursuit of the opposite sex ever to make a mistake. Now he realised she had met her nemesis.

Very deliberately he allowed himself to consider the figures of Alicia Carberry and James Mullineaux as they still circled the room in the waltz. They were not speaking now, but there was a dreamy smile on Alicia's face and James's dark head was bent very close to hers. Lady Corinna was almost scowling as she followed his gaze.

'And what would be my reward for helping you out, Corinna, my love?' he asked gently.

Lady Corinna made an effort to tear her gaze away from James

Mullineaux and smiled up at him. 'I'm sure I'll think of something,' she promised huskily, the sultry look in her dark eyes hinting at all sorts of delights to come.

Wickford did not trouble to tell her that she was wasting her time. He was willing to take her commission just for the amusement, but he felt she had gravely miscalculated. James Mullineaux was not the sort of man to fall at her feet just because she gave him the nod. She had become too spoiled, too used to conquest. Nor was Mullineaux's relationship with Lady Carberry so easy to dismiss. In the moment that Mullineaux had come to claim Alicia for the waltz, Wickford had sensed all kinds of complicated factors at work.

But Lady Corinna had taken his silence for assent. She pressed a soft, lingering kiss on his cheek and wafted away to position herself close to the edge of the dance floor in anticipation of the end of the waltz.

The music drew to a close and James and Alicia thanked each other with perfect solemnity. Alicia excused herself and slipped away to the ladies' anteroom, but not before she had had the irritation of seeing Lady Corinna Dawe drift back to James's side in a swirl of exotic draperies. The sight did nothing to calm her turbulent emotions, and she sat down rather heavily in an armchair to take several deep breaths.

A few moments of quiet reflection were sufficient to restore a degree of calmness, although Alicia still felt inclined to burst into tears and was quite exasperated with herself. She felt humiliated that, despite her best intentions, she had allowed James so much licence. She had let him take up exactly where he had left off at Chartley, and it was making a mockery of her feelings! Damn it, how could he remain so calm when he was wreaking havoc on her senses? And for him to behave in such a way, and then to go straight into the arms of Lady Dawe! Well, if James wished to avail himself of Corinna Dawe's blatantly offered charms that was no concern of hers, Alicia thought crossly, but if he intended to involve her in his little games as well he would find her less tractable in future! She checked her somewhat wan appearance in the mirror and emerged from the room as the quadrille began.

The ball was nearing its end and many guests had already left, mostly going on to other functions in the certainty that they had had full value of any scandal the evening could offer. The crowd in the ballroom was therefore thinning, but there were still plenty of couples dancing. Alicia's jealous gaze almost immediately picked out James's tall figure at the side of the room, still engaged closely in conversation with Lady Corinna. Neither of them seemed aware of anything except each other.

Alicia suddenly had no taste for the evening any more. She could see Patrick Wickford coming towards her, but the thought of resuming her flirtation with him irritated her, and none of her other suitors seemed remotely attractive. In a far corner behind some potted ferns Lady Stansfield still held court, but Alicia resisted the impulse to go across to her, for she could see Christopher Westwood hovering assiduously at her grandmother's side, plying her with refreshments. Alicia danced three more dances, had some desultory chat with the Renwicks and the Westons, and decided that enough was enough.

Marcus and Caroline Kilgaren were in the hallway, conversing with Charles Oxley and a few others, whilst James could be seen in the cluster of people around Corinna Dawe. He was helping her with her cloak and Alicia, as well as a score of other people, was able to see the way Lady Corinna put her hand over his with a brief, meaningful look and a soft word.

Alicia turned away hastily, unwilling to add to her own distress by dwelling on the imminent relationship between the two of them. Miss Frensham was tripping across the hall with her cloak and she grabbed it unceremoniously, determined to leave before James saw her. But it was too late. Leaving Corinna Dawe pouting, he crossed swiftly to Alicia's side, taking her hand.

'Am I forgiven for earlier, Lady Carberry, or are you still displeased with me?'

Alicia ignored the treacherous frisson of excitement that went through her at his touch and fixed him with her most quelling look. So he thought to play her off against Corinna Dawe, did he? This was the moment to end all play-acting and pretence!

'Displeased, Lord Mullineaux? Why, I do not even recall the incident...' She managed to hit exactly the right note of perplexity.

James laughed aloud. 'How bad you are for my self-confidence,

Lady Carberry! To have my attentions so easily dismissed... Shall I remind you?' The wicked glint was back in his eyes again. 'Perhaps I should—'

'James!' Lady Corinna, sharp as glass, was at his elbow. 'We are leaving now! Do you come with us or not?'

James turned to her unhurriedly. 'I shall be escorting Lady Carberry home, I think,' he said pleasantly. 'I look forward to seeing you again soon, Lady Corinna.'

Such a polite brush-off amazed Alicia and it was certainly not at all what Lady Corinna had had in mind. Her black eyes flashed furious fire as they swept over Alicia with comprehensive dislike.

'There is no need, Lord Mullineaux,' Alicia interposed hastily, anxious to avert a confrontation. She gestured towards Miss Frensham who was hovering on the edge of the group. 'It is but a step to Upper Grosvenor Street, and I have Miss Frensham to keep me company.'

James looked amused, whether at Alicia's reluctance or Lady Corinna's ire it was difficult to tell.

'No doubt,' he said smoothly, 'but I wish to speak to you. Good evening, Lady Corinna!'

Her ladyship could take a hint and flounced petulantly away without another word. Alicia sighed.

'There was no need for that,' she said, with a minatory glance up at him. 'Believe me, sir, your best interests lie in that direction!'

That earned her a flashing look, full of amusement. 'Do you say so, Lady Carberry? Whatever could lead you to such a conclusion?'

All Alicia's disappointment and frustrations seemed to lodge in a tight lump in her throat. 'Because she understands your games,' she snapped furiously, 'and she is willing to play them! And now, I fear, you will have to work hard to reinstate yourself in Lady Corinna's favours—she may not even be prepared to forgive you!'

'You are doubtless correct.' There was an absent look on James's face, as though Lady Corinna's tantrums held no interest for him. He took Alicia's arm, turning her towards the entrance.

'But how would *you* have me behave, Lady Carberry?'

Alicia thought she would burst at his persistence. 'With circumspection!' she said, angry with him for pursuing the subject and also with herself because she knew deep down she was lying. 'And perhaps you could start by confining your attentions to Lady Corinna rather than pestering me with meaningless flirtation!'

James laughed. 'Are my attentions really so unwelcome?'

Alicia gave him a fulminating look. 'Your reputation alone suggests that no woman of sense should take you seriously! And you are certainly undiscriminating, sir!'

Miss Frensham, who had been trotting along behind them, totally riveted by the conversation, gave a despairing squeak at such plain speaking. James winced and held up a hand in mock surrender. 'You are too cruel, Lady Carberry! Very well, you have convinced me!' He sketched a mocking bow. 'Your wish is my command! I'll bid you goodnight!'

He strolled off down the street in the direction of White's, and the only consolation Alicia was left with was that she had seen Lady Corinna's party depart in the opposite direction. Well, she had not wanted his false attentions, she told herself fiercely. Better that he should leave her alone rather than seek to entertain himself at her expense. Idle flirtation with him held no charm for her. She would only end up with hurt feelings and an empty, aching heart when it was all over.

The carriage drew up and Alicia waited patiently whilst the Bingleys' footman helped Miss Frensham inside. She settled herself on the opposite seat and they set off towards Upper Grosvenor Street, her mind still preoccupied with thoughts of James. And what if he had wanted to take it further than mere flirtation? the devil's advocate inside her suddenly prompted. Do you really want him to take up with Lady Corinna, when that could be you? Admit that you want him. You know how much passion there could be between you. You could persuade him easily. If you really love him, you would want him on any terms...

With a shock, Alicia realised that they had arrived in Upper Grosvenor Street and that Miss Frensham was watching her with puzzlement, waiting for her to descend from the carriage. The cold night air made Alicia shiver as she hurried into the house. It was utterly alien to her nature to be thinking in such a way, but then James aroused in her emotions completely different from any she had ever experienced before. She had lived to the age of twenty-six without ever feeling true desire, and now that James had awakened those feelings in her they demanded fulfilment. For a moment Alicia recalled the delicious weakness which invaded her senses at his touch, the pressure of desire building within her, consuming her. She trembled again, this time with remembered pleasure.

'I hope you have not caught a chill, my dear,' Miss Frensham said, with a worried frown. 'You look quite pale and I noticed you shivering earlier. I will ask Cook to make up a posset for you.'

Alicia turned a blank green gaze on her, which only confirmed her companion's worries about her state of health. As Miss Frensham hurried off to fetch her a drink and hot-water bottle, Alicia reflected that there was something ailing her, but that the remedy was neither simple nor indeed suitable for discussion with her eminently respectable companion.

Chapter Nine

To Alicia's private dismay, James took her at her word and confined his amorous attentions to Lady Corinna Dawe. It took him just one week to reinstate himself in her favours. Usually so casually cruel to her admirers, her ladyship was apparently besotted to the point of obsession, according to malicious gossip. James's own feelings were less clear, but he seemed prepared to indulge the lady, ostentatiously escorting her to parties, routs, soirées and picnics. He squired her to a Pantheon masquerade and to a fireworks display in Vauxhall Gardens, where Lady Corinna lured him down the Dark Walks and was observed behaving in an amatory fashion more suited to a cyprian than the wife of a peer. It was all highly diverting for Society—as good as a play, Lady Stansfield had commented, thereby earning herself a glare from her granddaughter.

Over the weeks, Alicia had also found herself in James's company, but in far more staid circumstances than Lady Corinna. He had been in a couple of theatre parties of Caroline's contriving and he had stood up with Alicia for a dance or two at the balls they had both attended. He had even taken her for a drive in the park on two occasions, but then Lady Corinna was seen driving with him at least three times a week. The only sensation James had caused when he had taken Alicia up with him had been occasioned by the presence of a small black and white dog, which had accompanied them on James's phaeton. The next day, everyone who was anyone had had a pet dog accompanying them on their ride in the park.

All the gossip about James and Alicia had withered once he had taken up with Lady Corinna, most people concluding that their relationship was indeed as tame an affair as they had always maintained. This was, in fact, close to Alicia's own opinion of the situation, for she had had no private conversation with James since the night of the Bingleys' ball, and the discussion they had had then seemed like a dream. What remained all too real to her, however, were her own private longings, which she found difficult to ignore. They made the blameless time spent in James's company even more difficult for her.

Though they could now talk about all kinds of subjects in public, from his impressions of London after his time away to the latest literary work of the shocking Lord Byron, the conversation never became more personal. James behaved with impeccable propriety, just as Alicia had demanded of him, and she was intensely irritated with herself for wanting matters to be different. In her heart of hearts she knew that James had simply been passing his time in flirtation with her and now Lady Corinna was offering him something much more exciting. She tried to ignore the welter of pain and jealousy this thought engendered, but this proved difficult. At the back of her mind were the thoughts that had not left her since the night of the ball—if only she had been brave enough, it could have been her...

To make matters even more complicated, she had found herself the unexpected object of Captain Wickford's persistent gallantry. This had amused her to start with, and it was consoling in a vague sort of way in the light of James's obvious lack of interest. However, Wickford was now starting to become most particular in his attentions, and Alicia knew she would soon have to dissuade him. She sighed. It was almost possible to believe that some malicious fate was deliberately designing torments for her!

Domestic matters provided little diversion from this absorption. Before her that morning were the household accounts, but the price of candles, however monstrously expensive, could hardly distract her thoughts. She looked out of the window at the bustle in the street beyond, and wondered idly whether a walk in the park would improve her spirits.

'Excuse me, madam.' Fordyce was hovering, a slightly mournful look on his face. Alicia welcomed the interruption with relief, although she recognised from experience that his long face denoted something distasteful to report. She put down her sheet of accounts in order to give him her full attention.

'Yes, Fordyce?'

The butler cleared his throat. 'I must apologise for failing to give you this information before, madam. It was most remiss of me.' He looked slightly embarrassed. 'Whilst you were out of Town, madam, your cousin, Mr Broseley, came to call on you.'

Alicia raised her eyebrows in surprise. She seldom saw Josiah above twice a year. She remembered that he had missed Annabella's wedding through ill health and frowned. 'A social call from Cousin Josiah? What did he want, Fordyce—money?'

'Well, yes and no, madam.' Fordyce's expression became even more lugubrious. 'He did mention a pressing need for cash, but I do not believe it was his primary motive in coming here. Mr Broseley arrived at three in the morning, madam, and was—' here he cleared his throat discreetly once more '—somewhat the worse for drink. He was most insistent that he see you, and when I explained that you were from home he begged to be allowed to stay here.'

Alicia waited without comment and after a moment Fordyce continued.

'As you were not at home, madam, I judged it unwise to allow Mr Broseley to stay. I hope that I did the right thing.'

'You did indeed, Fordyce,' Alicia agreed. It seemed unkind, but Josiah was a determined scrounger. One summer several years before he had taken advantage of Alicia's absence in Brighton to move himself and several cronies into the house and there had been a most unpleasant scene when she had had him forcibly ejected. So much damage had been done to the house and her possessions in the short time that he had been there that she had scarcely been able to believe it. After that, relations had been somewhat strained between them until Josiah had arrived with a huge bouquet and a most hangdog expression. Alicia had known it was mostly humbug, but she had not been able to prevent a smile.

'Pardon the liberty, my lady,' Fordyce was saying now, 'but Mr Broseley seemed badly frightened.' He hesitated, then added; 'I wondered whether he had had some disagreement over cards. He resisted most strenuously when Dawson and I ejected him—surprisingly so for a man so badly foxed!'

'Did he leave a message at all?' Alicia asked, frowning. She was very puzzled, for Josiah had not been in touch at all since her return to Town. She could only assume that whatever had been so important before must have ceased to matter.

'Not really, madam. He was too intoxicated to be coherent.' Fordyce's lips primmed with disapproval again. 'The only matter which appeared clear was that he had come to warn you.'

'To warn me?' Alicia echoed, even more at sea.

'Yes, madam. About what, Mr Broseley was not specific. As I said, he was in some considerable fear and ran off down the street as though all the devils in hell were at his heels!'

It was an unexpectedly picturesque turn of phrase from her usually staid butler, and it was possibly that which made Alicia's mind up for her. She could visualise the clear, moonlit night, her cousin's white, strained face, befuddled with drink and fear as he tried to resist the attempts to expel him from the house. He had wanted to see her urgently, yet he had not called in the four weeks since she had been back in London. She had no real reason to be concerned, and yet she was.

Alicia sighed.

'Fordyce, I think you had better send out to find Mr Broseley for me.'

Fordyce's face was schooled to calm though inside he was very surprised. Since when had Lady Carberry actually sought out her cousin?

'Yes, madam,' he said respectfully. 'Where might Mr Broseley be found?'

This was a good question. Depending on the state of his purse, Josiah could be in any one of a number of gambling hells or brothels. Alicia sighed with vexation, already regretting her impulse.

'Send Frederick to the Feathers in Southwark, for a start, then try the Guineas,' she suggested, reflecting that it was fortunate her grandmother was not there to hear her reveal her extensive knowledge of the London stews. 'Even if Josiah is not to be found there, I believe there is a maidservant who is—' She broke off at Fordyce's look of appalled horror, and finished carefully, 'Anyway, she may well know of Josiah's whereabouts.'

Fordyce bowed without another word and went out, stiff with outrage at the mission which had been entrusted to him. Alicia stifled a giggle. Really, he could be the most ridiculous stuffed shirt sometimes! Admittedly, Lady Stansfield had chosen him for Alicia particularly for his respectable qualities, but there was no point in trying to pretend that the seamier side of life did not exist—nor that it did not involve her cousin.

Fordyce had been unfortunate enough to have to deal with the aforementioned maidservant when she had arrived on Alicia's doorstep one day the previous year, demanding money for herself and an accompanying infant whom she had claimed was Josiah's progeny. Alicia had never forgotten his look of shock as she had led the girl and the baby into the drawing-room for a chat. The encounter had ended with the girl surprising both Alicia and herself by grudgingly admitting that Josiah was not the real father, asserting that he was no gentleman either. Alicia had been forced to agree with the latter comment, and had given the girl a sum of money for the baby anyway, which had had the girl kissing her hand in gratitude. Whether the relationship with Josiah had survived to this day she would find out soon enough.

She put the matter from her mind, glad to be distracted by a call from Charlotte Renwick, who easily persuaded Alicia to join herself and Caroline in a trip to Bond Street. They spent an entertaining couple of hours selecting gloves and hats before returning home to prepare for the evening's entertainment. Alicia had also engaged herself for a soirée at the Renwicks' house that night, but her secret hope that James might also attend was dashed when Marcus announced casually that his friend had gone to the theatre. Alicia did not need to ask who had accompanied him. She found the rest of the evening a dead bore and reproached herself for her lack of appreciation of Charlotte's hospitality.

It was in fact the following afternoon that she had the answer to her questions about Josiah's whereabouts, and they were not at all what she had anticipated. At the Guineas, Frederick had found the girl voluble in her accusations against Josiah, whom she had not seen for seven weeks and who had apparently left her without a feather to fly. She had suggested rather sullenly that Frederick should try Josiah's lodgings in Deptford, but the landlady had been away. Frederick had waited to see the landlady, and now he was standing in Alicia's library, a place which made him uncomfortable anyway, since he only felt at home in the stables. He twisted his flat cap around in his hands, his fair, weathered face flushed and unhappy.

'I'm sorry, my lady, to be the bearer of such bad news...I wanted Mr Fordyce to be the one to tell you, but he said you might have questions for me—' He broke off and stared fixedly at a patch of carpet.

Alicia waved him to a seat and he perched on the edge of it as though expecting it to explode under him.

'Please do not be worried, Frederick,' she said kindly. 'Just tell me what has happened. Am I to understand that some sort of accident has befallen Josiah?'

Frederick nodded unhappily. 'Oh, ma'am...' It came out in a rush. 'I'm sorry, ma'am—Mr Broseley's dead! They buried him in St Aldate's, in a pauper's grave!'

There was silence whilst Alicia sat quite still and Frederick waited miserably for her to speak. Alicia realised that she did not feel shocked or even particularly surprised. Josiah's excesses had always been going to lead him into trouble. But she did feel a sadness which took her by surprise. Josiah had been troublesome, ineffectual, exasperating, but he had still been her cousin and she had had an unwilling affection for him.

'How did it happen, Frederick?' she asked quietly. 'My father mentioned a couple of months ago that Josiah had been ill—was it some sort of disease that carried him off?'

The groom looked even more uncomfortable. 'No, ma'am. His landlady said he fell in the river when he was drunk. She was right sorry she did not let you know, my lady, but she said she knew nothing of how to contact Mr Broseley's relations. She was most sorry because he still owed her three months' rent when he died!'

Alicia smiled reluctantly. That sounded just like Josiah. 'I will send to pay her,' she said.

'Oh, no, ma'am,' Frederick said, eager to be able to impart some good news. 'That won't be necessary. The landlady said Mr Broseley's other cousin had arrived and settled his debts when he identified the body.' He lowered his gaze. 'Begging your pardon to have to speak of such matters, my lady.'

Alicia was frowning, but not at his reference to the corpse. 'Mr Broseley's other cousin? He does not have any other cousins, Frederick, apart from my sister. Are you sure she did not mean his uncle rather than his cousin?'

The groom looked confused. 'Oh, no, ma'am, for I remember it most particular! The landlady was surprised you did not know of the death on account of the fact that she thought your other cousin would tell you!'

Alicia digested this. 'What was the name of the other cousin, Frederick?' she asked, without much hope.

Frederick shook his head. 'Don't rightly know, my lady. I didn't think to ask. All I know is that this gentleman settled up and took all Mr Broseley's effects. All except the letter for you, that is.' He brightened. 'He must have missed that. The landlady found it in his room behind the washstand. She was about to send it on, but gave it to me instead.' He patted his pockets and brought out a dog-eared missive.

Alicia thanked him gravely and he went out with relief. She picked up the letter thoughtfully, turning it over in her hands. It bore her own name in Josiah's extravagant flourish, and was stained with something that could have been tears but Alicia suspected was really gin. She was about to slide the letter-opener beneath the seal, when she realised that she was not alone. The library door was half open and a figure was hovering in the aperture. A moment later Alicia realised it was Christopher Westwood and cursed the fact that he had chosen that very moment to pay a visit. She had never felt less like receiving guests.

Westwood, appearing oblivious to any tension in her manner, threw his gloves and cane in the general direction of Fordyce and sauntered past him into the room. The butler's figure was stiff with rage. He had already intercepted Westwood in the hall and intimated that Alicia was not receiving, only to be told that she would see family.

'How are you, Alicia?' Westwood enquired affably. 'Fordyce said you were not at home, but I knew you would see me!'

Fordyce's mouth turned down even more in disapproval. Alicia looked at him with resignation.

'Thank you, Fordyce,' she said austerely. 'And I am not at home to visitors.'

Westwood, in the process of divesting himself of his coat and hat, brightened to hear this. He had been very unsure of his welcome, for Alicia had been as cold as ice to him since he had made the scene in the Bingleys' ballroom. However, if she wished to be private with him it must augur well. He sat down close to her in a way Alicia found tiresomely proprietorial and she deliberately got up, choosing a seat as far away from him as possible.

Westwood did not appear discomfited. He picked up the letter from the desk, looking at its designation without even concealing his interest. Alicia stood up again, crossed to the desk, then with great deliberation took the letter from him and put it in a drawer. She resumed her seat to turn on him her most bland and superficial smile.

'Is aught amiss, Alicia?' Westwood's bright grey eyes dwelt on her with interest. 'You seem a little troubled this afternoon.'

'I am perfectly well, I thank you,' Alicia snapped. 'However, I have just heard that my cousin Josiah has died, which is why I am not receiving.'

Westwood raised his eyebrows. 'So Josiah Broseley is dead, is he? I am sorry to hear it,' he commented with so obvious a lack of concern that his words were robbed of any sympathy. 'You were hardly close, however,' he added, even more insensitively. 'Surely a formal period of mourning would be a little excessive?'

Alicia eyed him with dislike. 'I would not claim that Josiah and I were very fond of each other, but the news of his death was still a shock! Really, Christopher, I would have expected you to have a little more consideration!'

'I'm sorry, Alicia, but one might have foreseen that Josiah

would end in such a way.' Westwood gave a negligent shrug. 'What did he die of?' he added carelessly.

'I believe he fell in the Thames,' Alicia said shortly, and saw a smile she did not understand briefly touch Westwood's lips. For some reason this irritated her even more.

'Careless of him,' Westwood murmured. 'He was drunk, I suppose.'

'I was not aware that you were familiar with Josiah's habits,' Alicia said frostily, and wondered what she had said when he gave her a very sharp look, totally unlike his usual languid pose.

'Did you hear from him at all before he died?' Westwood asked, allowing his gaze to wander along the library bookshelves, as though Alicia's answer was of no real interest to him. The question put Alicia in mind of her father's enquiry on the occasion of her visit to Greyrigg, which made her even more irritable. She had managed to forget Bertram Broseley for the few brief weeks she had spent in London. Must matters always be reminding her of him? She decided that it was time to get rid of Westwood's unwanted presence.

'No, I did not. Did you want something in particular, Christopher, or is this just a social call?'

Even Westwood was not so insensitive that he could view this as a particularly encouraging comment. He straightened in his chair.

'I am here on an errand from your grandmother,' he said, with a return to his normal equable manner. 'She suggests that you dine at Stansfield House before the masquerade next Friday—nothing formal, just family. Will you come?'

Alicia hesitated. She felt tempted to cry off and anyway she suspected this to be a plot of her grandmother's making. Lady Stansfield had made it plain that she wished to see better relations established between her granddaughter and great-nephew. She had apparently not given up hope that Alicia would accept Christopher's marriage proposal since recent events appeared to dash any hope of Alicia marrying James Mullineaux. Still, there was nothing to be gained by sitting at home fretting over Josiah's death. Despite the insensitivity of Westwood's comments, he had been right in suggesting it would be hypocritical of her to go into formal mourning for Josiah. Westwood was awaiting her reply, his gaze full of eager hope. Alicia stifled her irritation.

'Please thank my grandmother for her invitation to dine, Christopher,' she said carefully. 'I shall be pleased to do so.'

'Capital! Lady Stansfield will be delighted!' Westwood had brightened considerably at her acceptance, not least because it meant he could now escort her to the masquerade and had a legitimate excuse for staying at her side all evening. Taking her hand, he pressed a fervent kiss on it. Alicia sighed. The day was proving to be very trying.

After Christopher Westwood went out, Alicia sat still for a moment wondering what it was about him that had been different during their conversation. It was Josiah's name that had prompted the change, she thought. Christopher had barely bothered to utter the conventional platitudes of sympathy over his death, and for a man who prided himself on his proper behaviour under all circumstances that was rather remarkable. She frowned. He was certainly acting uncharacteristically.

Shaking off her puzzlement, Alicia moved back to sit behind the desk, and took out the letter from Josiah again. This time the knife cut through the seal and she unfolded it to read the message.

Alicia,
Be careful. You may know that your father has plans for you,
but there are others closer to home you should watch.

Here there were some other words—a name?—heavily crossed out and illegible.

I can say no more, but I must see you. I am in fear of my
life. When you get the letter, send for me to the Guineas.
Your loving cousin,
Josiah.

Alicia pulled a face. Josiah's habitual penchant for melodrama had resulted in a letter which told her very little indeed. She could imagine him sitting in his shabby room, his bottle of gin by his side, plumped up with a sense of importance as he penned the theatrical words to warn her and summon her to his aid. She considered the letter again. Yes, she knew her father had wanted to marry her off again, but what did the reference to someone closer to home mean? There was no one closer than her father, unless one included the Countess of Stansfield, and it seemed ludicrous to imagine that she was plotting something sinister.

Alicia got up to put the letter in the fire, but as she was about to throw it into the flames she paused and looked at it again. Josiah stated quite plainly that he was in fear of his life. Fordyce had confirmed this when he had said that Josiah had resisted being thrown out of the house and had subsequently run off down the road in a frenzy. There could be any number of reasons for Josiah's terror—the money-lenders could have been foreclosing on him, or he could have fallen foul of some card sharp—but there was a definite implication in the letter that the matter involved Alicia in some way. She flung the letter down on the table in exasperation. Why did Josiah have to be so obscure? Now she would never be able to ask him what he had meant.

She remembered what Frederick had told her about the mysterious cousin, and frowned. She knew that Josiah had no cousins other than herself and Annabella. Perhaps this mystery man was some connection of her father's? Alicia was suddenly aware of a very strong desire to leave well alone. She did not want to become embroiled in Josiah's murky affairs, to discover things that were better left unknown. But Josiah had been in fear of his life. And Josiah had died. Alicia frowned. She thought about her cousin; he had been reckless, foolish and spendthrift, but was she really going to leave him in his pauper's grave and think no more about it? Surely she owed it to him to try to find out what had happened?

She rang the bell for Fordyce, and soon his stately tread could be heard approaching across the marble hallway. Alicia grimaced a little as she thought about the instructions she was about to give him for Frederick. Delving into Josiah's domestic arrangements had been bad enough, but now she would be fortunate if he did not decide to leave her service!

Alicia refused all invitations the following week as a mark of respect to her cousin. She had discussed this with Lady Stansfield, who, as an arbiter of taste, felt that her granddaughter had a fine line to tread between appearing to have no concern over her cousin's death and appearing hypocritical by going into excessive mourning for someone she'd hardly ever seen. Most of the *ton* barely knew of Josiah's existence anyway, and took the news of his demise without much comment. As for Alicia, she found the time alone quite soothing for once, giving her the opportunity to read and to write letters—and studiously avoid thinking about James Mullineaux.

One thing which Alicia did not discuss with her grandmother was her concerns over Josiah's death and the warning he had issued to her. She had no wish to worry the old lady unnecessarily. But she found herself in desperate need of someone to talk to. Christopher Westwood she dismissed almost immediately. She did not believe she could rely on him. She thought of talking to Caroline Kilgaren, but decided against it. Finally and imperceptibly her mind turned to James Mullineaux. She wanted to confide in him. She wanted to be able to trust him. A few weeks ago she might have followed her instincts and sought him out, but now matters were different. Any closeness which there had appeared to be between them had proved illusory.

By the time the Stapleford masquerade came round, she had made no progress in her pursuit of further information of Josiah's death. Frederick's enquiries had drawn a blank, for Josiah's landlady had been silently unhelpful and the girl at the Guineas had sworn she knew nothing. The beadle who had arranged the burial had been found, but he had had nothing helpful to add; it seemed they had reached a dead end. Alicia was tempted to forget the whole matter, but something nagged at her to persist.

Alicia was already regretting her decision to accept Christopher Westwood's escort by the time that the party from Stansfield House reached the masquerade. Lady Stansfield had insisted on attending a tedious musical soirée before the ball and Alicia had sat wincing whilst an off-key tenor had warbled in Italian about the miseries of true love. Westwood had sat beside her, requesting translations of the songs, once more the possessive lover.

The masquerade was well advanced as they made their way into the ballroom. Ostensibly a celebration of Lord Stapleford's birthday, it was also yet another attempt to matchmake for the Stapleford's' daughter Georgiana, who, at twenty-two, was now in every danger of being left on the shelf.

Because of the lateness of the hour, the ballroom was full and Alicia's hand was immediately solicited for a set of country dances which were forming. Etiquette was less strict behind the disguise of domino and mask, and Alicia observed that some fairly uninhibited behaviour was already taking place. No doubt that was why masquerades were so popular in the first place!

From her place in the dance Alicia was able to guess at the identities of some of her fellow guests—Caroline Kilgaren, in a white domino and matching mask studded with diamonds was in the next set, dancing with a gentleman in blue whom Alicia suspected to be Peter Weston. Marcus was over by the door to the refreshment room, chatting with another gentleman. In a group by the French windows stood Lady Corinna Dawe, voluptuous in a deep purple domino and playfully fending off the advances of a gentleman in grey in the sort of way that was intended to encourage rather than dissuade him. Alicia's heart missed a beat, but it was not James Mullineaux with Lady Corinna, for the gentleman was too short and stocky. Her ladyship was no doubt skilled in juggling her admirers, Alicia thought dispassionately.

Alicia herself was the recipient of plenty of stares, for even the relative anonymity of a domino and mask could not dull the instant impact of her beauty. The domino of jade-green complemented her colouring and she wore with it a mask of plain black silk. Indeed, the mask was a positive benefit since it hid her expression from view on a night when she did not suppose she looked very cheerful at all.

The dances became more lively and the crowds more animated, and still Alicia could not distinguish the Marquis of Mullineaux amongst the throng. She felt tired and depressed amongst such vibrant company. She had a constant stream of partners, but felt as though she was an outsider watching an event in which she had no part. Christopher Westwood watched her progress through the dances with jealous eyes, for his plans of spending the evening with Alicia had been overset from the first by Lady Stapleford. As one of the few acceptable young men who had shown Georgiana any serious attention, he was identified as a possible son-in-law by Lord and Lady Stapleford and they constantly threw him in her way. Georgiana herself, in celestial blue, was ably aiding and abetting this, gravitating to his side whenever she was free, attempting to flirt shamelessly with him.

The evening wound on. Lady Stansfield was holding court as usual in one corner of the room, surrounded by her elderly admirers. Alicia exchanged a few words with Caroline, who was obviously in high spirits and made her friend feel even more depressed as a result. Alicia danced every dance, smiled until her face ached and parried the more outrageous sallies of her partners. She realised that it had been a mistake on her part to try to distract herself at such a ball. The pleasure everyone else was having only served to underline her own worries all the more. The mystery surrounding Josiah's death dogged her heels and she could not shake it off.

Finally, to add to her woes, Westwood escaped Georgiana and came across to claim a dance, rudely cutting out Richard Pilton who had just approached Alicia on the same errand. Westwood's face was set in lines of deep displeasure and Alicia's heart sank even further.

'I have been trying to dance with you all evening,' he began peevishly as the orchestra struck up for a cotillion. 'Lady Stapleford has been pushing me in the direction of that spiteful cat Georgiana and I've barely been able to escape from her sight!'

'How flattering for you,' Alicia murmured, secretly thinking that Christopher and Georgiana rather deserved each other. 'No doubt she has her eye on you as a prospective son-in-law!'

Westwood grunted. 'Well, she'll catch cold at that! The whole of Georgiana's fortune is not enough to sweeten that pill!'

Alicia looked at him with a dislike fortunately hidden by her mask as Westwood continued in the same tone, 'I really wish you would reconsider my offer, Alicia! It would put an end to precisely that sort of speculation!'

'Thank you!' Alicia no longer tried to conceal her dislike. 'No doubt *my* fortune is sufficient to help you overlook those aspects of my character you dislike!'

Westwood looked affronted. 'Dash it all, Alicia, there's no need to be so sharp! You know I am at your feet—and have been for years!'

There was nothing remotely loverlike in his voice and Alicia wondered whether he had actually managed to convince himself that he loved her, or was merely repeating the fiction in the hope of convincing her. Either way, it only confirmed her belief that they would be badly suited and she was glad she had not seriously considered his proposal. A little while ago she might have been persuaded that he cared for her and that she was treating him badly. Now she felt that he no longer did care, if he had ever done so.

A moment later she was assailed with a jealousy far greater than anything Westwood could ever have felt. The Marquis of Mullineaux had come into the ballroom and had instantly been intercepted by Lady Corinna who was whispering intimately in his ear. Saturnine in a black domino, there was no mistaking his height and breadth of shoulder. He straightened up with negligent ease and the two of them disappeared together into the card-room. Alicia missed her footing, her anguish was so great, and Westwood caught her arm to steady her.

'Do take care, Alicia!' He guided her through the dancers to the edge of the ballroom without so much as a by-your-leave. 'I think you should sit this one out until you feel better!'

Resentment at his high-handed attitude now added to the mixture of miseries tormenting Alicia. She could not be bothered to speak, sitting in silence through the remainder of the dance and the polonaise that followed. Westwood attempted to engage her in conversation with determined cheerfulness.

Meanwhile, the Marquis and Lady Corinna had re-entered the room and joined the dance, which gave James the opportunity to study Alicia in a very similar way to that which she had been watching him earlier. His observation was subtle, but not covert enough to fool Lady Corinna, who was very shrewd in matters pertaining to her own sex. She gave an exaggerated sigh.

'Can it be that you still carry a torch for Lady Carberry, my lord? I fear that any hopes you may cherish in that direction are destined to be dashed!'

James raised an eyebrow lazily, not troubling to deny her allegation. 'Why might that be, Lady Corinna?'

Lady Corinna was too accomplished to disparage a rival directly. She pressed her body provocatively against his and gave him a melting smile. 'Oh, it is simply that Lady Carberry is renowned for her...coldness...to her admirers.' This was accompanied by a look which was the very antithesis of coldness. 'One might have expected that she would have wished for some fun after so tediously old a husband, but it seems not. One can only assume that such...pursuits do not interest her.' There was no mistaking the look she sent him with these words.

However, her statement did not appear to have the desired effect. As the dance ended, James renewed his scrutiny of Alicia with even greater interest. She was sitting quite still, head bent, with the unconscious grace which always seemed a part of her. For some reason he could not divine he was convinced that she was not at all happy. A man he took to be Christopher Westwood was talking to her animatedly and receiving little or no response.

'Of course,' Lady Corinna was saying to draw attention back to herself, 'she *is* very beautiful if one admires that style.'

The Marquis, who could recognise malice even when it was couched in such honeyed terms, agreed with deliberate obtuseness that Lady Carberry was indeed very beautiful. It earned him a sharp look and drove Lady Corinna further into indiscretion through sheer pique.

'Indeed,' she said spitefully, 'she has done very well out of those looks in the past. George Carberry may have been a nobody socially, but he was a very rich nobody and one who died very conveniently.'

Looking up into James's eyes, Lady Corinna thought she saw a flash of anger, but it was banished so swiftly by indifference that she thought she must have been mistaken. The movement of the dance took them onward and a moment later she knew she had miscalculated.

'Lady Carberry's marriage was very much a match forced by her father,' James said quite levelly, but in tones which could not be misconstrued.

Lady Corinna stared. Provoked into uncharacteristic jealousy, she gave a titter of artificial laughter.

'Lud, my lord, surely you cannot have fallen for that old excuse? Why, can it be that you are in love with her? How piquant! Or perhaps your relationship with Lady Carberry is not as innocent as the two of you like to make it seem?'

She knew it for a disastrous mistake as soon as the words had left her mouth. Before that moment the situation might have been retrieved with a tactful acknowledgement or a change of subject. But jealousy had driven her on and now it was too late. Lady Corinna had needed a reason to explain why James had not availed himself of her invitations to take their relationship further—much further. She did not think him obtuse, nor did his reputation suggest that he had lived as a monk. Yet all her most blatant invitations had been smoothly turned down in a way that could give no offence but which Lady Corinna had found both baffling and deeply frustrating.

But now she realised that her unguarded remark had hit quite literally on the truth, and that her next malicious comment had ended any chance she might have had of saving the day—or saving him for herself.

James caught her arm very tightly, swinging her round to face him. Until then their relationship had been characterised on his side by an indolence which had never revealed any deep feelings at all. Lady Corinna had, for her pride's sake, tried to make him fall in love with her, but he had shown no signs of doing so, no sign of any real feeling. Now, however, she could see genuine emotion in plenty and it chilled her to the bone.

James kept his voice discreetly low, but there was an edge of white-hot anger to it.

'I think it best, madam, that we forget your ill-judged observations. However, should I hear them repeated I shall know exactly where they originated.'

He did not wait for a reply, but dropped her arm with a contemptuous gesture and, turning on his heel, strode away without a backward glance.

Alicia was finding Christopher Westwood's presence beginning to grate on her. He lurked at her shoulder like a gaoler, glowering at anyone who looked as though they might ask her to dance. He had even managed to frighten away Caroline and Marcus, who had gone off with a certain relief to dance together. Caroline was puzzled that Alicia, normally so spirited in her refusal to accept Westwood dictating to her, appeared to have become completely passive. She did not have the opportunity to ask her friend what was going on, but as the dance ended she steered Marcus towards where James Mullineaux was moodily watching the game of piquet progressing in the next room.

'James—' Caroline never wasted time '—I need you to go and save Alicia from Christopher Westwood!'

Marcus almost choked but James did not seem impressed. He did not laugh, but shook his head slightly.

'I'm sorry, Caro, I don't think I can help you.'

Caroline frowned in vexation. 'What is the matter with everyone tonight? You're sulking in here like a schoolboy and Alicia is letting Christopher bully her! James, for my sake, please do as I ask!'

James turned to Marcus. 'What do you think, Marcus?'

His friend gave him a level look. 'I think it would be very dangerous, James.'

James smiled reluctantly. 'So you've read me like a book again, Marcus? Damn it, the only time I'm behaving with circumspection, and your own wife tries to persuade me otherwise!'

Caroline stamped her foot. 'I have no idea what you are both talking about,' she said stormly, 'but if you don't like my idea I'll have to think again—'

James put his hand on her arm. 'Keep calm, Caro! I am persuaded! But don't blame me if you regret it later!' He put his drink down and disappeared into the ballroom. Caroline turned to Marcus, still frowning.

'Marcus, if you don't tell me what is going on, I shall scream with aggravation!'

Marcus laughed. 'I rather think, my love, that James has been trying to avoid Alicia. Or at least,' he corrected himself scrupulously, 'trying to behave towards her with impeccable respectability. He wishes to put his estates in order before he takes matters any further, but I believe his intentions to be completely honourable!' He met her eyes, wide behind the jewelled mask. 'You may imagine how difficult it is for him to behave in such a way! And now you have thrown temptation in his path!'

Gradually the group around Alicia and Westwood had dissipated, seeking more congenial company, and as the music struck up for a waltz Westwood turned back to Alicia again clearly intending to ask her to dance.

The figure of a black domino interposed itself somehow between the two of them.

'You must not seek to monopolise this beautiful lady, sir!' The black domino's tone was mocking. 'This dance is surely mine!'

Alicia found herself swept onto the floor before a scowling Westwood could even draw breath to object. The black domino smiled down at her from behind his mask.

'I apologise if you feel that I have forced your hand, my lady, but I had the strong impression that your companion would not yield to more gentle persuasion! And how else would I then achieve a dance with the most beautiful lady in the room?'

Alicia's lips twitched but she was determined not to fall immediate prey to this outrageous flattery. 'A pretty compliment, sir,' she observed coolly. 'You must be a practised flatterer! In a gathering like this how is it possible to make such a judgement between ladies?'

The dark eyes behind the mask were intent on her face. 'Easily. Beauty such as yours cannot be eclipsed by a mere domino and mask, madam.'

Alicia laughed. The lilt of the music carried them onwards. He always chooses the waltz, she thought, feeling the hard strength of the arm that encircled her. She felt light-headed, as though she had drunk too much, dizzy with a mixture of excitement and anticipation. She forgot his previous coolness, forgot Lady Corinna, and gave herself up to the exhilaration of being in his arms again.

As they turned, Alicia caught sight of Christopher Westwood glowering in their direction and smiled at her partner with deliberation.

'You are too generous, sir. I shall begin to suspect you of insincerity soon!'

'Oh, you should not!' The lazy drawl held a note of teasing she recognised. 'I am in deadly earnest. But then, I have the advantage over your multitude of other admirers because I would recognise you anywhere, and in any disguise, madam. Just as you would know me.'

Alicia felt a shiver go through her. There was no point in denying his words and he had invested them with a significance deeper than their surface value. She looked up into the dark face above her and forgot all her worries in the pure enjoyment of being held so close to him. She could read the heat of desire in his eyes, see that he wanted her, feel it in the touch of his hand. It was intoxicating, pleasure distilled. She wanted to drink deep. It was so overwhelming that Alicia felt her doubts and fears melt away as the exhilaration took her.

The end of the dance found them by the doors which led to the conservatory. James let Alicia go slowly, with a speculative look which did nothing to calm her inner turmoil. 'Will you consent to walk a little with me?' he asked.

Alicia hesitated. He was very direct. There was no prevarication about the heat of the ballroom or the need for fresh air. Seeing her doubt, James smiled suddenly.

'Come, Alicia, you used not to be so careful of public opinion! Will you trust me if I promise to behave with the utmost propriety?'

He proffered his arm and they sauntered through the double doors which led into the green darkness of the conservatory. The air was scented and humid here the light dim. Spiky shadows of fern and palm mingled on the floor, and couples wandered slowly amongst the plants, conversing in low voices. They walked for a little while in silence, but it was a silence sharp with awareness on Alicia's part. She was very conscious of the hard muscles of his arm beneath her fingers and the brush of his body against hers as they walked. It was almost enough to fill her mind to the exclusion of her other concerns, but not quite. Unconsciously her head drooped as she felt the weight of her worries come back to haunt her.

James looked at her downbent head thoughtfully. 'I've been

watching you this evening, Alicia,' he said gently. 'There's something troubling you, isn't there?'

Taken aback by his perception, Alicia prevaricated. 'Something wrong? Whatever can you mean, my lord?'

She saw a shadow of a smile touch his mouth. 'Why, simply what I say. I hope you will not think me arrogant if I say that I know you well enough to tell when something is worrying you. But I have no wish to pry.'

Alicia immediately felt ashamed. She made a slight gesture. 'I'm sorry,' she said contritely. 'I know I sounded ungracious. You are right, of course, but I did not realise that it showed.'

'Only to me, perhaps. I will stand your friend, if you wish to confide in someone.'

Alicia looked at him. In the shadowy darkness her eyes seemed huge and troubled, almost luminously green in her heart-shaped face. Once again she was completely trapped by her feelings for him. The impulse to trust him and tell him the truth was terribly powerful.

She had wanted to confide in him, and here he was offering her that chance.

They walked on slowly in silence. There were other couples loitering beneath the palm trees and flirting in the alcoves. Water splashed into an ornate lily pond where lazy goldfish flashed a fin. It was no place for confidences, being too well-populated.

'I would like to tell you,' Alicia said at last, a little hesitantly, 'but we must step outside, I think, to avoid being overheard.'

James gave her a questioning look. 'That would not be very prudent, perhaps, given your previous wish that we both observe the conventions!'

He had a point and Alicia was forced to admit it. To stroll in the hothouse was unexceptionable, since other couples were doing precisely that, but to step outside would be pushing the bounds of acceptability. She could hardly insist on certain rules one day, then persist in breaking them herself the next. But then, he did not yet realise the gravity of her problem and therefore could not appreciate that the Staplefords' conservatory was hardly the place to discuss murder.

'I can vouch for my own good behaviour,' Alicia said, without a smile. 'Can you do the same, my lord?'

It was a provocative question and James gave her a searching look. The heat had gone from his eyes, but there was still a tension in his manner as though he held himself on a very tight rein. 'No, not really! If there is something you wish to discuss it would be safer for you to do it here!'

Alicia sighed. She seemed to have no choice. She waited until they were close to the terrace doors, then said, in a clear, quiet voice quite devoid of feeling, 'Very well, I shall tell you here, then. I believe my cousin Josiah to have been murdered.'

Whatever James had been expecting, it was not that. Alicia, still holding his arm, felt the shock go through him like lightning. Without another word he steered them both through the doors and out onto the terrace, letting go of her when they reached the balustrade. The air was fresh and chill after the warmth of the house and the sky was very clear. Alicia took off her mask and swung it from her hands by the ribbons.

James was leaning on the balustrade, looking out across a line of cypresses which disappeared into the dark gardens. Eventually he said, in the same quiet tones she herself had used, 'Whatever can have led you to make such a deduction?'

Reaction was now getting to Alicia. She wrapped her arms around herself for warmth. 'Fordyce tells me that Josiah called to see me whilst I was away in Somerset. He wanted to warn me about something but he was too drunk to be coherent. Fordyce put him out of the house, but I think he regretted it later, for he said Josiah was in terror of his life.' She shivered in the cold air. 'And then Josiah died. Am I at fault in thinking it more than a coincidence?'

James straightened up and turned to look at her, still preserving an irreproachable distance between them. In the moonlight his expression was remote, impenetrable. He put back the hood of his domino with an impatient gesture and took off his mask.

'Perhaps not,' he said noncommittally. 'And what have you done to discover the truth, Alicia? Knowing you, it would be impossible to believe that you have let matters lie!'

Alicia prickled with resentment.

'I could not just ignore it!' she answered hotly. 'Leaving aside the matter of Josiah's death, there was a letter he wrote me, and a mysterious cousin who does not exist!'

She saw James raise his eyebrows in faint exasperation. 'All the ingredients of a gothic romance!' he commented dryly. 'You had better tell me the whole, I think!'

Alicia leant on the balustrade, relating the whole story from the moment Fordyce had told her of Josiah's visit to the current state of Frederick's investigations. It was a huge relief to share her suspicions with someone, even if she did suspect James was likely to tell her that her imagination was running away with her.

'We seem to have reached a full stop,' she said regretfully, at the end of her recital, 'and to have made no progress. I am at a loss as to what to do next.'

'Not to meddle any further would seem a sensible course of action,' James said sharply.

'But I cannot just let it go,' Alicia burst out.

James took a step nearer to her without appearing to notice. 'I was not suggesting it. As you are determined to pursue this, I am offering to put investigations in motion at Bow Street for you.'

Alicia hesitated. James asked, with the smile back in his voice, 'What is it? Do you not trust me? Or have you perhaps changed your mind?'

Alicia shook her head. 'No, I have not changed my mind. And it is a relief to me that you do not dismiss my concerns out of hand! But—are you sure, sir? You are under no obligation to help me.'

'The offer still stands.'

'Very well, then. I accept with gratitude, my lord.'

There was a silence between them. Alicia turned to go back inside, oddly at a loss as to what she should say now. As she took a step towards the doorway, James caught her hand.

'Just a moment, my lady. We have been out here some considerable time. You know what people will think?'

Alicia paused. She could no longer see his expression, for the moon had dipped behind the cypresses, leaving them in darkness. She felt almost empty with the relief of sharing her problem, and too tired to care about anything else.

'Let them think what they will. It's better than the truth!'

'That's so, of course.' She could hear the smile in his voice, though she could not see him clearly. 'But you look, if you will forgive me, like someone who has just been discussing murder, rather than someone who has just been thoroughly kissed in the starlight. It would be preferable for the Staplefords' guests to be certain of the latter, not the former!'

He pulled her towards him and Alicia's free hand came up hard against his chest. The hood of her domino slipped back so that her hair spilled out, its colour muted by the dark. She caught her breath.

'My lord, I thought we had agreed... You should not—'

James just laughed. 'No, I should not. But I did warn you, and you should know by now that in this at least you cannot trust me!'

'Yes, but I scarce supposed—'

Alicia's words were cut off as his mouth captured hers. Afterwards, all she could remember was the strength of his arms holding her hard against him, and the brilliant, dizzying darkness of the kiss as their desire spiralled up to engulf them.

It could have been five minutes or several hours later that James lifted his mouth from hers, holding her at arm's length, scanning her face. He was breathing as hard as she as he gave a shaken laugh.

'Well, no one is going to have any doubts now! Go inside, Alicia, before I forget all my good resolutions and kiss you again!'

Alicia paused. She felt cold now that he had let her go, and almost dizzy with longing. 'I think I shall go home now,' she said, a little uncertainly. 'I have no taste for the masquerade.'

James's face was still and shadowed. He did not answer her. His hands fell to his sides and he stepped back punctiliously to let her pass. Suddenly, inexplicably, there was a tension between them. Still Alicia hesitated on the threshold of committing herself.

'Will you accompany me, Lord Mullineaux?' she asked softly. 'I find I do not wish to be alone.'

James shifted slightly. His voice was once more his own—cool, remote and a little hard. 'Are you sure that is what you really want, Lady Carberry? You might prefer to reconsider. Seeking out my sole company is hardly wise.'

Alicia put her hand on his arm and felt the tautness in him. 'Please,' she urged, very quietly. 'Don't leave me now!'

There was a very long silence. James's expression was unreadable.

'Then,' he said, very deliberately, 'you must go back into the ballroom and take your leave. It would not do for us to return together, so I shall join you in your carriage shortly.'

Alicia gave him a hesitant backward glance as she went in through the French doors. He was watching her with the same cool, remote expression in his eyes and somehow it chilled her. But it was too late now. She had made her decision and the die was cast.

Chapter Ten

James did not touch her at all in the carriage on the way back to
Upper Grosvenor Street, nor did he speak. Alicia would have been
happier if he had. She sat opposite him in the dark, watching in
the faint lamplight the stern set of his face, his expression distant,
almost severe. It daunted her. This was not as she had imagined
it would be.

Alicia was half-appalled, half-exhilarated at what she was doing.
It might have been the intoxication of the wine or the moonlight
which had actually brought her to this point, but she knew deep
down that it was what she wanted. She had been faced with the
growing conviction that she would rather be with James on any
terms than face the prospect of losing him. Whilst it was not in
her nature to give herself easily, she loved him too much to want
to live without him. She would settle for whatever he was prepared
to give.

She stole another look at James, very aware of him in the enclosed space of the carriage. He had removed the black domino
and the immaculate but severe cut of his evening clothes only
served to enhance his physique, doing nothing to detract from his
devastating good looks. His black hair was artfully dishevelled in
the windswept style and there was an expression in his eyes which
made him look, Alicia thought, the complete answer to any
maiden's prayer and the epitome of a chaperon's warning.

For a moment her heart skipped a beat out of sheer nervousness.
It's not too late to change your mind, a voice whispered inside her

head. She drew on all the courage she could muster. She had thought about this, carefully considered her options. The thought of losing him to some dewy-eyed debutante or experienced flirt was not to be borne. Besides, she might as well be honest. She wanted James, longed for his touch in a way quite alien to her previous experience. She could not draw back now, *would* not!

It was late and Fordyce had dismissed the servants in the expectation that Alicia would have stayed at Stansfield House for the night after the masquerade. Dawson, the night porter, was dozing at his post and woke with a start as the carriage drew up and its occupants descended. His eyebrows shot up into his hairline as he recognised the Marquis of Mullineaux with Alicia. He struggled upright, and desperately tried to regain a suitably bland expression.

'Madam! We did not expect—Do you wish me to wake the servants?'

'No, thank you, Dawson.' Alicia sounded far more composed than she felt. 'We do not require anything further tonight.'

Once again, Dawson, who had far less aplomb than Fordyce, fought to keep his amazement from showing on his face. 'Yes, my lady,' he said respectfully, and watched them cross the hall to the drawing-room. The door closed behind them with a firm click and Dawson stared at its panels in complete disbelief. He even pinched himself to check that he was awake. He was.

Alicia was finding this far more difficult than she had anticipated. She had not really thought beyond the point of making her wishes clear to James. Now she was not sure what she had expected to happen next, but whatever impassioned and ardent scene should have followed it was very different from reality.

James had taken the drink she had offered and was now standing moodily before the fire, his arm resting along the mantelpiece.

'Before we take matters any further,' he said quietly, 'may I be permitted to know why you have chosen this course of action? It seems somewhat out of character. Are you sure you know what you are doing?'

That was the last straw for Alicia. This clinical analysis of her behaviour was so far from her romantic dreams as to be a travesty.

'I thought that you were supposed to know how to manage these things,' she replied childishly. 'That's why I chose you!'

It wasn't true, but the words, born of disappointment and frustration, were out before she could bite her lip. James put his glass down on the mantelpiece with what seemed like exaggerated care and crossed to her with an intentness which belied his previous air of indolence. He leant on the arms of Alicia's chair so that she was pinned back and forced to crane her neck to look up at him.

'So now we come to the truth of it,' he said, very softly but with an edge to his words which frightened her. 'I did not believe you would go through with this, but it seems I misjudged you! A few weeks ago you were accusing *me* of a want of propriety, yet now I am to help you over the temporary inconvenience of your virginity, if I understand you correctly!'

Alicia winced at his words and the hot colour flooded her face. In all her calculations it had not occurred to her that he would react like this. She had assumed that were she to make her feelings clear he would take control of the situation. He had declined to play her game—worse, he had spoken with a cool calculation which only proved that he had no desire for her. Humiliated, she realised that she had misread the circumstances completely. True, James had indulged in a certain amount of flirtation with her, but it had not meant anything to him. And why should it, with the opulent charms of Lady Dawe all too obviously at his disposal? So she had made a complete fool of herself.

'You mistake me; I did not mean that—' she began desperately, concerned now only to retreat and cope with her embarrassment in private.

But James was not prepared to let it go so easily. She looked so young and vulnerable in the shadowed candlelight that it made her behaviour seem all the more outrageous. James tried to concentrate on her relative youth, her naïveté, her inexperience, but all his wayward mind seemed capable of presenting him with was a series of images which had nothing to do with innocence and everything to do with the deep, turbulent emotions which ran between the two of them. With his anger fanned to white heat by his own imagination, he cut her off ruthlessly.

'You did not mean what, precisely? To propose me as your first conquest in a career as a demi-rep?' He straightened up, still looming over her threateningly. 'Perhaps I misunderstood! Perhaps you intended only to become *my* mistress rather than to throw yourself open to the public? Thank you, but I prefer to do the asking myself!'

Since this had been precisely what Alicia had intended, her mortification now knew no bounds. She did not understand that James's anger sprang more from the temptation of her offer rather than its lack of appeal. And her pride was now seriously injured. How dared he humiliate her like this? She jumped to her feet.

'How very hypocritical you can be, Lord Mullineaux!' she said furiously. 'So the rules are different for you, are they, and for the likes of Lady Dawe? What blatant double standards!'

James clenched his fists with frustration. His mouth was a hard, angry line, but still he strove for self-control. 'My dear child, can you not see that respectable ladies simply do not behave in such a manner? Lady Corinna Dawe is the sort of woman whose behaviour should be as far removed from your own as…as the Prince Regent, and even you are not so naïve as to require an explanation of that!'

Alicia looked like an angry kitten, he thought dispassionately, all wide-eyed fury and sharp little claws. He almost expected her to stamp her foot.

'How dare you be so patronising, sir?' she stormed. 'I am a widow of twenty-six, not some immature child of eighteen! It is not for you to legislate for my behaviour! I have the right to act as I choose!'

James lost his temper finally and comprehensively. 'You have just proved your lack of understanding by your very words,' he said scathingly. 'You don't know what you're talking about! God damn it, this isn't some parlour game you can play and expect not to get hurt! What if half Society does behave as you describe? That is not for you!'

Alicia recoiled, her face stony, though her eyes were bright with unshed tears.

'Enough! You have said quite enough, sir! I understand you perfectly! But do not think that you have the right to dictate my conduct!' The sting was all too apparent beneath the sweetness of her next words. 'Though I may not appeal to you, I am sure that there will be others more...amenable...to my suggestions! I bid you goodnight!'

For a moment, James did not move. Alicia was standing between him and the door, so she was now perfectly able to see the almost murderous look of fury on his face as he started towards her. Her heart gave a sudden jolt as she realised that her bitter comment, meant only to salve her pride, had overstepped the mark by a long way.

James had given up the unequal struggle for self-control. Alicia's words had conjured up a vivid picture of her locked in Christopher Westwood's arms, or, worse still, Patrick Wickford's—he would not be so scrupulous in his treatment of her, at pains to protect the innocence which James had recognised and tried to preserve from both his own and Alicia's reckless actions. He took another step towards her.

Alicia quailed before his rage, instinctively taking a step back as he came closer to her. She recognised that her words had unleashed something elemental in him, something she could not control. Expecting him at first to walk straight past her and out of the house, Alicia was gripped by an unreasoning panic as he drew nearer. She backed away until she felt the door panels digging into her back and half turned in a desperate attempt to wrench the door open. But it was too late. James was already beside her, reaching past her to turn the key in the lock with a finality which both terrified and, at the same time, excited her.

'I've changed my mind,' he said roughly.

He was not gentle with her, but then, Alicia acknowledged numbly, she had pushed him beyond restraint through her foolish provocation. Suddenly it was a little too late to admit that she understood exactly what he meant about not playing games which were too deep for her.

His mouth took hers without tenderness, showing only an urgent desire which demanded satisfaction. It was shocking to Alicia to feel the immediate and perfidious response within her as her body recognised and welcomed his touch, even as her mind struggled to assimilate what was happening. She put her hands up to his chest, intending to push him away, but the thought was already lost in the clamour of her senses and instead she simply pulled him closer, sliding her arms about his neck.

The ribbon restraining Alicia's curls was coming loose and James put out an impatient hand to tug it free, spilling her hair around them in a rich auburn cloud. His mouth returned to hers with a ruthless intensity which incited feelings Alicia had never dreamed of. She would have fallen had he not held her, so completely was she at the mercy of her emotions. She felt his fingers trace a path of fire across her skin, easing the dress from her shoulders with a touch that was very sure. The low-cut bodice slid down to her waist, but before Alicia's shocked mind could even register the thought properly James's lips followed the path of his hands, brushing tantalisingly over the curve of her exposed breast until it closed over the sensitised tip, making her gasp aloud with pleasure. Alicia arched against him, conscious only for the need to be closer still, to appease the deep ache within her with his body on hers.

She had no recollection of how she came to be lying on the chaise longue, only that she was leaning back on the cushions, watching with languorous pleasure as James hurriedly divested himself of his jacket and pulled off his neckcloth. He crossed swiftly back to her side, and she offered her mouth to his with a total lack of shamelessness. Their kisses became wilder, as though they wished to devour each other, his tongue plundering the sweetness of her mouth. Alicia's head fell back as his lips traced the delicate line of her throat and took possession of her breasts again, teasing first one nipple and then the other with his circling tongue.

Her fingers dealt impatiently with the buttons of his shirt so that she could slip her hands inside, against his chest, pulling his nakedness against hers. She heard him groan and then his hand was pushing up her skirts so that they foamed about her hips and he could slide his hand up her silken stocking to the soft skin at the top of her thigh. Alicia gasped his name, digging her fingernails into his back in an agony of sensuous delight. She could feel his fingers parting her thighs and was within an inch of giving herself up completely to the searing pleasure which she knew was waiting for her, when suddenly James let her go, so violently that she almost tumbled to the floor.

Alicia caught her breath painfully, blinded by the swirl of her hair, bewildered, disorientated and deeply disappointed. Gradually, reality intruded. She was in her own drawing-room with the servants within call, and James, who had until a moment ago been making love to her to the exclusion of all other thought, was now shrugging himself back into his jacket, swearing most fluently under his breath. She had no idea what had gone wrong, but she instinctively straightened her bodice and smoothed down her crumpled skirts with hands that shook. Why had he stopped? He must have known that she had wanted him to take her there and then...

A moment's bewildered thought, and she rather imagined that she understood what James had done. No doubt he had set out to teach her a lesson and he had succeeded all too well, for she would remember this humiliation for as long as she lived! First, she had had the unutterable folly to try to seduce him, then she had responded to his calculated lovemaking with a total abandonment which made her burn with mortification at the recollection. And it must all have meant nothing to him, nothing at all. Her breath caught on a sob and she almost fled the room, remembering at the last minute that James had pocketed the key. Instead, she took refuge behind the huge desk she used for her business transactions, desperately hoping that her trembling legs would not disgrace her by giving way completely.

James himself was, in fact, no less shaken than she. He castigated himself silently and viciously for permitting his desires to overcome his self-control. True, Alicia had goaded him to it, but even so he could not blame her. He had wanted it as much as she. In fact, he was damn near being driven mad with desire for her! It had been bad enough to have to keep his distance after she had made it plain she thought his attentions meaningless. He had determined to show her the truth, but he had not wanted to propose until he could prove his estates were in good order and he did not need her money. In the meantime, Lady Corinna had proved a good distraction for the *ton*, who had been convinced they had been having an affair. Unfortunately, Alicia had thought so too.

Then, tonight, her unexpected proposition had completely floored him. He had known at the Bingleys' ball that her strictures to him to behave circumspectly had been almost in spite of herself. Alicia had wanted him, and only the fear that he might not care for her had held her back. Knowing that he would soon be able to declare himself, James had tried to possess his soul in patience. Then she had set out to seduce him.

At first disbelieving that she really meant to go through with it, James had been infuriated by her apparent attempt to use him. Deep down he did not really believe it to be true, but once he had let his self-control slip he had been as helpless as Alicia to avoid the torrent of passion that had followed. It was, after all, what he wanted. Now he could see no point in delaying further and intended to put his fate to the touch.

'You have nothing to fear from me, Lady Carberry,' James said dryly as he assimilated how she had chosen to distance herself from him, 'for I am determined to proceed with the utmost propriety from now onwards. It was not my intention to speak now, but it seems foolish for us both to carry on this most unsatisfactory of situations. I should therefore deem it an honour should you agree to become my wife.'

It was a considerably more handsome proposal than his previous one, but Alicia was no less surprised than she had been then. She had been waiting for his scornful denunciation and thinking that she preferred to have quite a large space between them, plus several pieces of solid furniture, when his words broke on her like a bombshell.

'No!' The word was wrenched from her. Seeing his frown deepen, she tried to move even further away from him and would have succeeded had he not caught her arm and held her still. 'This cannot be so, my lord! I thought...' She stopped and caught her breath while she tried to work out what she did think.

So he was not going to reproach her for her folly and wilful provocation. Alicia remembered Ottery, and James's determination to do the right thing despite his dislike of her. She must have misjudged him just now, she thought a little shakily. He had not manufactured the situation to punish her; instead, she had trapped him into a predicament where he felt the only solution could be to propose marriage and save her reputation. What had he said? That he had not intended to speak now... That, at least, she could believe to be true and it made clear to her her only course of action. She could not hold him to a proposal made under duress.

She freed her arm gently from James's grasp and looked up to meet the gaze that was fixed intently on her.

'I am sensible of the honour you do me, Lord Mullineaux,' Alicia said unsteadily, 'but I must decline. I cannot permit you to make me an offer out of pity, or propriety, or whatever else one might choose to call it!'

There was a taut silence. James was looking both astonished and annoyed. He ran his hand through his hair, only adding to its general look of dishevelment.

'My dear Alicia, what are you talking about? Is the prospect of marriage to me so disagreeable that you have to make excuses by crediting me with such false motives?'

'Yes! No! Of course not!' Alicia tried to get a grip on herself. 'I appreciate your reasons for asking me to marry you, sir, but it would not serve! It was foolish of me to meet with you alone tonight, and even more foolish of me to provoke you as I did—I see that now. But no real harm is done and, out of your generosity, I ask you to forget all that has happened. There is no necessity for anything more!'

A slightly grim expression came over James's face as he made a rapid reassessment of the situation. 'Alicia,' he said dangerously, 'do I understand you correctly? Are you suggesting that I have proposed to you only to protect your reputation, or even to make amends for what has just happened between us?'

'Certainly,' Alicia said, with a cool composure that was far from her real feelings. 'It is quite clear to me that both your recent proposals to me have been made out of chivalry! There could be no other explanation for your behaviour at Ottery, and, whilst I appreciate your kindness more than I can say, I cannot permit you to tie yourself to a loveless marriage just in order to do what you perceive to be right!'

At that moment, James was looking anything but kind. In fact, he seemed about to commit an act of violence. He could not believe that Alicia could have so thoroughly, so determinedly misunderstood him. Not long ago, he reflected with incredulity, he had relished the battle of wills between them. Now he was merely infuriated. Severe sexual frustration did not improve his temper.

'Well, here is a Cheltenham tragedy! I see that you are determined to martyr yourself, madam, so I shall leave you to do so in peace! It was too simple, I suppose, to have imagined I might have been prompted to propose because I love you—that *that* was the reason why I could see no point in us continuing to be apart! Allow me to say that you would try the patience of a saint! Goodnight to you, madam! I will see myself out!'

The door slammed behind him, leaving Alicia staring after him open-mouthed and, for once, silenced.

Deverson, James's very proper gentleman's gentleman, was startled by his master's reappearance so early in the evening, and in such a state of disarray. James's neckcloth was completely ruined and the jacket which had earlier fitted without a wrinkle now looked distinctly rakish.

Deverson's consternation grew as James's filthy temper became evident. Usually the most amiable of employers, he said barely a word from the time he entered the house to when he left it again thirty minutes later, with the air of a man setting out to get comprehensively drunk.

James did indeed turn in the direction of White's, but at his club fate decreed that he should meet up with Marcus Kilgaren, Charles Oxley and Peter Weston, who were in the card-room. They hailed him enthusiastically with the offer of a game of faro, but James declined and after a thoughtful look at him Marcus declared his pockets to let and got up from the table.

'You're looking pretty rough, old chap,' he commented critically as by common consent he and James moved off in search of a drink. He took two glasses from a passing waiter. 'Care to share the problem?'

He handed James the glass and watched with interest as his friend downed the contents in one mouthful.

'Steady on, James, this is quite a tolerable claret!'

James scowled. 'I have just proposed marriage to Alicia Carberry for a second time, and been rejected,' he said abruptly.

Marcus glanced round, but they were in no danger of being

overheard. A couple of elderly noblemen were dozing over their newspapers before the fire, but it was too early for the young bloods, who were all still out on the Town or gambling for high stakes.

Marcus raised a quizzical eyebrow. Alicia's refusal must rankle indeed for James to speak so openly of it. 'Now you have surprised me,' he observed quietly. 'From what I know of the lady, I would have said that your suit would be welcome—this time around!'

James's scowl deepened. 'Yes, well, I was coxcomb enough to believe the same myself! I could have sworn—' He broke off. 'My mistake was a simple tactical error: I did not prepare my ground well enough before I advanced!'

Marcus looked at him with concern and a hint of amusement. 'This really doesn't sound like you at all, James! Have you lost your touch?'

'Since when have I had it in my dealings with Alicia?' James put his glass down and reached for another. 'Marcus, you would not believe the way in which Alicia was prepared to ascribe my reasons for proposing to her to all but the most obvious motives! Pity, propriety, chivalry...she had thought of them all!'

Marcus hid his grin by taking a sip of wine. 'Whereas I can discern immediately that you are suffering all the symptoms of a thwarted passion, old chap! However did all this misunderstanding come about?'

James gave him a baleful look. 'Like I said, Marcus, I rushed my fences! I'll spare you the details, for I don't wish to shock you! Suffice it to say that I have been finding self-denial a little difficult where Alicia is concerned, and tonight I nearly lost what little self-control I had!'

'Ah!' Marcus required no further clarification. 'Don't tell me— you, realising that to postpone your proposal further would only lead to more pointless self-sacrifice, offered Alicia your hand but perhaps did not mention your heart, only to be told that she understood your chivalric reasons for proposing and could not possibly let you sacrifice yourself!'

James stared. 'How on earth did you know that?'

'Common sense, old chap! If you didn't mention first that you cared for Alicia, your cause was already lost, I'm afraid!'

James began to see the funny side of the situation. 'Thank you for the philosophy—how about some practical advice on how I put the matter to rights?'

'Hmm,' Marcus looked meditative. 'That's the difficult bit!' He started to laugh. 'I have to say, James, that this is the most amusing turnabout! Who would have thought that you would have such difficulty in persuading a lady to marry you?'

'Thank you!' James tried to sound sarcastic but could not help laughing. 'It is not a problem which I had anticipated, certainly! So what can I do?'

Marcus raised a hand to beckon the waiter across. 'Lay siege to her feelings—prove that you love her!' He made an expansive gesture. 'I don't know—you are supposed to be the expert in these matters!' He gave his friend a mocking look. 'Brought low by a slip of a girl, James?'

But James had regained his good humour. He smiled. 'It was only a matter of time,' he said.

Alicia did not discuss James's proposal with anyone. Her feelings on the subject were still too raw. On the day following their encounter she developed a sick headache and sore throat, and when Miss Frensham found her in tears in the drawing-room it was easier for her to admit to influenza than try to explain to her companion that her misery also sprang from another cause.

It was ten days before she felt any better. The fever was followed by lassitude and depression, and she was prone to burst into tears for no reason at all. She spent much time lying in her bed, gazing unseeingly out of the window while her miserable thoughts centred on James and the hopeless mess she had made of their relationship. On the fifth day of her illness, a huge bouquet of lilies and snapdragons arrived from him, which prompted her to burst into tears yet again. She knew that he had called but she had refused all visitors except Caroline Kilgaren, whose brisk common sense had been tempered with so much kindness that Alicia had almost cried again.

James, meanwhile, had been true to his word and had gone to Bow Street to put in train an investigation into the death of Josiah Broseley. His requests for information had met with little enthusiasm. Josiah's name was not known to the Runners, a gloomily helpful man named Dundry had informed him, although that did not prove that he had not been mixed up in all sorts of nefarious goings on. Dundry had agreed that they would do their best to find out what his lordship wanted to know, and James had left him with the instruction that he should let him know at once if he had any useful information.

James was, in fact, finding it deeply frustrating not to be able to speak with Alicia. At first he had been confident of his ability to persuade her of his true feelings, but the passage of two weeks without seeing her had gnawed away at both his patience and the assurance that he could put matters to rights. He had called several times in Upper Grosvenor Street only to be told by an urbane Fordyce that Lady Carberry was much better, but still not receiving guests. It had not improved his temper.

Matters became progressively worse. At the end of the week, James's grandfather, the Duke of Cardace, was holding a magnificently opulent ball and James had rashly promised to help his maiden aunt Eugenie with the last minute preparations. This allowed him little time for social calls, so he tried to make do with despatching another huge bouquet of flowers to Alicia, with a note saying that he hoped she was better and looked forward to seeing her. On the day of the ball he was suddenly assailed by doubts and wondered if she would attend. Given that he had not been allowed a chance to put matters to rights with her, it seemed all too possible that she would not. Too late, he wished he had made time to call on her that day and found himself to be in an even worse temper. Adding yet another ruined neckcloth to the discarded pile, James reflected that the course of true love was proving tiresomely riddled with difficulties.

In the event, however, Alicia was not so poor-spirited as to fail to attend the ball. James, involved in the tediously long and boring process of greeting the guests, as well as also taking on a fair proportion of the host's role as a result of his grandfather's infirmity, was nevertheless able to pinpoint the exact moment when Alicia came through the door.

She was formidably ranked by the Dowager Countess of Stansfield on one side and the ubiquitous Christopher Westwood on the other, whom James was beginning to detest. In lilac silk Alicia looked at once impossibly exquisite and fragile, and her expression as she greeted him was serene and remote. James tried to place her mood but was unable to read anything beneath the surface. Already in an advanced state of irritation and frustration, he had to subdue a violent urge to take her in his arms there and then and kiss her out of her Society calm. Could this ice maiden be the same Alicia who had responded to him with such searing intensity only two weeks before? It seemed impossible. Wishing that he could regain his own lost equilibrium, James took her hand.

'You had my note, I hope,' he said, with a polite formality he hoped would mask his true feelings.

'Yes, thank you, my lord. And the flowers were beautiful.' There was no animation in Alicia's voice at all. She could match his own courtesy effortlessly. A faint, distant smile touched her mouth, but left her eyes blank.

James gritted his teeth. He considered—and reluctantly rejected—a very real desire to pick her up and carry her out of the ballroom to somewhere more private where he could dispense with the tiresome business of trying to tell her how he felt by simply proving it in other ways. Something of how he was feeling must have shown in his eyes, for he had the satisfaction of seeing Alicia recognise his expression and withdraw her hand from his rather hastily.

The queue was buckling behind them. 'I look forward to a dance later, Lady Carberry,' James said with the same smooth courtesy, and turned to greet Lady Stansfield, who had been flirting with his grandfather. She gave him a very quizzical look indeed, but fortunately made no comment. Alicia and Westwood moved away, he holding her arm in a proprietorial grip which made James want to hit him.

The reception of the guests was almost over when Lady Corinna Dawe arrived. Exotic in clinging yellow gauze, she had certainly dampened her dress to make it even more transparent, and appeared to be wearing absolutely nothing underneath it. She greeted James with confident aplomb as though their quarrel had never occurred, and looked him over with a distinctly seductive glint in her melting dark eyes. She clung to his arm, then reached up to kiss him lingeringly, smiling with satisfaction as she caught Alicia's eye across the ballroom.

'I see Lady Carberry has chosen your ball as her first social engagement since becoming betrothed,' Lady Corinna observed, with an artificial tinkle of laughter. 'How absolutely charming of her, and such a good way to refute any rumours linking the two of you together!'

Not a muscle moved in James's face. 'Just so,' he said calmly. 'Westwood is fortunate indeed. But is it yet an official engagement, or do you expect an announcement tonight?'

Lady Corinna shot him a sharp glance, but James's face was impassive. For a moment she had the frightening feeling that he had seen through her words for the fabrication they were, for he was not really reacting in the way she had hoped, either by showing any chagrin or turning his attentions to her instead. She gave a light, petulant shrug, provoked by James's very lack of reaction into taking matters further.

'As to that, I only know that the happy couple are to be congratulated,' she continued mendaciously. 'I hear that Lady Stansfield is *aux anges* at having achieved a family alliance!' And so saying she tripped away, pleased to have had the chance at least to plant her barbs.

James turned to watch Alicia, conscious of his exasperation growing with every moment. Alicia's usual coterie of admirers had gathered effortlessly about her and she was shimmering among them like a pale flame. It was an accomplished performance and James found it grated on him. Westwood clung to her like a burr and she did not appear to mind at all. Could it be true? he wondered suddenly. He was not such a fool as to fall for Lady Corinna's spiteful needling, but Caroline had mentioned a little while ago that Westwood had made Alicia an offer. He looked at her again, as though he would be able to divine the truth simply from watching her. Surely Alicia could not simply disregard the affinity between them and tie herself to a man of Westwood's stamp? James could not believe it; but equally he could not quite ignore that nagging doubt. A feeling akin to rage rose in him as he considered Christopher Westwood's smugly satisfied expression.

Leaving some very late arrivals stranded, James abandoned the

receiving line and cut a path through the throng to Alicia's side.
He knew it was not the time or place for a serious discussion, but
at least he could try to establish some sort of contact. It was like
a repeat of the scene in Mrs Bingley's ballroom—all conversation
in the vicinity ceased as he reached her side.

'May I beg the honour of a dance with you, Lady Carberry?'
James asked, smiling down at her.

Alicia's green eyes opened very wide. She plied her fan in a
quick, nervous gesture. 'I am so sorry, Lord Mullineaux—' she
even sounded nervous '—but all my dances are already spoken
for.'

She saw the flash of real anger in his eyes before he bowed
abruptly and turned on his heel to walk away. Her heart, which
had been hovering in the vicinity of her feet, sank even further.

If James was suffering agonies of frustration, Alicia was feeling
even more miserable. Her fortnight's illness had given her too
much time to think. At first convinced that James had made love
to her to teach her a humiliating lesson, then that he had proposed
out of chivalry, she had been completely dumbfounded by his
parting shot that night. She considered herself to be an independent
lady, but she was aware that she could not simply ask him to
confirm if he was in love with her. For two weeks she had agonised over whether it was really possible and she shuddered to
imagine her embarrassment if she had misunderstood him. Besides,
he had had plenty of time to change his mind. Earlier that evening,
after all, she had seen him with Lady Corinna hanging on his arm
again in apparent possession.

She turned her head to meet with the unappetising sight of Lady
Corinna and James dancing the boulanger together with every appearance of enjoyment. Pain sliced through her and she damned
herself for a complete fool. Even if James had been sincere, he
hardly had a reputation for fidelity. In utter confusion, she wondered what she could have been thinking of, to consider committing herself to such a man. If she felt miserable now, it was nothing
to the grief she would feel were she to lose him to another woman
after they had married.

Christopher Westwood was pressing her to dance again. Alicia
turned listlessly to him and allowed him to lead her out onto the

floor. She could smile and chat and dance, but she felt as though all life and light had finally gone out of her, and it was a pale ghost of herself that was left in the Cardace ballroom.

It seemed as though the gods were finally smiling on James, for just after supper he went back into the ballroom and found Alicia waiting for her partner for the cotillion by the French windows, temporarily alone. He took his chance quickly, catching her arm and pulling her out onto the terrace before she even had time to realise what was happening.

'Disgraceful conduct!' observed Mrs Eddington-Buck, watching their departure with avid eyes. She turned to her companion, her turban wagging. 'A scandalous example to set, do you not agree? But then, I fear they are lost to all sense of propriety, those two!'

Once outside, James did not speak, but ushered Alicia back inside the garden door to his grandfather's study, which he had thoughtfully left open for just such an eventuality. That he succeeded at all was mainly down to Alicia's stupefaction at the manoeuvre which had rendered her temporarily speechless, but by the time they were in the study shock had been replaced by outrage and James kept hold of her arm, correctly surmising from her look of fury that she would run away if he let go. Now that he finally had her to himself he fully intended to have his say.

Alicia was furiously angry, both annoyed and nervous to find herself outmanoeuvred by his high-handed behaviour. One touch of his hand had been enough to awaken all the feelings that had tormented her since that fevered night in her drawing-room, and it just made her more distressed. She drew breath for a blistering attack. It was the only way she could think of to protect herself.

'Lord Mullineaux, what is the meaning of this? Let me go at once!'

James ignored the request. 'I want to talk to you.'

'Well, I do not want to talk to you! We have nothing further to say to each other!'

James realised that Alicia was afraid, but his own emotions were by now in such a state of pent-up turmoil that he was incapable of defusing the situation. He had intended only to tell her that he needed the opportunity to speak to her properly. What he actually said came out quite differently.

'I think that there is plenty to say! For example, what is the nature of the relationship between yourself and Christopher West-wood?'

Alicia wrenched her arm from his grip. Far from the protestations of love and devotion she might secretly have hoped for, he was actually daring to interrogate her! She remembered the way in which Lady Corinna had draped herself all over him and felt a wave of defiance overtake her. He took too much for granted, behaving as he chose and yet expecting her to act like some poor creature whose happiness depended on his notice!

'If you must know, sir—not that I consider it to be *any* of your business—Christopher and I are betrothed.'

James went cold with shock. Regardless of what Lady Corinna had said, he had not really believed that she would do such a thing, either to spite him or to escape from him. He felt all his good intentions for reconciliation slip away as the situation slid irretrievably into all-out war.

'Indeed, madam? And is Mr Westwood aware that I consider you to have made a prior commitment to myself?' he asked, with cold menace.

Alicia's shocked gaze searched his face. 'You are mistaken, sir. There never was such an engagement.'

James gave her a look which brought the blood rushing into her face.

'I am sure,' he said with slow deliberation, 'that your... betrothed...would be glad to know of the circumstances under which I proposed to you!'

The colour left Alicia's face as quickly as it had come. 'You would not dare!'

'Would I not?' Even James could hear the insulting drawl in his own tones. It was as though one part of him, icy cold, was watching the other half make quite the most unforgivable mess of his whole life and was incapable of intervening. 'I assure you, my dear, that if that was what it took to get you to marry me I should not even hesitate!'

'And you may be assured, sir,' Alicia said with a cold magnif-

icence that brought to mind her Stansfield forebears, 'that hell will
freeze over before I ever accept your hand in marriage! You have
clearly misplaced the manners of a gentleman during your sojourn
abroad—that is if you ever had them.'

She turned on her heel with a whisper of lilac silk and James
did not even try to stop her. The study door closed behind her
with a soft click which sounded to James very loud and very final.
A moment later he heard Alicia's voice in the corridor outside,
speaking in low, impassioned tones, and Lady Stansfield's quiet
response, then there was silence.

James reached automatically for the brandy decanter and noticed
with the same detached interest that his hand was shaking. He
could not even begin to analyse how he had managed to mishandle
the situation so disastrously, for his senses seemed mercifully
numbed except for a wholly understandable inclination towards
violence. It would have given him great satisfaction to smash the
brandy glass in the fireplace, but as it was one of his grandfather's
finest pieces of crystal he managed to restrain himself. The dispassionate observer in his mind chose that moment to point out
with sickening clarity that it was very unlikely that Alicia would
ever speak to him again. Clarity was not something that he wished
for at all, so he settled down with the brandy decanter and prepared
to get seriously drunk for the first time since his salad days.

Several glasses of brandy later, matters had not improved at all.
Marcus Kilgaren, coming in search of him, found James with an
empty glass dangling from his long fingers and an expression of
almost murderous intent on his face as he contemplated the things
he would like to do to Christopher Westwood. Marcus, quick to
define the cause, was not sympathetic.

'Devil take it, James, you really have made a deuced mess of
this whole situation!' Marcus moved the brandy decanter beyond
James's reach, and fixed him with a severe frown. 'You may come
out now, for Lady Stansfield has retired from the ball with a sick
headache, taking Alicia with her. It didn't exactly require Dr John-
son to tell which of them really was feeling sick—I've seldom
seen Alicia looking so bad! Anyway, I am sent by your grandfather
to recall you to a sense of duty!'

He took his friend's unresisting arm. 'Come along, you might as well go to the card-room. You know you play your best piquet when you are half cut!'

Deverson knew better than to disturb his master so early in the morning, particularly when he had had a heavy night. Or, he corrected himself morosely, a series of heavy nights. First there had been the Cardace ball, which had apparently had some kind of transforming effect on the Marquis. Gone was the fair and considerate master he was used to, to be replaced by an ill-tempered, impatient gentleman frequently the worse for drink. To be fair, James had not vented his bad moods on Deverson, but merely being in the same house with him was uncomfortable. Two nights of heavy drinking and heavier losses had followed the ball, and Deverson knew that his master would not appreciate being disturbed from his much needed rest.

However, the gentleman of the law who was currently standing on the doorstep had been most insistent that he should see the Marquis, and while they had been arguing the Earl of Kilgaren had also arrived, demanding entry. Deverson could not withstand the combined onslaught, but it was with a great deal of trepidation that he pulled back the bed curtains now and cleared his throat apologetically.

He addressed the heaped pile of sheets and blankets somewhat nervously.

'There is a gentleman to see you, my lord, by the name of Dundry.' He paused, then said in the tone of someone relating information in questionable taste,' I understand that he is a Bow Street Runner.'

James groaned as he turned over and the light struck his eyes. 'For God's sake, Deverson, what time is it?'

'Ten o'clock, my lord.' Deverson was quite expressionless. 'The Earl of Kilgaren is also here to see you, sir. I have shown him into the drawing-room.'

James struggled to sit up and winced as his head swam. 'Quite a host of early morning callers,' he observed crossly. 'What the devil can they want at this hour of the day? Tell them I will join them shortly, Deverson, and bring me some hot water. And an ice bag might help matters, too!'

'Very good, my lord.' Deverson backed hastily from the room as James, still clutching his head, attempted to swing his legs over the side of the bed and stand up.

When James entered the drawing-room a little while later, he found Marcus Kilgaren at his ease reading the *Gazette*, and Mr Dundry of Bow Street still on his feet, looking very uncomfortable. He was twisting his round hat by the brim and his equally round face was a florid red colour. On seeing James he immediately burst into speech.

'Begging your pardon for disturbing your lordship at such an hour, but you did say that if it was urgent—'

James winced as his head gave him a fresh spasm of pain. 'You did quite right, Dundry,' he interrupted abruptly, unable to cope with too many profuse apologies. He looked at Marcus, who was calmly folding up the paper. 'What can I do for you, Marcus? I hardly expected to see you so early.'

'Caro has sent me,' Marcus said, unruffled. 'She had a message from Alicia this morning which I thought to convey to you, to the effect that she has left Town for Somerset. But perhaps you should hear what Dundry has to say first? I collect that his is the more urgent business?'

'Caro must have the constitution of an ox to be up so early in the morning,' James grumbled, eyeing the entry of Deverson and the ice with disfavour. 'Well, you'd better start, then, Dundry.'

Mr Dundry cleared his throat awkwardly. 'It's like this, your honours,' he began. Then he frowned. 'Perhaps I should say at this point—as background, like—that we have been pursuant on our enquiries concerning the death of a certain Josiah Broseley ever since your lordship came to us with a request for information.' He nodded respectfully in James's direction.

Marcus, who had not previously had the pleasure of meeting Mr Dundry, began to perceive that the explanation might be a long one. James, however, had other ideas. His head was not up to taking any circumlocution.

'Any luck?' he asked directly, slumping in an armchair and applying the ice bag to his head.

Dundry looked scandalised at being hurried along in this manner. 'Yes, my lord,' he admitted, 'which is as why I'm calling.' He paused for thought.

'Mr Josiah died of drowning,' he said sententiously. 'That wouldn't be so rare in a man supposed to be a drunkard, but word is that before he died there were those out looking for him.'

Both Marcus and James were now listening intently. 'And do you think they found him?' James asked quietly.

Dundry permitted himself a small, grim smile. 'Aye, sir. A man—tall, fair, well-spoken and well-dressed—was seen talking to Josiah Broseley the night he died. The same man went to identify the body and claimed Broseley's effects.'

'It's not much of a description.' Marcus observed. 'Why, it could have been me!'

'You're pleased to jest, sir!' Dundry gave another small smile. 'I'll not deny it was difficult to put a name to the cove, but in the end we got him!' His tone conveyed his satisfaction. 'Name of Westwood, as is great-nephew to the old Countess of Stansfield.'

The effect on his audience was electric. James sat up a little straighter, his eyes narrowing. Dundry, gratified by this rapt attention, continued. 'Seems Mr Westwood, like Josiah Broseley, also owes a lot of money,' he commented thoughtfully. 'To moneylenders, to his tailor, and most of all to a certain Mr Bertram Broseley, who bought up his debts going back a long way. In fact, Westwood's done some work for Bertram Broseley, by way of payment, like.'

There was complete silence in the room. Marcus Kilgaren, who had guessed nothing of this, was looking incredulous.

'Westwood and Bertram Broseley? Why, I was not even aware they knew each other!'

'Why should we have known?' James said intently. He had abandoned the ice bag, Dundry's news having cleared his head more effectively than any other treatment could have done. 'I dislike the sound of this, Dundry. What sort of work does Westwood do for Broseley?'

'We're still making our enquiries, sir,' the Runner said, 'but I understand that it covers a little extortion here, a bit of blackmail there... Bertram Broseley is as nasty a piece of work as you'll find, sir, but word is that his business is failing and he needs

money fast. Which brings me to the other aspect of Mr Westwood's plans which I think is germane to your interest.'

A brief spasm of pain crossed Marcus's face at the effort of
following Dundry's parentheses. James, however, had completely
shaken off his headache and was watching Dundry with a look
that was grimly alert.

'I think that I can hazard a guess—Westwood has resolved to
marry money,' he said levelly, the quiet tone belied by the keen-
ness of his gaze.

'Just so, sir.' Dundry looked gratified at such quick deduction.
'Some time ago he apparently devised a plan to marry Broseley's
widowed daughter—with Mr Broseley's connivance.'

'He needed no subterfuge,' James said, with bleak bitterness.
'She told me herself that they were betrothed. My God, if only
she knew—' He broke off, for Dundry was frowning heavily.

'Oh, no, sir, pardon the liberty, but that can't be right! My
sources told me that the lady had turned him down two months
ago! Which is why,' he said with a triumphant flourish, 'Mr Westwood decided to abduct her—the lady being not willing!'

Both men looked at him incredulously. 'Are you mad, man?'
James demanded. 'Lady Carberry told me quite clearly that she
had accepted Westwood's suit! He had no need to carry her off!'

Dundry looked offended, but it was Marcus who interposed
quietly; 'Just a moment, James. That may have been what Alicia
told you, but was it true? Caro told me at least a month ago that
Westwood had proposed and Alicia had rejected him! And even
if Alicia told you at the ball that she would marry Westwood I
would venture to suggest that it was mere bravado!'

'That's what I've been trying to tell you,' Dundry said eagerly.
'Her ladyship rejected Mr Westwood's offer, so he has abducted
her!'

James clutched his head before the conundrum could revive the
pain. 'This makes no sense,' he complained. 'Wait, let me think.
Broseley and Westwood have been in business together for some
time. Both are desperately short of cash. Westwood proposes to
Lady Carberry but is rejected.' His gaze sharpened on Dundry.
'Are you saying that both Broseley and Westwood together are

after her money? And that Westwood has carried her off to force her into marriage?'

Mr Dundry drew himself up with full, offended dignity. 'I've been trying to explain to your lordships! Lady Carberry decided two days ago to go back to Somerset and Mr Westwood offered his escort when he heard of her plans. All was falling out very conveniently for him! Now do you see, my lord? Mr Westwood has taken his chance to abduct her!'

Chapter Eleven

Two hours later the tension was beginning to tell on James. He had ordered some strong coffee and sat drinking it moodily, having been restrained from setting off immediately to the West Country. Marcus had pointed out quite reasonably that they needed to check first that Westwood had not re-routed the carriage from the start—even now he could be heading up the Great North Road. James had chafed at the delay, but had had to acknowledge the logic of this.

Other than having his curricle put to, there was little he could do at this stage. Dundry had gone off to check with the coaching inns on all the major routes out of London, and Marcus had sent a message to Kilgaren House to alert Caroline. He had insisted that they would follow James once they knew which direction Westwood had taken, and, bearing in mind that Alicia might need Caroline's comfort, James had not demurred.

It was a bare few minutes later that Dundry returned, remarkably succinct now that immediate action was required.

'They're on the Bath Road, my lord!'

'How many?' James questioned swiftly.

'Two ladies and a gentleman, sir. They passed that way yesterday, and I make no doubt that we should be able to trace them along the road quite easily. I have a good description of the carriage. The innkeeper said that all three seemed quite amicable, but I imagine that is because Lady Carberry thought that she was going home, rather than—' He broke off at the expression on James's face. 'It's definitely our party, for the landlord described Lady Carberry.' He smiled reminiscently. 'No one is likely to forget that lady, sir!'

'I'm going after them now,' James said decisively. 'We won't be able to catch up with them, but we might be able to track them down in the end. I just pray we will not be too late, but if so—' He stopped, his face set.

'If only we knew where Westwood was intending to go,' Marcus said thoughtfully as James opened the door and shouted for his groom. 'It won't be Chartley Chase, for sure.'

'There's Broseley's place at Taunton,' Dundry suggested, a little diffidently. 'If the two of them have planned this together...'

'Good man.' James clapped him on the shoulder. 'It's worth a try at any rate! You'd better come with me, Dundry. Marcus, I take it you and Caroline won't be far behind?'

'Try and stop us!' Marcus replied cheerfully. 'Don't break your neck,' he added as James shrugged himself into his caped driving coat. 'That would be no use to Alicia at all—or Miss Frensham. I wonder what Westwood intends to do with Miss Frensham?' he added as an afterthought.

James swore. He had very little concern for Miss Frensham's welfare at that moment, but the vision of Alicia trying to defend herself against Westwood's advances was with him constantly.

'Leave us messages at the posting houses,' Marcus was saying urgently to Dundry. 'We might even catch up with you, given the speed at which Caroline likes to travel! And don't let him do anything too rash.' He looked at James thoughtfully. 'Damn it, he's been wanting an excuse to call Westwood out for months!'

For Alicia, the journey down to Somerset was assuming nightmarish proportions. When she had left Cardace House on the night of the ball, her only thought had been to escape from London and all future contact with James Mullineaux. She did not understand how everything had gone so irretrievably wrong between them; every true feeling was twisted and spoiled beyond recognition. All she could do was instinctively head for the place where she had been happiest, and that was Chartley Chase.

A long-suffering Miss Frensham had set about packing up in

preparation for their departure the following day and they had left Fordyce impassively arranging to close the house in Upper Grosvenor Street indefinitely. Lady Stansfield had not spared her granddaughter's feelings, accusing her of rash, impulsive action, and Alicia had been vaguely surprised that Christopher Westwood had actually supported her to the extent of offering his escort for the journey.

She had not questioned his actions particularly, for her mind was obsessed with thoughts of James and she seemed incapable of making much sense of anything else. She had completely forgotten about Josiah's death and the fact that she had asked James for his help in finding out what had happened to him.

Now, as they neared Bath and the end of their journey, Alicia was beginning to regret her hurried departure. They had stayed overnight in a busy coaching inn where she had lain awake listening to the carriages coming and going, trying not to dwell on every encounter she had ever had with James. She had not been very successful. It was rather like a replaying of the dreadful time when she had first lost him, when every waking and sleeping moment had seemed to be haunted by his presence.

Her head ached from lack of sleep and her heart ached even more. The enforced inactivity of the journey gave her too much time to think, to try to retrace the progress of their relationship up to this miserable point. The rumble of the carriage wheels was making her head ache even more. She leant back against the cushions and allowed her eyes to close. Suddenly she felt very tired. Well, if there was nothing else she could do, she could at least sleep. The noise of the journey blurred and faded away, and Alicia was dead to the world.

When she woke up she knew instinctively that it was a very long time later. She was very cold and she felt horribly sick. Other sensations returned to her slowly. She lay still, listening halfconsciously to the faint, plaintive call of birds outside. There was also an almost imperceptible smell...sandalwood...spices...which jogged a very faint memory deep in her unconscious, reminding her of her childhood... With an effort Alicia pulled herself awake, opened her eyes and flinched as the dim light caused her head to ache abominably.

She closed her eyes again immediately. The nausea ebbed a little and she tried to think. What had happened to her? She seemed to be lying on a lumpy sort of mattress and could feel the coarse material of a blanket rough beneath her fingers. Surely this could not be another inn? She moved her hand slightly and discovered to her relief that she was not physically restrained in any way. Not that she could move much in her present state. She felt as though any attempt at movement would result in violent sickness. What on earth was going on? Try as she might, she could not remember anything beyond falling asleep in the carriage.

The second time that she opened her eyes it was marginally easier to keep them open. She moved her head cautiously. She seemed to be lying on her back looking up at a high, shadowed ceiling. Meagre light was coming from a dirty window in the wall to her left, and she could make out rough plaster walls and bare boards on the floor, deep in dust. The iron bedstead on which she was lying was one of the few pieces of furniture in the large, empty room. The scent of spice was still there, faint but discernible, and the sound of the birds drifted into the room with no other noise but the lowing of cattle as a backdrop. It was all rather pleasant, and Alicia was tempted to allow herself to float back into unconsciousness and worry no more about anything.

However, it was too late. As she turned her head slightly to look about her there was a movement about the bed and someone spoke.

'So you are round again, my dear. How very fortuitous. I was afraid that I had completely overdone the dose and you would die. Even the Reverend Mr Skittle might draw the line at joining me in holy matrimony with a corpse!'

It was unquestionably Christopher Westwood's voice, and Westwood's face which hung over her. His words made no sense to Alicia at that moment, for she had more pressing preoccupations.

'I am going to be sick,' Alicia said, as distinctly as possible, and was gratified when a bucket appeared underneath her nose within a moment. Although unpleasant, the interlude made her feel much better. The nausea receded and her headache dimmed a little.

Westwood had removed the bucket with an expression of dis-

taste on his face. Now he relocked the door and came back towards
her. The first thing Alicia noticed about him was that he was very
drunk. There was a hectic flush to his cheeks and a feverish glitter
in his eyes, and, if further testimony were needed, a three quarters
empty brandy bottle stood on the nearby table.

'Not quite your elegant style, is it, my dear, being sick in a
bucket?' he jeered. 'But then, I suspect you will need to become
accustomed to a few changes!'

There was a sneering tone in his voice which Alicia had never
heard before. It was the voice of a bully, one who was very confident of himself. She tried to sit up but pain shot through her head
and she sank back on the dirty pillow with a groan.

'I don't understand.' There was a quiver in her voice which was
all too real. 'What's going on? Where am I? And where is Miss
Frensham?'

Westwood stood looking down at her with odious complacency.
'Calm yourself, my dear. Miss Frensham is quite well, though no
doubt a little distraught by now!' He giggled unpleasantly. 'I abandoned her at an inn near Bath, having encouraged her to step down
to partake of some refreshment. You were asleep and nothing
could have been easier than to trick her. I helped her down and
said I would go back to wake you, but, of course, I simply gave
the order to drive on and left her in the inn yard!' He giggled
again with evident enjoyment. 'I can still see the look on her face
as the carriage sped away!'

Alicia remained silent. It seemed the most sensible course of
action until her head improved and she could think straight. At
least the debilitating sickness had retreated, but she felt very weak
and all the dust of the journey appeared to be clinging to her skin.
Once again she attempted to sit up and this time she was successful. Propping herself against the iron bedpost, she cleared her
throat painfully.

'Could I have a glass of water, please, Christopher? I feel very
unwell.'

'Hardly surprising, I feel, with the dose of laudanum I gave
you.' Westwood sounded pleased with himself rather than anything else. 'I think I must have overestimated the amount, but I
did not want to run the risk of you waking too soon. As it is, you

have slept the clock round, and very inconvenient it has been, too!' He sounded as though he expected her to apologise for her lack of consideration.

He passed her a rough beaker of water, which was brackish and warm, but tasted wonderful to Alicia. So this had been the reason why he had supported her when she had announced she was leaving London—and why he had offered the use of his own carriage. Alicia thought she already guessed why, but would make no assumptions.

'Why have you brought me here?' she asked, hitting just the right plaintive note. Westwood had seemed to appreciate her meek approach, so she decided she would try to maintain it, although it went rather against the grain. It would be foolish to provoke him when she appeared to be so thoroughly at his mercy—there was a lot she needed to learn.

Westwood drew his chair up beside the bed and gave Alicia a rather unpleasant grin. It was obvious that he was enjoying himself hugely.

'Why, to marry you, my dear!' He stretched out his legs before him and admired the high gloss of his boots. 'I asked you once before—do you remember?—but you refused me. This time I was taking no risks.'

So she had been right, Alicia thought. He was determined to marry her, and not because he was suffering from unrequited love either! His attitude towards her could scarcely have been more contemptuous.

'But you don't really care for me, do you, Christopher?' she asked, trying to sound piqued by his indifference.

Westwood gave a crack of laughter and swung backwards on the chair. 'Does it hurt your feelings that I don't bother to pretend any more? But then you ain't my type, Alicia! You're as cold as ice and I prefer my bedmates to have a little more spirit!' He tilted the brandy bottle to his lips. 'No, you hold no attraction for me, but your money...well, that's another matter!'

'Money? You mean Carberry's money?'

Westwood wiped his sleeve across his mouth and looked at her thoughtfully. 'Well, certainly that's part of it, of course.' How heartless he sounded. 'But I know Carberry's money is tied up in your do-good trusts, and it will take me a little time to break those. No, what I really need is ready cash and the promise of more. Your expectations as your grandmother's heiress are enough for now!' His tone changed from smug self-congratulation to bitterness.

'The old witch always meant to leave her fortune to me—I'd been living on the expectation of it for years, borrowing money to maintain the style of living I was entitled to! Then you had to come along and spoil sport! I thought she could at least be relied upon to disinherit you after you married Carberry, but the two of you always were so close she wouldn't even abandon you then!' He glared at her. 'So I had to spend the next seven years kowtowing to the old besom for the pittance of an allowance she granted me!'

Alicia marvelled at the casual cruelty of his words. Apart from his insensitivity over Josiah's death, none of this corrosive spite had ever spilled over onto the surface before. Westwood had always charmed Lady Stansfield with his attentiveness and anxiety to please, a consummate actor bent on gaining a fortune at any price. Alicia shivered.

'And if I refuse you again?' She tried not to sound aggressive, simply curious. Westwood laughed again, without mirth.

'You ain't in any position to refuse, my dear! In the first place you're hopelessly compromised and I doubt if even your grandmother would stand by you now! Besides, the shock might kill her if you claim to have been forced into marriage for a second time! She is not as strong as she was. It would create yet another monstrous scandal and you would be obliged to live retired.

'Anyway, there's no one here to listen to your cries for help and the Reverend Mr Skittle has been well paid to ignore your objections.' He paused and looked at her thoughtfully. 'And if you cut up really rough I expect I could manage to overcome my aversion to you sufficiently to ruin you. You would not really be in any fit state to refuse me after that!'

Alicia winced. The thought of marriage to Westwood under duress was horrible, but she knew he spoke the truth. She was hardly in a position to escape him and even if she did he would create another hideous scandal. She could never inflict that on Lady Stansfield.

Westwood had moved over to the door, presumably listening for the arrival of Mr Skittle. There was no sound, and once again Alicia became aware of the noises outside the room—the country sounds of the birds and cattle, the wind in the trees. So where was she? Not at Chartley Chase, although they were certainly somewhere in the countryside. If they had not altered direction after Bath, could they have carried on to Taunton, perhaps…?

Her mind was still working very slowly, for it was at least half a minute before she put together the elusive threads that were now all in her mind…the dusty, high-ceilinged room, the sounds of the country and the smell of spices…her father's plans for an arranged marriage for her, and an associate of his waiting in the wings… She had all the pieces of the jigsaw now, and they gently slid into place, to form the most incredible and horrifying whole.

'Christopher, what is your connection with my father?'

He had no warning and was too drunk to dissemble. She watched his mouth hang slackly with shock, an expression of stupefaction in his eyes. Finally he licked his lips and looked at her with a curiously wary expression.

'How the devil did you guess? Damn it, I've never said a word and I'm damned sure he hasn't! How did you know?'

Alicia shrugged. Despite her predicament she suddenly felt stronger, as though the balance of power had shifted away from him to her. He was on the defensive and she was determined to keep him there.

'It was you, wasn't it?' she said flatly. 'It was you who killed Josiah and pretended to be his cousin when you went to collect his possessions. You knew he had tried to warn me of the plot you'd hatched with my father and you wanted to make sure he never had the chance!'

An extraordinary expression came into Westwood's eyes, part malice, part triumph. 'That fool Josiah—he was a weak reed! He did some work for your father, but he could never bear to sully his hands! I tolerated him for as long as your father chose to protect him, but then he found out that we planned to use you and your fortune and he became nauseatingly sentimental!'

There was no expression in the glittering grey gaze as he turned to look out of the window. 'He said you'd always been good to him and you didn't deserve to be tricked again—the mawkish fool! He threatened to tell you all our plans. I went after him—he had to be silenced. And just when I thought all was safe I came to call on you and saw a letter from him sitting on your desk!'

Alicia closed her eyes against the memory of Christopher Westwood sitting in her library, immaculately self-possessed, with Josiah's blood on his hands. But Westwood was continuing.

'I took a big risk then,' he said cheerfully. 'I thought Josiah was too much of a fool to tell a straight tale, and I gambled on the fact that he would not have named me. And I was right, wasn't I?' He turned to smile triumphantly at Alicia and she could feel herself shrinking back against the hard iron of the bedstead, chilled to the bone by the madness she could see in his eyes. 'We knew you were already wary of your father, but you acted just the same to me. Same Alicia, cold as the driven snow! But I knew I had to move quickly. And you gave me the opportunity, didn't you, my dear?'

Alicia did not really feel that he required an answer. He must be quite mad to speak of murder and marriage in the same breath, but she was not going to test him further. She sat huddled on the bed, frozen at the thought of what she had uncovered. What could she do now, circumstanced as she was? To be forced into some conspiracy of silence was as bad in its way as being forced into marriage with him. When Westwood came back across the room and sat down beside her she tried not to cringe away. It was difficult, but he appeared not to notice her anyway, engrossed as he was by his own thoughts.

'I think I'll tell you it all,' he began conversationally. 'It'll pass the time until that tiresome priest gets here.' He drained the brandy bottle and some of the liquid ran down his chin, splashing on his shirt. Alicia felt a spasm of disgust go through her, but Westwood merely wiped it away impatiently with the back of his hand. He was flushed with high colour now, a triumphant glitter in his eyes which gave the lie to any claims of charm or good looks. Putting down the empty bottle, he thrust his hands into his jacket pockets.

'Where to start...?' he mused. 'I suppose that you are the start of the story, my dear, for you came to London and, as I've already said, supplanted me as your grandmother's heir. I'd always had a penchant for deep play and I was fathoms-deep in debt. In one of the dens I frequented I met your cousin Josiah.' He paused, picked up the brandy bottle and looked surprised that it was empty. 'Well, Josiah was very helpful. I confided all my troubles and he suggested that I should go to see your father. I knew nothing of Broseley's reputation then, but Josiah said he might help me.'

'And he did?' Alicia kept her voice neutral, allowing none of her horror to show. Fatal to make a slip now and draw his anger onto herself.

'It became apparent that we could do business together.' The self-satisfied tone had returned. 'Broseley bought up all my debts and in return I did some jobs for him.' Westwood looked at Alicia consideringly. 'No need to offend your sensibilities with the details, I suppose, though it's as good a joke as any that he is your father. Chalk and cheese!' He laughed. 'I expect you get your airs from your mother. He was always complaining of her vapours and die-away airs. Said he should never have married her, for she brought him nothing, and her death had been a great release for him... What was that?'

'What? I heard nothing.' Alicia's mouth was suddenly dry. Like him she had heard a faint noise on the stairs, but she did not dare to hope that any help was at hand. No doubt it was the corrupt priest whom Westwood had hired to perform his dubious nuptials. She waited, but there was no knock at the door and after a suspicious look Westwood appeared to lose interest.

'No doubt Castle is keeping an eye on things downstairs,' he murmured. 'You've guessed we're at Greyrigg, haven't you? But we've sent the servants away, so don't get any ideas about calling for help, my dear! Now, where was I?'

'You had done some work for my father,' Alicia reminded him quietly.

'Ah, yes.' Westwood settled himself more comfortably. 'Well, after a while your father called me in to discuss a proposition. He planned to marry you off to his business partner, George Carberry. They had plenty of plans for joint ventures. He thought the proposal would do me some good, too. He was sure that the marriage would be anathema to your grandmother and that she would disinherit you! I think he saw it as a fitting punishment for her,' Westwood said thoughtfully. 'She had always refused to receive him, and he knew your marriage to Carberry would humiliate her before the *ton*, when she had supported Mullineaux's suit!'

Alicia felt her eyes fill with tears. So, in the end, the whole tawdry affair had centred around Broseley's need for money and revenge. There was some kind of irony, she thought numbly, in the fact that Broseley's plans for vengeance had turned out to be the ruin of Westwood's own hopes of the Stansfield fortune.

'So my father removed me from your path by marrying me to Carberry,' Alicia observed. 'And what did you do in return?'

She saw Westwood smile. 'I owed him a favour—and eventually he called it in! Josiah was becoming more of a liability than an asset to Broseley's organisation those last few months. He would get drunk and spill dangerous information, in addition to his threat to destroy our plans by going to you. So he had to go. Your father had no compunction about losing a member of the family!'

There was no trace of remorse in his voice. Alicia, struggling with a feeling of unreality, felt as though she was trapped in some outrageous nightmare. How could he simply relate all of this without expression, without feeling? He had no concept of morality, for all that mattered to him was centred around the needs and wishes of Christopher Westwood. Broseley had indeed found a man after his own heart when the fates had sent him Westwood.

'I suppose,' Westwood said lightly, 'that the real villain of the whole piece was George Carberry, for dying so inconveniently. If he had lived you would have been shunned by Society and no doubt disinherited by your grandmother. Trust the old fool to make a mess of even that. He was only ever good for his money—but you inherited all of that, didn't you, my dear? Yes, Broseley was too clever for his own good there, and it has rankled with him ever since. Nor did you endear yourself to him last time you met, with your wilful rejection of his plans!' He turned to look at her, and there was something in his eyes which was thoroughly unpleasant.

'I suppose you were always my intended suitor,' Alicia said tiredly.

'I told your father that you would never agree to another marriage of convenience!' Westwood laughed again, clearly relishing the situation. 'He always thought he knew best! But I knew you, and I knew it was madness to suggest either a business arrangement or a match! All I could do was insist that he did not disclose my identity so that he did not queer my pitch with you. I knew it would hardly be to my advantage if you realised I was in league with him!' He sighed. 'You are always so headstrong, my dear! But that is all in the past now. With me as your husband I am sure you will conform!'

Alicia was sure that he knew any number of ways to enforce his will and she shuddered at the thought. She drew the rough blanket closer around her for comfort. Thank God he had not yet exhausted his story—she did not like to think what he might do if once his attentions became focused solely on her again. Without flinching she faced the fact that he was quite capable of fulfilling his threat of forcing himself on her to compromise her beyond saving. She was not sure how she could cope with that.

'Anyway, I decided to try my luck with you under my own colours,' Westwood was saying. 'I thought I had a good chance of persuading you to marry me—you seemed to enjoy my company and I knew you were lonely. I invested a lot of time and energy in being pleasant to you, Alicia.' He kicked moodily at a loose floorboard. 'Unfortunately, I'd left it too late, hadn't I? You had already met Mullineaux again and were no doubt cherishing some sweet romantic dream that the two of you might be reunited!' There was an ugly expression on his face. 'Damn it, if only I had proposed sooner I'm sure you would have accepted me!'

Alicia shuddered to think that this could be true. The Christopher Westwood she had known until recently had been charming and good company, solace in her loneliness, kind and pleasant. She might well have accepted him simply to enliven her solitary existence, little knowing that she had a tiger by the tail. But James Mullineaux had changed all that. Meeting him again had shown her just what a sham it would be to accept any other man, and no one else could ever be a substitute for him. Suddenly Alicia un-

derstood the change in Westwood's behaviour of late, as he had
realised that he had left his proposal for too long. He had become
sharp with frustration as he had seen his chance with her slip away.
The mask of his good nature had faltered, but not sufficiently for
her ever to suspect the truth.

Once again, her attention was attracted by a slight noise outside
the door—the scrape of something on the wooden floorboards. It
stopped almost immediately, but Alicia frowned a little in puzzlement. Surely Mr Skittle had no reason to be surreptitious in his
approach?

Alicia's head was beginning to ache again with the effort of
holding back the tears. To think that she had told James in a fit
of pique that she had accepted Westwood's offer. Now she was
well-served for all that foolish pride which had prevented her from
telling him that she loved him. She imagined him receiving the
news of her marriage to Westwood and the contempt it would
engender. Little would he know of the truth of the matter, and she
could never tell—not while Lady Stansfield lived. And when Lady
Stansfield had died could she really come out with the truth of
Westwood's criminality—and her own enforced connivance in it?
She struggled against the fog of tiredness and misery that was
clouding her mind.

At last there was the sound of steps on the stair. Westwood
jumped up with barely concealed impatience.

'Can that be that damned priest at last? God alone knows what
is taking him so long to get here!' He hurried across to the door,
and unlocked it again.

Alicia was hoping that God would indeed be very tardy in sending his dubious representative along to conduct the marriage service. It was not, in fact, Mr Skittle who came into the room, but
her own father. She was not surprised to see him. Westwood had
confirmed that her prison was one of the attics at Greyrigg, albeit
one in which she had never been before. The top floor of the house
was riddled with interconnecting rooms and passageways which
could conceal any number of dubiously imported goods or an entire army of men. She steeled herself as Broseley strode across the
bare floor towards her, an oleaginous smile pinned to his face.

'Well, my dear, history repeats itself, does it not? I hope that

Christopher has been persuading you of the good sense in accepting your fate this time!'

'I find him no more acceptable as a bridegroom than I did George Carberry,' Alicia said coldly. 'Furthermore, you cannot possibly think that a marriage conducted here by some questionable priest will ever be recognised as valid. I certainly will not honour it!'

Broseley turned his slimy gaze on Westwood. 'My dear Christopher, have you been wasting your time here? You assured me that she would be eating out of your hand by the time I arrived to act as witness to your marriage!' He turned back to Alicia. 'You must allow that he's a finer figure of a man than poor Carberry, my dear, and unlikely to die from the exertions of your wedding night! Indeed, I had quite expected to find him anticipating those delights already!'

Alicia's expression showed her contempt, but she would not lower herself to answer him. It was Westwood, apparently piqued at the aspersions thus cast on him, who burst into speech. 'Your daughter, sir, holds no charms for me besides her money!'

Broseley just laughed. 'But you'll marry her just the same, my boy! All we need now is the Reverend Mr Skittle to set the seal on matters!'

As if on cue, there was a knock at the door. Westwood caught Alicia's arm and practically dragged her off the bed as the door opened. Alicia had intended to struggle as much as she could, but to her horror she found that her legs were as weak as cotton-wool and she could barely stand, let alone put up a fight.

'Mr Skittle—' Westwood began, then broke off.

'Skittle is temporarily indisposed, I fear, my dear Westwood,' said the Marquis of Mullineaux in very smooth but infinitely dangerous tones. 'Your butler, sir,' the Marquis added, turning to Broseley with utter courtesy, 'has also succumbed to a mysterious ailment which has rendered him completely unable to move.'

He made a slight gesture with the wicked-looking duelling pistol he held negligently in one hand. 'I must beg you to unhand that lady, Westwood.'

Broseley had not moved, but Westwood took this instruction very badly. 'Be damned to you,' he snarled. 'You'll have to kill me first.' He shot a furious glance in the direction of the doorway, saw Marcus Kilgaren lurking there, and turned back to James like an animal at bay.

Mullineaux's mouth twisted in a travesty of a smile. 'If I must, I will,' he murmured, 'but much as I would wish to rid the world of you, Westwood, I am reluctantly compelled to leave you alive to stand trial.'

Westwood burst out laughing. 'Trial! You jest, Mullineaux!'

'I fear not.' James was so expressionless he might have been discussing the weather. 'You have just confessed to Lady Carberry that you murdered her cousin. Both myself and the excellent Mr Dundry of Bow Street heard every word through this door. We were here long before your proposed father-in-law—' he nodded grimly towards Broseley '—came stumbling along to act as a witness at the wedding. And, of course, as well as murder there is the matter of the abduction of a lady. Plenty of work, I feel, to keep Mr Dundry busy over the next few weeks!'

Westwood had lost colour as James spoke and the extent to which he had condemned himself out of his own mouth became apparent. His mouth hung slackly in a face of pasty white. He turned to stare at Broseley. 'You old fool, how the hell did they get in? Castle's supposed to be a professional! Damnation take it that I ever trusted you to organise any of this!'

'Shocking lack of servants in this part of the country,' James drawled. 'Certainly not enough of them to keep an eye on all the comings and goings in a big house like this! But we waste time, Westwood. Let the lady go.'

Neither Westwood nor Broseley paid him much attention, for they were too wrapped up in their mutual hatred. Westwood was still muttering, 'Of all the stupid, incompetent fools—' when his employer turned on him with a fury beyond anything Alicia had ever seen in her father before.

'Hold your tongue, you dolt! Haven't you done enough damage? I can't believe what I'm hearing here!' His West Country accent was very strong. 'So you thought you'd pass the time in telling tales of your exploits, did you? Something to impress your future wife? God damn it that I should ever have soiled my hands with you, you worthless bastard!'

For a split second Westwood's grip on Alicia's arm slackened out of sheer shock, and it was all the chance she needed. With more strength than she realised she possessed, she drove the elbow of her free arm into his stomach with a satisfying impact and twisted herself out of his grip. Westwood let out a gasp of both surprise and pain, and doubled up, coughing.

James, with great presence of mind, caught hold of Alicia and dragged her free of the maelstrom as Broseley hurled himself upon Westwood. Whilst he was twice the age of his opponent, he was not drunk and fury gave him an added strength to counteract Westwood's relative youth and agility. It was not much of a fight, however. As the two of them locked bodies with a grunt, Westwood got an arm free and Alicia suddenly saw the glint of a knife in his hand.

She drew breath on a scream as Broseley also saw the knife, but too late. As it slid between his ribs he had a look of ludicrous surprise fixed on his face. His weight fell against Westwood, setting him off balance, and the drink did the rest. Westwood lost his footing, stumbled sideways and fell onto the bare floorboards, Broseley's body half across him and a choking cloud of dust rising from the floor. The knife slipped from his fingers and went skittering away, aided by a well-aimed kick from James Mullineaux. Then it was all over as Dundry rushed into the room and began the words which spelled doom for Westwood.

'Christopher Westwood, I am arresting you for the wilful murders of Josiah Broseley and—' he cast a significant look down at the prone body on the floor—'Bertram Broseley...'

Some time passed, but Alicia was not really aware of it. James carried her downstairs, wrapped in the noxious blanket from the bed, which Alicia had half-heartedly tried to push away. In the drawing-room was Caroline Kilgaren, pale and distraught, who jumped up eagerly as they came in, her worried gaze going to Alicia's face.

'You have her safe! Thank God! And James—you are not hurt yourself? I was beside myself with worry... Put her down here...I will fetch some water...'

James put Alicia down gently on one of the lumpy sofas and

drew Caroline aside, speaking to her in a low voice. Their voices
washed over Alicia, who lay with her eyes closed, in a state between waking and sleeping. Presently Caroline came across to her
and tried to encourage her to drink, but she merely turned her head
away on the cushion and did not open her eyes.

An unquantifiable time later she was recalled from this dream-
like state by the unpleasant smell of burnt feathers being wafted
beneath her nose. She opened her eyes crossly and met the amused
gaze of the Marquis of Mullineaux.

'I thought that would do the trick,' James said cheerfully. 'Pity
the poor fowl we had to pluck them from! Don't frown at me like
that, Alicia—you may sleep presently, but for now I need to talk
to you!'

To her complete horror, Alicia immediately burst into tears. She
felt the puffy sofa give as James sat down next to her and gathered
her into his arms without a word. She just clung to him, her face
turned against his chest. None of the questions such as why he
was there or how they had found her mattered at all for the time
being.

For a while James said nothing, simply holding Alicia close so
that the warmth and reassurance from his body transmitted itself
to her and she began to relax. It was so amazingly comforting to
be held like that that after a time Alicia found herself yawning
involuntarily, and felt rather than saw James laugh. A little shyly,
she raised her head and looked at him.

'I haven't thanked you yet for rescuing me...' she said diffidently. 'How did you find me? And so quickly!'

James loosened his grip a little, much to her disappointment.
He smiled down at her. 'Quickly! It didn't seem quick to me, I
can assure you! You do know that you were unconscious for a
whole day, don't you? It was two days ago that you left London!'

Alicia blinked a little, but she was too tired to make much sense
of this. 'I didn't realise...so I had been asleep all that time!'

'Fortunately for you,' James said, his tone grim. 'Otherwise you
would probably be married by now—or worse! He didn't hurt you,
did he?' he added, his tone suddenly so sharp that Alicia jumped.

She shook her head tiredly. 'No... He didn't beat me, if that is
what you mean!' Her mouth curved in a slight, sleepy smile. 'Nor

did he molest me—he told me that I was not at all appealing to him, and too cold for his taste!'

She felt James's arm tighten about her for a moment as he smiled.

'Well, we must be grateful for your shortcomings in that respect, my love! Though I doubt I will have much complaint to make in the future!'

Alicia just snuggled closer to him. She was bored with talking, feeling so happy and warm that she simply wanted to sleep. There had been some disagreement between them, she remembered vaguely, but none of that mattered now. Nothing mattered, except—

'Miss Frensham!' she exclaimed, sitting bolt upright. 'Whatever has happened to her? Christopher said something about leaving her behind at a coaching inn...'

James laughed. 'Yes, indeed, we found Miss Frensham at Bathampton, ensconced in the landlord's best bedchamber with three doctors in attendance! She had such a strong fit of the vapours after she was abandoned that they feared for her life! She is a little recovered now, and Marcus has arranged for her to be taken to Chartley Chase, so you need not worry about her any more!'

He glanced down at Alicia and realised that the finer points of any explanation would have to wait. She was almost asleep where she sat, her head resting against his shoulder, her eyes closing irresistibly. He gave her a little shake.

'Listen, Alicia, it's going to take a bit of time for you to sleep off this stuff Westwood gave you, particularly with the shock you've had as well. Caroline and Marcus are going to take you back to Chartley and look after you. I must return to London with Dundry and sort things out once and for all. I'll come back as soon as I can, I promise.'

None of this made sense to Alicia except the unwelcome news that he was going to leave her. Her mind slid over the bits she did not understand—who was Dundry, and what were the Kilgarens doing there?—and fastened on what really mattered to her. Her face puckered like that of a petulant child.

'Why must you go? I want you to stay here with me!'

James pressed his mouth against her hair. More than anything he wanted to stay there too, not least to prevent anything else going wrong. But he knew that someone had to break the unwelcome news to the Countess of Stansfield. It was the least she deserved.

'It won't be for long, Alicia. By the time you are feeling better I shall be back, I promise. I don't want to go.' His serious gaze sought hers. 'You must understand that. But I have to.'

He gave her a quick, hard kiss. Caroline was hovering in the doorway and it was time to go. James stood up and wrapped the blanket closer around Alicia, as though she were a child. By the time he had reached the doorway she was already asleep.

The day was warm with the promise of summer as James Mullineaux rode into Chartley village almost two weeks later, and he felt his spirits lift with the hope of one who felt that he had at last reached the end of a long journey. He had stayed with friends near Bath on the previous night and had left his luggage to follow as he took advantage of the fine weather to ride the rest of the way.

It had not been a pleasant couple of weeks. Christopher Westwood had sung from the rooftops in an attempt to incriminate others and free himself from blame. To James had fallen the uncomfortable task of telling Lady Stansfield the truth of Westwood's corruption and she had aged almost visibly as she had absorbed the news. Her main concern, however, had been for Alicia's welfare. Only James's reassurance that Alicia was safe and would visit her as soon as possible had prevented her from posting down to Somerset immediately. Finally, James had been to see his grandfather to gain his blessing for his forthcoming marriage and had at last set off for the country with a heart lighter than it had been in weeks.

The village was very quiet. A few ducks splashed lazily on the pond and the sound of children's voices floated on the air. Over the heather-clad hill lay Monks Dacorum and James suddenly felt a rush of uncomplicated pleasure to be back. They would settle in the country, he decided, then laughed aloud at the change in his own outlook. He turned into the approach to the Chase and the pebbles of the driveway scattered beneath his horse's hooves. A groom, alerted by the noise of his arrival, emerged from the stableblock to take the horse and James dismounted to hurry up to the front door with sudden impatience.

His anticipation was now almost at fever pitch. Chartley Chase, always peaceful, seemed almost sepulchrally silent. James knocked vigorously on the door and a moment later Fordyce's firm tread could be heard crossing the hall to the main door.

'Good day, Fordyce. I hope that you are well?' With barely concealed impatience, James hurried into the hall, divesting himself of his coat. The sunlight dappled the polished floor, and the scent of lilies filled the air. It was beautifully serene and tranquil, just as he remembered it. But James could not help wishing that the calm might have been broken. He felt that he really did deserve a hero's welcome.

'I am very well, my lord, I thank you.' Fordyce was closing the door with what seemed to James to be agonising slowness.

'And Lady Carberry? How is she?'

Fordyce paused. James could barely curb his frustration. What was the matter? Where was everyone? Fordyce spoke with lugubrious deliberation.

'Her ladyship is much better, my lord. However, she is from home. The Earl and Countess of Kilgaren are in the drawing-room, should you care to—'

But James was gone.

Caroline had never seen James enter a room so precipitately. She had been sitting on the window-seat in the sunshine, dozing contentedly over a book, listening to the soft rustling of the pages turning as Marcus read a two-day-old copy of the *Gazette*. Then the door slammed and James had erupted into the room like a tornado.

'I understand Alicia is from home!' he began, without preamble. 'What the devil is going on here?'

Marcus put down his newspaper and got to his feet in a leisurely manner.

'Good day, James,' he said mildly. 'How nice it is to see you again!'

James had the grace to look a little ashamed of himself. He shook Marcus's hand and came across to the window-seat to kiss Caroline.

'I beg your pardon. I hope that you are both well. I have but this minute arrived, and been told by Fordyce that Alicia is not at home! I apologise for the fact that it put all other thoughts out of my head!'

Caroline put down her book and rose to her feet, smiling. 'It's too fine a day to be cooped up indoors. Come outside and we will tell you what has been going on here! But first tell us what happened in London. Is Westwood safely locked away?'

She slipped her hand through James's arm and steered him out of the French windows. Beyond the formal terrace stretched the woodland garden, and the three of them strolled through this as James gave them the details of what had been happening in London. The grassy glades were thick with bluebells and they sat down on a couple of rustic benches in a patch of sun as James turned expectantly to them.

'Well? You must know that I am positively expiring with impatience! How can it be that Alicia, who should by rights be considering herself an invalid, should go off visiting or whatever at such a time?'

'You mean,' Marcus corrected dryly, 'how can it be that Alicia, who should be here waiting for you in a fever of gratitude and impatience, should have the bad taste to be from home when you choose to call!'

James scowled at him. 'Well, I'll allow that I did expect some show of appreciation, even if it was too much to expect the wretched girl to fall into my arms!'

Caroline sighed, propping her chin on her hand. 'I don't know what's going through Alicia's mind at present, James, for she does not speak to me. At first when we brought her home she simply slept all the time. We called Dr Pym from Bath, but he said that no real harm had been done, though, of course, she was deeply shocked and distressed. After a few days she seemed a little better, but she was quieter than I have ever seen her and she barely spoke a word. She wasn't difficult about anything,' Caroline added thoughtfully. 'In fact she was quite docile and passive, but it was most odd—and most out of character!'

James raised his eyebrows, struggling to come to terms with this completely alien description of his beloved. One might describe Alicia in many ways, but mild and submissive she was not. God forbid that her experiences had turned her into a mouse!

Marcus smiled slightly. 'Yes, I must admit I've never seen Alicia like that before! Caro finally got her to talk about Westwood and the ordeal she'd been through, but Alicia showed no emotion whatsoever and when Caro tried to turn the conversation to you James, Alicia simply wouldn't speak at all!'

Caroline's mouth drooped despondently. 'It's true, James,' she said unhappily. 'Then two days ago we got your letter telling us to expect you soon, and Alicia said nothing, but—'

'Yesterday she rose very early and left without a word!' Marcus finished for her. 'She left a note apologising for abandoning us like that, but said she could not face you at the moment and needed time to think. Nobody knows where she has gone!'

'Well, Fordyce knows,' Caroline amended, 'but he told us that Alicia had sworn him to secrecy. Oh, it really is too bad of her! When I see her again—' She broke off with a rueful smile as Marcus took her hand in his in a soothing gesture.

James was tight-lipped with annoyance. 'So Fordyce knows, does he?' he asked, getting purposefully to his feet.

'James,' Caroline called after him, hopelessly, 'don't make him tell you... Don't!' But it was too late. James's tall figure could be seen cutting across the terrace and into the house without a backward glance. Marcus gave a resigned sigh and pulled his wife to her feet.

'What a delightful place this is—when our friends are not here to cause us problems! Come along, my love! We may be needed to keep the peace!'

'Fordyce,' James said directly when the butler had made his usual stately entrance in response to the bell, 'I understand that you know of Lady Carberry's present whereabouts. Is that so?'

Fordyce permitted himself a small, discreet nod of the head. 'It is so, my lord.'

'Where is she?'

'Her ladyship gave instructions that her whereabouts be divulged to no one, I fear, my lord.'

James gave him a hard stare. He had his impatience well in hand now, but he was still taut with annoyance.

Fordyce maintained a prudent silence. Every last one of the servants was behind the Marquis of Mullineaux in his courtship of Lady Carberry, but it was evident to them all that she was making things extremely difficult for him. Fordyce considered Lord Mullineaux thoughtfully. He suspected that he was the sort of man who could be relied upon to bring matters to a successful conclusion and would very likely brook no opposition. The delicate question from Fordyce's own point of view was how much help he should offer. He decided to test the water.

'Her ladyship is expected back in a few days, my lord,' he offered. 'If your lordship would be good enough to wait—'

'No, thank you.' James was polite but firm. 'I have an alternative plan. I wish to go and meet Lady Carberry.'

Fordyce swallowed hard. Both Caroline and Marcus, who had not said a word, were looking at him with identical quizzical expressions. Fordyce capitulated.

'I hope, sir,' he said severely, looking at James very straight, 'that you will understand my motives for divulging the following piece of information. Her ladyship is visiting her sister, Mrs St Auby, in Taunton. She has sent a message to the effect that she expects to set out for home the day after tomorrow.'

James's face broke into a grin. 'Thank you, Fordyce. You're a good man! I know you have your mistress's best interests at heart, and I assure you that in that we are at one!'

Fordyce could not be said to have smiled, but he almost did. 'Very good, sir. Shall I give orders for the carriage to be prepared?'

James laughed. 'Certainly, Fordyce.' He turned to look at Caroline and Marcus as Fordyce made his stately exit from the room. 'We are all three going on a journey to Ottery!'

Marcus groaned. 'You push the bounds of friendship a long way, James! In the last few weeks you've dragged us halfway across the country!'

James came across the room to them. His face was alight with amusement and a new determination now that he could at last plan a course of action. 'Patience, Marcus! I know you would both wish to be present at my wedding! Here is what we shall do...'

It was a sunny afternoon on the road to Ottery. The sky was a bright, clear azure without a cloud in sight and a light breeze blew across the levels, carrying the scents of summer.

The brilliant splendour of the day suited Alicia's mood ill. She had spent a miserable few days visiting Annabella, who had been loud in her discussions of their father's death and tiresomely superior about her own married state. It was easy to see, however, that matters were not very happy in the St Auby household. Although Annabella had proved to be Bertram Broseley's sole heir, his fortune had not been as great as expected and tempers were short.

Annabella's ill-concealed enquiries about Alicia's future plans all too obviously stemmed from her own self-interest, so in the end Alicia had told her that she was thinking of retiring from Society and living as a recluse. Annabella had appeared delighted, pressing her to stay as long and as often as she wished, exchanging a glance of obvious complicity with her young husband. Alicia had felt vaguely sickened and was glad her visit was but a short one.

Now, of course, she had ample time to consider her own situation. Once the shock of her abduction had faded, she had chafed at the idea of sitting waiting for James to come back to Chartley. She really did not feel that she could bear to face another proposal from him. Would he forever be rescuing her from the consequences of her own folly? It was intolerable to consider. Despite her own deep feelings for him, Alicia was even more determined that he should feel under no obligation to offer for her. If the only way to avoid him was to live retired, she would quite happily do so. She even considered living abroad in order to ensure that she kept out of his way. It was a miserable thought, but it had to be considered. Once James realised that she was determined not to accept his suit, surely pride would ensure that he left her in peace?

Alicia was so lost in her thoughts that it was a moment before she realised that the carriage had stopped. They were a couple of hundred yards away from the village of Ottery, for she could see

the spire of the church against the sky and the stone walls of the
first cottages. Alicia would have chosen just about anywhere else
to be delayed, the village bringing as it did memories of her first
encounter with James a bare few months before. She sighed with
vexation and pushed the carriage window down.

'Jack! What is going on? Why have we stopped?'

There was a pause before the voice of the coachman, noticeably
expressionless, floated down to her.

'There's a gentleman here wishing to have speech with your
ladyship. He requests that you step down from the carriage.'

A strong premonition seized Alicia. She could not see around
the front of the coach, but then she did not really need to in order
to know who was there.

'Ridiculous!' she snapped. 'I will do no such thing! Drive on
at once, Jack!'

There was another pause before Jack spoke again.

'Begging your pardon, my lady, I cannot.'

'Cannot?' Alicia stuck her head out of the window in exasperation. 'From whom do you take your orders, Jack?'

'Why, from you, ma'am, of course.' Jack sounded infuriatingly
placid. 'The trouble is, my lady, that the gentleman has a pistol.'

Inside the carriage Miss Frensham heard this and began to twit-
ter. She had been extremely highly strung ever since the episode
at the inn outside Bath, where she had spent a very uncomfortable
time until being rescued by Marcus Kilgaren.

'Oh, Lady Carberry, I cannot bear it! Do as he says, I implore
you!'

Alicia ignored her. 'You surely cannot believe that he would
use it, Jack! Drive on, I say!'

'I have a responsibility to my passengers and for the horses,
ma'am,' the coachman returned. 'I cannot risk injury or damage.
Please dismount, ma'am.'

Alicia slammed the window shut in fury and wrenched the door
open. There was no doubt about it—she would have to face James,
for she was sure it was he. As she let down the steps he came
alongside the carriage, smiling wickedly at her furiously flushed
countenance.

'Alicia, did your grandmother never tell you that it is very bad *ton* to cause a scene on a public highway?'

Alicia's voice was squeaky with annoyance. 'You are the one causing the scene, Mullineaux, with this outrageous behaviour!'

'Then step aside to speak to me, my love,' James said whimsically, 'before I add to the scandal further by dragging you bodily from your carriage!'

Miss Frensham, an interested bystander, gave a little scream. Having been robbed of her chance to defend Alicia on the previous occasion, she threw herself into the part now.

'Oh, that I should ever live to see such goings on on the King's highway! You, sir—' she pointed her umbrella at James '—are a blackguard and a bounder masquerading as an honest gentleman! To think that Lady Carberry should be subject to such an outrage...'

James was smiling broadly. 'Doing it too brown, ma'am! Never fear, I mean Lady Carberry no harm! My apologies for interrupting your journey—Jack will convey you to Ottery Manor, where you will find the Earl and Countess staying with the Squire and Mrs Henley. If you would be so good as to ask them to join us at the church, we may proceed with the nuptials!'

Miss Frensham subsided on the seat, her face the picture of affronted dignity. 'A runaway match! And with the connivance of the Earl and Countess of Kilgaren! Well I never—'

'Just so, ma'am!' James turned back to Alicia and held out his hand with a grave courtesy to help her descend.

Alicia, who had stood by all this time in astonished silence, looked at him thoughtfully. He was looking particularly handsome, but also definitely unyielding. In an undignified tussle of wills or, worse, a physical struggle, she was certain that she would lose. She put her hand tentatively in his and felt his fingers close round hers strongly. There was a glimmer of a smile in the look which he gave her, then he closed the carriage door on Miss Frensham, gestured to Jack, and the carriage set off at a brisk pace, leaving James and Alicia alone in the road.

'Don't say a word!' James ordered as he heard Alicia draw breath to speak. 'Hear me out and then you may say whatever you wish, but do not, I beg you, refuse my offer of marriage before it is even made!'

Unusually persuadable, Alicia remained silent, and after a moment James's stern demeanour relaxed slightly, although he did not let go of her hand.

'On the first occasion that I proposed to you, Alicia, you accepted me without question. Things were very easy then—you knew that I loved you and you trusted me. A lot has happened since then to dispel that love and trust, but I can only hope that it's not too late and that you do still care for me.' He took a deep breath. 'Because, whatever has happened, I know that I have always loved you. I might have pretended otherwise—I tried very hard to convince myself I disliked you—but in the end I knew it was not true. Now *that* is what I should have said when I proposed to you last time and I beg you to believe me, because you have put me to an unconscionable amount of trouble just to find you and say it!'

That sounded more like the real James, Alicia thought as, suddenly shy, she concentrated on one of the large mother-of-pearl buttons on his driving coat. Looking up after a moment, she saw that he was watching her with unwonted seriousness.

'If you are really sure...' she said hesitantly, and was swept into his arms in a way which left no room for doubts.

A breathless, shaken time later, James let Alicia go sufficiently to turn her in the direction of the village and start walking.

'I almost forgot...' The wicked smile was back in his eyes. 'Our wedding guests will be wondering if you are cutting up rough at my high-handed tactics! No doubt Theo March will be trying to decide how long to wait for us! Come along, before I kiss you again in the middle of the road and scandalise this entire village!'

'James!' Alicia stopped dead in the road. 'You really meant what you said to Miss Frensham, then...you had arranged the wedding before you even asked me?'

'How many times am I expected to ask?' James enquired with perfect reasonableness. 'Twice you have rejected my suit with no consideration for my feelings and I did not intend to give you the chance to do so a third time!'

'And now,' Alicia said, looking down at her crumpled green

travelling dress with disfavour, 'I am expected to get married in this, and I don't doubt that I look a shocking fright!'

James removed a leaf from her hair. 'Indeed, my love, you look delightful! You had all the traditional trappings of a wedding at your marriage to George Carberry—this time I hope you will accept that the advantages of the groom far outweigh any superficial considerations of dress or decoration!'

'How obviously complacent you are,' Alicia marvelled, trying to sound cross. 'And to think I have not even said that I love you!'

James gave her a look which made her retreat a step. 'Not in so many words,' he said thoughtfully as he followed her, 'but I am reasonably certain! Perhaps, however, I should put it to the test—'

Alicia warded him off with both hands. 'I am content to admit it!' she said, with a wary look for an old crone who had emerged from the nearest cottage and was eyeing them suspiciously. 'Save your demonstrations for later, when we do not have an audience!'

As they approached the lichened church, the carriage from Ottery Manor could be seen drawing up at the lych-gate. Alicia stopped again.

'James...'

'Yes, Alicia?' There was a sudden tension in his voice as though he expected that she was about to change her mind.

'When we are married, may we go and see my grandmother straight away? I feel that I have neglected her of late, leaving her alone to hear of Christopher's arrest and now this...I don't want her to hear from anyone else that we are married!'

'Of course.' Tension had given way to amusement in his voice. 'We will go up to London at once—but I hope you do not intend to stay long, for I have other plans for our honeymoon!' He stopped to kiss her again. 'Well, maybe we won't go immediately,' he said thoughtfully, when they had stopped for breath, 'for I also have other plans for tonight!'

He let her go at last very reluctantly. 'We must see if we can get as far as the church,' he finished, a little huskily. 'I have had a special licence burning a hole in my pocket for four days now and if we do not manage to get married soon I cannot answer for the consequences!'

He took her hand and they completed the final thirty yards to the church gate. Theo March was waiting in the church doorway, and his anxious face broke into a smile as he saw the two of them.

'James, my boy! Alicia! I was so glad when James told me... And thrilled to be able to be of service...' He looked at their radiant expressions. 'No need to ask you if you are sure,' he said comfortably, 'for it is written all over your faces!' A slight frown of puzzlement touched his features. 'It's strange,' he reflected thoughtfully, 'for when you met at the vicarage I was sure you did not even like each other. Yet now...'

Alicia, glancing at James a little shyly, saw that he was smiling. He took her hand again. 'We were just extremely good at hiding our feelings, sir!'

Theo beamed. 'So even then...'

'Yes, sir,' James said, giving Alicia a look which made her feel both warm and dizzy at the same time. 'Even then!'

The Dowager Countess of Stansfield was feeling disconsolate. The news of Christopher Westwood's criminal activities had quite overset her and, to make matters worse, Alicia had chosen to bury herself in the depths of Somerset without a word. Only that morning, Mrs Eddington-Buck, in the most gently malicious of terms, had hinted that Alicia's reputation was now so tarnished that she doubted Alicia would ever dare return to Town. Lady Stansfield had given her the rightabout, but when the outraged matron had left she had slumped back in her chair, feeling sick at heart.

She stabbed viciously at her embroidery to give relief to her feelings. To think that she had been driven to take up needlework to pass the time, she who was used to so many more exciting occupations! But there was no Christopher Westwood now to flatter and cajole, no Alicia to bring light and youth into her life.

The door of the drawing-room opened softly, but her sharp old ears still caught the butler's tread.

'I do not wish to be disturbed, Masters!' she snapped irascibly. 'I am at home to no one!'

'Of course, your ladyship.' Masters was even more smoothly deferential than Fordyce. 'However, I am persuaded that you would wish to see the lady and gentleman who are waiting below. Indeed, I have already told them that you will receive them.'

Lady Stansfield stared at him in outraged amazement. Had he taken leave of his senses?

She swelled with wrath. 'Ho, have you indeed? Well, Masters, you can now go and tell them that I am not at home!'

'No, madam.' The butler appeared impervious to her wrath. 'I am certain that you will make an exception.' He executed a slight bow, then turned to throw open the drawing-room door with more than his usual aplomb.

The embroidery fell unheeded from Lady Stansfield's lap as she got to her feet. Alicia ran into her grandmother's arms. She was followed across the room by James Mullineaux with the broadest smile on his face that Masters thought he had ever seen. Not to be outdone, he cleared his throat with great deliberation.

'The Marquis and Marchioness of Mullineaux!' he announced grandly.

* * * * *

THE YOUNGEST MISS ASHE
by
by Paula Marshall

Paula Marshall, married with three children, has had a varied life. She began her career in a large library and ended it as a senior academic in charge of history in a polytechnic. She has travelled widely, has been a swimming coach, and has appeared on *University Challenge* and *Mastermind*. She has always wanted to write, and likes her novels to be full of adventure and humour.

Also by Paula Marshall
in Mills & Boon® Historical Romance™

LORD HADLEIGH'S REBELLION
RINALDI'S REVENGE
THE MISSING MARCHIONESS★
JACK COMPTON'S LUCK
A CHRISTMAS ROSE
(short story within *Safe Haven for Christmas*)
AN UNCONVENTIONAL HEIRESS
MAID OF HONOUR ^
THE BLACK SHEEP'S BRIDE ^

★*The Steepwood Scandal* mini-series
^*The Elizabethan Season* quartet

The author would like to thank the staff of the Wolfson Library of the Royal Zoological Society, London, for their kind assistance in helping to make the visit of my characters to the London Zoo in 1828 as authentic as possible.

Chapter One

'**O**h, do hold still, Margaret,' complained Mrs Ashe
to her daughter, the youngest Miss Ashe, 'you know
how important it is that you look perfectly proper
when Sir Simon comes to propose to you. And here
you are, your hair awry and your gown creased,
and he almost about to arrive. How is it, I ask myself, that however carefully Simpson dresses you, in
half an hour you look as though you have
been bird's-nesting with that wretched Julian
Wentworth?'

Julian was the Rector's son with whom, not so
long ago, eighteen-year-old Margaret *had* enjoyed
bird's-nesting.

'I wish I were going out with Julian, or helping
Wilkinson to pot plants in the hothouse. Anything
would be better than sitting here like a prize heifer,
waiting for its owner to claim it!'

'Dear me, Margaret, you do say the most indeli-
cate things,' moaned her mother, trying to tidy her
daughter's errant and undistinguished brown hair.

'No wonder your London Season was such a disaster.'

For the hundredth time she wished that Margaret was more like her sisters, who possessed bright golden curls, blue eyes, beautiful regular features and elegant figures, together with biddable dispositions. All of them, though virtually dowerless, had made grand marriages in consequence.

'Really, Mama, you mustn't expect me to chaperon Margaret again,' her eldest and most beautiful sister, Jane, Lady Vancourt, had told her mother. 'She makes no effort to please, finds polite society a dead bore and frightens off any pretty young fellow who might wish to marry her. Instead, she spends all her time either in the library with Vancourt's librarian, or in the stables with the grooms. . .

'No, she must stay in Leicestershire and marry some rustic squire who won't object to her lack of manners. Hetty and Phoebe are both of the same mind, so it's no use asking *them* to drag her about, either.'

Margaret, who much preferred to be called Meg, or Meggie, shrugged her shoulders and took her canvaswork from her mother with the instruction that Sir Simon Darrow must find her usefully employed when he arrived. It was, her mother thought despairingly, perhaps Margaret's most annoying attribute that she was so much more capable in everything she did than her elder sisters had been.

Her stitchery, her embroidery, her tending of the flowerbeds, her piano playing, her singing, her riding, as well as her ability to speak both French and Italian so fluently, were all to no avail if she despised marriage and the social round which were, after all, what women of their class were trained and destined for.

Such useful attributes would be sure to please a husband who was looking for sense rather than mere beauty in a wife, so it was more than ever distressing that the youngest and only plain Miss Ashe was so set against marriage.

'No one,' said Meg crossly to her mother, 'seems to understand that I don't want to be married, at least not yet. I'm not at all like Jane and the rest, you know. They never talk about anything serious and would faint if they saw a calf born. . .'

'Margaret!' shrieked her mother. 'What a thing to say! I knew no good would come of your father allowing you to run wild among the grooms and the gardeners. You really do need a husband to keep you in order. And, for goodness sake, don't say anything like that to Sir Simon—or to any other man, for that matter. Your reputation would be gone in an instant, and you would end up like your great-aunt Griselda, an eccentric old maid.'

But happy, thought Meg mutinously, giving a resigned sigh and beginning to stitch doggedly away at the tail of the peacock she had drawn upon a square of fine linen, which was destined to be a firescreen. I daren't upset Mama by telling her that, even though Lord Vancourt was the catch of the Season and Jenny caught him, she is most unhappy.

For what did he do, once the honeymoon was over, but start chasing bits of muslin again, even

though he had vowed to her that his wild days were
behind him. When I lived in London with them they
only met at meal times—and not always then.

But that, she thought, doesn't explain why I don't
wish to marry Simon. After all, so far as I know,
he's never been interested in the muslin trade, and
I'm sure that he would be faithful. Except that, like
the heroine of that old play Papa gave me to read,
The Way of the World, I think it was, I don't want
to dwindle into a wife.

I suppose that it's all Papa's fault for encouraging
me to read and to think, as well as learning what he
calls the womanly arts. Jenny and the others certainly never wanted to talk about anything but
lovers, dress, trimming bonnets and the season, and
poor Papa needed *someone* to talk to!

Mrs Ashe had not ceased to harangue her about
how she should behave before, during and after she
had accepted Simon's proposal and was about to
become young Lady Darrow instead of the youngest
Miss Ashe.

'It will be such a relief to have all four of you
married,' she proclaimed. 'And all of you so well,
particularly since you—'

She stopped and coloured, realising it was
scarcely tactful to tell Margaret quite so bluntly that
her value in the marriage market had been so low,
not only because of Margaret's lack of obvious
charms, but because the Ashe family had been as
poor as church mice ever since grandfather Ashe
had gambled away all their land and property. He
had left them just enough to live on, but not to

keep Highmount Hall in the state in which their great-grandfather had left it.

'Are nowhere near as beautiful and biddable as any of your more fortunate sisters,' finished Meg for her. 'Say it, Mama. Tell me how lucky I am that Simon is willing to overlook my brown hair, green eyes and lack of figure, and marry me.'

'I am sure, Margaret Ashe, that you are the most contrary child a mother could have the misfortune to give birth to. I will leave you now to do your duty to your name and family,' was all that her unhappy mother could manage in answer. Margaret had always been able to run verbal rings around her.

'If I didn't marry, I should at least do my duty by keeping my name,' retorted Meg perversely. 'But I promise that I will give Sir Simon a fair hearing and then make up my own mind as to whether I accept him or not. Will that do?'

It would obviously have to serve. Before she left her to await Sir Simon's arrival, her mother could not resist offering her yet another piece of advice. 'Do not disarrange yourself once I am gone. A man does so like a tidy woman for his wife.'

But not for his mistress, thought Miss Ashe irrepressibly and irreverently, having had some of London's most notorious ladybirds pointed out to her, including Miss Laura Knight, who had been the *belle amie* of more than one great man. There had been nothing conspicuously tidy about *her*. Quite the contrary. She was more like the lady in the poem by Herrick, which Papa had once begun to quote when Mama had reproached her in front of him for untidiness.

' "A sweet disorder in the dress",' he had murmured slyly.

Only Mama had said sharply to him, 'Fie on you, sir! Not in front of the child.'

Seventeen-year old Meg had looked up the rest of the verse which went on 'kindles in clothes a wantonness'. So perhaps it wasn't surprising that Miss Knight, although richly dressed, had a certain air of invitation about her, which was best expressed by a curl which had sprung free from her otherwise carefully ordered *coiffure*, and a scarf which kept falling away to reveal more of a beautiful bosom than might be considered seemly. Another example, she thought wryly, of her Papa's fatal influence on her speech and conduct.

So she said nothing, and allowed her mother to leave her, unaware that a large part of her daughter's perversity had arisen as a consequence of another conversation between her parents: this time on the previous evening.

Her mother had been expressing surprise at the news that Simon had asked her father for the youngest Miss Ashe's hand in marriage.

Her father had replied in the pleasantly harried voice which he always used to her mother, 'But, my dear, consider. Simon is getting no younger. He is twenty-seven and unmarried. He has only that wastrel cousin, Peverel Darrow, for an heir, and needs a child of his own. Marrying Margaret would be most convenient for him, seeing that he does not wish to waste time running round the London Season, looking for a wife in the marriage mart.

'He knows that our Meg is a sensible girl of good

breeding stock, since all her sisters have provided
their husbands with heirs with commendable prompt-
itude. Besides, given everything, she is the homely
sort who will always be faithful to him. She will be
content to live quietly in the country, since she loves
country pursuits and will never be the belle of the
Season.'

'I had thought,' her mother had said, a trifle plain-
tively, 'that he might offer for Jenny, but he never
did. She married Vancourt instead—which was, of
course, a much better match than any Margaret is
likely to achieve.'

'Marry Jenny? Never. That's not Simon's way.
She was far too flighty for him. No, you may depend
upon it, my dear, my practical and clever Meg is
the one he wishes to marry. And I, for one, do not
blame him. She will make him an excellent wife.
We have trained her well between us.'

No, I shan't, Meg had thought savagely, I shan't
make Sir Simon Darrow a wife at all. He's obviously
only marrying me to have his children because I am
of good breeding stock—like he chooses his cows
and horses, I suppose.

And because I'm convenient. Convenient! As well
as being plain and unlikely to attract any other man
once we are married. Not that I should want to, of
course, but it's horrid to be so taken for granted. I
don't consider any of *that* makes marriage to him
an honour at all.

Not that he was so bad a catch, all things considered, even if he were nowhere near as grand as
Lords Vancourt, Wallasey and Zealand, her sisters'
husbands.

Darrow Hall, its parkland, its tenant farms and adjacent coalfield in the heart of the Leicestershire countryside, not far from where the Quorn hunted, brought in a largish income. He could probably do far better than marry the only ugly sister in a beautiful family. He was a kind man, Meg was sure, but he wasn't the kind man the youngest Miss Ashe wanted, not now.

Now she would rather die an old maid like Great Aunt Griselda than marry him. Let him marry some other plain girl. The good Lord knew that there were plenty of them about for him to choose from. Which all went to prove that the old adage was true: listeners never hear any good of themselves.

Tears had filled her eyes as she had walked desolately away. Oh, if only she had not overheard them! If she had not done so, the prospect of marrying Simon would not have seemed so dreadful—he had always been a kind of jolly brother to her.

What is it that I do want, then? she had asked herself. I don't know. The only thing that I do know is that I don't want to get married—yet. I haven't seen the world. More importantly, I haven't seen anyone in it I wish to marry—marriage being such a lottery.

Now, stricken all over again, she pricked her finger and gave a slight moan just as there was a knock on the door. It was the butler, who announced that Sir Simon Darrow was here to see her if she were in.

'Of course, I'm in,' she replied. 'I couldn't be more in if I tried. Tell *him* to come in, too.'

She tried to smile as the butler bowed Simon

into the room. He was perfectly dressed for such an important occasion, which was also what she had expected. He was always so exceedingly proper in every way. And old. Racing towards his thirties.

With his deep-blue coat, cream breeches that were not skintight, perfectly blacked boots—without gold tassels—and a not-too-elaborate cravat, he was the very model of a country squire, neither carelessly dressed nor a dandy.

He might, Meg conceded, even be thought handsome if you liked big, strong men with harsh faces, grey eyes, slightly hooked noses and dark, waving hair prematurely shot with silver. Her own taste ran to blond Apollos who resembled the milder-looking Greek gods, of whom there were a number of statues in the entrance hall of her run-down home. Her father was considering selling them.

To her astonishment, Simon took her hand and bowed over it as solemnly and reverently as though she were the Season's toast, a beauty of the first water. Which was all a nonsense, of course.

He rose, and when she waved him to a chair, said, in that kind, fatherly voice of his which made him sound so much older than his years, 'Allow me to stand, my dear. I have something to say to you which I think would be better said standing.'

Well, what was she to say to that? Not the truth, which would have been something in the order of, Save your breath, Simon, I have not the slightest desire to marry you! So she said nothing, which was the cue for him to continue. 'My dear Margaret. You will allow me to call you Margaret, will you not?'

He stood there, head slightly bent, waiting for an answer.

What an odd way for him to begin! He had been calling her Meg, or Meggie, ever since she had run behind him in short skirts at the age of five. Then he had been a tall boy of fourteen, come to fly his kite with her big brother Jasper, who was now a cavalry officer in the Army, and she had been a little pest, wailing after them, 'Let me come with you, please. . .'

Or had he? Wasn't it true that lately he had taken to calling her Miss Margaret, as though she were already ninety? She really ought to give him an answer, for his air of pleasant command as he stood before the empty hearth was growing a little strained as a result of her delay.

'I'm sorry,' she stammered, 'I was woolgathering.' Which was hardly a gracious thing to say to a man who had come to propose to her, but never mind that. 'Of course, you may call me Margaret, Sir Simon.'

Belatedly, Meg realised how badly she was behaving. If Margaret, then Simon, of course; and so, politely and inevitably, he told her.

'Oh, I think that I may be Simon again, don't you?' he said. 'Particularly as I have come to ask you something, which I hope will result in what has been a pleasant friendship for both of us becoming something closer, much closer.'

Now his smile had taken on a genuine warmth, softening his harsh face, making him seem younger, more like his true age. If only. . .

If only, what? Meg couldn't think. What she

wanted to do was to prevent him from proposing, but none of the books of etiquette which she had read had ever given her any advice on that. There was a general assumption in them that all sensible young ladies could only have one thing to say in such a situation and that was 'yes'. Would he be very cross when she said 'no'? Might it not be better to say 'yes' and please everyone?

Except herself, of course.

Better to bite the bullet. Let him have his say and then decline him politely. She remembered Jenny making them all laugh in the schoolroom when she had told them how she had turned down some impossible younger son of no fortune. Which was not the same thing at all, for Simon was not a younger son, and he certainly had a fortune, and he did not deserve to be laughed at.

'My dear Margaret,' he was saying. 'I have known you since you were a child, and have watched you grow into a most attractive young lady of great practicality—a virtue which many young ladies lack. . .'

Was she really hearing this? Of course, she knew what he meant. He had seen her doing groom's work with Brutus; potting plants with Wilkinson and helping him to prune shrubs and roses; working in the still room and, once, he had caught her churning butter in their small dairy at the back of the stables.

He surely didn't know that she had been working in the library, listing books for Papa so that he might know which would fetch money if sold and which would not. Or perhaps Papa had told him.

But most attractive? Now that *must* be a joke.

He was ploughing on, listing her virtues which

apparently and mainly included common sense and not much else. How little he knew of her! He was quite unaware of the Meg Ashe who read Minerva Press novels and imagined herself amazingly beautiful—like Jane—and running off with the errant and bedazzled heir to a dukedom, and saving him from the plots of his wicked uncle. . .

'And so,' he finally achieved, 'seeing that we have always been great friends, I thought that we might seal that friendship by becoming man and wife. Make me a happy man, Margaret, by accepting the hand which I offer you.'

At least he didn't go down on one knee as Jane had said Vancourt had done. Instead, he put his large and shapely hand out to her, doubtless certain that she would take it—and him.

Now that the moment for refusing him had come, Meg found that she had no heart for it. Yes, he had been a good and kind friend and his grim face no longer looked so grim. It was the face of the patient young man who had always had time to talk to her, lift her on to her horse, and make up for the fact that she had lost her brother Jasper to the Army.

He had always been kind to her—unlike her sisters. Simon, who had shown her how to hold his pet macaw and stroke his naughty monkey, trophies his sailor uncle had brought him from strange lands overseas. Simon loved all animals.

Alas, while she hesitated, he settled the matter for her and, in Jasper's slang, dished himself.

He smiled encouragingly and said, 'Come, my dear girl, do not be coy. This is not like you. I know how forthright you are, how free from the fashionable folly of most young women—how little you value sentimental flim-flam. Give me your answer.'

He meant it kindly, no doubt, Meg thought afterwards.

He believed that he was offering her a compliment by differentiating her from the pretty girls who were allowed to dither charmingly, prevaricate and titter before they made an answer. Had he not spoken so, she would have accepted him, and her whole life—and his—would have been different.

After all, she knew him to be a good man, kind even to his tenants when many landowners were not. He had never taken part in the careless round of pleasure like many young men of his station. He would make a splendid husband and father.

Alas, all her life she had been 'only Meg', and, in a sense, the manner of his proposal had betrayed that, to him, too, she was different from her sisters. So he had spared her—spared her!—'sentimental flim-flam'. Oh, if only. . . And that 'if only' had her disregarding his offered hand so that he dropped it, his face beginning to change a little, becoming sterner, the kind smile disappearing.

'I'm sorry, Simon,' she faltered, her voice breaking a little, 'but I have always thought of you as a brother, never as a husband.' Well, that at least, was true. 'So I am sure that, on reflection, you will agree that it would be wrong for me to consent to be your wife. I am sure, also, that there are many young ladies who would be pleased to accept you, but I cannot.'

'And this is your considered answer? You have

made it very quickly—you do not wish to ask for time to reflect on my offer?' His face had darkened, but to Meg's relief his voice was as cool and calm as ever.

'Yes, it is my considered answer. I do not think that I shall wish to change my mind.'

'Then I am sorry, Margaret. I had thought that we might deal well together as man and wife.'

Deal well together! Where was love? Where was passion in that? Vancourt might have been a deceiver, but Wallasey, Hetty's husband, had looked at her, and she at him, with such fire in their eyes. Where was Simon's fire when he looked at her? And, more to the point, where was hers when she looked at him?

'Your father thought. . .' Simon began. For once Meg saw him at a loss, which surprised her.

He stopped, started again. 'Your father thought that you would be very happy to accept me. He knows that we share the same interests—which is a good foundation for marriage.'

Meg thought fleetingly of kneeling beside Simon and his herdsman as they examined a newborn calf. Of his tenderness for the calf, and the pride with which he had shown it to her. He had told her that it was the first of a new breed. It occurred to her that he had never talked of such things to Jenny, to whom her mother had thought that he might propose.

Even so, she had made up her mind. She was tired of being the youngest Miss Ashe, taken for granted. She quailed a little at the thought of what her parents would say when they heard that she had refused such a desirable marriage, but it was her life, not theirs, and she was not afraid to live with the consequences.

In many ways Simon Darrow knew the youngest Miss Ashe very well, even if he did not know enough of her to frame his proposal correctly. He could tell by the set of her face, the tilt of her head, her whole posture, that her mind was made up. She would not have him. Or at least, not now. He was a patient man, he told himself and there would be another day—when she was a little older, perhaps, and marriage did not seem so daunting.

He would wait.

'Refused him!' her mother almost shrieked at her when Simon had left, his carriage disappearing down the drive. 'You wicked, thoughtless child! You are unlikely ever to get a better offer—or, indeed, any offer at all, considering how little *you* have to offer!'

Her father was more measured, and kinder in his speech, but Meg could tell at once how disappointed he was.

'Oh, Meggie,' he said sorrowfully, 'I thought you liked Simon. You have been friends for so long, and he would make you the best of husbands. On the other hand, it is your life, and I don't believe in arranged marriages, or I would have arranged your marriage to Simon.'

There was nothing she could usefully say to that, but, 'I don't think that I love him, and I'm not yet ready to be married.'

Her mother made a great scoffing noise, but her father looked thoughtful, and nodded.

'You may be right, my child. You are not like

your sisters.' He paused, then said rapidly before her mother could speak again, her colour high, her face set in lines of temper, 'My dear,' and now he was addressing his wife.

'My sister, Léonie, is coming to stay with us shortly. I think that it would be helpful if we asked her to take Meg back to Paris with her when she leaves. It would be good for her to learn to live away from us and her sisters. She has grown too used to being the youngest—and the least considered. A change of air might work wonders.'

Mrs Ashe's expected snort of disagreement would have amused Meg at any other time.

'*Margaret* does not need pampering. She needs informing what her duty is, and doing it. You must order her to write at once to Sir Simon and tell him that she has changed her mind. Going to Paris with Léonie, indeed! What will that achieve other than to convince her that she may do as she pleases—and be rewarded for it.'

Mr Ashe passed his hand wearily over his face. He knew that his wife detested her sister-in-law Léonie. Not only had she married a French *émigré* Vicomte and changed her name from an unpronounceable English Leonora to a pronounceable French Léonie, but she had the effrontery to be charming, civilised and witty—a great lady, in every sense. Everything, in fact, Mrs Ashe considered, which was not sturdily English.

'I have made up my mind,' he announced, his tone as mild as he could make it. 'If Léonie will agree to take her, Meg shall go to Paris.'

'Oh, I know that you only call her Meg to annoy

me,' her mother proclaimed. 'But you will have your way, I suppose, as she does.'

'No one,' said Meg, 'has asked me whether I wish to go to Paris.'

'Now, Meg,' said her father. 'Is that a declaration that you do not wish to go—or simply one of independence? If the latter, then I will ask you.'

She smiled. All was well again. Papa was not really cross with her; perhaps he even understood something of what had made her refuse Simon. He was already making the kind of mild joke that her mother would never understand.

'Really, Mr Ashe! Tell her what you wish her to do. Do not raise her spirits by asking her anything. *That* is what has brought us to this day!'

'Yes, Papa, I will go with aunt Léonie, if she will have me,' Meg said swiftly, in an attempt to prevent her mother from continuing to berate her father. To see Paris! Recently defeated at Waterloo though the French had been, Paris was still the *Ville Lumière*, the city of light and culture.

'Then that is settled,' replied her papa, equally swiftly, ignoring her mother's scoffing.

'Light in the attic, both of you. Nothing good will come of it, I can tell you, Margaret being what she is and Léonie what she is.'

And so it was decided.

Aunt Léonie, when she arrived at Highmount Hall in her usual continental state, took one look at a dejected and rumpled Meg and agreed that Paris was the only cure for such determined megrims.

'What is it, child?' she asked Meg when they

were alone. 'Are they determined to wed you to some elderly ogre?'

Meg shook her head. 'No, not at all. It was Sir Simon Darrow—Jasper's friend, who lives nearby—whom they wanted me to marry.'

Inwardly, she was marvelling at her aunt. Would she ever be like her? She made her beautiful sisters look like dowdy milkmaids, and even if she went to Paris to be groomed by Aunt Léonie—for that, of course, was what Papa intended—would she ever achieve such effortless elegance?

Her aunt had dark hair and green eyes, exactly like her own, but her resemblance to Meg ended there. She was so absolutely, exquisitely polished: a perfect example of Parisian chic and sophistication. Her spoken English now had a pretty accent to it—which added to her attractiveness.

Meg could see at once why her mother resented her husband's sister so much. She was almost frightening in her total command of life. The fact that she was a rich widow was yet another offence to be added to the long list that Mrs Ashe kept.

'Ah, yes. I remember. Somewhat older than you are. Exactly the right age for a husband for you. A good man—and kind. So why the refusal?

'I don't know.' Meg's eyes filled with tears. 'I wake up in the night sometimes, and wish that I had said yes. And then by morning I think no again. I believe that the real truth is—and Papa agrees with me—that I am not yet ready for marriage.'

'But not your mother? She would have you married and off her hands. Hmm.' She pulled Meg to her feet—they were alone in the big drawing-room—and held her away so that she was looking at her from a distance.

'I agree with you. You are so raw, so young, so *farouche*. Your Papa tells me that not only are you clever, but that you are practical as well, and that is why Sir Simon wishes to marry you. Tell me, are you tired of being clever and practical? Is that why you refused him? Do you wish to be, oh, so pretty and flirt, and have the young men at your feet, la, la?'

'Sometimes.' Meg was honest. 'The truth is, I don't know what I want.'

'Then you shall come to France with me and you shall find out. I shall make such a fine lady of you that no one will know you—and then, perhaps, you may come to know yourself.'

And when I do, what then? thought Meg, who was not sure that she wanted to go to Paris to learn to be a fine lady, until her aunt said,

'I will make you someone who will eclipse your sisters, for you have character and they do not.'

Oh, that did it, did it not! For then she would no longer be 'only Meg', the youngest Miss Ashe. Who knew what the future might bring?

'Yes, I will come to Paris with you,' Meg said, hanging her head.

Her aunt put her finger beneath her chin, saying briskly, 'No slouching, mind, no round shoulders, for deportment will be your first lesson.'

Meg had set her foot on a new path in life and she had no idea where it would take her, nor what pains, as well as pleasures, she would find as she walked along it.

Chapter Two

'**I**f you must know, I am at *point non plus*, my dear, and I have no one to turn to—except you. I would never have thought, years ago,' she went on slowly, 'that. . .' Jane, Lady Vancourt paused, and looked across the room at Marguerite de Vaux, Madame la Comtesse de Mortaine, widowed these two years, who stood in the bow window of the drawing-room at the Vancourts' Piccadilly home, a book in her hand.

How to finish her sentence without saying the unsayable, '. . .I would need to ask you, of all people, for help and advice,' but something in the calmly serene expression on her sister's face stopped her.

Instead, she began again.

'I know that I was foolish to do what I did. But, as I suppose you know, Vancourt has never done me the honour of being faithful to me, not since the day we were married. I was so bored with being dull and faithful and good, and all the things that perfect wives are supposed to be.

'When Peverel Darrow made such a dead set at me, I was foolish enough to give way for once and have an *affaire* with him. Such a mistake. And I made it worse by writing him letters—and now he is blackmailing me with them. Well, aren't you going to say something?'

'Only, why Peverel Darrow, of all people? You have known for years what a charming rogue he is, never to be trusted. Did his pretty face seduce you? It can't have been his character—*that* is not pretty at all.'

'Easy for you to talk,' retorted Jane. 'I suppose that you were never tempted before André died— and not since, either.'

Her sister did not answer her, simply shook her head, put down her book and arranged herself carefully on the sofa opposite Jane, who stared at her in frank disbelief. Such coolly charming perfection of appearance and manner was an art in itself.

Marguerite's chestnut-coloured hair, smoothly polished and sleek with golden lights in it like a ripe conker, enhanced her green eyes. It was dressed in the latest, severer style, without clustering ringlets and the usual deep fringe. The lack of curls emphasised the austere planes of her face, giving it a grave and individual attractiveness.

'You are so like Aunt Léonie,' burst from Jane, 'so much so that it's almost unnatural.'

'*Vraiment*? Truly? And you are so like Mama— as are Hetty and Phoebe. One of us had to resemble Papa's family.'

'And that is not what I meant—it is your manner which is most like hers, as you must know.'

Marguerite inclined her head. 'What I do know—'
and her tone was gentle '—is that you need my
help. What can I do for you?'

Recalled to the point, Jane resumed her sad story.
'He has threatened to send my letters to Vancourt
unless I pay him five hundred pounds—when he
promises to return them. Despite the fact that
Vancourt trades with every member of the muslin
set and has a *maîtresse en titre* as well, he would
never forgive me for having an affair. He would
send me into the country forever.

'But. . .' and her voice degenerated into a wail
'. . .I can't raise five hundred pounds, and he has
told me that unless I pay it over to him at Lady
Leominster's reception tomorrow evening, he will
offer them to Vancourt for the same amount, and if
he refuses he will sell them to Bayes who will pub-
lish them in his Radical paper as evidence of
aristocratic corruption, and the need for reform. It
might even bring the government down.'

Despite herself, Marguerite began to laugh. 'Oh,
I doubt whether your letters will bring the Ministry
down—' Vancourt was a minor member of the cabinet '—but I agree, the scandal would be *formidable*.
Yes, I will help you. Do not trouble yourself about
the money, I will lend you that.'

'Oh, thank you, thank you. I know it's a great
deal to ask, but I wonder if you would take my
place, hand him the money and collect the letters?
I haven't the courage to face him. I'm sure I would
do something stupid. . .but you. . . Oh, please,
say yes.'

Marguerite had no wish to do any such thing, but

Jane had dropped her face into her hands and had begun a low dry sobbing which was more distressing than loud watery keening would have been.

'Yes,' she said, at last. 'Tell me exactly where your rendezvous is tomorrow.'

Jane sprang to her feet and flung her arms around her sister. 'Oh, thank you, thank you. I am to meet him in Lady Leominster's Chinese room tomorrow evening at ten of the clock. Oh, I knew that you wouldn't let me down! After all, we meant a great deal to one another when we were children, did we not? I am on my high ropes that you have returned to England in time to help me.'

Marguerite de Vaux, Comtesse de Mortaine, who, after eight years in France, was no longer 'only Meg', the youngest Miss Ashe, but a great lady of consequence in her own right, smiled a wry smile as she stared across the room at a group portrait of Lord and Lady Vancourt and their two children, prettily disposed in an Arcadian garden. Whatever she had expected when she returned to England, it was not this. Neither the knowledge of how much she had changed, or how little Vancourt and Jane had!

'There, there,' she said, as though she were comforting a child. 'No need to worry.'

'Oh, what a tower of strength you have become, Margaret. Whoever would have thought it when we were children together? You were such a gauche little thing. And you have become quite a beauty, too. Vancourt was making sheep's eyes at you, as I'm sure you noticed.'

'And that's a Banbury tale,' retorted Marguerite

de Vaux, who still thought of herself as Meg, the youngest Miss Ashe, 'that I am a beauty. I make no such claim for myself. And you may rest assured that I have no designs on Vancourt, or anyone else for that matter. I am content to remain a widow.'

'You've no need to. Others will make the claim of beauty for you. As for being a widow, that is the one thing about you which I do criticise. After all, André died over two years ago, and here you are, still in lilac, still in half-mourning.'

'It suits me,' said her sister, as simply as Meg Ashe would once have done.

'True, it goes with your eyes. How was it that, when you were a girl, we never noticed how beautiful they were?' sighed Jane who, at least, Meg thought, had the decency not to be jealous of her now that the tables were turned. For between two children, three miscarriages and Vancourt's overt unfaithfulness, she had not worn well.

The pretty plump girl with blonde ringlets and blue eyes had become faded and harried-looking before she had reached thirty-five. Meg, on the other hand, knew how much she had changed and bloomed after two years grooming in Paris by her aunt Léonie, her four years of marriage to André de Vaux, and her two years of widowhood.

Apparently inconsequentially, Jane asked, 'Have you spoken to Simon Darrow since you returned to England?'

Simon Darrow! How long was it since she had thought of him? In those early, dreadful days in Paris spent trying to live up to Aunt Léonie's apparently impossible demands and commands, Meg had thought of him often. Mostly in terms of bitter regret that, had she accepted his offer, she would have been back in the country with him and his dogs, cows and horses, instead of being pulled in and out of fine clothes, and being rebuked for her gauche behaviour.

At what point had the change come when she had turned from Meg to Margaret to Marguerite, Aunt Léonie's charming and amusing niece, who had half the eligible young men in Paris at her feet? Not until after a long and arduous tutelage, that was for sure! And when exactly had she forgotten Simon, so that to hear his name was something of a shock?

'He's never married, you know,' said Jane, watching her sister for some kind of telltale response. But, as usual, she was wasting her time. Behind that calmly perfect mask acquired in France, nothing showed.

'No, I didn't know.'

'And he's an MP, now. Doing well, Vancourt says. Won't be long before they offer him a post in the Government.'

Simon an MP! Simon, who always claimed that he loathed London and politics whenever the suggestion had come up in the days when she had known him. What a turn-up! Had he changed, too?

'He's greatly changed,' Jane offered, mind-reading a little, perhaps. 'Vancourt always thought him a bit of a prig—particularly where women were concerned. But he's certainly not a prig these days. Quite the rake, or so the rumours say.'

Simon a rake! Staid, somewhat solid, if not to say stolid, Simon Darrow. Decidedly, whilst she was out of England, forgetting all that she had left behind, things had changed more than somewhat.

What surprised Meg most of all was that learning that Simon was a rake hurt her—it was as though, at the back of her mind, she had always thought of him as her husband, so that to hear Jane say that he was a womaniser gave her a strong feeling of betrayal!

Which was ridiculous, to say the least. For if she had the right to turn herself into a Frenchified belle, and to marry a rich and powerful French aristocrat, then Simon certainly had the right to turn himself into a ladies' man.

For once, Meg was nonplussed. Fearful that she might betray her odd turn of thought to Jane, she was carefully considering her answer when Vancourt entered with a young man at his heels.

Watching him carefully, Meg saw that Jane's statement that he was attracted by her was no less than the truth. His manner to her was gallant in the extreme, and when he introduced the blond young man as 'my cousin, Mr Will Osborne', Will's answer betrayed that Vancourt had spoken of her in admiring terms.

'Delighted to make your acquaintance, Madame la Comtesse,' he said, bowing over her hand, his accent atrocious. 'I have heard so much of you, and all to your advantage.'

Meg smiled and inclined her head to him graciously in a gesture which Meg Ashe would have mocked, but which slew young Mr Osborne, who turned scarlet at her graciousness. He decided that all he had heard of the Comtesse de Mortaine's charm, sophistication and *savoir faire* was true.

'Vancourt tells me that you are accompanying him and Lady Vancourt to Lady Leominster's ball tomorrow evening. You would do me a great honour if you agreed to allow me to act as your escort.'

Jane watched, fascinated, as yet another pretty young fellow threw himself metaphorically at her sister's feet. She was no more surprised than Meg herself.

In France it had, even before she had married André, seemed perfectly natural for her to enter a room and capture the attention of nearly every man in it, but here in England—that was a different matter. She had feared that the shadow of being the youngest Miss Ashe might still hang over her and affect her confidence. But no such thing!

She took Will's homage as her due, and accepted his offer. She would arrive at her first public appearance in London on the arm of one of the Season's greatest catches. Jane had already told her that Will was the cousin and heir of the Earl of Stanyon and every mother in the marriage market was desperate to secure him for her daughter!

And if she saw Simon Darrow—but why was she thinking about Simon? He was part of her past, which was dead and gone.

Another dead bore of an evening, thought Sir Simon Darrow glumly. Ever since he had broken with Caroline, Lady Kenilworth, that lovely widow, who had been determined not only to add him to her list of conquests, but to marry him as well, he had found such occasions as the Leominsters' ball wearying.

Every Mama in society was in headlong pursuit
of him.

It was not that he hadn't enjoyed his six years as
an MP, although he hadn't expected to. Before his
first Season had begun, he had decided that the end
of it would see him married, and now, here he was,
still a bachelor—and in the eyes of the polite world,
a confirmed one.

He had taken up a position near the top of the
stairs, watching Lord and Lady Leominster greet
their guests: the strains of a waltz came from the
ballroom behind him. George Vancourt was
escorting a small party on to the landing at exactly
the same moment that his cousin Peverel
accosted him.

'How do, Sim? Thought you might not be here.
Hard day in the Commons, wasn't it?'

Peverel had Jasper Ashe with him, a blond giant
resplendent in full regimentals. It was some years
since he had seen Jasper, although as boys they had
been chums, always in and out of scrapes. Then
Jasper had joined Wellington's army, in time to see
action at Waterloo, and they had drifted apart.

'Happy to see you again, Darrow. How many
years has it been?'

'Too many,' said Simon cheerfully—he preferred
Jasper's Darrow to Peverel's over-familiar Sim—
and then stopped.

His attention had been caught by an unknown
woman in Vancourt's party. Her escort was that
eager young puppy, Will Osborne, who was visibly
dangling after her, adoration written in his eyes. She
was just under middle height, with a perfect figure,

a slightly haughty carriage and was dressed with extreme elegance and perfect style in amethyst silk; a colour which enhanced both an ivory face of great character and her lustrous chestnut hair.

The jewels she wore were discreet, not vulgar, but were worth a small fortune none the less. A tiny tiara of amethysts and diamonds adorned her shapely head, amethyst and diamond tear drops her ears. A single amethyst on a thin silver chain beautified a neck like that of a swan in its elegance, and a slender bracelet of the same stones showed to advantage an exquisite tiny hand. She was carrying a large fan— amethyst coloured, inevitably—with pale mauve lilacs painted on it.

Altogether she was a sight to draw every eye, male or female—and was obviously used to doing so, for the murmur which followed her progress apparently moved her not at all.

Simon drew in his breath. He remarked abruptly to his cousin Peverel, who knew everything and everybody in society despite his dubious reputation, 'Who is the polished piece of perfection with Vancourt who is causing all the excitement?'

For some reason his question appeared to amuse both Jasper and Peverel inordinately. Jasper laughed openly, and Peverel's accompanying smile was more than usually knowing and cynical.

'Come on, Simon,' Jasper said, grinning. 'You needn't bam us. We're old friends, remember?'

'Bam you?' Simon was genuinely puzzled.

So puzzled that Jasper, choking a little, said, 'Doing it too brown, old fellow. It's m'sister—as you well know.'

This merely served to confound Simon the more rather than enlighten him.

'Now *you*'re bamming *me*. That's neither Hetty nor Phoebe and well you know it.'

It was Peverel's turn to try to bait him. It was too good a trick to miss. Simon was usually the one coldly in charge, not the gull which he was now pretending to be.

'Not Hetty nor Phoebe, nodcock, but Margaret— Jasper's youngest sister—the Comtesse de Mortaine. Don't pretend you can't recognise her.'

'Margaret! *That's* Margaret?'

Vancourt's party was passing them at some little distance. The woman whom they claimed was his long-lost Margaret was walking quietly along, her eyes lowered. Suddenly, as though she had become aware that she was being closely watched, she lifted her head to turn to look in his direction, so that Simon caught a glimpse of a pair of brilliant green eyes.

Something clicked in his brain. It was as though Madame de Mortaine had been wearing a mask that had suddenly dropped to reveal a face far different from that which it had hidden. He briefly saw Margaret Ashe again, the youthful hoyden who had followed him and Jasper about.

The look of pain which passed across his face astonished Jasper, who moved between Simon and Peverel so that Peverel should not see it. So, Simon's proposal to Meg must have been more than one of convenience—even if Simon had not consciously known that when he had made it.

He had spoken lightly of it to Jasper when he had

seen him in London a year later, and Jasper had
believed him. After all, Meg had scarcely been a
great prize, either in looks or wealth, and Simon
could have been expected to marry both.

Now, of course, she was one of the greatest prizes
in society!

What had they done to her? His Margaret. His
Meg. . .his Meggie. The pet names they had called
her by, years ago, sprang unbidden to Simon's mind.
Worse still, what had she done to turn herself into
a fashion plate, a sophisticated houri? By all appearances she was no better than she should be! Oh, he
knew them well, these cool and haughty sirens;
knew all the tricks they used to ensnare men. And
his Margaret—for she should have been his—had
turned into one of them.

When was it that he had realised that he had loved
the wild little girl who had refused him because he
had made such a ham-fisted mess of his proposal?
He looked away from Jasper and Petterel. Jasper,
quick-witted, thought that there was only one thing
to do, and that at once. Simon must take his
medicine.

He seized him by the arm, and said, 'Come on,
old fellow, and meet her again. How long is it since
she left England? Eight years, is it not? You could
scarcely have expected her to remain the same, could
you now? Especially after living for so many years
in France and marrying into their nobility.'

Whilst he spoke, he was urging Simon into the
ballroom and towards Vancourt's party. By now
Simon had sufficiently recovered himself to remark
coolly, 'I should never have known her. Not only

is she not in the least like you and your sisters, but she doesn't resemble the little girl I used to know in any way.'

'True,' said Jasper, nodding vigorously, to be supported by Peverel who was walking with them, determined to see the fun when Simon met Meg again. He had been greatly relieved when she had turned his cousin down. For, no doubt about it, had she not done so she would have dished any hopes that he had of inheriting Darrow Hall and all that went with it.

The Ashes were a prolific lot, and by now Simon would have been the father of a number of squalling brats, and all of them—to spite his former heir— sons. No need to think that Simon might up and propose to the merry widow, his former choice of wife, if the expression on his face, when he had discovered who the fancy madam was, was any guide.

Which was exactly what Simon was thinking, agreeing for once with his wastrel heir. The nearer he got to the woman who had once been Margaret Ashe, the less he liked the look of her. Meretricious in every vein of her body, and proud of it, was his savage conclusion. For some reason that he didn't understand, he had a burning desire to punish her for having changed so much that she was unrecognisable.

Oh, but she had recognised him, without a doubt! For as he drew near and she saw him coming, her eyes widened, and there was the smallest, slightest shift in the hands which held the big fan.

Simon had found, during his years as an MP and

in London society, that he could read not only animals, but also men and women. Now, eight years later, he would not have made the mistakes in his proposal which had lost him Margaret—except that now he did not wish to propose to her. By no means.

He was immediately before her, bowing, as Jasper said, 'Marguerite, I have brought over an old friend to see you,' and as she did not respond other than by a cool nod of that haughty head, and the holding out of a small hand to be kissed, he added, 'You remember Simon, surely?'

Marguerite, Jasper had called her. What the devil kind of name was that for Meggie Ashe? It took him all his strength not to say so. Instead he remarked, politely, if coldly, 'I would not have known you, Margaret, without Jasper's help—and scarcely with it.'

'Oh, I knew *you*,' she responded, unsmiling, and withdrawing the hand which he had refused to kiss. 'You have become London fine, I admit, but that has added polish, not change.'

She even had the temerity to speak English with the slightest of accents—something which doubtless charmed fools like Will Osborne, who stood there, worshipping her. It didn't charm Simon Darrow, and he would have liked to tell her so. At the same time, something inside him was wondering why he was so angry with her.

Jasper had drawn Peverel away, and was talking to Vancourt, another old friend of both of them. Judging by the way he was looking at Madame la Comtesse he was yet another of her admirers. Well, good luck to him, unless she was as cool in bed as she was in public. . .in which case he wouldn't be lucky. Damn him either way!

Margaret knew only too well that Simon was seething with rage. Like him, she had learned to read people in the years since she had last seen him. She had not lied when she had said that she recognised him. The only changes in him were for the better.

She had forgotten, or perhaps had never really understood, how attractive his harsh craggy face and powerful body were. There was more silver in his glossy black hair, but that merely served to add to his attraction, not diminish it.

He was quite different from the men she had known in Paris, and quite unlike her late husband, that blond Apollo.

'I understand that you are now a member of Parliament. When we last met, you always said that you would never be tempted into public life, that you had no talent for it, but Vancourt tells me that you are in line for a government post. Quite a transformation.'

'You are not the only one allowed to change,' riposted Simon drily. 'It was pointed out to me that if I did not like the way that the country was run, then I had a duty to take up a position where I might try to change it.'

She inclined her head, ignoring the first part of his answer. 'Very proper of you, and much to be commended. I trust that leaving your rural interests for so much of the year was not too great a wrench.'

Such patronage! And from little Meg Ashe! Simon's thoughts were savage. His face registered only cold politeness, so that something wrenched inside Meg. Had they descended to this? Banal and boring chit-chat which she could practise in her sleep. She was not surprised when, oh so frostily, he replied in kind.

'It is my rural prowess, I believe, which has given me a Parliamentary reputation. But—unlike many— I have not said goodbye to my roots. I am still Darrow of Darrow, you understand, not a fine gentleman.'

Unspoken were the words, 'As you are a fine lady who *has* renounced her roots!'

'Ah, but you are a remarkably good imitation of a fine gentleman, are you not, *Sir Simon*?' Meg paused, then added meaningfully, 'In every way. . .or so rumour says.'

They were icy with each other, but Jasper, who had rid himself of Peverel and was watching them both, could almost feel the fire beneath the ice. Hostility was in every line of their bodies, although their faces gave nothing away. That last *double entendre* from Meg, twisting Simon's tail about his amorous career, was enough to have any right-minded man thirsting for her blood.

Why in the world were they behaving in this odd fashion? Were they both light in the attic? He had hoped that, once Simon and Meg met again, they would realise that they were made for each other.

But were they?

Meg had turned into a haughty belle with a cruel tongue and Simon into a rake. Who would have thought that possible eight years ago?

Only by hanging on to her self-control as hard as

she could was it possible for Meg not to flinch at the silent fury on Simon's face after she had flung her insult at him. But it was her own fault, was it not? Whatever had provoked her to be so unpleasant to him?

'My dear Madame la Comtesse,' he told her softly, 'it would please me greatly to demonstrate to you the truth of your innuendo in the most time-honoured fashion! You understand me, I'm sure.'

So she did. But she had never thought to hear Simon be so unpleasantly cool to her, and at the same time offer to seduce her!

'Oh, I do hope not.' Her tone was as sweet as her smile. 'Sometimes, I fear, my understanding proves faulty. A feminine frailty, perhaps.'

Frail! She was as frail as a six-foot-tall Grenadier Guardsman, and apparently about as sensitive! What, though, was appalling was that the mere sight of her, added to his covert suggestion, sent a spasm of desire through him so strong that it was shocking.

For the one thing which he had never done was lust after little Margaret Ashe! But this woman was a different proposition altogether.

He had heard some of the unpleasant gossip about Madame la Comtesse de Mortaine, never thinking— for how could he—that she was *his* Margaret; that she was accustomed to men who wanted nothing more than to bed her, and was happy to oblige them. Damn everything, he now had a burning desire to be obliged, and a determination to achieve it.

Well, she was his Margaret no longer, just a Frenchified barque of frailty, fair game for any man. Fair game for Simon Darrow. He could only hope

that his good friend Jasper Ashe had no notion of
what he was thinking!

'I'm sure,' he returned, his smile both sweet and
false, 'that there is nothing wanting in your understanding which I could not easily supply. You have
only to say the word.'

'But if that word has been torn from my diction-
ary, Sir Simon, what then?'

'That I will lend you mine—to our mutual
advantage.'

Meg was torn between a desire to laugh at his
impudence, and an equally strong desire to slap his
face for his easy supposition that she and virtue
were no longer bedfellows—and endure the scandal
which would follow such a public act.

So this was what Simon Darrow was really like
beneath the mask of virtue which he had shown the
world—and her—eight long years ago. Would she
have accepted him then, had she known? Especially
since she had partly refused him because of his supposed iron rectitude. Now, where on earth had that
gone to? Or had he been a hypocrite then?

An overwhelming desire to end this surprising
conversation before she said something unforgivable
caused Meg to end their tête-á-tête. She raised her
large fan to look at him over the top of it, and said,
'I really must ask you to allow me to leave you. I
see that there are a number of friends present from
my days in France whose acquaintance I wish
to renew.'

Simon stared into the brilliant green eyes which
were, he was sure, mocking him, and murmured as
softly as he could, 'So long as it is understood,

Madame la Comtesse, that this is *au revoir* and not goodbye.'

She lowered her fan for a moment, to reply in kind, 'Oh, that is entirely up to you, sir,' which she was sure was the kind of flirtatious coda which the siren he obviously supposed her to be would make.

Simon almost laughed aloud as she moved away, but refrained out of respect for Jasper's hurt feelings.

'What in the world has happened to your old rapport with Meg, Simon?' Jasper asked mournfully. 'You used to be such friends.'

Simon parried Jasper's criticism of the pair of them by remarking easily, 'Oh, too many years have passed for us to take up where we left off—and I'm not quite sure what our true relationship was then. Meg was such an unformed child.'

Jasper opened his mouth to say something further, then shrugged his shoulders. Oh, to the devil with both of them—no one else would want such a cross-grained pair!

'You're sure that you are really happy to do this favour for me, Meg? It is a great imposition, I know—but I shall be truly grateful.'

'I wouldn't say that I am exactly happy to meet Peverel Darrow for such a reason—but I am willing. Will that do?'

Which was exactly the kind of barbed remark which her sister was fond of throwing into the conversation, was it not? Meg saw by the shadow on her face that she had hurt Jane's feelings. Remorse seized her. Jane's life was unhappy enough without her being needlessly teased.

Dropping her mask of cool control, Meg impulsively put an arm around her sister and hugged her. 'Oh, Jane, forgive me. I'm a little overset tonight. Forget what I said. Remember only that in about an hour, with any luck, you will have your letters back—ready to throw into the nearest fire after you have checked that he has returned them all.'

'Oh, dear, I never thought of that. Surely even Peverel wouldn't do such a thing!'

'Always as well to be sure. Just tell me where the Chinese room is, so that I arrive in time to beard the wolf in his den.'

'Oh, how serene you are! I suppose it is all those years in Paris with Aunt Léonie, and then being married to André. I wish that I possessed your composure.'

Meg forebore to tell her sister the hard price which she had paid to acquire that composure. Later, when she quietly left the Vancourts' party to make her way to the rendezvous with Peverel Darrow, she wondered ruefully whether jousting with him would be easier than jousting with his cousin Simon.

He was far more handsome than Simon, that was for sure, and far more easy in his manner. Where Simon was harsh he was soft—in every way.

Meg found him standing in a dimly lit room, by a fire place flanked by two large bronze urns with roaring Chinese dragons twined around them. The mantelpiece was adorned by a pair of blue and white Chinese vases. All that was wanting was a haughty mandarin to preside over them. Peverel's brows rose in surprise when she entered. Her arrival, instead of that of Jane, did not put him out of countenance.

'Ah, an emissary, I see,' he murmured, offering her a low bow, and motioning her to a seat on to a long divan, which she refused. 'But then, your late husband was a diplomat, was he not? I suppose that you learnt something of his trade. Have you come with a yea or a nay for me?'

Meg lifted the reticule which depended from her waist. She had not done him the honour of acknowledging his bow, or his attempt to take her hand. Instead she took a piece of paper from the reticule, but she did not give it to him as he expected.

'I have here that which you have demanded, sir,' she told him, her voice as frosty as she could make it. 'But I shall not hand this bank draft to you until you give me *all* the letters that you are misusing so wantonly. Blackmail, sir, is not a pretty word, and you are far from a pretty fellow to practise it.'

He bowed again. 'Oh, what a fine lady the little country cousin has become! And so worldly wise. I congratulate you, Madame. Your caution, however, is uneccessary. I am prepared to hand over all the letters, retaining none. I am not a complete villain, you see.'

If it were not for the pain which he had caused her sister, Meg might have been amused by his impudence. Caution had seen her refusing to speak Jane's name, someone might enter, and hear them, and she would rather risk her own reputation— which she knew to be shadowed—than that of poor Jane, who had too many crosses to bear already.

Peverel was also employing caution in naming names—presumably for similar reasons. His eyes on the bank draft which Meg was holding, he pulled from an inner pocket of his fine coat a small packet of letters tied with blue ribbon.

'Reputation restored again,' he had the effrontery to say. 'I need not tell you that burning them would be an excellent notion—never having written them at all, a better.'

Meg did not deign to answer him. It was bad enough to act as a go-between in such a sordid affair without having to endure the excesses of a villain's impudence. He laughed soundlessly at her silence when she handed him the draft, and took the little bundle of letters from him.

As she withdrew her hand, and before she could stop him by moving away, he seized it and kissed it saying, 'Allow me to assure you, Madame la Comtesse, of my utmost admiration for your courage and daring in coming here tonight, and for the manner in which you have behaved. You have surpassed all that I know of you.'

It was plain that, having seduced Jane, he was now prepared to seduce her sister.

To no avail. Meg withdrew her hand as haughtily as she could, gave him a cold stare and averted her head. He was not in the least distressed by her rebuff, merely smiled and murmured, 'One day, Madame la Comtesse, one day you shall give me a different answer. Even the strongest fortress falls at last.'

Still she made him no reply, simply watched him kiss the bank draft, signed by her, proving to him that Jane had not dared to ask her husband for the money, before he left her alone. Meg gave a great sigh, patted her reticule, which now held Jane's letters, and prepared to leave herself.

But as she put her hand on the door knob a sardonic voice said behind her, 'So, Madame la Comtesse, not so discreet after all since you had to hand over money to my rascally cousin Peverel to recover your incriminating love letters and save what is left of your reputation. I cannot say that I admire your taste. . .'

Simon Darrow had been afflicted by an excess of remorse as soon as Meg had left him. How could he have spoken to her so cruelly? What devil had possessed him, so that first he lusted after her and then insulted her because he had done so? Useless to say that she had been as rude to him as he to her. Jasper was right to reproach the pair of them.

The rumours must be wrong. His little Margaret could not have changed so much for the worse. Behind the mask of experience was surely still the frank child she had once been. It had been his duty to find her. Instead, he had most likely driven her away for ever. He was so disgusted with himself that he could no longer bear to be in the company of so many visibly enjoying themselves.

Shame had driven him out of the ballroom and along the corridor to seek solitude. He would have left Leominster House immediately, except that he had engaged to meet Jack, Earl Devereux, later. Jack was coming on from another engagement in order to discuss two matters with him. The first related to the agricultural policy of the present government, which was of great concern to all landowners, and the second to the business of the new Zoological Society of London, which he hoped to join.

He had opened a promising-looking door to discover a dimly lit room furnished in the Chinese style. He remembered that he had been told once that the present Earl's father had been a great Chinese fancier. There was a low divan before an empty hearth. Another, a high-backed one, faced away from the door towards long curtained windows.

Having no mind to be found by any passing busybody, he picked an interesting-looking book from a shelf in a niche by the fireplace, sat on the high-backed divan out of sight of anyone entering, and began to read. . .

And then, after a time, he dozed—he had passed a long and hard day—to be awoken soon afterwards by the noisy entry of someone whistling happily. He peered over the back of the divan to discover that it was his cousin Peverel—on some dubious assignation, no doubt.

For a moment, Simon debated whether to make his presence known, but decided against it. The devil which had possessed him earlier now prompted him to wait in silence in order to discover exactly which light-minded woman it was whom his disreputable cousin was expecting.

Alas, when she arrived, it was none other than Marguerite de Vaux, Countess de Mortaine, late the youngest Miss Ashe!

Oh, how stupid he had been to feel remorseful, to doubt that his fondly remembered Margaret had turned into the lightskirt which gossip said that she was. He was compelled to believe that all that he had heard of her was true: that her husband had died in a duel over a woman's honour, and that woman

his wife. That her conduct was no better than it
should have been, and had brought her husband to
his death.

Every word in the conversation which he was
overhearing struck his heart like a dart piercing it.
What was worst of all was that she should not only
engage in an *affaire* with his worthless cousin, but
that she should be foolish enough to write him incriminating love letters as well.

He was not to know—as Meg did not—that her
care never to mention Jane's name, in order to protect her, had only succeeded in proving to Simon
that his suspicions about her were true. Worse than
that was the knowledge that he had behaved in such
an ungentlemanly fashion by continuing to listen to
their conversation without revealing himself.

He should have announced his presence the
moment that they had begun to speak, but at first
their voices had been low, and he had not been sure
immediately that it was Meg he was overhearing—
and by the time he was, it was too late.

The anger which he felt over his own misbehav-
iour found relief in being turned on Meg—who,
having had an unwanted encounter with one cousin,
was now faced with a verbal duel with the other.

For a moment she was bewildered, then understanding flooded in. Her carefully worded tête-à-tête
with Peverel had only served to convince Simon that
she had been Peverel's mistress; that the letters she
had recovered were hers.

She opened her mouth to confound him—only to
realise that, in order to do so, she would have to
betray Jane who had trusted her. No, indeed, she

would deny nothing. If Simon was intent on believing her to be a Jezebel, then so be it. He did not deserve to know the truth—even if she could tell it.

Oh, she had weathered worse than this, although the sight of his hostile, condemning face was enough to make her feel physically ill. Holding her head high, keeping her voice level and her hands still— she knew that twisting and shaking hands betrayed an inward confusion—she confronted him. He thought that she was Jezebel: then she would behave like her.

'Why, Sir Simon, I do believe that you are jealous of your cousin. Is it because open rascality appears to conquer, whilst hypocritical virtue cannot?' This sword thrust to the heart was all the more cruel for being so calmly delivered. Its effect on Simon was immediate and shocking—it broke the fine control on which he had prided himself all his life.

He was around the divan in a trice, and was upon her, saying hoarsely, 'Why, Madame la Comtesse, seeing that you are any man's whore, why should you not be mine?' His arms were about her, his lips were on hers, and if Meg's first instinctive reaction was to welcome him and his insistent searching mouth, her second and more considered response was to tear her betraying mouth from his and push him away from her, while still retaining her composure.

'No, indeed. I always choose my lovers myself, they do not choose me, and I certainly have no intention of choosing you. You are more of a savage than Peverel was. He, at least, had the decency not to continue to pursue me when he saw that I was no longer willing.'

On hearing this further insult Simon, who had begun to feel ashamed all over again at yet another breach of his precious self-control, lost both his temper and his newly recovered remorse.

'That being so, Madame, if I am the savage you proclaim me to be, then I beg leave to enjoy the privileges of a savage.'

He was almost upon her again before Meg, seeing that she had unwittingly roused a tiger, had it by the tail, and could not control it, ran to the door.

But he was there before her, a strong arm holding it shut, demanding, 'What, may all the world have you, but not I?' A sentence which afterwards, when cold reason ruled him once more, set him shuddering. What in the world had possessed him to make him rant and behave like the villain in a Drury Lane melodrama? And how, in the name of everything precious to him, had they reached such a pass so quickly?

Even at the time, the enormity of his conduct suddenly struck him as he began to take Meg in his arms—to do what? He released her, and stood back, visibly fighting for self-control, so roused was he.

If he continued in this fashion, logic said that there would be only one end, and that something which he had always believed that as a man of honour he could never commit—the rape of an unwilling woman. Whatever had happened to the man of virtue he had once thought himself to be?

Meg refrained from asking him that question, which had also sprung into her mind. She leaned back against the door, paralysed, shocked by her own response to his wildness. One part of her wanted him to go on, wanted to lie in his arms, was hatefully pleased that she was able to rouse the devil in him.

The other, sane, part, said to her, 'If you surrender to him, then afterwards, he will hate both himself and you for such a betrayal of all that he lives by. And do you wish to lie with him in despite, with him thinking you a lightskirt, and you resenting that even as he pleasures you? What would the pleasure be worth that was founded on an untruth? How hatefully fleeting would it be?'

The same thing which had shocked Simon was shocking her: the speed with which they had found themselves in this situation. It was barely two hours since they had met again after eight long years, and here they were, at such surprising odds that they had almost consummated their unruly passion on the floor of the Leominsters' Chinese drawing room!

Still composed, although inwardly shaking, Meg began to try to placate him. 'If I were to assure you that I have nothing to reproach myself with so far as your cousin Peverel is concerned. . .'

Alas, Simon allowed her to say nothing further.

'Oh, no lies, please, Madame. I heard you both— remember? Accept my apologies that I assaulted you so rudely, that was scarcely the act of a gentleman— but I was most damnably provoked, not only by what I had earlier heard, but what you said to me afterwards.'

This only served to enrage Meg once more. She knew that she should leave, that she was in danger of rousing him again, but she could not prevent herself from saying, 'Provoke you, sir? You are as amusing as a comedian in a play by Sheridan.

'In the first place, were you the gentleman you pretend to be, you would have made your presence known when I came in, not skulked in the shadows listening to what was no concern of yours—and then claiming to be provoked by it. In the second place, whatever I said to you was in response to *your* unwarranted conduct, and should have driven you to reconsider your own behaviour and not animadvert on mine!'

Such a piece of cold-blooded legalistic pont-ification in the middle of a passionate amorous encounter, by the woman who had been subjected to attack, apparently struck neither party as at all untoward or odd. On the contrary, Simon replied in kind, saying stiffly, 'You cannot reproach me more than I reproach myself. But I must ask you to subject your own conduct to the same scrupulous examin-ation to which you have subjected mine.'

This was really the outside of enough! To blame her for his own misconstruing of her character! Meg would have stamped her foot had she not been so busy living up to her own legend as a woman of experience whom nothing could annoy or shock.

'It is plain, sir,' she told him, 'that we shall never agree on anything, so that further conversation is useless. Let us try to bring this unfortunate meeting to an end, and agree to avoid one another in future, since intercourse between us appears likely to bring out the worst in us both.'

Simon nodded a miserable assent, bowed, and held the door open for her. So this was how the friendship between the youngest Miss Ashe and Simon Darrow was to end—in hateful antagonism.

Walking along the corridor to the ballroom, looking around her for Jane, to reassure her that her letters were recovered, that her reputation was saved, Meg was astonished to find that her eyes were wet with tears.

Whether they were for herself or Simon, she did not know.

Chapter Three

'I cannot thank you enough, Meg, for what you have done for me. Peverel seems to have returned all my letters—which was more than I expected—and last night when I was alone, I burned them.'

Jane and Meg were seated in the Vancourts' pretty drawing-room, waiting for Jasper and Vancourt to arrive home after a session at a gymnasium run by an ex-member of Jasper's regiment.

'No thanks are required, Jane,' replied Meg, looking up from her work—she was painting Jane's portrait in watercolour. 'I was only too pleased to be able to help you.'

She had told no one, least of all Jane, of her unfortunate encounter with Simon. Since she appeared to be doomed to keep a large part of her life in France a secret from her friends and relatives, to keep quiet about this latest incident should not have seemed too great a burden—but it did. She felt like the old man of the sea himself, his back bowed beneath the weight of his past and his knowledge.

'Now that I can breathe freely again,' Jane continued happily, 'I can spend some time introducing you to as many eligible *partis* as possible. I am sure that you will wish to marry again—life can be hard for a widow, I am given to understand.'

Meg shook her head. 'Oh, no. I have not the slightest desire to remarry, so you may rest easy. And I have found that there are many advantages in being a widow.'

'So you say now, but you may not think so when you are a little older. And there is one match that one would expect you to make, one which we all thought that you would agree to long ago.'

'Really, Jane?' replied Meg with false innocence. 'And, pray, what match is that?'

'Oh, come now. You must know that I am referring to Simon Darrow. Mama and Papa thought it inevitable that you would accept him and were shocked when you did not.'

'I would have been more shocked if I had accepted him,' riposted Meg without looking up from her work.

Jane ploughed on regardless. 'Oh, it wasn't just Mama and Papa, you know. The rest of us, particularly Jasper, were equally surprised. After all, you worshiped him when you were a little girl—you never left him alone.'

'Well, I am not a little girl now, and I don't worship anyone, least of all Simon Darrow. Is that Vancourt arriving?' For there were voices in the corridor outside and this was not a topic which Meg wished to pursue.

It was not Vancourt, however, but Caroline, Lady Kenilworth, come to call in a cloud of French perfume and, Meg naughtily noted, a cloud of false French hair, neatly adjusted to hide her own thinning locks. She was dressed *à outrance*, and had a manner to match.

'I have heard so much about you, Madame,' she trilled at Meg, once the niceties were over, 'and I regret that I never found an occasion to be introduced to you at the Leominsters' ball. Simon Darrow told me that you were staying with your sister, so here I am.'

She strolled across the room to stare at Jane's portrait, which was nearing completion, then swung away again, without further ado, saying over her shoulder to Meg, 'Of course, as you may not know, Sir Simon and I are bosom bows these days.'

Meg offered Caroline her sweetest smile. It was plain that someone had informed Caro that Simon had proposed to Meg eight years ago, and now she was being warned off, as Jasper said of some punter at a cheap gaming hell who could not pay his dues. Well, she could have Simon Darrow, and welcome to him, nasty tongue and all.

'Oh, I know nothing of London society and its *on dits*,' Meg announced cheerfully, in a tone which hinted at an unspoken 'and have little interest in hearing them'. Instead, she added, 'And am I to offer you congratulations, m'lady?'

'Call me Caro, do. Now that Caro Lamb is no longer with us, the name has become respectable again. As for congratulations, you may defer them for a little. The gentleman and I are in full agreement that, being of mature years, we need not rush matters, but may settle them in our own good time.'

You may settle them in Hell, for all I care, remarked Meg's internal devil nastily. Aloud she said, 'Very wise of you, very proper. Second marriages for the bride are always dangerous—particularly when the groom has been such a determined bachelor as Sir Simon.'

'You speak from personal knowledge, Madame?' Caro Kenilworth was being as poisonously sweet as Meg whom she undoubtedly—and mistakenly—saw as a rival.

'Not at all. From observation, not experience. It was a first marriage for both my poor André and myself.'

Meg wondered if a handkerchief to her eyes might be a useful piece of business at this point. If nothing else, it might shame Lady Kenilworth into silence. She was not to know how little Meg mourned her lost husband. The real question was: how could Simon have become so lacking in taste as to have this aging houri for a *belle amie*? Opportunity, doubtless, was the great thing here!

Behind Caro's back Jane was mouthing something, her pleasant face a little alarmed. She had always been frightened by women of the world like Caro, but Meg had no intention of being warned off, put down, or battered into submission by such an elderly charmer.

The elderly charmer was roaring on. 'I believe that you are expecting Vancourt and Sir Simon here this afternoon. If so, it would be a great convenience for me to let him know that I am attending the Devereuxs' outdoor fête. They are so rarely in London and their grounds are so fine that it is an occasion not to be missed. You will be there, of course?'

'Of course,' murmured Meg.

Jane said, 'I am expecting Vancourt and my brother, but not Sir Simon. I fear that you will be disappointed.'

'Oh, I think not,' drawled the ineffable Caro. 'My understanding was quite otherwise.'

Fortunately for Jane, whose *savoir faire* had been greatly undermined by Vancourt's continued and open unfaithfulness, voices in the corridor announced that this time it *was* her husband and Jasper who were arriving and who would assist Meg in fending off Caro's practised nastiness.

Unfortunately when they came in, laughing and talking, and all aglow from what Vancourt cheerfully announced was a famous piece of exercise, Caro was proved to be right, much to the inward consternation of both sisters. Simon Darrow was with them, being congratulated by Jasper and Vancourt on the splendid state of his athletic prowess despite 'sitting about in the Commons, prosing', as Jasper inelegantly put it.

Meg had already realised that it was plainly going to be impossible for her and Simon to avoid meeting one another frequently. London society—the cousinry, as it was always known—was numerically small and inter-related, into the bargain, to such a degree that everyone knew everyone else and was constantly coming across them.

Meg privately thought of it as a public quadrille with partners, advancing and receding, sometimes in a group, at other times separately.

Simon's bow to her was impeccable, if indifferent; Caroline received a similar accolade, Meg was pleased to notice. Not that Caro took any notice of *that*. She had a hide like one of the rhinoceroses in the new Zoo which the London Zoological Society had recently founded at Regent's Park.

'And then we played tennis, or rather Ashe and Darrow did. And Darrow won.'

'As usual,' grumbled Jasper, who had walked over to where Meg was finishing her watercolour. But his grumble was a friendly one.

'Of course,' cooed Caro, in Simon's direction, 'one expects it of Sir Simon. To win, I mean. I can only say that I am sorry that ladies are not permitted to be spectators.'

'You would be bored,' announced Simon somewhat ungallantly. 'The fun is all for the players.'

'In that case,' remarked Meg, sparking at him before she had time to tell herself not to, 'it is a pity that ladies are not allowed to play and join in the fun.'

Exactly the sort of thing a forward, Frenchified hussy might come out with, thought Simon, but had enough self-control not to say so aloud. He had to admit, though, that annoyingly enough, Caro's faded charms looked the more so beside Meg's fresh elegance, French though it might be.

She was wearing lilac again, and the green eyes looked even more remarkable—and even more challenging when they were turned in his direction. He did not pause to think that his own stern grey ones, when turned on her, were equally challenging. Abandoning the importunate Caroline, he walked over to join Jasper and Meg, whereupon Jasper moved tactfully away to pacify Caroline, by employing all the charm with women that he had learned during his Army career.

Meg looked up at Simon. He said, without preamble, staring into the distance to avoid the distraction of those amazing green eyes, 'I have been thinking over what you said the other evening at the Leominsters'—that we should avoid one another. I agreed at the time, but I think that I was wrong. We are civilised human beings. It should not be beyond us to practise common politeness when we meet. It is my earnest wish that you will agree with me over this.'

Meg swished her brush around in her water pot in order to clean it, and avoided looking at him.

She said, using her most aloof Parisian manner, 'Indeed, Sir Simon. London society is so small that we should occasion remark if we were to be seen at odds. Particularly when there are many who will remember how close our families were in the past.'

He bowed. Punctiliousness was to be everything, it seemed. Meg, for once, had difficulty in keeping a straight face, so serious was he.

'Let us begin now,' he said as he straightened up. Then, in what Meg privately and naughtily thought of as his House of Commons voice, he remarked politely, 'I see that your painting skills are greatly improved. That is an excellent portrait of Jane.'

'Thank you, Sir Simon. I fear that you flatter me—but I did have lessons from an excellent French master in Paris.'

The moment she had spoken Meg was dismally

aware of the possible *double entendre*.

Matters were not helped by Simon producing one of his own. In an effort to mend matters between them, by complimenting her on something more, he offered unluckily, 'Ah, but one sees quite plainly that this is not your only talent which excellent French masters have enhanced. . .'

If Meg's first reaction was to be angry with him all over again for this revived memories of the way he had taunted her at the Leominsters', her second—when she saw his scarlet face—was to remain silent and do nothing.

'Forgive me. I did not intend to say anything which would provoke you.' This was so unwillingly wrenched from him—he was a man who had rarely needed to apologise—that Meg not only forgave him, but sought to reassure him.

'Why, sir—what should you mean? Pray do not spoil your compliment. It was doubtless expressed from the heart and will be received as such. And now I must show Jane her portrait. She has been most patient with me whilst I have been at work. I know from experience how wearying it is to sit still for an afternoon whilst a painter expresses him—or her—self.'

It was neatly done, Simon had to admit. He had been forgiven. And perhaps it would be possible for them to start again. He bowed and watched Meg walk over to Jane and the others. The only troubling thing was that merely to see her was to undo him. He had little time to reflect on this, however, for Caro was beside him in an instant as soon as she saw that Meg had left him.

'So *that* is the famous Madame la Comtesse de Mortaine. I cannot say that I am impressed.'

'No? Madame appears to me to be all that is claimed of her. But one lady can hardly be expected to see the charms of another—as you have frequently told me yourself.'

Even Caro's brass-faced composure was scarcely proof against this rebuff, so icily delivered. She was not to know how two-edged Simon's comment was!

She recovered herself, and replied smoothly, 'Ah, I had forgotten. Rumour says that you knew her when she was little more than a child, and have not seen her for many years. The change in her from being a country mouse must be remarkable. But I would have expected her to have more. . .' She paused significantly, largely because she could not think what to say that might not invite a further barbed remark from him.

'More what, Caro? And yes, the change is remarkable.'

'More. . .nothing. . . Oh, this is becoming tedious—like the lady. Let us *parlons d'autres choses*, talk of other matters. Say you will escort me to Devereux House tomorrow.'

Well, one thing was for sure. Caro's French was not a patch on little Meg Ashe's these days, was Simon's inward and ungallant comment. He had no wish to escort Caro anywhere. They had agreed to part, but the lady was not living up to her agreement. Nevertheless, his conscience told him to make up for his earlier rudeness to her by acceding to her wishes.

Simon wondered what in the world had come over

him during the last twenty-four hours or so, and reached the sad conclusion that he might not be behaving like a savage if Margaret Ashe had not taken his cousin Peverel for a lover and chosen to visit England!

All the world—or rather, most of the cousinry—was at the Devereuxs' afternoon party, as Jane and Caro Kenilworth had foretold. The gardens of Devereux House were as delightful as Jane had told her they would be; Countess Cassandra was as charmingly eccentric, and her husband as physically impressive, as rumour had said.

The Countess was wearing what looked like an Indian sari in vermilion and saffron, belted at the waist with a narrow cloth of gold sash. This should have appeared a very much overdone toilette, but she wore it with such careless panache that it looked entirely appropriate for an English summer afternoon.

Her husband, the Earl, was an Englishman out of the same mould as Simon. Large and craggily handsome, he looked like the cavalryman he had once been. They both greeted Meg as though they had longed to meet her. Will Osborne, who was her escort for the afternoon, was obviously an old friend. He recommended them to take a stroll down a pretty path that led to a small lake at the far end of the gardens.

Walking along it, being stared at by half of London society, it soon became plain to Meg that her presence was creating a great deal of excitement—her dubious reputation had obviously preceded her, she decided wryly.

Peverel Darrow came towards them when they reached the lake. An elegant wooden summerhouse or gazebo stood before it. Like all the company he was dressed *à outrance* by one of London's most fashionable tailors. His royal blue coat was by Stultz and his shiny black, gold-tasselled boots were by Weston. His cravat was a dream of a thing. More than one spectator wondered where the money was coming from to pay for such elegance.

No need to wonder, was Meg's irrepressible response to that thought. It was the banker's draft, which she had handed to him the other night, that was doubtless responsible for his impeccable turn-out. He greeted her and Will as though they were his dearest friends.

'Osborne, Madame, delighted to meet you both. The gardens are all and more than they are claimed to be, are they not? And the Countess even more so. A true original, if ever there was one. I believe that you thought so at one time, eh, Osborne?'

Will's honest face crimsoned. 'Oh, nothing to that, Darrow. It was long ago—and we were friends only.'

'Oh, I don't doubt you. Devereux a bit of a wild man, you see, Madame. Not a man of peace, like Osborne and me. By the by, Osborne, your Mama was asking after you. Told me to tell you that, if we met, she was seated on the terrace and wished to speak to you. I'll look after Madame whilst you do your duty like a good son.'

This brash and cold-blooded attempt to detach a rival from Meg's side could only succeed because

Peverel was older and brazen and Will was younger and naïve.

'If Madame does not object. . .' Will began a trifle desperately, only for Peverel to say in a cheery voice,

'Of course, she won't, old fellow. Must do your *devoir*, mustn't you? A single man's duty is to his mother first, after all.'

If anything had been needed—which it wasn't—to convince Meg that Will was too lightweight to be considered as a serious suitor or a possible husband, his surrender to Peverel's overt blackmail would have done the trick.

As he galloped away, Meg put up her parasol—she was wearing lilac again, and the parasol was a deep purple with a long white fringe—and drawled at Peverel in her most distant great-lady manner, 'It would have been better-mannered of you, sir, to ask me first whether I wished for your company before you sent Mr Osborne away.'

He offered her a deep bow, remarking in his most carelessly charming manner, 'Oh, I am sure that you would infinitely prefer to be escorted by someone less of a puling boy with his mother's milk still around his mouth than Mr Will Osborne. Besides, you made no objection to my proposal, none at all.' His smile was complacent and self-congratulatory.

'Only because I had not the slightest desire to be turned into a public bone to be fought over by two dogs. Moreover, you might be able to bam poor Will in such a high-handed manner, but you must remember, Mr Darrow, that I know you for what you are, and I will have no problem in bidding you *adieu*—which I do now,' and she made to go.

'One moment, Madame,' he said, and put out a hand to detain her. 'I do not choose to allow you to leave—yet.'

'Choose, sir, choose? I will tell you what I told your cousin. It is I who choose my companions, sir, not they me,' and Meg turned to go again. His impudence was unsufferable—and it was not yet over.

'I think not, Madame. I have no further interest in your sister. You have fire and spirit beneath that cold mask you wear, whilst she—like Will Osborne—is shallow. I have a mind to marry well, and you, unlike your sister, are free to marry and I am assured were left a vast fortune by your husband.

'We should, I believe, deal well together as husband and wife. When you handed me that bank draft drawn on your account, you created the assumption that *you*, and not your sister, were paying me for something—services rendered perhaps, or the return of *your* incriminating letters. It is your reputation which is now at stake, if I choose to be indiscreet.

'Furthermore, I know something of your life in France, which you would not care to become public knowledge—particularly since your reputation is already a trifle. . .spotty, shall we say? My courtship of you will be both short—and public. You would do well to take me seriously.'

Perhaps the worst part of Peverel's blandly threatening speech were not his threats but the words 'We should, I believe, deal well together.' They revived in Meg unfortunate memories of his cousin Simon's otherwise quite different proposal.

But he had Meg's attention, and knew it. Unknown to them both, however, their seemingly intimate *tête-à-tête* was being watched by his cousin Simon, who had come upon them as he strolled alone through the gardens, having abandoned his unwelcome companion, Caroline Kenilworth, to another gentleman whom she was hoping to fascinate.

So, Madame had no more sense than to be up to her tricks again with his worthless cousin, having managed to shake off that fribble Osborne! Would she never learn sense? He watched them, watched Peverel put an intimate hand on Meg's arm when he said, 'Oh, I have your attention now, Madame, have I not?'

'For a moment, only,' returned Meg coldly. 'I am not poor Jane. I will not be blackmailed, sir. And, in any case, I do not believe that even you would stoop to blackmail me into marriage.' Alas, she knew him only too well, and that he would stoop to anything—but she would fight him to the end. Peverel's smile told her that she had read him aright.

'I would advise you to stay—' he began, but before he could say any more, Simon was upon them, remarking,

'Ah, Peverel, I see that you are already acquainted with Madame. I was not aware that you knew her.'

They had been speaking in such low tones that Simon had heard nothing of what was being said—only that it was being said intimately. He was unaware that the intimacy was unfriendly. He only saw that they were close together and his suspicion of Meg was so strong that he always drew the worst conclusion about her behaviour, particularly when she was associating with such a known bad hat as his cousin.

Meg read Simon's body language correctly—and was furious with him. He was judging her to be a whore again, which was particularly galling when she was being bullied so determinedly by Peverel— who had, as usual, an answer for anything thrown at him.

'Oh, Madame and I knew one another in Paris,' he began to say in a way that suggested a much deeper relationship than the passing one they had enjoyed, if that were the right word. 'When Madame was married to André de Vaux.' This was also said as though André had been his dearest friend instead of someone with whom he had exchanged a few brief sentences—and none of them amicable.

Which successfully served to convince Simon of Meg's perfidy. She closed her eyes and her parasol, and said, 'I am sure that you have much to say to one another, since you meet so rarely. I will leave you. Lady Devereux is to give us a harp recital; as I understand that she is a most accomplished performer, I do not wish to miss it.'

She bowed to the cousins, who were glaring at one another, heads down, like a pair of angry buffalos, and moved away, amused at herself for taking a leaf out of Peverel's book and disposing of the unwanted third in a group without asking the others' permission. That unwanted third being herself.

Lady Devereux was an accomplished performer

and Meg enjoyed her playing, even though at the back of her mind she was worried by what it was that Peverel knew—or thought that he knew—about her.

Chapter Four

'**M**y dear Madame,' said Cass, Lady Devereux, to Meg, who had approached her after the recital was over, and had complimented her on her performance, 'I believe that we met briefly in Paris some years ago shortly after your marriage. Pray allow me to commiserate with you on the sad death of your husband.'

Meg inclined her head graciously and murmured her thanks. The acid voice of her inner demon commented that she was becoming so practised at this kind of polite nothingness that she would soon be able to do it sleepwalking.

Something of this perhaps showed, for Cass, one of the most shrewd members of London society, said briskly, 'Now that we have got rid of the niceties, may you also permit me to say that, if ever you become bored with conversations confined to *on dits* and the discussion of how best to trim a bonnet, there will always be a welcome for you at Devereux House. Something tells me that you suffer fools gladly no more than I do.'

Meg's laugh was, for once, a genuine one. This she had not expected. 'Oh, dear,' she exclaimed, 'was I so obvious? Were my good manners so excessive that they were enough to induce nausea?'

Cass's smile was as genuine as Meg's laugh. 'Indeed not. Jack, my husband, sometimes accuses me of mind-reading, usually after I have detected him in some monstrous piece of crinkum-crankum designed to deceive me as to what he and his one-time corporal got up to in one of their periodic reunions.

'You may or may not know that he served as a cavalryman in the ranks during the late wars and rose to the ineffable height of being a sergeant. Better that I tell you that than someone who might wish to cause trouble between us. You see, my dear, my mind-reading has told me that we are to be friends, nay, bosom bows.'

She was in no way pretty, Meg decided, but was something better. She had character and a sense of fun. As Cass was to say to her later on in their acquaintance, 'The trouble with me is that cheerfulness will keep breaking in, however determined I am to be solemn.'

In that sense, she was a happy counterbalance to Meg, who had, these days, a tendency towards sadness, and consequently solemnity. But this was to be in the future.

For the present, Cass, whilst drawing her attention to a portrait of a pretty boy carrying a hawk who turned out, improbably, to be her craggy-looking husband as a very young man, concentrated on saying as she turned away from it, 'Jack does not look

like that at all now—he rather resembles Simon
Darrow than his cousin Peverel, and not merely in
looks. Peverel, as I am sure you know, is not to be
trusted.'

Now this was mind-reading with a vengeance! Or
someone had been talking. But the look Cass turned
on her was so innocent that Meg decided that she
was reading meanings into what was being said that
were not there.

The rest of their conversation was innocent
enough, with Cass offering her a friendship which
Meg was coming to understand that she needed.
'You will,' she said, 'visit me soon, my dear
Comtesse, won't you? For if you do not, I shall
haunt Vancourt House until you do.'

To her astonishment, Meg found herself saying
something quite unexpected and of which she had
not previously thought. 'I shall not be staying
overlong at Vancourt House. I am determined to set
up my own establishment, and would value your
recommendation of a *dame de compagnie* to keep
me respectable.'

Now where had that come from? Perhaps the
knowledge that Vancourt's manner to her was
becoming over-warm, and Jane had enough to contend with without suspecting that her husband had
designs on her sister. Not only Jane, perhaps. It
was bad enough to have Simon suspecting that she
possessed no virtue and Peverel having designs on
her pocket, if not her virtue, without having to suffer
Vancourt having designs on her virtue, if not her
pocket.

Or was it the effect of Cass Devereux's downright

commonsense, which was reminding her that to remove the temptation which she apparently presented was, like discretion, the better part of valour?

No matter. At least, if she had her own establishment, Peverel's attempts to visit her would not arouse the suspicions of Jane and her husband, and she would be able to refuse to see him without causing comment. Meg was growing tired of living her life in public.

'Oh, I know just the person for you,' Cass said eagerly, 'A Mrs Hollis, a young widow who lost her husband, General Hollis, last year. He left her with very little to live on. She is a dear friend of my old governess, Mrs Dickson, and is so upright that she could almost confer respectability on the King himself! My husband's secretary will give you her address before you leave.

'In return, you will do something to rescue my guests from possible boredom. I understand from your brother that you and Sir Simon Darrow used to entertain your father's guests—he by singing, and you by playing for him. I would be greatly pleased if you would agree to do so again, this afternoon.'

Jasper! thought Meg wildly. It was Jasper who had put Cass Devereux up to this. . .this. . .trick, to try to get us together again.

Well, he would not succeed. She would refuse, politely, but still refuse. And then she looked at Cass Devereux. There was a transparent honesty about her, which she proved by saying gently, 'Oh, I know that you will feel that you are being coerced into this. But your brother—who knew my husband when he was in the ranks—believes that you and Sir Simon should be friends again, and asked me to do him this favour. You can, of course, refuse.'

After that, how could she? But first she had a question for Cass. 'Sir Simon? Has the request been made to him?'

'Oh, indeed, and he has agreed to it—but only on the condition that it would be pleasing to you.'

An olive branch from him, no less. She could scarcely, now, be so graceless as to refuse Cass.

Simon was waiting for her in the Devereuxs' splendid drawing-room, where the company were already seated for a resumption of the afternoon's entertainment. Caro Kenilworth was standing near him, her whole posture betraying the anger which she had felt on hearing that 'that woman' and Simon were to sing and play together.

He bowed over her hand as Cass's major-domo announced them. Caro flounced to a seat near the front, announcing loudly, 'Oh, I do so detest being compelled to listen to amateurs,' a statement that endeared her to no one.

Meg found that she was trembling. Simon said, below his breath. 'Come, we must not disappoint Jasper and the lady. I know that it is many years since we sang and played together but, knowing you, I am sure that you have not neglected your music. Here is the score for the "Last Rose of Summer". I remember that it used to be a favourite of your father's.'

So it had been. He had liked all the songs in Tom Moore's collection of Irish airs. Meg took a deep breath and sat down. She said nothing to him. Indeed, he did not seem to expect it. Her simple agreement had apparently been enough.

She sat down at the Broadwood pianoforte and played a few tentative chords. Simon placed the score before her, but it was not needed. Meg had played it so often in those long gone years that she knew it by heart. But again, she said nothing but a simple thank you—which appeared to serve.

Simon was ready, too. He was standing by the piano as he had done so many times before, waiting for her to begin. Meg was suddenly overcome. Panic struck her. She could not do this. And then Simon looked down at her, and smiled. For a moment it was almost as though she were little Meggie, the youngest Miss Ashe, again, and he was the tall young man whom she had adored.

Courage ran through her. She lifted her head and began to play the introduction, pausing at the end of it for a fraction of a second to allow him to begin.

Tom Moore's poignant and well remembered-words, sung by Simon's mellow baritone, filled the drawing-room. And if there had been a few who had, beforehand, silently echoed Caroline Kenilworth's unkind judgment on them, they were silenced by the simple purity of their performance.

The applause, which followed a short silence once the song had ended, was long and sincere. 'Another,' said Simon, and it was not really a question. 'You will consent to join me in another song.'

Meg nodded dumbly. Astonishingly, she was near to tears—she, who never cried.

'I thought,' he murmured, a trifle tentatively, 'that "*Partant pour la Syrie*" might go down well, you being a Frenchwoman these days.'

It was, Meg acknowledged, a suitable choice, being a French love song written during the late wars that had been adopted by France's enemy, England. It told of a young soldier leaving behind his own true love in order to go to war, and promising to win her hand by his bravery.

'And you will sing it with me?'

The tears were near to the surface again. Meg told herself that he was simply being kind because Jasper had put them in this impossible position, and he did not wish society to know that they were at odds.

Time turned back upon itself again. The lost years were gone. She was fifteen-year-old Meg Ashe, practising her singing, her piano playing and her ability to do both in public. Singing, she remembered how Simon had always encouraged her and, as contralto met baritone, their voices mixed and mingled as though they had never been parted.

When the song ended, he looked down at her, and she looked up at him. Their eyes met: tenderness in his, hope in hers. But for a moment only. In a trice Simon's eyes on hers were as hard as ever, and hopelessness took over again in Meg's. Their moment of rapport was over.

This time the silence after they had finished was long and profound. Cass led the applause. She rose and walked over to them. Something in the set of Meg's shoulders told her of the strain she was under.

'That was quite splendid,' she said. 'Particularly since this was sprung upon you both without warning. It is quite plain, though, that you have sung together before. I offer you my congratulations as well as my thanks.' If she thought that Simon, like

Meg, was also somewhat constrained in his manner, she said nothing to indicate that she was aware of it.

'I was right,' Simon told Meg coolly as they walked away from the piano to receive the thanks and congratulations of many of the company. 'You had not forgotten your past entirely. And your technique has improved immensely.'

'Nor had Jasper forgotten, apparently,' said Meg drily. 'I wonder that he does not consider joining the *corps diplomatique* since he seems to be so adept at arranging cunning plots. I take it that he also proposed that you, as well as I, should perform without a word of warning.'

Simon gave a short laugh. Like Meg, he thought that at least Jasper's ploy had set them talking in a reasonable fashion—which was doubtless what he had intended.

'Indeed, and I shall have words with him before we leave. I must, however, remark that eight years in France has done wonders for the purity of your accent. It quite shamed mine.'

Meg made no direct answer to this, other than to say, 'And here comes brother Jasper, who needs a little shaming of a different sort—from the pair of us.' She was not sure whether Simon's remark on her French accent was meant to be a compliment or not.

Jasper was as forthright as usual; as forthright as Meg had once been and was no longer.

'Well done,' he offered cheerfully. 'And at least my suggestion had the pair of you speaking to one another again in a civilised manner, not snarling like dogs over a bone!'

United for once, both Meg and Simon glared at

him. Meg, retaining her aloof self-control, merely murmured, 'You might at least have had the courtesy to speak to Simon and myself before approaching Lady Devereux. I had not expected such blackmail from a brother.'

Jasper's withers were quite unwrung, 'Oh, if I had done *that*, neither of you would have consented. As it is, no harm done, and the company was entertained. I must compliment you, sister, on your playing and singing. You have become quite the professional since you went to Paris.'

'And for my part, Ashe, I shall not forget this piece of arm-twisting, I assure you. I shall take my revenge in the gym, or the *salle des armes*, a true duel being a trifle overblown as a form of punishment.' Simon's tone was jovial enough, but there was more than a hint of savagery in it.

'Oh, come.' Jasper was all smiles, and ran an arm through Simon's. 'It's time for the tea board, I see, and Will Osborne is panting towards us to look after Meg. Why don't you put Caro K. out of her misery, and I will bring Lucy Seymour along.

'You may then inform us about the new Zoological Society of which *The Times* tells me you are a member, and after that you may invite us all, including our host and hostess, to stroll around the gardens in Regent's Park and feed buns to the bears.'

Unwillingly, Simon began to laugh. 'I had forgotten what a fellow you are, Ashe. I suppose, knowing you, that you have already made this suggestion to Lady Devereux.'

'Now, Darrow, there you are wrong. I spoke to Jack Devereux, not Cass, and he wishes to enrol as a member also, and would be delighted if you saw fit to propose him and to show him around the celebrated five acres of Regent's Park that Lord Lansdowne managed to gouge out of the Commissioners of Woods and Forests. Quite an achievement, that.'

'Nothing to yours, Jas,' said Simon, suddenly as cheerful as Jasper, and using his boyhood name to him to show that no real offence had been taken by his trickery, 'in manoeuvring me before a piano again. I suppose that you expect me to invite the whole Vancourt brood and young Osborne as well. In for a penny, in for a pound.'

Will, who had just arrived, heard this last statement with some surprise. He quite thought that Sir Simon Darrow had taken against him, as the slang saying had it.

'Eh, what's that?' he asked after claiming Meg as Jasper had prophesied. 'The new Zoological Gardens? I should be delighted to make up the party—if I am invited, of course. Have always wanted to see the bears.'

'So that's settled,' proclaimed Jasper cheerfully, before Simon, or anyone else, could demur. 'All that remains for us now is to set a date for this delightful expedition!'

And so it was arranged. Simon, who had every intention of having as little to do with Meg as possible, had been coerced by her brother into agreeing that she should be one of his party, in an expedition which he had not arranged!

All in all, Meg left Devereux House feeling happy for the first time since she had arrived in London.

Despite Jane's many quiet virtues, she could not share in most of Meg's interests: to find in Cass Devereux someone who did, and who could enjoy her witticisms almost before she had uttered them, was a boon indeed.

Not only that: Cass Devereux had become such a power in London society that if she accepted Meg, then so would all the other hostesses. It seemed that she was not destined to be a pariah after all.

And for a few happy moments she and Simon had shared—if only briefly—a little of the rapport which had once been theirs. Perhaps, when they were at the Gardens together, they might recover a little more ground.

Sir Simon Darrow was not quite so happy. The even tenor of his life had been disturbed by the reappearance of Meg Ashe to a degree that he would not have believed possible had he known of it beforehand. At least, he thought, unaware that Meg was spending her days dodging Vancourt's advances, she would have to behave herself whilst she was living with her sister, and she had been much more quietly reasonable with him during their songs together.

'Oh, Aunt Marguerite, are we really going to see the animals today? Oh, I do hope Papa wasn't teasing us when he said that we could go with you.'

Little Georgie Vancourt turned a pleading face to his aunt. He had already discovered that she was much more reliable than either his mama or his papa, and if she said something would be so, it was so. Now Papa would promise one thing one day, and quite another thing on another. As for Mama—well, she never seemed to know quite what she was doing.

His sister, Harriet, who was not sure that she wished to see wild animals—she remained unconvinced that they were safely penned away from visiting little girls—added a rather doubtful voice to Georgie's pleadings.

'Of course you shall go, my darlings. See, Nancy is coming to dress you. It is a cold day for June so you must both wear your pelisses.'

Meg was not quite so calm about this Sunday afternoon trip to the Zoological Gardens at Regent's Park as her comforting words to her niece and nephew suggested. One part of her was looking forward to seeing Simon—they had not directly encountered one another since the Devereuxs' afternoon party—the other part was asking herself why she should look forward to being hurt again.

Simon had made it quite plain that he considered her to be a loose woman, corrupted by her marriage and her years in France, and nothing she could say or do appeared to be able to change his mind.

Peverel's behavior was not calculated to improve matters, either. He haunted her, constantly reminding her that she was, to some extent, in his power, and that the day of reckoning might be soon. Until she had her own home, it would be difficult to avoid him. Vancourt had taken a fancy to Peverel—probably to annoy Jane who disliked him—and he was constantly at Vancourt House.

The rumours about her own past had died down a little since Cass had taken her up, and today's party would help to silence them even further.

The irony was that Vancourt's patronage was conferring respectability on her although he was the loosest fish around, whilst she, whose own conduct had been impeccable, was regarded with suspicion. It was enough to make the angels weep!

Nevertheless, she was calmness itself when she walked into the massive hall of Vancourt House, ready to be driven by him to Regent's Park, Jane by her side, and the children following in a dog cart driven by the chief coachman.

'How splendid you look, Meg. Exactly right for a fine day in the open with the animals. Neither too elegant, nor too *farouche*.'

Meg looked down at the pretty blue cotton dress she was wearing. It had a round linen collar embroidered with forget-me-nots. The sash which cinched her slender waist was of a deeper blue. Her shoes were made of a serviceable but light cream kid, ornamented with the tiniest silver rosettes. Silk forget-me-nots decorated her straw hat, and she was carrying a white parasol decorated with the same modest flowers. The shawl, draped so artistically around her shoulders, was a dream of a thing in the finest cashmere, and was also blue and white. She was slipping on exquisitely delicate white lace gloves as she turned to Jane.

'Parisian chic,' sighed her sister, whose own sage-green toilette did neither her figure nor her colouring any favours. She saw at once that her bonnet, her shoes, her everything appeared irretrievably clumsy beside Meg's elegance. 'Aunt Léonie's tutelage, I suppose.'

And so, unkindly, Vancourt told her when he

drove the carriage round to the front doors for them to be handed in by various subservient footmen. As usual, he was very late: he liked to keep his wife and children waiting.

'Really, Jane, if you can't manage a more suitable turnout than the one that you're wearing, then do have the goodness to ask your sister for advice.'

Jane flushed an unlovely crimson and his brutality set Meg shuddering. He had ruined Jane's day for her before it had begun.

She put an arm around her sister's shoulders. 'Certainly not, Vancourt,' she said, her voice icy. 'Jane is far more sensibly dressed than I am. Indeed, if there were time, I would beg leave to return to my room to put on something less suited to a drawing-room. I find the afternoon cooler than I thought. But I will not cause you further delay.'

'Thank you,' Jane whispered as she settled herself in her seat.

Meg being on Vancourt's other side afforded him the opportunity to whisper into her ear, once the grooms let go of his horses' heads and they set off, 'I like a woman of spirit, m'dear, and God knows my poor wife has little enough.'

'And small wonder at that,' retorted Meg in a fierce undertone, 'seeing that, by your behaviour, you have extinguished what little she had!'

If she thought this would deter him in any way from his pursuit of her, she was wrong. Rather, her spirited response to him and his behaviour served only to encourage him the more.

By God, it would be a pleasure to have such a proud filly beneath him. She was like an apparently extinct volcano with passionate fires beneath a cold exterior. Unlike her suet pudding of a sister, she was strawberries and champagne of the very best! His greatest pleasure would be to tame that proud spirit and have her his submissive slave. How to bring her to his bed was his present problem, particularly with that sly devil Peverel Darrow after her. Probably not such good tactics to have him constantly in his home in order to annoy his wife by his presence.

Meg knew quite well what her brother-in-law was thinking, and had there been room would have shuddered away from him. Fortunately for her and Jane's composure, the world and his wife were taking the air that morning, and it needed all of Vancourt's concentration to manoeuvre his way through assorted gigs, dog carts, curricles, broughams, landaulets and chaises, to say nothing of gay young bucks on horseback.

Many of them were on their way to Regent's Park. The Zoological Society was now so large that, even though only its members were allowed to visit the Gardens on Sunday, they were nearly as busy as on weekdays when the general public might pay to enter.

'God damn the traffic,' cursed Vancourt morosely. 'We shall be late.'

'And so I told you,' nagged Jane unwisely. 'And I do not, my lord, appreciate blasphemy indulged in before myself and my sister.'

'Damn that for a tale,' swore Vancourt. 'You never appreciate anything, so that is no matter to me. Your sister has heard worse in Paris, I dare swear.'

'Not often,' retorted Meg sweetly as they neared

the entrance to the Zoological Gardens, after they had negotiated the splendid Nash terraces which ran alongside them. 'And then only in the worst possible company.'

Her reward for that was a roar of happy laughter from her brother-in-law.

'Would hardly guess you were my poor wife's sister, Madame. Why in the world did you always tell me she was a plain, poor-spirited little thing, m'lady? Might have known that you were wrong, as usual. You should try imitating her.'

If Meg could have borrowed a pair of angel's wings and flown out of the carriage, she would have done so. As it was, she remained quiet with some difficulty. To say anything at all to Vancourt was merely to encourage him to torment poor Jane the more. Best to ignore him and hope that the drive would soon end.

To her great relief, it was not long before they reached the Grand Drive that ran round Regent's Park, which meant that their journey was nearly over and she and Jane and the children would be free to leave the carriage and roam around the Gardens. Her recent experience with Vancourt had served to confirm her in the belief that she must find another place to live.

I am becoming a nomad, she thought wryly, as Vancourt drove them to the entrance, a female wandering Jew who has no place which she can truly call her own: I must shuffle the cards and deal again. . .

Chapter Five

Simon was waiting for them by the gates. He was driving a stylish curricle picked out in blue and silver, a tiger behind, and Caro Kenilworth up front with him. She had a discontented expression on her face, most probably because the Vancourt party was late and she was being compelled to wait for it in public. Will Osborne had arrived on horseback, and his steed was being led away by his attendant groom.

Outside the entrance to the Gardens, which was flanked by two small rustic sentry boxes, Jack and Cass Devereux and their children were already dismounting from a staid family carriage.

'I told you that we would be late,' fretted Jane unwisely to Vancourt. 'They have been waiting for us.'

A further angry explosion from her husband was only averted by Simon's approach, Caro on his arm. Simon had his own reason for being annoyed: Peverel had just driven up, also in a spanking new curricle, and was now walking towards them, arm in arm with a stranger.

Now who the devil had invited him? Peverel read Simon's face correctly, and remarked gaily, 'No need to frown, cousin, I'm not a gatecrasher! My sponsor today is Acland, here like yourself as one of the Society's founder members. A splendid day to see the animals, is it not?'

Watching Simon bow stiffly to Peverel and his friend, Sir Thomas Acland, who was by way of being one of Vancourt's, too, Meg could not help being amused by Peverel's jaunty insolence, and by his flaunting of his new curricle, doubtless bought with the money that she had given him on Jane's behalf. Rogue he might be, but she could see exactly how he used his charm to achieve his criminal ends and stay afloat in an unforgiving society.

'Like my new turn-out, do you?' he asked Simon confidentially. 'Thought I might pamper m'self a little. Tired of driving round in other men's hand-me-downs.'

And where did he get the money from for *that*? was a question Simon would have liked to ask, but Peverel was moving on, a smile on his lips, and the friends whom Simon had invited were waiting for him.

'No need to pass me in,' announced Jack Devereux jovially. 'I was accepted as a member last week. Promised to help buy a giraffe when one becomes available. Cass says that she's always wanted to see a giraffe.'

He gave a great burst of laughter, and said affectionately, 'Mark you, I wouldn't put it past m'lady wife to ask to lead it round with her! Most disappointed that she couldn't bring her dogs in today; but rules are rules.'

This brought more laughter from all those who knew that Cass Devereux was famous for the size and splendour of the dogs which always accompanied her on walks and jaunts to Hyde Park. The lady herself enjoyed her husband's teasing most of all.

'And parasols are banned, also, I'm afraid,' said Simon, 'so I must ask the ladies to hand them to Stephen to take back to the carriages before we enter.'

Meg and Jane handed theirs to the waiting groom, but Caro complained angrily, 'Oh, this is really the outside of enough. I am sure that the sun is about to become over-warm at any moment and, of all things, I do detest a brown face! What can be the reason for such an absurd rule?'

'Not absurd.' For once Simon was short with Caro. 'The members have decided that the danger of visitors poking the animals with walking sticks, umbrellas and parasols and thus causing injury to them is too great a risk to take. I should have warned you all beforehand,' he admitted, 'but rarely carrying a stick or an umbrella myself, I quite forgot.'

He saw with pleasure that the guard at the sentry box was making Peverel surrender his elegant silver-topped cane.

To the delight of all the children, it was not long before they were through the gate and walking along the broad path on either side of which were animals exhibited in a variety of cages and houses.

George Vancourt and Ritchie Devereux, who had

already become great chums, were urging Ritchie's father to take them to the bearpit, 'at once'. Georgie had seen immediately that Jack was quite a different sort of papa from his own, who was sauntering along, looking supremely bored at the prospect of spending his afternoon with a pack of children gaping at animals, since he possessed not the slightest interest in either species.

Jack, on the other hand, had taken his small Sophie in his arms to show her the kangaroo, and was promising George and Ritchie that, as soon as they found the kiosk which sold food for the animals, he would buy them some buns to throw to the bears.

Harriet Vancourt was holding tightly on to Aunt Marguerite's hand. Her nursemaid had taken a light fever and was thus unable to join the party, but Meg had promised Jane that she would look after her, rather than allow her niece to lose her treat. Simon, who was walking parallel with them, Caro by his side, watched in some surprise as Meg gently helped her niece to kneel down in order to inspect more easily the cranes and bustards which were running around an enclosed lawn with a pond at one end.

For a moment he saw again the little Meg Ashe whom he had thought he had lost, so tender was the expression on her face as she cared for the child whom both her parents were ignoring, lost in their own grievances against one another. Impulsively, he moved forward to speak to her—but a possible moment of *rapprochement* was lost when Will Osborne, who had detached himself from Acland, moved forward to attach himself to Meg.

Will was big with information about the Gardens,

gleaned from Acland, who was strolling along in his wake, and which he was bursting to impart to Meg in order to impress her with his knowledge.

'Decimus Burton, the great architect, has designed the Gardens, and the Gothic building in which the llamas are to be found,' he announced portentously. 'They say he intends to build a turret with a clock tower on to it.'

'Oh, can the llamas tell the time, then?' asked Harriet eagerly: she was having difficulty in learning to tell the time herself, and was prepared to admire the llamas for being able to do so.

This naïve comment completely overset Will, whose understanding of small girls was as deficient as his understanding of their elder sisters. Meg rescued him by saying, 'Not at all, my dear, but the grown-ups walking around the Gardens will be pleased to be able to check their watches with it, I am sure.'

Will's attempt at an answer was drowned in the noise of George and Ritchie running up and exclaiming together, 'Oh, Aunt Marguerite,' from George, and 'Oh, Mama,' from Ritchie, 'we are all going to the bear pit to feed the bears. You must come with us. The bears are simply not to be missed, Uncle Peverel says, and they are nearby.'

Uncle Peverel! Both Simon and Meg reacted to this remarkable statement in the same way. So, it had not taken the wretched swindler more than five minutes to win the hearts of two small boys.

Well, if Meg and little Harriet were to decide to join 'Uncle Peverel', then he, Simon, was bound to go with them to keep Meg apart, if possible, from his worthless, blackmailing cousin. He was, however, checkmated even before he could announce his intentions, by Caro passing a fine lace handkerchief over her face and announcing that she needed a seat: she was far too tired to walk any further.

'But we've only just arrived.' Simon uttered this incontrovertible truth as gently as possible. 'So far you have only seen the kangaroos, and the bears are not far away.'

'And seeing the kangaroos is quite enough for me,' shuddered Caro. 'The wretched animal is an offence against nature. Carrying its young in a pouch, indeed! Quite improper to allow little children to see it—or the bears either, nasty dangerous things!'

Nothing to do but summon one of the young keepers and ask him to arrange for a chair to be brought for Lady Kenilworth, 'who is feeling the heat,' Simon explained as he watched Meg, Harriet, Cass Devereux and all the little Devereuxs, plus Will Osborne, join Jack Devereux, his Sophie and 'Uncle Peverel' in front of the bear pit. They were all busy buying buns to throw to the bears—particularly to the one who had climbed up his pole to watch *them*.

At least Peverel couldn't get up to any of his underhand tricks in the middle of that mob, was Simon's glum thought as he left the main party behind on his way to the beavers' enclosure.

And where were Jane and her husband, who had apparently abandoned their offspring to others? That question was partly answered a few minutes later when Jane suddenly appeared, scarlet in the face, at the exact moment when the young keeper was

reverently setting out a light chair for Caro by the
beavers' pond, which was situated in the shade of
some trees, far away from the offending kangaroos
and bears.

'Oh, splendid,' she exclaimed. 'I am already quite
exhausted, and I had no notion that one might obtain
seating. Vancourt is too busy staring at the camels
to care for my comfort.' The young keeper was
promptly despatched to fetch her a chair also.

'In that case,' said Simon, ever ready to seize
opportunity by the forelock, 'you may keep Lady
K. company whilst I rejoin the main party. I have
a mind to throw buns to the bears, too!'

'Buns to bears!' shuddered Jane. It appeared that
she was as impervious to Zoological delights as
Caro. How in God's name, thought Simon, did I
become entangled with such a silly. . .woman? And
she wasn't even very good in bed, either, despite all
the rumours.

Simon did not leave the two women until he had
seen Jane settled beside a discontented Caro, who
had expected him to remain with her. They had a
good view of the American beavers inside their little
enclosure, if nothing else. Acland had gallantly
joined them. 'Have thrown buns to bears before,'
he announced. 'Nothing to it,' before sending the
keeper off to find him a third chair. As Simon strode
away he could hear him recounting to his uninterested, but captive, audience a short history of the
early days of the foundation of the Gardens.

Grinning to himself, Simon found his party standing before the wooden hut next to the bear pit where
a stout lady in a mob cap was selling buns, fruit and

nuts to a large assembly of interested spectators. Other apparently exhausted women had been provided with chairs where they might watch the animals in comfort.

Meg and the Devereux party were made of sterner stuff, however. They were already equipped with a supply of goodies and the bear up the pole was waiting for the buns to begin raining in his direction again. Little Harriet Vancourt was relieved to see that all the bears were in a pit which was surrounded by a tall iron fence, and their pole was far enough away from it to make it unlikely that the bear might vault the fence in order to eat her instead of a bun.

Meg, unaware that Simon had joined them, found herself between Peverel and a rather stern-looking woman who had a little boy by the hand.

'Have a bun?' Peverel invited her, oozing charm, only for Meg to say coolly,

'No, thank you, I have a supply of my own.'

'In the land of double meanings,' he announced, 'great play could be made of your reply.'

'Could it?' she replied, still cool. 'But we are not, are we? Harriet dear, throw this piece of bun towards the bear.'

She had heard the woman beside her stifle a laugh when she answered Peverel so cavalierly—not that that troubled him.

Fortunately Cass Devereux, who had been inspecting the goats, provided a diversion. She came strolling towards them, exclaiming when she saw the stern-looking woman, 'Oh, Stroody—I mean, Emma—what a delightful surprise, and Thomas, too,' and she gave the little boy a kiss. 'I had never thought to see you here. I suppose George is with you?' and she gave the stern woman an affectionate kiss.

'Oh, indeed, he has taken Johnny to see the kangaroos again. He cannot get enough of them. Every time he visits the gardens, he bounces about the house afterwards as though he were one himself!'

'And this, my dear Comtesse—' Cass swept on in her impulsive way to Meg '—is my oldest friend and former companion, Mrs George Dickson, who is married to my husband's oldest friend. Is that not convenient! And this, dearest Emma, is my new friend Marguerite, Comtesse de Vaux, from Paris, on whom you may practise your excellent French. Appearances to the contrary, she is as English as you are, but her accent is a miracle.'

'My lady—' began Mrs Dickson, only to have Meg say, for once as impulsive as Cass,

'Oh, pray call me Meg, we cannot be friends else.'

The look Cass gave her was a glowing one, and Mrs Dickson said quietly, 'Then I insist upon being Emma. If you are from Paris, I must ask you if you were acquainted with my oldest friend, the late Vicomtesse de Chavannes—we were at Miss Pinkerton's Academy together. She was a number of years ahead of me, but I remember with gratitude the many small kindnesses with which Léonie favoured me.'

'She was my aunt,' Meg replied, her face sad. 'And she was kind to me, too. But stern. I miss her greatly.'

'I'm sure that you do,' nodded Mrs Dickson. 'How strange to meet you here. I lost touch with her many years ago when she went to France.'

She did not say that, after her father died and she had descended into poverty, she had been compelled to earn her living by being a companion and governess to young girls of good birth—Cass being her last pupil—until she had married George Dickson.

No conversation in the Gardens could last for very long, for too much was going on. First Johnny Dickson ran up, or rather, jumped towards his mama, his amused father following him. After that came Peverel, Vancourt, Will Osborne, and Sir Thomas Acland, who had abandoned Jane and Caro to the beavers. Simon was a little way behind them, talking to Jack Devereux. Surrounding *them* were all the small fry.

Everyone was duly introduced to the Dicksons, upon whom Peverel turned his charm despite the fact that they were obviously low Cits in trade, and to whom Vancourt gave only a less than deep bow and a passing stare.

'I have made arrangements for a cold collation to be served at four of the clock, in the paddock where the moveable aviaries are situated,' Simon announced. 'As that time is almost upon us, I suggest that we adjourn there, after we have collected the Ladies Kenilworth and Vancourt and seen the beavers.'

He bowed to the Dicksons, 'You will, of course, do me the favour of joining us. There will be more than enough for a party twice the size, if my housekeeper and chef live up to their usual reputations!'

'Oh, famous,' cried little Johnny Dickson, imitating a kangaroo again in his excitement. 'An open-air picnic in the Gardens, what fun.'

'All food taken in the open air is referred to as a picnic, my love,' his mother informed him, 'and even kangaroos must be quiet when they eat, so I hope that you will imitate them.'

This half-reproof flew over Johnny's head, but set George and Ritchie Devereux laughing.

'Oh, Aunt Meg,' Harriet Vancourt complained. 'I'm too tired to walk to Mama.'

'No need to worry, chicken. I will carry you,' and Meg picked up the little girl, who was still clutching the rag doll which she had carried all the way from Vancourt House.

Simon, who could not keep his eyes off Meg— he had begun to worry if there were something wrong with him, she obsessed him so—was watching her as she lifted Harriet up. Astonishingly, the mere sight of Meg tenderly kissing the little girl's soft cheek as she settled her into her arms caused a strong surge of desire—or was it lust mixed with affection?—to sweep over him. So strong was it that it shocked him.

Always, in his dealings with women, as when he had proposed to Meg, he had kept the sensual side of his nature under firm control. Caro Kenilworth had complained once that he always kept something of himself in reserve even when he was love-making—an unusually perceptive remark for her to make, he now realised, as he was confronted with his inability to control his emotions when with Meg, or when thinking of her in her absence.

He became aware that Jack Devereux was speaking to him, asking when the Society's next scientific lecture was being given, and he tried to answer him sensibly whilst keeping a half-watch on Meg. It was plain that Harriet was too heavy for her to be able to carry the little girl any great distance. In the middle of a sentence from Jack, without a word other than, 'Pray excuse me, Devereux,' he walked over to Meg and said, 'Allow me, Madame, to take over your burden. She is too much for you.'

This came out so abruptly and so unloverlikely— it was almost as though, Cass and Emma Dickson agreed later, he was giving an order to a recalcitrant underling—that Meg retaliated by saying firmly, 'No, indeed, I am stronger than I look.'

Simon gave a half-laugh, said, 'I know that, but it is not right that you should carry Harriet when there are gentlemen about who have no burden at all.'

He then looked meaningfully at Peverel, who had been walking beside Meg, unwilling to spoil his appearance as a well-dressed dandy by carrying a small child *à la* Jack Devereux.

Peverel chose to ignore him, saying instead, 'Quite true, Madame. If my cousin wishes to carry your charge, then I suggest that you allow him to do so. I suspect that he will only fall into the sulks if you cross him, and you do not wish to spoil the afternoon with *that*, do you?'

Meg's instant agreement to allow him to take Harriet from her as a result of his cousin's insolent comment did nothing to improve Simon's temper— more erratic these days than he cared to acknowledge to himself. It was all Meg's fault, of course. And if his own jealousy of any man who went near her appalled him, then that was one more annoyance to add to the tally of offences that she was unwittingly running up!

He stifled an angry response to Peverel's remark for the sake of Harriet, who offered him her doll to kiss, saying loudly, 'Next to Aunt Meg, I like you best, Uncle Simon.' Simon was a frequent visitor to Vancourt House, mostly out of pity for Jane, whom he had known since she was a small girl, rather than through any friendship with Vancourt. Flighty she might be, but she had not deserved *him*.

What had also shocked him was that when he had lifted Harriet from her aunt's arms and had touched Meg only lightly, that light touch had served to rouse him again, as it had at the Leominsters' party—something which had never happened with any other woman before. Truly, he was a driven fool!

What he did not know was that Meg had suffered—if that were the right word—the same experience, with the same result. If Simon was listening half-distractedly to Jack Devereux as a result, then she was undergoing the same experience with Peverel, who had insinuated himself between her and Cass.

Gossiping and laughing, much of their true thoughts being concealed by the mask of politeness, the little party reached the spot where Jane and Caro had been left, in order to collect them for lunch. Caro, an expression of supreme boredom on her face, was engaged in walking around the enclosure where the American beavers played, leaving Jane to sit in silence, contemplating all her many grievances against her husband, who had put himself on Meg's other side, and was rivalling Peverel in his attempts to charm her.

Harriet, she saw, was in Simon's arms, demanding to be set down so that she might run to Mama. It had not occurred to Jane, until that moment, that her faithless husband might take it into his head to pursue Meg, and the thought made her feel so ill that she could hardly pay proper attention to her introduction to the Dicksons.

Fortunately for everyone's good temper, by the time that they had returned to the aviaries' paddock, Simon's servants were already arriving, carrying chairs, hampers of food, plates, cutlery, damask napkins, and a large number of wine bottles and glasses.

'At last,' drawled Vancourt, seizing on a glass of good red wine and accepting a large beef and horseradish sandwich from a Darrow footman. He threw himself into a chair as soon as was decently possible, after all the women were seated. He dismissed young George, who tried to tell his Papa about the wondrous beasts he had seen, with a curt, 'Not now, boy,' so that George was compelled to tell Mrs Dickson all about them instead. With the innocent shrewdness of childhood, he had already grasped that she would be a more willing audience than his selfish Papa.

The sun had come out as Caro had prophesied, something which she insisted on telling the company in an insufferable, I told you so, voice which had them all wincing, while she loudly complained of her dissatisfaction at being deprived of her parasol earlier, and of the shade of the beavers' pond later.

More to create a diversion than anything else, and

in an attempt to start a hare which might put some of the party in a better humour, Meg said thoughtfully, on picking up a chicken sandwich—a dainty one, made especially for the ladies—'When I am observing the animals I sometimes have the oddest thought: that *their* behaviour may afford us insights into our own.'

Her audience reacted to this statement each in his, or her, own fashion.

'Very odd, indeed,' was wrenched from Jane who was frowning, not being sure how much Meg was encouraging Vancourt.

'Dear Madame,' exclaimed Will Osborne, his honest face earnest, 'there I must correct you. We have it on the best authority of all, that of God himself, that we humans most resemble the angels, rather than the animals. We are of a different kind and of a different creation, so that any likeness between us must be accidental—if it exists at all.'

Jack Devereux paused in his demolition of a ham and mustard sandwich to say in his dry, but straightforward, fashion, 'Those of us who have engaged in warfare, Madame, might echo your opinion rather than that of Osborne's—eh, Dickie?' This last to George Dickson, who rewarded it with a silent nod of the head.

Simon's response was an internal one, and devoted to a quite different point, being of the order of, What kind of life has Madame been living to give vent to such a sentiment? More evidence, if such were needed, to support the notion of her loose-living, amorous career since animals were notoriously lax in that department!

For his part Peverel merely offered negligently, 'Such a remark, Madame la Comtesse, whatever its truth, serves only to display the witty liveliness of the mind that provoked its utterance.'

So, dear cousin, Simon silently glowered, you hope to follow the example of the animals with Madame, and take your pleasure with her as carelessly and as often as possible. Jealousy almost had him choking over his cook's excellent Shrewsbury biscuits.

Cass and Mrs Dickson, by contrast, said nothing at all, merely contenting themselves with exchanging amused glances, which said, What a splendid friend we have gained in Marguerite de Vaux. We shall have some excellent *causeries* with her, to be sure, if that is a sample of her thinking.

'For my part,' announced Caro Kenilworth, 'I consider it to be demeaning to my sex that such a comparison should be made at all, and by a lady. . .I have not the slightest wish to be compared to any animal.'

Meg, amused by the furore which her remark had created, had the greatest difficulty in not retorting to Caro, Not even with an honest cow, Lady K.?

The discussion that she had initiated received its death blow after Sir Thomas Acland, a silent man who had rarely uttered once during the afternoon, said in grave and bishoplike tones, 'The great Goethe, himself, Madame, discussed the matter at length in similar terms to your own, and reached the conclusion that we are more similar to the animals than we care to think.'

He paused, portentously, and it was plain to all

assembled that he was going to make up for his previous reticence by giving them an informed lecture on the matter, except that Cass Devereux exclaimed happily, 'Oh, if the great Goethe has spoken on the matter, then we must all hold our tongues and pass on to lower things, or do I mean higher ones?'

A general laugh in which even Sir Thomas joined, ran round the party—only Cass Devereux could get away with such charming irreverence. Will Osborne could be heard whispering to Simon, 'Now, who the devil is the great Goethe?'

Naughty Simon, delighted to see off a rival, muttered to him, 'If you really wish to know, Osborne, then have a word with Acland; he will be sure to enlighten you.'

Which would serve to keep him away from Meg for the rest of the afternoon, was his private, gleeful thought—one rival despatched for the time being. He was suddenly aware of Meg's sharp eyes on him—if he were watching her, she was watching him and she knew perfectly well that he had just dished Will! His respect for Madame's acuteness grew.

To Meg, the whole afternoon had been a revelation as each member of the party seemed determined to reveal their true selves, good or bad, without knowing what they were doing. She immediately amended that; some knew quite well, Cass Devereux among them, and Simon also, who was surprising her by his sharp eye to the main chance where she was concerned. If only he had not overheard that wretched conversation with his cousin Peverel and misunderstood it

No use repining, though. Or crying over spilt milk, as her old nurse used to say—and Aunt Léonie, who had said the same thing in French with more Gallic wit. What was done was done, and the real damage had been done that day long ago when she had refused Simon. Or later, perhaps, when she had married André. . .

The bright afternoon seemed to turn cold. She shuddered a little. No, she would not think of that, not now, not here, with the shouting children about her, and Jack and Cass Devereux present to show that a happy marriage could be achieved between two people who appeared to be quite different.

Peverel saw the shudder, and leaned officiously over to murmur, 'You are cold, Madame. May I lend you my jacket?'

Meg instinctively distrusted this chivalrous offer. Recovering her previous light-heartedness, she wondered what Simon's reaction would be if he saw Peverel in his shirtsleeves, and his jacket around her shoulders.

'How very kind of you, but no, I am not really cold. A passing frisson, I assure you.'

Cass Devereux, who was on her left, murmured in her ear, 'I am a little warmer than I care for, Meg. Take the shawl I am wearing, I do not really need it.'

Meg allowed Cass to drape it around her shoulders. It would be churlish to refuse a kind offer which would cause her no such embarrassment as Peverel's would have done. Simon's judgemental eyes were on her again, and she was sure that he had heard Peverel's offer. Perhaps he would think of her a little more kindly now that she had refused it.

Vain hope! Unknown to her, Simon had already decided that he would have words with his cousin as soon as he could decently contrive an opportunity. One came when all the children decided that they wished to visit the bears again before they went home. All except Harriet, that was, to whom Aunt Meg had promised a visit to the pelicans instead.

He caught Peverel by the arm, saying curtly, 'A private word with you, if you please.'

'What, here?' exclaimed Peverel. 'I have come on pleasure, not to be rebuked, for I see by your expression that some sort of rebuke is intended.'

'Yes, here.' Simon's voice was dangerous. 'I am not about to spend valuable time chasing you around town when all I need to do is detain you for a few moments. You will do me the courtesy of agreeing.'

He did not use the words the 'honour of agreeing' for he thought, rightly, that his cousin possessed no honour.

'Oh, very well.' Peverel shrugged his shoulders. 'If you must, you must.' He watched the rest of the party disappear into the distance, Madame among them. Another opportunity lost, thanks to his interfering cousin.

'I feel compelled to ask you not to pursue Madame. I have reason to believe that your intentions towards her are not honourable.' Simon could be no more definite than that, seeing that he could not reveal that he had overheard the conversation where Meg had given Peverel money.

'Oh, you are quite mistaken about that, Sim. My

intentions are purely honourable. I mean to marry her.'

'Do not call me Sim—' Simon began saying, only to be interrupted by Peverel's careless laugh.

'Cousin, then—if that is what you prefer.'

'Not that either. I do not wish to be reminded that we are cousins—' only to be interrupted again.

'Don't you, by God? But we are cousins, and I am your heir—or had you forgotten?'

Simon did his best to rein in his temper, aware that he was allowing Peverel to sidestep the true subject of the conversation. 'I suppose,' he said, cool again, 'that you are after her for her fortune.'

'What a low opinion you have of the lady's attractions,' drawled his cousin. 'I admit that her wealth is an inducement, but not the only one, I assure you.'

'Oh, I do beg leave to doubt that. Meg and I have had little to do with one another of recent years, but I should not wish to see her married to someone with your reputation.'

Peverel began to laugh. 'My reputation! That's rich. The lady's reputation is such that she should be grateful that anyone wishes to marry her!'

Only with difficulty did Simon prevent himself from striking the grinning face of the man before him. He had heard whispered and indefinite slurs against Meg before, but nothing so apparently downright as this. He contained himself by saying between his teeth, 'Now what the devil do you mean by *that*?'

'You mean that you haven't heard?' Peverel mocked him. 'Oh, I always knew that you were strangely innocent, *cousin*, but I thought that even

you knew how André de Vaux came to his death.
Why, when I was in Paris, it was the one topic of
conversation: that little Meg Ashe, now a Comtesse,
was Talleyrand's latest mistress, that André was
twitted over it, and consequently was compelled to
fight the duel in which he was killed. Rumour said
that she had other, nameless, lovers.' He paused,
adding with a significant wink and grin, 'As I was
in a position to know.'

Simon stared at him, stunned. Of all the things
that Peverel might have told him, he had not
expected this. Oh, he had known from the conversation that he had overheard at the Leominsters' that
Meg must have had an *affaire* with Peverel.

But what he had just learned was worse than that,
much worse. His once innocent Meg had been the
mistress of an old man who had been one of the
most notorious *roués* of the last forty years! A man
whose notoriety as a skilled seducer was only
equalled by his notoriety as a wily politician and
diplomat, who had managed to keep his head on his
shoulders through all the changes of regime in
France since the Revolution of 1789!

So *that* accounted for Meg's polish, her self-
control, her worldliness, her damned double-dealing
appearance of injured innocence. She had been
taught by a master. He seized on a straw. Peverel
might be lying. He told him so, fiercely.

'Oh, believe that if you will. I was in Paris at the
time. Of course, being such a man of honour yourself, so highly principled, *you* could not forgive her,
or wish her for a wife, but I, why. . .I am happy to
accept her for what she is, and marry her. A truly

Christian attitude to adopt under the circumstances,
I think you will agree.'

What could he say? Not, My blessings on the pair
of you, you are a splendid match for one another.
To do so would reveal the depth of his feelings for
a woman who had turned out to be totally unworthy,
and would also give Peverel the triumph over him
which his cousin had always wanted.

Instead, he was almost indifferent. 'Well, if that
is how matters lie, then I withdraw my objections.'
But he didn't mean what he said.

'And, of course,' Peverel pursued, 'the sooner we
are married, the sooner Darrow Hall and Darrow
lands will have an heir of the second generation.
You, I believe, still have no intention to marry.'

Simon felt like retorting that he would marry a
hag from Hell and get a child on her to save Darrow
from falling to Peverel and any of *his* get. His own
dignity and sense of fitness prevented him from saying any such thing. Which, he knew, meant that he
would always be at a disadvantage when arguring
with his unscrupulous cousin.

'Forgive me,' Peverel said into the silence that
had followed his last words, 'but if that is all that
you have to say to me, *cousin*, then I will join the
others.' He bowed, and strolled off, happy in
the knowledge that he had hurled a bombshell named
Talleyrand at Simon, and for the time being had
gained himself a respite from his advice and his
reproaches.

As for the lady, well, whether the rumours were
true or not, he didn't care a tinker's damn. As far
as Peverel was concerned, she was merely a source

of possible wealth—with the bonus that he had begun to care for her—so any lie, or innuendo, would serve to gain him a clear run at it.

Simon, for his part, spent the rest of the afternoon in an unhappy daze. As Peverel had guessed, almost more than the news of Meg's possible immorality was the revelation that one of her partners had been Talleyrand. He almost felt that he could have stomached a handsome young buck rather than the monster who had betrayed everyone in turn, man and woman.

Oh, damn everything, he was lying, he knew he was. He would have hated anyone with whom she had cared to be faithless. The very worst had happened. Of all inconvenient things, he knew beyond a doubt that, whatever he had felt for the youngest Miss Ashe all those years ago, he now loved her— as he must have done then, without knowing it.

Nothing to do but trudge after the others, thinking that, being a mindless bear, happy to climb a pole and catch buns, might be a better fate than being born Simon Darrow. Best of all was to try to do what he had originally suggested and avoid meeting Meg altogether.

In the meantime, he must try to enjoy the remainder of the visit to the Gardens as the others were doing and pretend, like Voltaire's Candide, that everything was for the best in the best of all possible worlds!

Chapter Six

A week after the visit to the Zoological Gardens, Simon met Jasper at Louis Fronsac's fencing academy. Meg's brother was improving his ability with the sabre, and told Simon of a piece of news about her that had him seething all over again, and immediately breaking his resolution to avoid her.

'Care to come with me and visit m'sister in her new home, Darrow?' Jasper offered as he towelled himself off between bouts. 'Time you made it up with her.'

Simon ignored the second statement, and seized on the first, surprise and indignation in his voice. 'New home? I thought that she was staying with the Vancourts whilst she was over here.'

Jasper eyed him, and his indignation, over his towel. 'Changed her mind. Staying longer. Something about settling her late husband's affairs in England. She's rented Templestowe's place off Piccadilly.' Alex, Lord Templestowe had recently been appointed Ambassador to Spain.

So, Madame wanted a nest of her own where she

could entertain whom she pleased, did she, without being observed? Suddenly Simon wanted most desperately to see her again. Why, God alone knew, because since Peverel's revelations about her loose life in Paris, seeing her—even at a distance—set him off into such a froth of anger and annoyance that he could barely think straight. A phrase he had not heard or used since the days when he had been a small boy and possessed a nanny.

'Alone?' he managed. 'In that great barracks?'

'Not exactly,' said Jasper through his towel. 'She's offered me quarters there, and she's taken on General Hollis's widow as a *dame de compagnie*, chaperon, what you will. Meg has nicknamed her my watchdog—which both ladies seem to think an excellent joke.'

'Oh.' For some reason Simon felt quite deflated. 'I wouldn't have thought that Meg needed a watchdog. She seems well able to look after herself.'

Jasper peered curiously at him, before throwing his towel down and picking up his sabre. There was a virulence in Simon's comments about his sister which was at odds with his normal equable self. What in the world was the matter with the pair of them? He had tried speaking of Simon to Meg as a possible brother-in-law, only to have her say in her most freezing French great-lady voice, 'Quite out of the question, Jas. Apart from the fact that I have no intention of marrying again, if I were to do so, Simon Darrow is the last person whom I should choose.'

And then she had swept out of the room, ending all further conversation.

'So you will come with me?' Jasper offered as carelessly as he could.

Simon could scarcely bring himself to speak, so he nodded instead. Light in the attic, fit for bedlam, a glutton for punishment, were all phrases which passed rapidly through his tormented mind.

He repeated them to himself all over again when he reached Templestowe House, for who should be there before him but Peverel!

He was not to know how little Meg wished to see his cousin, who had set about ingratiating himself from the moment he had walked through her drawing-room door and bowed over her hand, saying, 'You must know, my dear Madame, that I could not wait to visit you when I heard of your move. I have such happy memories of Templestowe House and the dear Countess.' He sighed sentimentally, offering Meg his most killing expression.

Meg was not killed by it. She had no wish to entertain Peverel, but had been unable to refuse him entry—he had cunningly arrived with Will Osborne in tow. He had obviously brought him along to confer respectability on himself, and his smiling near-impertinence told her that he knew that she was well aware of what he was doing. He was still treating poor Will in the same offhand fashion which he had used to him at the Devereux's party and at the Zoological Gardens.

Meg's only consolation was that, with Charlotte Hollis present, there was little untoward which Peverel could do or say to her. Like Will, he was dressed absolutely *à point* and was just as determined to please her.

'I have never met the Templestowes,' was Meg's cool reply. 'I rented the house from their man of business.'

She had a piece of canvaswork in her lap, showing a peacock in full display—an apt symbol, she thought, for the smirking man opposite to her, so sure of his charm.

For all his good looks and his wit she could not like him, knowing of his blackmailing of Jane and his proposed treatment of herself. This was merely the opening shot of his threatened campaign to win her, she was sure, and to do so he was concealing his villainy behind a mask of charm. Meg could not help contrasting his subtlety with Simon's blunt honesty.

What's more, she was also sure that he had bamboozled Will into bringing him along as a supporter of Will's courtship! Once arrived though, he was busy cutting Will out—in the most charming way, of course—so that Will could not take offence. There was only one thing for it.

'Charlotte,' she said to Mrs Hollis, who, in her early thirties, had turned out to be a much younger woman than Meg had expected—she had been the late General's second wife—'Charlotte, you might care to show Mr Darrow the new album of *Views of the Great Houses of Britain*, which is on the map table in the corner. I am sure that he would find it most interesting.'

Having, as she thought, dismissed Peverel successfully, she turned to Will who was gazing at her in mute adoration, and asked him about his new curricle, which he had christened in Hyde Park the day before.

She had reckoned without Peverel's impudence. He stood up, bowed in her direction, and said gaily, 'Mr Darrow, indeed! How can you speak to me so formally, my dear Madame? Why, your family and mine have been neighbours and friends for the last five generations, at least. And, although we were not childhood companions as you and my cousin Simon were, I think that you might do me the honour of calling me Peverel, in exchange for me being allowed to address you as Marguerite—or even, dare I say it, as Meg.'

He ended this remarkable speech by taking Meg's hand, and offering her a deep bow before kissing it.

It was at this inopportune moment that Jasper, who had told the butler not to trouble to announce them, walked in, followed by Simon, whose first sight of the female thorn in his flesh was of her being publicly saluted by his worthless cousin!

An unknown woman, the chaperon presumably, was certainly not doing her duty and protecting her mistress as she should. That unmitigated ass, Will Osborne, had apparently nothing better to do than to watch this pantomime, his jaw slightly dropped.

Meg refrained from withdrawing her hand hastily when Simon entered. She would not allow him to think that his opinion of her mattered in the least. Indeed, Simon's thunderous expression had the perverse effect of inciting her to encourage Peverel further. How dare Simon presume to judge her!

So she allowed Peverel to hold her hand a little longer than she should—he was undoubtedly baiting

Simon by clinging to it—but denied him what he had begged for.

'Alas, my name is only for my relatives—and those—' and she dropped her voice so that Simon should not hear her '—whom I can trust. May I now add you to that list?'

Meg saw that she had wrong-footed him slightly, but his recovery was rapid. 'Oh, I hope so, I do hope so,' he murmured but, even as he spoke, his eyes mocked her.

She was not Jane, to be over-awed and intimidated by him. During her marriage she had refused to be put down by a greater master of the devious arts than Peverel Darrow.

Instead, she moved over to her brother, offered him her cheek, which he duly kissed, before she turned her attention to Simon. He was glaring at her as though she were an unlovely cross between Jezebel and Messalina. Meg thought that it was fortunate for his friendship with her brother that, although Peverel could read Simon's expression, and was amused by it, Jasper could not.

'Sir Simon,' she said sweetly, acknowledging his bow, but not offering him the hand which Peverel had so recently kissed. Given everything, that might be going a step too far. 'I am delighted to see you here. I believe that you are not acquainted with my *dame de compagnie*, Mrs Hollis. She was recommended to me by one of your old friends, Lady Devereux.'

Well, that last fact ought to spike his guns and no mistake! Having wrong-footed one cousin, she had now done the same to the other. It was growing to be quite a habit, and a delightful one this time, since Simon could surely have no fault to find with such a paragon of perfection as Mrs Hollis was reputed to be.

'So pleased to make your acquaintance at last,' Simon told the lady, who was beginning to understand that being an Anglo-French Countess's watchdog was not going to be either as simple or as boring as she had at first thought.

'I met your late husband some years ago when I first entered Parliament. I was truly sorry to learn of his death. Madame la Comtesse could have no more proper or pleasing a companion.'

And so he told Meg a little later, after Jasper had suggested that he stay for supper, Peverel having left, spouting promises that he would visit again in a few days' time, when he proposed to escort Meg and Mrs Hollis to the theatre, Will Osborne also in attendance, of course. Peverel's contempt for Will was so great that he did not fear his competition for Meg's hand. He rightly judged that such a feeble ass could have no attraction for her.

Meg was unable to refuse this apparently kind offer out of hand without betraying her difficult situation *vis-à-vis* Peverel to Mrs Hollis. Her acquiescence earned her a glare from Simon.

Supper might have been an uncomfortable meal, but surprisingly was not. Jasper was in great form, teasing Charlotte Hollis about trying, unsuccessfully, to be his sister's dragon.

'When she told me that she was acquiring a companion,' he said, raising his wineglass to her, 'I naturally assumed that I was going to meet a dear little old lady with a mob cap, a large canvas bag, and an elderly smelly poodle, not someone who looks as though she needs a chaperon herself.'

Even for Jasper, this was a little extreme. He was a great man for the ladies, mostly those ladies who were kindly known as opera dancers, or bits of muslin for want of a better name. Charlotte Hollis with her gravely pretty face, her simply dressed brown hair and her modest toilette, was not one of his obvious targets.

'You will have to guard one another,' remarked Simon drily. 'Especially if you are to keep away such adventurers as my cousin Peverel,' he could not resist adding. 'A trip with him to the theatre is sure to cause comment about the particularity of his intentions, especially if repeated.'

'Mr Will Osborne will add respectability to the party,' offered Charlotte swiftly. She knew that Peverel's reputation was not good, although not bad enough to bar him from polite society. 'And I don't believe that either Madame or I wish to repeat the experience.'

Simon could say nothing further without appearing churlish, and the rest of the evening passed happily enough—even though both Charlotte and Jasper privately noted that the polite formality between Simon and Meg was excessive, to say the least.

Except that when Simon had left, Jasper—who was staying the night—walked into his sister's little sitting-room, adjacent to the large best bedroom, and sat down opposite her. Meg was reading before retiring. He said, quietly for him, 'What is wrong between you and Simon, Meg, that you are at such odds? The air is positively sulphurous when you are together these days.'

Meg decided to treat him to a little of the truth: not too much, for Simon and he were old and valued friends, and she did not wish to spoil their friendship.

'Oh, Jasper, do not refine overmuch on what I hope is only a passing thing. Simon has heard a little of the stupid gossip about me, I believe, and it is making him unhappy. After all, he did propose to me once, so I don't suppose he feels very pleased if someone tells him untruthful *on dits* about my life in France.'

'I suppose Peverel has been trying to queer his pitch with you,' remarked Jasper shrewdly. 'Want me to have a word with him? I could tell him something of the truth.'

'Of all things, no,' exclaimed Meg, showing agitation for once. 'The matter is trivial, seeing that he and I are merely acquaintances these days.'

'As you wish, sister, but I don't think that Simon quite views you in that light. I know a jealous man when I see one, but least said, soonest mended, I suppose. However, if you should need my help, then you merely have to speak. What are brothers for, but to protect their sisters?'

He rose. So did Meg. She walked impulsively over to him and kissed his cheek. 'You are a good fellow, Jasper, the best of brothers. Always remember that you may come to me, too, although I cannot imagine that you will ever need my help.'

She sat for a time after he had left, listening to the peacocks screeching on the terrace outside. She

was thinking of Simon. He was seldom out of her
thoughts. When Charlotte came in to bid her goodnight, after her maid had dressed her for bed, she
found Meg standing at the window, looking out
into the darkness, as though trying to find
something there.

'May I be of assistance, Madame?'

Meg turned, startled. She had been far away. She
understood at once that Charlotte was referring to
what had passed with the Darrow cousins and, like
Jasper, was offering her aid and comfort.

'You are very kind, but I do not believe that anyone can help me. It is for me to help myself. What
you may do is join me in discouraging Peverel
Darrow without causing any form of scandal. Jasper
twitted you with not being my dragon—perhaps you
could be my dragonette instead!'

This set Charlotte laughing at the mere idea that
she could be a baby dragon, and the moment passed.
Only, as she made to leave, Meg said, 'Not Madame
in future, but Meg. There are so few left to call
me that.'

'In private,' agreed Charlotte. 'In public, it would
not be proper.'

Meg considered saying, 'Oh, I am beyond propriety,' but kept the thought to herself. As with
Jasper, she had to consider carefully how much of
herself she gave away. It was growing harder and
harder for her to be frank with anyone.

So matters stood throughout the summer that followed. Jasper's care for Meg took the form of
constantly escorting her and Charlotte to all the

events of the season. They visited Ranelagh, the theatre—only once with Peverel—boated on the Thames, went to the Opera, and all the balls, receptions, and ridottos that filled the lives of the cousinry who ruled Britain.

Once Meg went to the House of Commons with Jane and Charlotte to hear Simon make a short speech on Reform, of which he was an advocate, since he believed that only through careful and progressive change could a revolution be averted.

Polite formality continued to reign. On one thing she and Simon apparently agreed: not to waltz with one another. To do so would have meant a physical contact that neither of them could bear, for it immediately revived all the suppressed passion which lay between them.

Of the two, Meg was the more astonished by this. When she had known Simon at the time of his proposal, his touch had meant nothing to her, although the sight of him had excited her after a fashion which at the time she had not fully understood.

Marriage to André changed me, she thought one evening at a *bal masqué* given by Princess Lieven, as she watched Simon waltzing with Caro Kenilworth, who was still doggedly pursuing him with a view to marriage. If he taught me nothing else, he taught me what passion could mean. He awoke my sleeping senses. And that is why I feel such a pang when I see Simon with Caro. Are they going home together, I wonder? To. . . And if to think of *that* pains me so, what does it tell me about my feelings for him?

She was not to know that Simon's feelings for

her, when he saw her, lightly clasped in Will
Osborne's arms, circling the dance floor, were
equally strong, if not stronger. To the devil with him
and her, and Peverel, too! For his worthless cousin
always seemed to be hovering nearby.

Commonsense told him that Jasper Ashe's
constant hovering about Meg was proof of his intention to safeguard both her and her reputation—or
was it that Jasper was after the chaperon, despite
her difference from all the other women he had
pursued?

He taxed Jasper with this immediately. Simon's
only concession to the Princess's masquerade had
been to adopt a long dark cloak and a black bird
mask with a long beak. Jasper, however, was splen-
didly turned out as a Cossack, and not for the first
time Simon wondered where Jasper's money, to pay
for all the trappings of high life, came from.
Although he was a half-pay officer in peace time,
from a family which was notoriously poor, he
appeared as rich and improvident as the young heirs
to vast fortunes who were his friends.

'Tell me, Ashe,' he remarked, apparently carelessly, 'is your constant dancing in attendance on
Meg and her friend on behalf of your sister's
honour—or is the chaperon your true target?'

For once Jasper was not frank with him. 'Why
should it be for either reason? Can't a man have
a pretty woman on each arm without his friends
immediately consigning him to the duelling field or
the altar?'

Nevertheless, it was becoming increasingly clear
to Meg and Simon that Charlotte Hollis had suc-

ceeded in doing something which no other woman
had done before—she had captured the heart of that
fickle cavalier, Jasper Ashe.

For the Lievens' ball, she had adopted the pretty
rustic clothing of a shepherdess, and its delightful
simplicity had enchanted Jasper even further. That
night it was obvious, by their manner to one another,
that Charlotte was as attracted to Jasper as he was
to her. Meg, dressed daringly as Cleopatra, and still
alienated from Simon, had the dubious pleasure of
watching their happiness. Fancy Jasper being caught
at last, and by someone so good and modest: who
would have believed it? The pity was that she was
as poor as he was—thus proving the purity of his
intentions, for there was no reason to believe that
Charlotte's attraction for him was her fortune.

'But reformed rakes always marry good women,'
explained Cass Devereux to Meg, as they sat
pleasantly chatting to one another whilst watching
the fun. 'Safer so. Jack says its always better to
know that your sons are your own, and not someone
else's.'

'Is that the only reason?' asked Meg, entertained,
as usual, by Cass's witty down-to-earth conversation.

'Not entirely. Flighty women choose bad house-
keepers, too, and a man prefers a comfortable home
when he reaches mature years, rather than a trumpery love nest. Now here comes someone who has
never wished for a trumpery love nest. Good
evening, Sir Simon. Have you arrived to take
my friend away so that I shall have no one left
with whom to talk sense? I'm sure that you are

determined to talk nonsense to her!'

'If she will allow me,' retorted Simon gravely, openly light-hearted for once. Perhaps it was the mask he was wearing—or was it that Cass Devereux could always disarm him? Meg thought enviously. Shall I ask her how she does it?

Instead, as Simon bowed and asked her to stand up in the quadrille with him, she accepted, putting out her hand for him to raise her to her feet. She was aware of Cass's shrewd eyes on them, so she was as gracious as she could be. So much so that Simon remarked, still retaining her hand in his so that her whole body quivered and silently sang, 'You are pleased to be at evens with me tonight.'

'I am always at evens with you,' riposted Meg tartly. 'It is you who are at odds with me.'

Normally she might have expected her dart to be thrown back at her as she came out with this, but for once it was no such thing, since he continued by saying, 'Jasper's presence seems to have sobered you, Madame, or is it the example of Mrs Hollis? My cousin Peverel appears to be in exile so far as you are concerned, which pleases me even if it does not please him.'

'I was not aware that my conduct ought to be arranged so as to please either of you,' was Meg's answer to that, immediately before they separated to bow at one another before the music began.

'Oh, our conduct ought always to be arranged so as to please our friends,' replied Simon as they passed one another in the dance.

Meg, on their next encounter, asked sweetly, 'And do I count as a friend so far as you are concerned,

Sir Simon? I was not aware that I had that honour.'

'Good God, Madame,' he said as he passed her again. 'I thought that we had been friends since you were in short skirts.'

'But not, apparently, when I wore long French ones. Unless you have changed your mind recently.'

Against his will, this set Simon laughing, but his face had regained its normal composure when next they met. This impelled Meg to remark, 'You are suddenly grave, Sir Simon. Is it French fashions that you object to? If so, I cannot promise to reform— English ones seem so dull.'

This should have annoyed him, served to confirm her frivolity, but this evening he could not be angry with her. The laxness which *bals masqués* invariably imposed on those who attended them was doing its work. Everyone knew everyone else, even though they were masked; but eyes glittering through slits and bodies wearing unfamiliar and exciting clothes had a strange effect on their wearers.

Simon's mask gave him the air of a predator, and he could convince himself that Meg's disguise as Cleopatra was a disguise and that she was quite unlike the free-living Egyptian queen, and so he was kinder to her than usual. Or was it, he thought afterwards, that he had a mind to lull her? Once the dance was over and they stood bowing, before he consigned her back to Cass again, instead of doing so he took her hand, and said, 'Come.'

Whether it was his bird mask which transformed him into an eagle ready to pounce on its prey, or whether it was the mere sight of Meg as Egypt's queen which caused him to lose all his stern resolve to keep their relationship distant, Simon never knew.

Using his considerable strength, he urged her through the milling crowds, through a glass door and, closing it firmly behind them, led her on to a terrace from where they could see London and its gas lamps below them.

Meg's initial wish to struggle rapidly disappeared. Easier to let him pull her gently along. In any case, without making a scene she could not refuse him—and did she wish to?

Once on the terrace, he released her. She thought that he was about to step back; indeed, he began to do so, but no, instead, he looked down at her, tense and silent. His eyes glittering through the mask were exactly like those of the eagle it was portraying. He stepped forward instead, saying hoarsely, 'Unfinished business, Madame,' and took her in his arms.

It would be true to say that Simon was as astonished as Meg by his actions. He had had no intention of doing any such thing. He had meant to speak to her carefully and seriously, to ask her to deny the rumours about her reputation that were running around society; to praise her, perhaps, for her recent circumspect behaviour.

Alas, all such good resolutions flew away when Meg stood before him, her lips parted, her eyes shining, her head a little thrown back, her whole beautiful body displayed to advantage in the trappings of the desert temptress!

Tempted he was. And fell.

Mouth met mouth. Body met body. Hands misbehaved. Simon said something hoarse and broken,

Meg echoed him. They clung together as though they were a stone nymph and satyr making love in the gardens below them.

An idyll out of time, Meg thought later, alone in her chaste bed. What would have happened had it been allowed to continue might have given a whole different course to their subsequent lives. But the door to the terrace opened, and a familiar voice said, mocking them, 'Ah, there you are, cousin. Enjoying the night, I see.'

It was Peverel Darrow. He must have seen them leave, and had followed them, giving them just sufficient time, Simon thought savagely, to begin to misbehave themselves. Slowly, reluctantly, they fell apart, their bodies protesting at joy denied.

'I believe, Madame,' Peverel said, grinning as he advanced towards them, wearing the trappings of the Devil—Mephistopheles in person, down to a small tail—'that you agreed to dance the cotillion with me, and the music is about to begin.'

It was true. Meg had so agreed, as much to keep him quiet, without conceding a lot to him, as for any other reason. She and Charlotte had agreed on such a ploy. Simon, however, thwarted, took matters differently.

'Oh, indeed,' he almost snarled. 'Dance with him, by all means, Madame. Please the Devil, if no one else.'

You might, thought Meg bitterly, have believed that in their recent encounter *she* had fallen on *him*, instead of the other way round.

'Oh, so I have your permission, Sir Simon,' she shot at him, Peverel grinning the while at Simon's discomfiture. He had been shocked to see them disappear, even more shocked to discover them in one another's arms: it was no part of his plans for Meg that she and Simon should become reconciled.

He held out his hand to her and, perforce, Meg took it. She could almost feel Simon seething behind her as they walked through the garden door and re-entered the ballroom. For a moment it had seemed to Meg that what lay between them had been forgotten, that they might take up where they had left off when she had so foolishly refused him.

But she had reckoned without Peverel, and it might be wise not to reckon without him again.

Chapter Seven

The blue skies of summer are frequently spoiled by the appearance of unexpected clouds. So, too, life may deceive the unwary into thinking that all may be well—and will remain well. Just as Meg had begun to hope that she and Simon might be coming to terms again, and that Jasper was at last prepared to settle down, dark clouds arrived to spoil her summer, which had begun to be a happier one.

Simon's friendliness to her had been destroyed by Peverel's breaking in on them at the Lievens' *bal masqué*, whilst Jasper, who had begun to spend more and more of his time with her and Charlotte, suddenly retreated into the wild life that he had led before coming to stay at Templestowe House. They rarely saw him during late June and early July, and Charlotte, whose cheeks had become rosy under Jasper's attentions, grew sallow again.

Better, thought Meg sadly, that he had never paid her any attentions at all, rather than show her such particularity and then withdraw. To make matters worse, Peverel and Will Osborne haunted them, or rather haunted Meg, for Charlotte, having lost her one devoted cavalier, now had no cavalier at all.

'I would wish,' Meg said brightly to Charlotte as they were busy with their canvaswork one afternoon, 'to visit Astley's Amphitheatre. I have never been there, but it would not be proper for us to go without a gentleman dancing attendance on us. I shall ask Jasper to take us, but I do wish that it were possible for ladies to look after themselves a little more than we are allowed to.'

Charlotte stitched on in silence, her head lowered, before she muttered, 'I do not think that Major Ashe cares for our company these days. We rarely see him, and I have no wish to impose on him. I would prefer you not to ask such a favour of him.'

'No!' Meg's answer was spirited. 'Why should it always be presumed that men may do exactly as they please whilst we are always condemned to please them? I do not greatly care what Jasper's wishes are. He should be prepared to sink his own wishes for once and oblige us. Besides, his recent conduct is most strange. He has always been a good and loving brother to me, particularly in the past when the rest of my family showed me little consideration.'

This surprised Charlotte and roused her from her apathy a little. Meg rarely talked of personal matters, and for the first time it occurred to her companion that perhaps her employer's life had not always been a bed of roses.

'That is true,' she said slowly, and then in a rush, 'Oh, do forgive me, Meg, but I have been so foolish. . .I had thought. . . No, no, I must not say it,' and she began to cry, wildly and loudly after a fashion quite unlike that of her usual equable self.

'No, Charlotte, no!' Meg threw down her stitchery, in order to cross to where Charlotte sat sobbing. She put her arms around her to comfort her.

'You were not foolish. I, too, thought that Jasper had a *tendre* for you, and it is most unlike him to play fast and loose with a good woman such as yourself. If you were deceived, so was I, so do not call yourself foolish. If he has really treated you so lightly then you may call him wicked for all that he is my brother.'

Charlotte's response was to cry even harder, so that Meg began to rock her, murmuring, 'There, there, cry for a little if you must, but then be brave and show the world a bold uncaring face.'

Even as I do, she thought sadly. Even as I do.

After a time Charlotte stopped weeping, pulled out a most inadequate handkerchief, mopped up her tears and blew her nose.

'I was a fool,' she muttered, 'to think that a sought-after and handsome man like your brother could care for a dowd past her last prayers such as I am. Who would want to marry a penniless widow when the world is full of well-dowered young girls?'

What to say? Nothing was best. Meg made comforting noises until Charlotte recovered herself and picked up her stitchery again, saying, 'Oh, dear, Meg, I have wet you through, and it is my duty to comfort you, not you me.'

All the same, decided Meg, after she had rung for the tea things to be brought in and life had resumed its normal tranquil way, I shall have a word with

Jasper. He had no right to raise Charlotte's hopes as he did, and then drop her so unkindly. I shall try to see him tonight, however late he returns home and, as Cook said of a misbehaving kitchen boy, I shall have it out with him. Best to do it when all the world is safely asleep and none may overhear us.

Late it was. The clock in the drawing-room nearest to the big front door was striking four before Meg heard the noise and clatter attendant on Jasper's return. She had decided not to speak to him immediately, but would allow him time to retire to his rooms before she challenged him.

His progress up the grand staircase was slow. He was obviously half-cut, and for a moment Meg considered the wisdom of challenging him when he was in such a state. The image of Charlotte's wan face rose before her. No, she would not wait. If he was not fit to talk to her, then he must tell her so. He was by no means the first drunken man she had had to cope with. . .

She knocked on his door. His valet, Tyler, had passed her on the landing and had stopped to say, 'Madame, the Major is not himself. He will not allow me to undress him. . .'

Whether or no he was shocked by Meg's riposte, she did not stay to find out. 'I have no wish to undress my brother, but I do need to speak to him.' Afterwards, she was to ask herself what had driven her to be so urgent and to thank God for it. At the time she thought of nothing but knocking on the door.

To hear Jasper call in a blurred voice, 'I told

you to leave me alone, Tyler. Go away.'

'It isn't Tyler knocking, Jas. It's Meg.'

'Doubly go away, then. You've no business with me tonight, or ever.'

He wasn't so overset that he could not answer her. Meg stared at the panelling. She made a decision.

'If you don't let me in, Jasper, I shall fetch the butler and a couple of footmen and have the door broken down. I don't think that Alex Templestowe would be too happy about that, do you?'

Silence. Meg stood, her heart beating rapidly. Something was wrong, she was sure of it. Jasper had been so unlike himself recently, and now he didn't resemble himself at all!

Please God, let him open the door, she prayed.

She heard footsteps. The door opened. Jasper stood there swaying a little, but somehow she thought that he was not very drunk. There was something else very wrong with him.

'Come in if you must,' he growled and retreated back to a small table in the middle of the room, sat down on the far side of it and stared at her.

'What is it, Jasper?' Meg said slowly. 'What's wrong? There is something dreadfully wrong, isn't there? I wouldn't have expected the Jasper I know to have treated Charlotte so unkindly.'

At the mention of Charlotte's name, her brother dropped his head into his hands. His shoulders heaved.

'Go away, Meg. Let me—' He stopped.

'Let you what, Jasper?' She advanced into the room as far as the table.

And saw on it a pistol.

She put her hand to her mouth, looking at her usually smartly dressed, self-controlled brother, who was hunched in a posture of complete abandon before a loaded pistol.

'Tell me, Jasper,' she said steadily. 'Tell me what is wrong. I once said that I would offer you help if you needed it, but I cannot do so if you will not tell me the truth.'

Jasper shuddered. He lifted his head to show her his ravaged face, his red eyes, the disarray of his clothing. 'You can't help me, Meg. I'm ruined.' He dropped his head again.

'Ruined, Jas? How ruined? Lift your head and tell me. At once.'

She had played this scene before, or one very like it, and Meg knew that she must be calm, be the voice of reason when all she wanted to do was shriek.

'I've lost everything. I. . .owe thousands—the moneylenders for my debts and to the people I played cards with when I tried to recoup my fortunes. I wanted to win enough so that Charlotte and I might marry—as well as pay my debts. I did win at first, and then I lost. . .I was plucked like the pigeon I am.

'In my position as heir, I pledged our parents' home, all that is left to them, as security for my debts—and now it is gone. My debts are being called in and I cannot pay them. Not only am I ruined, but so are they. All that is left to me, in honour, is that—' and he pointed to the pistol '—so go away.'

'Honour—? In that?' Meg's voice was icy. 'And how will killing yourself, here in my home may I remind you, save Mother and Father from being put

into the street? All that will do is save you from
suffering for your folly whilst leaving the rest of us
to pay for it. No, Jasper. That is not the answer.
How much do you owe?'

Bleary-eyed, he stared at her. 'Thousands, more
than I care to think of. Why?'

'How much?' she repeated.

Jasper told her. 'You fool,' she said calmly, 'to
lose so much, but if that is the sum of it—and you
must pledge your word, for what that is worth, that
it is—then I will pay your debts for you. But you
must promise me never to gamble again—or run up
debts of any kind.'

He shook his head. 'How can I promise to stay
out of debt? I am only a half-pay officer, for God's
sake, with no other source of income, and in peace-
time, no possibility of promotion, since I haven't
the money to purchase a commission. So, unless I
borrow money, I can't live.'

'Then resign your commission and be my agent
for the estate I am buying in Berkshire. If you wish,
and I think you do, to marry Charlotte, then you
may do so after a decent interval, providing you stay
away from London and the high life. You have told
me often that you love country living, and I know
that you are capable, when you are not busily
engaged in ruining yourself by living beyond
your paper.'

Her brother said, slowly and painfully, 'Are you
so rich, Meg? And so. . .hard-headed?'

'Both, Jasper, both—life has made me so. Say
yes, and we will go to Coutts Bank tomorrow and
arrange matters. I warn you that you must tell me

everything you owe, and sign a document that will commit you never to gamble in the future because, if you do. . .I shall not rescue you again.'

'Yes, yes, I understand you.' His voice was heavy. 'You must know that I can never repay you.'

'Only by living a good life in the country—and by the by, you will tell no one, not even Charlotte, that the estate is mine, until I am ready to acknowledge ownership. Let them think it is a friend's. So you see, I am not so hard-headed, after all, for I am giving you a second chance.'

'Oh, Meg,' he began, his voice husky, 'I promise you. . .'

'No, Jasper. Promise me nothing. I have had my fill of promises. . .and all of them broken. Just do as I ask. And if you truly love Charlotte, marry her.'

'Oh, indeed.' He was eager for the first time, more like his old self. 'I did it to gain her, you know. Because I could not afford to marry her. I have never gambled heavily before—I was always careful.'

'Then continue to be so.' Meg leaned forward, picked up the pistol and said, 'You will not be needing this.'

'No.' his voice broke. 'Meg. . .I can never thank you enough.'

'Thank me by doing as I ask. We shall visit Coutts in the morning. Goodnight.'

She was halfway down the grand staircase, holding the pistol away from her, before the irony of what had happened struck Meg. First Jane and now Jasper.

What next?

*   *   *

Peverel Darrow, wearing a Chinese dressing-gown, was drinking coffee at half past eleven in the morning in his rooms in the Albany. His valet, George Jackson, put his head around the door, and said in a disrespectful voice, 'There's that clerk fellow again, asking to see you. He says that his business is urgent.'

'Then take your Friday face away, and send him in, at once.'

Living as he did on the edge of ruin, one step ahead of a debtors' prison, Peverel had a number of dubious acquaintances and informants of whom his valet visibly disapproved. Well, damn him, let him disapprove away. Without them, and their information, Peverel could hardly have afforded a valet, and so he had told him more than once.

The clerk fellow? That was probably Lewis, a dogsbody at the moneylending house of Strauss and Sons. Now what particular useful titbit had brought him along this morning to earn a few pennies—or, if the information was important enough, perhaps a few guineas?

He was soon to find out. Lewis sidled in, his greasy top hat in his hand. Jackson had not deigned to dirty his hands by taking it from him. Peverel made no attempt to rise, saying brusquely, 'Well, what is it brings you here today?'

'Something I'll be bound you'll pay good money for, master,' whined Lewis.

'Fire away, then. And it had better be good, mark you, to be worth disturbing me at this hour.'

Lewis, whose day usually began at eight of the clock, nodded as though he, too, ate his breakfast at half-past ten, bowed his head and muttered, 'You said as how you wanted anything—rumour, gossip or facts—which I heard about the French Countess. Well, yesterday I had through my hands a draft from Coutts Bank, drawn on the account of Madame de Mortaine, to pay off a large debt which had been outstanding for some time. . .'

'How large?'

'Very large. To the tune of twenty thousand pounds, allowing for the original loans and accrued interest. It seems that Strauss bought up a lot of paper signed by the debtor.'

'Spit it out, man. Was it Madame's debt? And if so, for what? She's supposed to be as rich as Croesus, so it would be damned odd if she needed to borrow money—unless all the *on dits* are wrong.'

Lewis shook his head. 'That I don't know. Old Strauss keeps his business close to his chest. Only he knows who his clients are. I took the draft, with some others, to Coutts to be honoured. But my fellow clerk, Dickie Dobson, maintained that the debtor weren't Madame, by something Strauss said. It were a man, he thought, some nob.'

He made no apologies for breaching the confidential nature of either Coutts's business, or that of his employer. Poorly paid as he was, Lewis believed that he had the right to supplement his earnings in any way he could.

'But had he no notion of who she raised the money for? I'll give you a guinea for what you have told me, and I'll double it if you tell me the name of the man whom Madame was bailing out.'

A regretful shrug answered him. 'Nay, master.

I'm sorry to lose an extra guinea, but Dickie only knew that it must have been a man, nothing else. Besides, Strauss don't do business with women. Only takes their money if they clear a debt for someone else.' Then, a sly expression on his face as he pocketed the coin which Peverel handed to him, he offered, 'Ain't it a possibility, master, that you might know who the lucky man is? Some lover, perhaps?'

Or her brother, thought Peverel, although he had heard no rumours to the effect that Jasper Ashe's pockets were to let. On the other hand, the Ashes were as poor as church mice, and Jasper wouldn't be receiving much from them in the way of an income to support his half-pay.

Knowledge being power, though, there must be some way in which he could use this information. 'Keep your eyes and ears open,' he told Lewis before he left, 'and there'll be more than a guinea for you.'

One piece of information that Lewis had passed over was worth as much as the knowledge of the banker's draft: that little Meg Ashe, turned French Countess, was even richer than he had thought that she might be. A prize worth winning, and by fair means or foul he would have a go at winning her! But first he would have to destroy his cousin Simon's chances. By her behaviour, it was plain that Madame had a *tendre* for him, even if the idiot wasn't aware of it.

On second thoughts, though, from what he had seen lately, cousin Simon had been busy destroying his chances himself.

* * *

He took this comforting thought with him when he drove to Hyde Park that afternoon to look for her. If he made the Comtesse his wife, then Simon could keep Darrow Hall, and the measly fortune which went with it. With Meg's money he would buy himself a palace.

The sun shone and there was a gentle breeze, when Peverel turned into the Park. As was customary, all the polite world was on parade there that afternoon. Cass Devereux was driving a perchphaeton, her children and husband for once not with her.

She was wearing an outrageous habit based on a grenadier's uniform, something which only she could carry off. The Duke was there, Wellington himself, on horseback today, talking animatedly to Cass—twitting her on her turn-out, no doubt.

But where was Madame de Mortaine? Peverel looked about him and saw that his cousin Simon was present, but alone, thank God—he had feared that Meg might be with him. Simon was riding a powerful grey stallion, which only a strong man could tame sufficiently to make him behave in the over-crowded Park.

And there she was. She was neither on horseback, nor driving any kind of phaeton or gig. Instead, looking enchanting in the palest green, she was in a modest landaulet parked in the shade of a large tree. That plain prude Charlotte Hollis sat by her side. Meg looked so charming that Peverel was surprised all over again to discover that it was not only for her money that he wished to win her. Lust—or could it possibly be love?—was driving him, too.

So much so that, for once, sincerity rode on his face as he approached the landaulet. His pleasure at finding her was genuine. The other, baser, pleasure he felt was that, seated as she was, she could not avoid him, and what was even better, in Simon's absence there was no one to queer his pitch with her.

Meg had seen him coming, but she misread his expression, translating it as merely predatory. She muttered below her breath to Charlotte, 'We are finely trapped with no escape from him, but never mind, we may practice our politeness—and our indifference.'

Charlotte, who had been looking around for Jasper, who had promised to meet them there, nodded agreement. For all his good looks and his easy charm, she could not like Peverel. It was plain that he was chasing Meg for her fortune. Charlotte did not believe that he loved Meg: she believed that, like many men in society, he loved only himself.

'Good afternoon, ladies,' he said gaily. 'It is a fine one, is it not?'

Of such banalities was conversation in society made up, thought Meg acidly, but she gave him her cool agreement whilst looking around to see if Simon was anywhere near. She could not find him, but instead saw Jasper, who was riding a spirited chestnut, and was plainly making for her and Charlotte.

He had already begun to arrange his resignation from the Army, and was due to visit Meg's new property in Berkshire in the near future. Beside him was her sister Phoebe's husband, Fred Zealand, a discontented expression on his face.

Peverel had no objection to them joining Meg. On the contrary, their willingness to be seen talking to him proved that he was still acceptable in the best society. Jasper was only interested in Charlotte, and Zealand, happily married to Phoebe, could not expect to attract Meg, even if he was attracted by her.

Which was nothing less than the truth. What would have amused her with anyone but her sister's husband, pained her when Zealand began to contend with Peverel for her favour. Oh, the devil was in all men. The one she wanted despised her, and she despised all those who wanted her. Perhaps it was life she was complaining of.

She thought so even more when Simon suddenly appeared, flung himself off his magnificent grey and walked over to join the party and add his mischief to theirs.

'Well met, cousin,' Peverel taunted him. 'I had not thought that you lent yourself to such frivolous occasions as these.'

To Meg's fascination, Simon showed his cousin his splendid teeth at once. 'Indeed? Then as usual, *sir*, you are wrong!' He trod heavily on the word 'sir' to demonstrate his dislike at being addressed as cousin, before he acknowledged Jasper and Zealand, and after he had done his polite duties to Meg and Charlotte.

Charlotte, indeed, not for the first time, thought what a splendid specimen of manhood he was, putting even her beloved Jasper into the shade, and making Peverel look effete.

Meg was busy thinking the same thing, as Simon came out with, 'I had a mind to take the air this afternoon. The House is sitting, but as it is not treating with any of my interests today, and as I am summoned to a meeting of the Zoological Society this evening, I have taken the opportunity of a little exercise. I shall grow fat if I do nothing but sit on the Commons' benches every afternoon.'

'If you were a member of the opposite sex, Sir Simon, you would be instantly accused of fishing for a compliment, but since you are not a female then I must assume that you are doing no such thing. I will simply assure you that you appear to be in no danger of rivalling Daniel Lambert.'

This reference to the man who was reputed to be the largest and fattest England had ever bred amused all Meg's hearers and even brought an unwilling smile to Simon's lips.

'Rightly rebuked,' he said.

'*Touché*, cousin,' came from Peverel, delighted to see the 'haughty baronet', as he privately thought of him, being put down for once.

'You are severe today, Meg,' Jasper put in, smiling affectionately at her, robbing his words of any possible sting. The gratitude that he felt for having saved him from ruin was so great that he knew that he could never thank her enough. He had said so on the day he had handed her draft to Strauss in his pokey office in the City.

But she had shaken her head and said simply, 'Don't try, Jas. Words mean nothing. Show me your gratitude by managing Monks Lovell for me and keeping out of trouble.

Well, he would try to do that, and his visit to the Park was in the nature of a farewell to his old life.

He would go to Berkshire, find out what being Meg's agent would mean and, after a suitable interval, he would return to ask Charlotte for her hand.

In the meantime, he was busy watching Simon, Peverel and, of all people, Zealand, dance around Meg. He had never thought of Phoebe's husband as a loose fish, and rumour had not touched him, as it had touched many others.

Meg, thinking the same thing, was equally surprised, particularly when, in a diversion created by a group of Jasper's fellow officers arriving, she was temporarily left to her own devices and Zealand leaned forward and muttered to her in an urgent voice, 'May I have your permission to call on you tomorrow, Madame? There is a matter of some import which I must discuss with you privately.'

Now what in the world can Zealand possibly have to say to me? was her immediate and private response after she had agreed to his request, but she was allowed no time to puzzle over the matter. Simon, who had overheard Zealand's question and her reply, immediately jumped to all the wrong conclusions.

So! Madame was up to her tricks again, was she?—and with her own sister's husband this time. Had she lost all sense of shame during her stay in Paris?

Meg looked up to see him glaring at her. Her heart sank—something which she had believed was a physical impossibility until she had met Simon again.

'Pray, Sir Simon,' she enquired sweetly, 'what wrong am I supposed to have committed now? For, by your expression, you plainly believe that I have done or said *something*.' Not even the presence of Charlotte sitting quietly beside her could prevent her from challenging him.

Nor did it prevent him from replying fiercely, 'You know perfectly well, Madame, what your offence is. No need for me to answer you in detail.'

'But if I have a desire to know, sir? What then?'

Simon opened his mouth to speak, to say something unforgivable, for he seemed to lose all sense of what was proper whenever he encountered Madame la Comtesse. He was stopped by the sudden knowledge that Peverel was now listening to them, and that Charlotte Hollis was staring at them both as they broke all the rules of polite conduct in public.

This would never do. He must speak to her privately, he must. Rage and desire, mixed in equal parts, swept over him. Meg had never looked more charming than when she had been having her half-private *tête-à-tête* with that. . .that. . . Adequate words to describe Zealand failed him.

He became aware that Peverel was also staring at him. He turned away, only for Peverel to touch him on the arm and say, 'I must have a word with you in private, cousin, before you leave. Pray walk over with me towards the tree where Cass Devereux is holding court.'

For a moment Simon hesitated before he decided against a refusal. He was in danger of making a raree-show of himself. 'Yes,' he replied stiffly. 'What have you to say to me which is so urgent?'

'This. I am troubled in my mind where Meg de Mortaine is concerned.'

Oh, the bare-faced hypocrisy of the swine, who had not only blackmailed Meg over her affair with him, but had also blown on her reputation to himself, and doubtless also to others! Peverel was not to know that he had overheard him taking Meg's money from her, and something kept him from telling the scaly swine so.

'Indeed, Peverel, and why should that be? More to the point, what is it that you think you know?'

'This. That she has been blackmailed once before, and now the rumour is all about town that she has been tricked into paying off the huge debts of one of her lovers. As we are all old friends from our childhood days, I do not like to think of her being up the River Tick where her fortune is concerned, nor barred from good society because of whispers about her reputation.'

Simon was not to know that there was not a word of truth in what his cousin was telling him. There were no rumours, and the ones about Meg's supposed wicked past, which Peverel had started on their way, had died the death in the face of the purity of her appearance and her behaviour.

As for the money supposedly paid over to a paramour—only Peverel knew of that through his bribing of Lewis, Strauss's double-dealing clerk. He saw Simon's face change and wondered again at the power of jealousy that left his cousin at his mercy.

'And I am to believe this?' enquired Simon glacially, for once refusing to credit Peverel's lies.

'Alas, I have it on the very best authority.' Peverel was solemn—so solemn, so grave, that Simon admitted with a pang that what he was saying might be the truth. He looked away to where Meg was now entertaining the Iron Duke himself, who had driven over from one of society's known successes, Cass Devereux, to one of the new ones.

Wellington had always had an eye for a pretty woman, and there was no doubt that that eye was now on Meg. The very sight of yet another besotted *roué* pursuing her—even if he were the great Duke himself—was enough to set him grinding his teeth all over again.

Simon made a swift resolution. He would call on Meg, this very day, before Zealand could visit her, and try to help her out of the pit into which she had fallen. Unwittingly Peverel had overdone things for, whilst inciting Simon against Meg, he had also spurred him on towards a confrontation with her in which anything might happen.

Chapter Eight

'You are sure that you do not wish me to remain with you this evening, Meg? If you are not feeling up to snuff, then I really should stay with you and give Lady Cowper's ball a miss.'

Charlotte and Meg were in the small drawing-room on the ground floor of Templestowe House. It was an exquisite miniature of all the other large rooms there. The portrait of an earlier Templestowe Countess hung above the fireplace.

Even the chairs and the sofa were more comfortable, more suited to the human body than those elsewhere, including one monster sofa, deep and wide. It was drawn up before a hearth that was filled with flowers and not with fire, since it was summer.

'Now that really would be beyond the call of duty, Charlotte. I know that Jasper wishes to escort you to one last London jaunt before he journeys to Monks Lovell, and I would be distressed to think that my slight malaise had deprived you of that. And since the Vancourts are calling at seven to take us there, my sister may act as your chaperon, and allow you to enjoy yourself without having to consider me.'

Charlotte could not prevent her pleasure at not losing the delight of one last evening with Jasper from showing on her face.

'But my duty—' she began.

Meg refused to let her finish her sentence. 'Oh, run along, my dear, at once, or you will not be ready when their carriage arrives. It would not do to keep Vancourt waiting—you know how uncertain his temper is these days.'

Charlotte needed no more pressing on the matter, and her and Jasper's pleasure in one another as they left for the ball was Meg's reward—if any were needed—for dispensing with Charlotte's company for the night.

Not that it was a sacrifice for her on this particular evening. She felt tired to the bone. Jousting with Simon gave her a perverse pleasure when she was engaged in it, but once away from him an enormous sadness overtook her at the realisation of the great gulf of misunderstanding which had opened between them. Explanation and reconciliation seemed alike impossible.

Neither her temper nor her mood had been improved by reading her mother's latest letter. Some busybody had apparently passed on some unpleasant gossip about her character and reputation, and the litany of complaint and reproach which always filled her mother's letters to her was worse than usual in her latest missive. Missile might have been a better description of it!

One might have thought, Meg mused sadly, that my having made such a splendid marriage, so splendid that I have been able to assist both her and father in their financial difficulties, would have changed her carping attitude towards me. But that was apparently fixed at my birth when I became merely another daughter instead of another son. All my title and wealth have done is to change the nature of mother's complaints, not silence them altogether.

She was minded to throw the letter in the fire, except that at the end of it her father had written a few kind words—all that he could manage now that his hands were crippled with a painful rheumatism.

Her sad and solitary reverie was broken by the butler who asked her if she was prepared to receive a visitor—Simon Darrow, no less.

For a moment, Meg contemplated the notion of snubbing Simon by sending him a message that she was receiving no one at this late hour. Something stopped her, and later she was to ask herself whether her subsequent life would have been better or worse if she had done so.

Instead, she nodded her head and remarked as indifferently as she could, 'Send him in and, James, do not allow anyone to interrupt us until I ring for you.'

She wondered afterwards what had impelled her to order any such thing. Perhaps she had thought that she and Simon might soon be at odds again, and did not want any servants as possible spectators of their differences which might mean gossip about them later. In any case, James seemed to find nothing odd about her instructions, and showed Simon in as impassively as ever.

Simon was obviously on his way to the Cowpers'

ball, by the splendour of his clothing. Meg rebuked herself for feeling overwhelmed at the sight of him. After all, he was scarcely the most handsome man in the world, and well dressed though he was, there were others in society far more dandified than he.

But no one else had such a superb and athletic physique, similar to the statues of the ancient Greeks which filled the houses of the cousinry. It was that which gave his clothes distinction, and not the other way around.

It was also that, perhaps, which made her feel so weak whenever she saw him, even before they began their verbal sparring. No other man, not even André when she had first met him, had succeeded in creating such a strange and immediate response in her.

But why had he come? Meg was soon to find out. 'I wished to speak to you,' he began after the politenesses were over. 'I had hoped to see you at Lady Cowper's, but when I arrived there, Mrs Hollis informed me that you were feeling a little under the weather and had decided not to attend. It is good of you to receive me, if you are not feeling A1 at Lloyds.'

A compliment! He had paid her a compliment. Wonders would never cease. Were there any more to come? Alas, apparently not, for he went on to add, looking earnestly at her, 'I hope you will forgive me for what I have to say to you, but please accept that I am only trying to play the part of a true friend and adviser to you.'

He paused, thinking perhaps that this might sound a trifle presumptuous, and attempted to placate her a little by adding, 'I have, after all, known you since

you were a child, so pray overlook my apparent
impertinence.'

Goodness, whatever could be coming? Meg
answered him as cryptically as he had been addressing her, 'Until I hear what is is you have to say, Sir
Simon, I am not in a position to determine whether
it is impertinent or not.'

Simon had hoped that her answer might help him
in what he now understood to be a difficult and
tricky task. He tugged nervously at his perfectly tied
cravat, of a kind known as a waterfall. Unfortunately, his tug was stronger than he had intended;
it turned the waterfall into a positive torrent, which
cascaded in a cloud of billowing white linen down
his shirtfront and his black and white striped
waistcoat.

Meg tried to repress a giggle, turned it into a cross
between a blurred 'ahem' and a snort, but to no
good purpose, since Simon had immediately realised
that both his senatorial gravity and his self-
possession had been destroyed. Nevertheless, he
decided to plough on, but unfortunately it also
became apparent that his tact had deserted him, too.
Being alone with Meg was continuing to bring out
the worst in him

'Is it,' he asked passionately, 'impossible these
days for you not to conduct yourself in a manner
which will draw censure upon you?'

Now what, in God's name, had made him say
that? Whatever had provoked him into coming out
with such a mealy-mouthed and impertinent question? He was not her husband, her father, nor her
brother. It was really no business of his what the

Comtesse de Mortaine, once little Meg Ashe, did.

Apparently she thought so, too. Her voice was as stern as steel when she spoke. 'And who, Sir Simon Darrow, gave you leave to be the arbiter of my conduct?'

'Forgive me,' he began, which was acceptable, but what followed was not, 'but it hurts me to hear that you are busy dragging your good name through the dust.' Oh, hell and all the devils in it, what had his unlucky tongue come out with now?

Meg sprang to her feet and pointed to the door. 'Go,' she said, 'please go. You once asked me to marry you, but that gives you no right to speak to me after such a fashion. I do not know who has been spreading lies about me, but it is hurtful and demeaning to learn that you have hanged, drawn and quartered me without asking yourself whether any of the gossip about me is true before you came here to accuse me.'

How to rescue himself? He had only meant to help her, but his clumsy tongue had let him down again for the simple reason that he cared so much for her. Like all good men he had difficulty in articulating such delicate and involved sentiments.

Perhaps if he asked her one question, and one alone, she would answer him in such a way that he would be reassured that she was unchanged; that behind the mask of continental sophistication she was little Meg Ashe still. And then he might sleep again.

He said, attempting to make his tone more humble and placatory, but signally failing, 'I shall say nothing further, if you can assure me that the rumour, that you have paid out large sums of money to silence persons who have a hold on you by reason of your. . .conduct, is untrue. The *on dit* is that your latest transaction took place as recently as this week.'

Meg, now at the double doors, glared at him. 'I shall tell you nothing, for it is no business of yours. Now leave at once. I will ring for James to show you out—but if you refuse to leave, a pair of sturdy footmen might persuade you to change your mind.'

Whirling through her mind was the question: who has told him about the draft with which I paid off Jasper's debts? To clear myself in his eyes, I could tell him the truth: that the money was not for a lover, but for my brother. Alas, I am bound by my honour to say nothing, for I agreed with Jasper that only he, I and the moneylender should know the truth of the matter.

Simon stood stock-still. So, Madame had denied nothing, and, what was almost worse, she had threatened to have her footmen throw him from the door! She stood proudly before him in her pure white gown, with its high puritan collar, and its prim long sleeves. Her beautiful chestnut hair was severely dressed, giving her the air of an affronted vestal virgin.

How dare she? How dare she look so chaste, yet so desirable? And oh, by God, he desired her so much that it hurt. As on the night of the Leominsters' ball, one wicked thought pounded at the door of his honour, demanding that what others had enjoyed, he, who for his punishment loved her, might also share and enjoy.

Something in his expression and the set of his mouth frightened Meg as he strode towards her, pulling off his damned cravat as he did so, as though it were strangling him.

'No,' he said hoarsely, 'you shall not dismiss me. And I don't care if you have bedded every man in London and Paris, if you will only—' Before he had finished the sentence, he pressed her against the door and stole from her the kiss he now so desperately wanted.

Held prisoner, not by his arms but by the strong body which she had earlier admired, his mouth on hers—a treacherous mouth which opened itself to him, for she could resist him only so long as he did not touch her—Meg felt herself drowning in sensation.

A moment ago she had wanted to shriek at him, 'Oh, you wrong me, you cannot conceive how much you wrong me. And that being so, I never want to see you again.' But now, what did she wish to do *now*, now that his arms were around her—and her arms were so willingly stealing around him?

He lifted his mouth and his body from her, only to give her his mouth again, once they were apart. This time his touch was not violent, but tender, so that, had she wished to, Meg could have thrown him off. He cupped her face, oh so gently, in his two big hands, and when the kiss ended, murmured, 'So sweet, oh, so sweet.'

It was Meg, impatient for more of him, who put her arms around his neck and pulled his face down to hers, to resume where he had left off.

This time, when he pulled away, it was to lift her

in his arms and carry her over to the big sofa, whilst Meg, witless with desire, caring nothing at this moment for what he thought of her, but wanting him, and only him, made no effort to stop him.

Once there he took her on his knee and began to stroke and pet her, kissing her so gently, but so thoroughly, that Meg thought she would die of the delight of it. She felt like a flower being delicately ravaged by a bee, except that it was no bee who began to push her backwards and pull down the prim collar of her dress.

She had made no attempt to stop him, indeed, as Meg later ruefully conceded, at every turn she had encouraged him, rather than thrust him off. His cravat had gone long ago, his shirt followed it, and Meg knew that it would not be long before they were naked together in front of the summer flowers: as naked as father Adam and mother Eve.

But long before they reached that point, shortly before kissing became more passionate than tender, he had reared back a little, and said, his voice hoarse with emotion, 'Meg, I have no wish to force you. Much though it would pain me, I will stop now if you ask me to.'

Stop! Now? Whatever did he take her for? Regardless of the consequences, and whether her behaviour would convince him that she was the lightskirt she had been branded, and which he obviously took her for, she would offer the man she loved everything that was hers to offer. She knew that he would only take what she would freely give—and knowing this, she chose to give, even if it proved to be the only time that she would ever hold him in her arms.

'No,' she whispered, 'no, Simon, don't stop.' Even the prospect of a possible child could not deter her, for it would be his, and God knew, that whatever else André had done for and to her, he had left her rich enough to ensure that neither she nor the child would suffer. It would have a name, even if it were not hers or Simon's, and a place in society.

He was strangely gentle with her, as though to prove to himself, as well as her, that he was not taking anything from her, only accepting, and paradoxically that was more exciting to them both than if he had been roughly passionate.

His body respected her more than his mind did, Meg thought afterwards. And what a strange thing that was, when with most men it was the other way round. It was almost as though he were proving to her that, whatever she was, he would treat her as though she were the most precious thing he knew.

With the result that together they achieved a harmony given to few, and if Simon found surcease from the pain and jealousy which had consumed him, Meg found peace from the misery that the knowledge that he was at odds with her had created.

No one came to disturb them, and afterwards, all passion spent, they lay in one another's arms in a tranquillity so perfect that it could not last. Nor did it. Once he was himself again, Simon was wracked, not by jealousy, but by regret, and by a remorse so strong that it drove every other thought away. Even his recent passion could not stand before it.

The clock striking eleven awoke him from a light

sleep and recalled him back to the world of consequence and consequences again. He knew one
consequence at once. The fact that he and Meg had
been closeted alone for several long hours would be
the talk of the servants' hall.

As, indeed, it already was. One of the footmen, with
whom Meg had threatened Simon, said knowingly
to James as he began to put out the lamps in the
servants' hall—the kitchen maids had long ago
picked up their candles to light them to bed—'Be
Sir Simon *still* alone with Madame? Whatever can
they be at?' His sly expression betrayed perfectly
well what he thought they were at.

James, the long candle snuffer in his hand, said
equably, 'Nothing to do with you, George. Their
business, not yours.'

'Oh, aye? Reading together, be they? Mighty
int'resting book, no doubt.'

James brought the candle snuffer down on
George's head. 'Nothing to do with you, I said. Off
to bed with you.'

George, rubbing his head, was irrepressible. 'And
who's to show him to the door, then—if he chooses
not to stay the night, that is?'

'My business, not yours. You heard what I said.
Do as you're bid, if you value your position here.
You'll not easily get one as good without a
reference.'

All the same, as he watched George go, chuckling,
to his room in the attic, he could not resist a private
grin at the thought that the gentry were at their
games again. But a good servant did better in the

end by being discreet than by having a gabbing tongue.

George, on the other hand, annoyed by being reprimanded, remembered something which one of his cronies from another establishment had told him—that Peverel Darrow was paying good money to anyone who would sell him information about the saucy French Countess and his cousin, Sir Simon. No need to have your pockets to let if someone was willing to fill them in payment for tonight's little titbit.

In the drawing-room, matters were little more harmonious. Simon, a sleeping Meg in his arms, discovered that he had gone beyond jealousy and desire fulfilled merely to achieve guilt! He had not meant to compromise her, only to lead her by gentle means into a better way of life.

And what had been the consequence of that? He had behaved with her exactly as all those who had gone before him had done. He was no better than they were: he was worse. For he knew how he ought to behave and they—the 'they' including his cousin Peverel—did not.

As an honourable man, there was only one thing left for him to do and, when she awoke, he would do it. This resolution pleased him so much that he had difficulty in not allowing that pleasure to lull him to sleep again, but common sense said no.

Whatever would Jasper and Charlotte Hollis think, if they were to return and find them here—like this? He looked down at his naked body, and at the clothes strewn around the floor, mute evidence of the passion of the pair who had recently worn them.

Meg stirred a little in his arms. He lifted them both into a sitting position and the movement, as he had intended, woke her up.

'Oh,' she said, her opening eyes starry. 'I see that I didn't dream this!'

Such a frivolous comment was hardly in tune with Simon's newly made determination that the pair of them would behave with stern rectitude and propriety, after having been so abandoned.

'My dear,' he said urgently, 'we must talk.'

'What, now? At this hour? What about?' and she cuddled closer to his warm body. The sensation which this produced in him nearly destroyed all Simon's good resolutions, but he clung determinedly on to what he saw as his honour and his duty.

So he stared sternly at her. Nothing but plain speaking would do. And with that resolution he sealed his immediate fate. He had quite forgotten how useless and unprofitable his plain speaking before their. . .recent encounter. . .had been.

'There is nothing for it,' he announced ungallantly. 'I have ruined you, and therefore we must marry as soon as I can obtain a special licence.'

Meg's high spirits, which had given her the sensation of floating among the clouds rather like the painted gods and goddesses on the ceiling in Templestowe House's great dining room, plummeted to earth again.

Nothing had changed. If Simon had lived among the clouds for a brief space, which she now begged leave to doubt, the aftermath of their love-making

had restored him to the position of the cruel and
stern arbiter of her fate. All that had changed was
that he now wished to marry her; presumably in
order to be able to reproach her more easily. She
sat up, and became suddenly aware of her nakedness,
which had the effect of making her feel more vulnerable than ever.

Simon said nothing further: doubtless waiting for
an answer to his scurvily made offer. He deserved
nothing for it, and she would give him nothing.

'What for?' she asked, her tone and posture
defiant.

Simon stared at her even harder. He had the face
of a hanging judge, not of a man who had pleasured,
and been pleasured, twice, both times right royally.
'What for?' he echoed. 'And what, pray, does
that mean?'

The dignity with which he posed this question
was somewhat marred by his nudity. If ever Meg
had doubted that clothing gave men and women
consequence, formality, and gravity, she now knew
that her doubts were idle.

Unclothed, Simon showed a majestic body,
powerful, well proportioned, muscular; in short,
exactly what she had expected. But dignity and grav-
itas, the traits of a Member from the British
Parliament, were alike missing. He looked ready to
perform in one of the Greek Olympiads rather than
lay down the law in the grave surroundings of
Westminster.

Once more she gave him the answer he deserved.
'It means what I said. Why should you offer me
marriage? And why should I accept such an offer,

made only to confer respectability on us, rather than
as a consequence of the passion which we have just
enjoyed? A passion that I thought was mutual, but
which was evidently not, seeing that you appear to
regret it—whilst I do not.

'You are offering me marriage as a duty, not
because what we recently shared meant so much
that marriage was the inevitable consequence of love
expressed.' She paused and added, 'I will be your
mistress, but I will not marry you on such terms.'

Meg had not meant to say this, but temper moved
her so strongly that wisdom and caution had deserted
her. Besides, if what Simon was offering her was the
product of wisdom and caution, she did not want it.

'My good woman,' he began solemnly, obviously
aghast at her suggestion that she should be his whore
rather than his wife.

Meg leapt up, picked her discarded clothing from
the floor and began to dress herself with more speed
than precision.

'No,' she flung at him. 'Say no more. You do not
consider me to be a good woman. Do not spoil for
me the delight I felt during our love-making by
passing judgment on me, yourself and the whole
business which lies between men and women.'

This passionate speech was somewhat marred by
the difficulty which she was experiencing in manoeuvring herself into her elaborate clothing without
the assistance of her maid. Simon was now off the
sofa and was also attempting to dress himself, a task
made difficult by his fashionably skintight clothing.
Even with his valet's assistance, this was usually a
lengthy task.

Meg, almost decent again, watched him cover what had so recently delighted her, and exclaimed with exasperation as he fumbled with buttons and fastenings. The aftermath of passion should never be ludicrous—but cold reality always took over once the business of pleasure was completed.

'Goodness,' she exclaimed. 'I never thought that men went through such a tohu-bohu in becoming clothed. Here, permit me to help you,' and before he could stop her, she was assisting him, as deftly as his missing valet, into tight breeches, by fastening buttons, and with tying his cravat, so that very shortly he was nearly as *à point* as usual, and more respectable than she was.

Once clothed, formality in them both did not seem nearly so comical to Meg. She was more prepared to listen to him, but no more prepared to accept him. If only he had once said, I love you. But, then, she had not said it to him. Three words, and that was all they were, words. She had given him her love with her body, and in reply he talked of marriage as a duty he was to perform to prevent her from being a fallen woman.

This thought excited her to more excesses. As he opened his mouth, doubtless to propose marriage again, she announced gaily, 'Do you know, Simon, I rather fancy I like being a fallen woman. No ties, no responsibilities. I'm surprised that you don't enjoy being a fallen man—but then, men don't fall, do they? On the contrary, they do the pushing. Comfort yourself with the thought that I don't feel exploited or depraved, but fulfilled.'

'Oh, Meg, Meg,' he cried hoarsely, showing

emotion for the first time since their mutual transports. 'Supposing there is a child?'

'Somewhat late to think about that, isn't it?' she carolled. 'And it's my worry, not yours. You really must go, Simon. Charlotte and Jasper won't want to be late home tonight. He is off to Monks Lovell tomorrow afternoon. Should you require me again, you have only to write me a little note, or call in person. But no more talk of marriage, please. The notion does not attract, either with you—or with anyone else.'

She had driven him mad, and now *she* was mad, was Simon's mournful conclusion. He opened his mouth to offer for her again, but she jumped back, saying wildly, 'No more, tonight, please. Just go, Simon. And if you must marry, pick a hymn-singing Methodist, and then you may be proper together.'

Somehow he managed to leave Templestowe House, his dignity in shreds, wondering how he had come to make such an infernal cake of himself. He fell into his lonely and comfortless bed, having drunk so much port—in order to find oblivion— that he could hardly walk to it.

But oblivion refused to oblige him. His buzzing head once on the pillow, all that he could think of was Meg in his arms on the sofa, the joy they had shared, and his own folly in antagonising her all over again.

He would never understand women, never. Why should she be so insulted when all that he had wished to do was make an honest woman of her?

As for Meg, she reached her room just before Jasper and Charlotte returned, to sit on her bed, eyes

wide and smarting with unshed tears, too distressed
to ring for her maid, to sleep, or even to cry. Was
she a fool not to have accepted him on his terms?

And then she remembered that she had accepted
André on his terms, and look what *that* had led to.

Chapter Nine

Meg was standing by the window, staring out at the magnificent formal gardens at the back of Templestowe House when her brother-in-law, Zealand, was announced the next morning. She was alone and, theoretically speaking, she should have rung for Charlotte to be present when she received him.

But she was suddenly tired of formality and conventions. Charlotte was enjoying a late breakfast in her room, having stayed at Lady Cowper's ball to the very end. Besides, she had the impression from Zealand's manner, when he had spoken to her the day before, that he might prefer to consult with her alone.

Her guess was correct. His manner to her when he came in was perfectly proper, but she thought that she detected relief in him when he looked around and noted that her companion was absent.

Once they were seated, he began without preamble, using her pet name to establish a family intimacy since it proved that he had called to discuss a family matter.

'Oh, Meg, Phoebe and I are greatly in need of your help. You are aware, I am sure, that when your father and mother come to town for the Season, they have always stayed with us. It has been their custom since Phoebe and I were married.'

Puzzled, Meg said cautiously, 'Yes, Fred, I was aware of that.'

'Well. . .' he swallowed and looked uncomfortable '. . .it's like this, my dear. You know that Phoebe and I have never been fortunate enough to have children. It is a matter of great grief to us. We both dearly want them, and not simply because I need an heir, but because we both—particularly Phoebe—love children.'

He stopped, and Meg nodded agreement—to what, she wasn't quite sure—but it seemed to encourage Fred to continue. Looking away from her, he began again.

'The trouble is. . .it's your mama. These last few Seasons, every time she comes she talks non-stop about all her grandchildren, and constantly seems to hint that it's somehow Phoebe's fault that we haven't given her any. Phoebe spends a large part of her visit crying in private. Two days ago, when your father's letter arrived with the dates of their proposed visit this year, she had a violent fit of the hysterics, took to her room and hasn't come out since. Most unlike her, as I am sure that you will agree.'

Meg nodded again. Yes, most unlike. Phoebe had been the equable, the placid sister, always cheerful and uncomplaining.

'Oh, Meg,' he said despairingly. 'What am I to
do? I know it's unfashionable, I know it's not quite
the thing, but I dearly love Phoebe, and it hurts me
to see her so distressed. I hardly like to write and
tell them not to come. Your mama would be sure
to take that amiss. Part of the problem is that our
place in Bruton Street isn't very large and there's no
easy way Phoebe can hide from your mama without
causing offence.'

Meg knew immediately how much Fred Zealand
was troubled, for only if he were in dire distress
would he have said such a personal thing to her.
But she knew her mother. Once she had an idea in
her head, she was like a dog worrying a bone which
it refused to give up. Worse, she always required a
whipping boy to vent her life's disappointments on,
and Meg had once been that boy. Now it seemed
that Phoebe was her mother's target.

A way out for Fred and Phoebe occurred to her.
It was not a happy one. It meant a considerable
sacrifice on her part, but so be it.

'I have a notion which might save Phoebe, Fred.
Suppose I were to write and ask my parents to stay
with me this summer? Templestowe House is large
enough for an army, and as I am a widow, Mama
cannot reproach me for not providing her with a
grandchild.'

'Would you, Meg? Would you really?' Even Fred
knew that Meg had never managed to please
her mama and that she would simply be a revived
target for her bad temper. He did not say, 'You are
making a great sacrifice', for it had been difficult
enough to confess the truth about Mrs Ashe and her

treatment of Phoebe without saying more.

And so it was settled.

And now I shall have Mother reproaching me as well as Simon, thought Meg with wry amusement. I shall surely achieve heavenly salvation, having endured so much on earth!

There was more for her to endure later that day. Charlotte was with her when Will Osborne was announced; Meg knew immediately why he had come, without Peverel in tow. He intended to propose to her. He had been working himself up to do so for the last few weeks.

Nevertheless, she was bound to see him. Nothing had happened between them which could justify her snubbing him. Perhaps, in the end, it would be better for both of them if he proposed to her sooner rather than later—at least it would be out of the way.

The trouble was that, as soon as he had asked to see her alone, and she had sent an agog Charlotte out of the room, she knew that her refusal of his proposal would be bound to hurt him. All his life everything he had wanted had fallen either into his lap, or his open mouth.

Without being unpleasantly spoiled, he yet considered that everything which Will Osborne wanted, he ought to get. Even the cavalier treatment that he received from Peverel could not daunt him, since he scarcely recognised it.

So here he was, not exactly on one knee, but charmingly bent before her, offering her himself, his future title, his vast fortune and approximately one-tenth of the entire acres of England, Wales and

Scotland. Surely she could not refuse *that*?

But she could.

And did. In the gentlest possible manner.

Will pulled himself slowly erect. It was plain that he was finding it difficult to believe what he had just heard.

'You have done me a great honour, sir,' Meg had said, 'by proposing to me. Alas, it is not an offer which I can accept, however. While I both like and esteem you, I do not love you, and I think that you deserve to receive the last sentiment from your future wife, as well as the first two.'

'Oh,' he said, bravely trying to conceal his chagrin by smiling kindly at her, 'I understand that many ladies' modesty is such that they find it difficult to accept a proposal from a gentleman at its first offering. I had flattered myself that matters between us were such that you would feel able to accept me immediately. I am, however, prepared to wait.'

Meg, appalled at the prospect of watching Will wind himself up all over again, said, 'I must emphasise that my "no" to you is unlikely to turn into a "yes", however long you wait. It is not my custom to say what I do not mean, particularly when to do so might raise false hopes. I would be happy to remain your friend, even if I do not intend to be your wife.'

It was plain that he could scarce take in what he was hearing. Somewhat bewildered, he came out with, 'You do understand that, if you marry me, you will be Lady Stanyon when my cousin goes to his last rest—surely a prospect which any woman might find difficult to refuse.'

Meg could hardly retort that she was already the Comtesse de Mortaine, owned a large part of France, and had not found that either fact had brought her much in the way of happiness. She doubted whether marrying a man she did not love in order to acquire yet another title would bring her any more.

Instead, she said gently, 'If I married you, sir, it would not be for your title, but because I loved you enough to wish to be your wife. Since I do not, however, I have no desire to be a party to a loveless marriage, for I have observed that such arrangements frequently end in misery.'

'But if you did marry me, I am sure that you would come to love me in the end,' he said eagerly. 'Reconsider your answer, I beg of you.'

'You must,' Meg returned, 'accept that I am unwilling to take that risk. Moreover, I do not yet feel prepared to venture into marriage again at all—even with someone whom I might love.'

She was thinking of Simon when she said this, and of how and why she had refused him. The burned child fears the fire. It was the notion of marriage itself which Meg found fearful, not the act of love. But she could hardly tell Will that, when he was prepared to prattle about female modesty to a woman who had been married to André, Comte de Mortaine.

Meg could see by his face, his whole posture, that he was attributing her refusal of him to female whims, the unaccountably flighty behaviour of her sex, which must be the only reason why she would not accept him: the most desirable catch of the Season.

She sighed. 'Come,' she said. 'Bite the bullet—
if you will allow me to be so brusque—and accept
that I am unlikely to change my mind. There are
other young women, younger than I am, who would
be only too happy to become Lady Stanyon.'

'But I don't want those other young women, I
want you,' he told her mournfully. 'And I do believe
that, if you think things over, you are likely to
change your mind. So I will leave you to reconsider
my offer, so that you may the sooner decide to do
so.' Nothing which she could say would change *his*
mind, and so she sadly told Charlotte when he had
gone in a cloud of ill-conceived optimism. Fortune's
favourite could not believe that he was not every
woman's favourite, and that where he pitched his
desires, there would not be a woman panting for him.

'Refused you, did she?' said Peverel Darrow when
will told him his sad news. 'I could have told you
that she would, if you had cared to consult me
beforehand, and saved you the trouble of offering
for her. She needs a seasoned man, not a boy, does
Meg de Mortaine!'

For once Will neither ignored nor swallowed this
insult. 'I don't care for your manner to me these
days, Darrow. I believe that you are trying to deter
me because you are after the lady yourself. I suppose
that you consider yourself a seasoned man.'

Peverel stifled his inward amusement at Will's
sudden discovery of what everyone in their circle
had known for weeks—that he was after Meg de
Mortaine, too. It would not do, though, to try Will's
patience overmuch. To be one of his friends gave

Peverel access to social circles which he would have otherwise found it hard to enter, and the money he gained from cheating Will at cards was a useful bonus for a man always strapped for cash. He made sure never to fleece a victim so much as to rouse his suspicions.

'A cat may look at a queen,' he remarked carelessly. 'And the lady is there for the taking.'

'She told me that she had no mind to marry,' retorted Will, who was at last beginning to grow up and therefore be ready to throw off the patronage of such as Peverel. 'So there is no point in you spending your time making a leg at her, either!'

'True,' agreed Peverel, but despite that he was relieved to discover that he had seen off one rival for Meg in Will. Now, if he could only be sure that his cousin Simon was also *persona non grata* with Meg, his day would be made. He took no note of Meg saying that she had no wish to marry, for in his experience women frequently made such a claim, but rarely lived up to it.

He would be seeing Meg in a couple of days' time at a reception given by the French Ambassador. Her late husband had once been part of France's *Corps Diplomatique* shortly after the restoration, in 1815, of King Louis XVIII to the throne that his brother had lost nearly twenty-five years before. He had resigned immediately before he had married Meg, but she was still invited to all the Embassy thrashes.

It was said that the famous, or infamous, Monsieur de Talleyrand—according to the way you looked at him—was to be present. He was paying a short visit to London, and rumour had it that he was being considered as the next French Ambassador to the Court of St James.

But the rumour that Peverel was interested in was the one he had passed on to Simon, which said that Talleyrand had been Meg de Mortaine's lover, even though he had then been in his early seventies. He would dearly like to see his cousin Simon's face when the pair of them came face to face again, as they surely would. . .

It would be exactly the right time for him to propose to Meg himself; it would prove that he cared nothing for society's *on dits*, but only for her.

What Peverel could not know was that Meg was not entirely sure that she wished to meet Monsieur de Talleyrand again. Oh, it was not that she no longer liked him, or no longer wished to converse with a man of such intellect, wit and charm, to say nothing of his immense learning. No, it was the knowledge of the unpleasant gossip, which had painted his kind friendship in such ugly colours.

She had met Talleyrand at a time when her life was at a low ebb: when her marriage, which had once seemed to open before her a long road of love, offered instead only a cul-de-sac with a bleak wall at its end.

Astonishingly, since there was some fifty years between them, they had struck up a friendship based on mutual interests. Behind the mask of age, behind his monkey face which many had mocked, behind the devious mind which had enabled him to keep his head and his life through all France's turbulent changes of government since 1789, Meg had seen something of the bright and charming young man that he had once been before France's *ancien régime* had ended.

By his manner to her, she could only imagine that he saw her as the grown-up daughter whom he had never fathered. It was this last memory which persuaded her to meet him again. They had done nothing wrong, and she would not forgo the pleasure of his company.

She knew, as she walked up the grand staircase at the French Embassy with Charlotte Hollis and Fred and Phoebe Zealand by her side, that curious eyes and salacious whispers followed her slow progress.

She had dressed herself with particular care in a gown of the deepest topaz with the new lower waist. The neck of it was high, consisting of a straight slash from shoulder to shoulder, revealing little of the shapely bosom beneath it. Its sleeves were long, reaching to the wrist and ending in a small cream ruffle. The cream motif was repeated in the two flounces on her skirt.

Her jewellery was magnificently simple and consisted of a parure of topazes set about with pearls which André had given her as a wedding present. Her fan was a tiny one, as was her tiara.

Altogether she considered that her turn-out had given the gossips something to get their teeth into— something worth staring at, as well as her encounter with her supposed lover. She knew very well that they would watch her when she was presented to

Talleyrand to try to discover what their true relationship was.

They learned nothing. Simon, who was watching her, not jealously—for jealousy, oddly enough, seemed to have flown our of the window since their passionate encounter—but with the deepest interest, saw nothing but the cool politeness of old friends meeting again. To his astonishment, when he had seen her enter with the Zealands, he had discovered that jealousy had been replaced by a deeply protective feeling for her.

Because he feared that he had hurt her, he wanted no one else to do so. If only she would consent to be his wife, he would make sure that the scandalmongers would never again have cause to look sideways at her.

Meg saw that Talleyrand had grown older, and more dependent on his friend, almost certainly his secret wife, Dorothea, the Duchess de Dino. For his part, Talleyrand could see at once that his good friend the Comtesse de Mortaine had not only grown more beautiful, but had gained more *savoir faire* than ever before.

'My dear Comtesse,' he said gravely to her in French, as she curtsied before him, 'you have grown up, and in the doing you have become an even more accomplished woman. If my companion—' and he looked at the Duchess de Dino '—will forgive me for saying so, were I fifty years younger, I would be storming your front door. Are all Englishmen bloodless, that you are not married yet?'

Meg smiled. 'Oh, Monseigneur—' for she could

never forget that he was a Prince '—I have no mind
to marry.'

'Now that, Madame, is a pity, for you were meant
to be the mother of prodigies. Besides, I do not
believe you. I think that you are particular, and that
only the right man will do for you. Meet him soon,
I beg of you.'

Given the formality of their circumstances, it was
her *congé*, and she moved on, after another curtsy,
pleased that the rapidity of their conversation meant
that few near them could have followed it. She wondered if Simon were present, and whether the sight
of her talking to her supposed elderly lover, had
fuelled his jealousy. She had not met him since she
had refused him, and was not sure whether she
wished to.

The person she did meet, almost immediately, was
Peverel. She always seemed to be encountering him
these days. He bowed to her companions, but it was
plain that Meg was his target.

'May I compliment you this evening, Madame?
Your turnout is superb. I wish you will do me the
honour of allowing me to take you into supper.'

As usual, without causing offence, it was difficult
to refuse him. He walked along with them, bowing
and nodding to their mutual aquaintances. Despite
the late war with France, everyone in society wished
to be seen at their Embassy.

Peverel was engaging in his greatest accomplish-
ment: light conversation. Behind it, his brain was
working furiously in order to use his recently learned
information to the best effect.

Earlier that day he had been standing in the mews

where his curricle and pair were kept, ruefully wondering how long it would be before the cost of maintaining them became so prohibitive that he would have to sell them again.

He had bought them after he had paid in Meg's bank draft, elated by the picture of himself driving into Hyde Park in a spanking carriage behind two prime specimens of horseflesh, at last the equal of those upon whom he preyed. But elation would not pay his mounting bills.

Even as he had been thinking this, he had become aware that a hovering presence was now directly approaching him. A respectable-looking young fellow of the servant class, his hat in his hand, bowed servilely at him, saying, 'Master, I have been told that you pay good money for information about my mistress, Madame de Mortaine. I have a little titbit which you might like to hear of,' and he held out his hand.

'Information first, money afterwards,' replied Peverel curtly. 'I like to know what I'm buying.'

'Oh, indeed, master. It's this. Your cousin, Sir Simon Darrow, visited my mistress late in the evening two nights ago.' He licked his lips and paused.

'And?'

'And stayed in the drawing-room alone with her for three hours, so he did. Mrs Hollis was out with friends. And she gave orders when he arrived that on no account was they to be disturbed while he was with her. . .' He paused again.

Peverel pulled a guinea out of his breeches pocket and held it out to his informant. 'That's for you when you've finished your story.'

The man bowed again, 'And a right generous fellow you are to be sure, master. James, the butler, told us to say nothing, it worn't our business, but the old girl who cleaned the room said as how all the evidence was that they'd been having a bit of. . .hanky-panky. . .if you take my meaning. She'd served in other houses and knew the signs.'

Peverel stared at him before handing his money over. 'You're quite sure of this?' He could scarcely imagine his upright cousin and Meg engaging in illicit. . .hanky-panky on a drawing-room sofa. Nothing he had seen of the pair of them together had suggested that any such behaviour was likely. Quite the contrary.

And then something which he had read at University came back to him—that the philosopher Aristotle had said that hate and love were two passions which were closely intertwined.

'Oh, yes. Quite sure. Or I wouldn't have troubled you, master. I'm an honest man He bowed and moved away again, pocketing his reward.

Peverel said after him, whilst savouring his informant's quaint understanding of honesty, 'There'll be more for you, mind, if you have more to tell me.'

And now here was Meg de Mortaine, walking along beside him as though butter wouldn't melt in her supposedly virtuous mouth.

And here came cousin Simon, the damned hypocrite, whose two-faced dealings rivalled those of the characters in Moliere's old play *Tartuffe* which some rich widow, whom he had vainly pursued, had made him sit through. They, too, pretended to virtue whilst practising vice. Hanky-panky indeed! It was all enough to make an honest man of the world choke.

But knowing what he knew was a bonus. He smiled engagingly at Simon.

Simon was not best pleased to see Peverel. He bowed stiffly at him and his companions. He tried not to look too hard at Meg. He had spent the day consumed by pointless remorse after they. . .he could think of no polite word for what he and Meg had done. . .after they had consummated their passion was the flowery, literary phrase for it, he supposed. For he was sure that, one way or another, he had dished himself with her for ever.

He could not imagine what had happened to the Simon Darrow who had once seen women, whether mistresses or wives, as part of the background of his life, not to be taken seriously by a serious man.

But Meg, and that one short bout of pleasure with her, had changed all that. Oh, he wanted more than a passing affair—he wanted her in his bed and his life, no matter what she had got up to in their years apart.

Without her, a long vista of loneliness opened up before him. He could not now imagine asking some characterless girl to be his wife. He also understood why he had never wanted Caro Kenilworth to become Lady Darrow. He could not imagine that, in either case, he would wish to hurry home to be with them.

He had considered going round to Templestowe House and asking to see Meg, to speak to her, to try to change her mind. But fear that she might turn him away kept him from doing so. Loving Meg had made a coward of him.

For the first time, he felt a bitter regret for what he now grasped was the careless way in which he had proposed to her, not once, but twice. What a jackass he had been to throw his pearl away so lightly—and all because he had not understood that she was his pearl.

He felt ill, but did not look it. Was Meg in the same case? This evening she was glowing. Was she, like him, suffering behind a cheerful exterior?

He was, without knowing it, looking at her so ardently and so hopelessly, that even Freddie Zealand noticed his unlikely state, and said in his cheerfully inconsequential way, 'You are alone, I see, Darrow. We are going in to supper. Why not join us? Phoebe told me once that you and the Ashe girls were playmates when you were children.'

This was the last thing which Peverel wanted— Simon to be one of their party, but he smiled his agreement all the same. As did Meg. Seeing Simon again, after an absence of nearly three days, was doing strange things to her, as it was to him. Desire took no heed of time or place, it just *was*, whatever the circumstances in which it manifested itself.

'Not exactly,' Simon found himself saying. 'Phoebe and I, yes. But Madame de Mortaine was a mere baby when Phoebe, Jasper and I considered ourselves fully grown.'

'But Madame is fully grown now,' put in Peverel slyly, trying to discomfit him, for he at least understood why Simon and Meg were so constrained in one another's presence. 'So there is no objection to you being play. . .I mean friends, now, is there?'

This extremely oblique *double entendre* affected both Meg and Simon, even if it passed straight over the heads of Fred and Phoebe.

That Peverel was in some way twitting them both was plain. But surely he could know nothing of their. . .joint contretemps. . .could he? Oh, but he could. The servants always knew everything about their masters, and one or more of them might have talked.

Silence, they both decided, was the best thing. Meg offered Peverel and the company an enigmatic smile.

Simon said, 'I saw you introduced to the great man, Madame.' He had decided to be formal with her in public to quieten doubts about their possible free and easy. . .intercourse, in private.

'He favoured me with a smile and a nod of the head which I suppose passed for a bow, but he was much less formal with you.'

'And all in French, too,' commented Phoebe, a trifle enviously, as they settled themselves around one of the tables laid out with food and drink, 'and so fast that no one could understand a word of what they were saying. You used not to be so accomplished a linguist, Meg.'

'Oh, eight years in France does wonders for one's command of the language,' Meg replied with a smile. 'And what we were saying was innocuous enough. Except that, as usual, I was twitted about not marrying again!'

She tried not to look at Simon as she said this. Or at Peverel. The latter muttered, half under his breath, 'And is there no one who might tempt you to do so, Meg?'

This somewhat daring personal remark had several members of the company showing disapproval. Meg took it in her stride whilst accepting a vol-au-vent from a large salver offered her by a white-gloved footman. 'Oh,' she said, carelessly, 'marriage, and whomsoever one might marry, is too serious a topic for discussion at an Embassy party.'

'Quite so,' uttered Charlotte Hollis repressively, playing the stern companion for once and shooting a glance of dislike in Peverel's direction. 'Might one enquire, Lady Zealand, if your mama and papa are to stay with you again this Season?' Unknown to her, this topic was no more a welcome one than that of Meg's marriage or her possible suitors.

'Not this year,' replied Phoebe a trifle stiffly. 'I believe that Meg has invited them to stay at Templestowe House.'

Now here was a facer for Simon and Peverel, who had both hoped for a clear field with Meg. Peverel was the more dismayed, seeing that Mrs Ashe had always favoured Simon's suit in the past, and would surely do so in the future. On the other hand, he consoled himself with the thought that if Simon had privately hoped for future entertainment either in Meg's bed or her sofa, he was scarcely like to find it with the Ashes hovering in the background.

As for Simon, he glumly considered that Mrs Ashe's favouring of him, far from encouraging Meg to accept him, would most likely achieve the opposite. Of such contrary stuff is life made up!

The training in perfect manners to which all

members of the supper party had been subjected saw
them behaving as though there were no under-
currents to mar the equally perfect surface of social
life on which they were all skating. Only the fact
that Simon was drinking rather more than he ought
betrayed that anything was wrong.

The sight of Peverel making even Charlotte Hollis
laugh by retailing some pointless anecdote did his
temper no good at all, since he had thought of
Charlotte as an ally, and here she was, consorting
with the enemy. He must speak to Meg privately, he
must, to warn her yet again about Peverel although
surely, after her experiences with him that had
caused him to blackmail her, she ought to need no
warning?

He was about to take another swig of the
Embassy's good red wine when it occurred to him,
a little belatedly, that perhaps getting himself blind
drunk was not the way either to put himself in Meg's
good books, or be able to give her the high-minded,
disinterested advice which she so badly needed.

He leaned towards Fred Zealand and whispered
urgently to him, 'Fred, be a good fellow, get rid of
Peverel and the rest for me in such a fashion that I
might have a word with Meg alone.'

Fred, catching firm hold of the wrong end of the
stick, thought that this must mean that Simon wanted
to propose to his sister-in-law, not read her a lecture,
and was only too delighted to oblige.

'Of course, Darrow, at once, and good luck to
you. Deserves a good husband, does Meg. She's not
only a good catch, but a jolly good fellow. More
sense than most men, as I have reason to know.'

Simon suppressed a sigh. 'I'm not about to propose, Zealand,' he said hastily, for he did not want that *on dit* flying round to dish him even further with Meg. 'It's a. . .' He cast about frantically for something to say, ended up by coming out with, 'It's a matter of business, merely.'

This seemed to satisfy Fred, although in similar case it wouldn't have satisfied Simon. 'Well, yes,' he beamed, 'even a clever woman like my sister-in-law needs a man's help in her business dealings. Leave it to me. Tact is everything in these matters.'

Fred's idea of tact consisted in taking Peverel by the arm and literally dragging him away, saying loudly, 'I have an old friend I would like you to meet, Darrow. He's over there, in the party around the Ambassador. Quick march, old fellow, or they'll send him off with the diplomatic bag or something equally mysterious, before I have a chance to introduce you.

'And you, Mrs Hollis, you, too. I know that Meg is already acquainted with Jack Fawcett, and she won't want to meet him again, I'm sure. Look after her for us, Darrow,' he continued remorselessly, dragging Phoebe—who was wondering what had got into her usually somewhat lethargic husband—along with him.

A trifle bemused, Meg watched them go. Short of actually frogmarching Peverel, Fred Zealand could scarcely have been more insistent on tearing him away from her. She turned to see Simon grinning after them. Her eyebrows rose.

'Oh,' she exclaimed, 'I suppose that I have you to thank for Fred's exceedingly odd behaviour. You put him up to this in order to be alone with me. Well, I will not be tricked in such a scurvy fashion. He'll be informing half of London by tomorrow morning that you and I are almost at the altar!'

She rose to go, but Simon put out a beseeching hand. 'Don't hurry away, Meg. I told Fred I wanted to speak to you on a matter of business, and that was not actually a lie. It's the business of asking you if you have considered my offer of marriage, and telling me what you have decided.' He had already forgotten, now that he was alone with her, that his original intention had been to warn her of Peverel's possible machinations.

His smiling impudence, heightened by the fact that, for once, he had drunk more than was good for him, almost overset Meg. The spectacle of him being impudent at all, smiling or not, was so surprising that she found herself unwillingly captivated by it.

His harsh face was softened. The smile which curved his mouth was a true one, for it had reached his eyes as well; they shone at her with earnest entreaty. Almost was she beguiled.

Only almost. Something, she knew not what, held Meg back. She said, and her voice was soft when she spoke, neither harsh nor angry, but sorrowful, rather, 'Oh, Simon, I gave you your answer the other night, and it was a refusal, as well you know. I also refused to promise to think the matter over, for I know my own mind. My yea is my yea, and my nay is my nay, and there it stands.'

She must be honest with him, but her heart almost failed her when she saw his face change, and the light in his eyes begin to die out. Desperation in her voice, she added, 'Oh, Simon, it is not you. It is marriage. I meant it when I said that I would rather be your mistress.'

'But I don't want you for a mistress, Meg. I want you for my wife.'

'No more,' Meg said, the tears not far away. 'I cannot bear this, Simon. I know that I am hurting you, and that I deeply regret. You have had your answer. Do not torment me any more.'

But he must. For he had really meant to warn her yet once more against Peverel. He opened his mouth to do so, but before he could utter a word she had picked up her fan from the table, and had arranged her face so that she presented a perfectly composed aspect to the world before she said, resuming her best great-lady manner, 'I really must rejoin the others, Simon. We shall cause unkind comment if we remain here alone. We are already being watched.'

He could not stop her, and then she was gone from him, leaving him to wonder what her marriage must have been like for her to reject the notion of marrying again with such horror that she was prepared to become his mistress, but never his wife.

Chapter Ten

Charlotte was writing a letter to Jasper. Meg was reading the accounts and documents relating to her estates both in France and England that her agent, George Paton, had presented to her that morning. L'Angelier, the steward who ran her French possessions for her, had come over from Paris a few days earlier, and he and George had spent the time since his arrival going over them together.

George was a middle-aged man, the younger son of a poor gentry family, and she had been recommended to hire him by Jasper, who knew his nephew. They had been fellow officers in the army. Meg had found George so useful that she had come to use him as a kind of secretary. His command of French was good, and he was pathetically grateful to her for employing him.

His previous post had been with an elderly Marquess whose profligate heir, on succeeding to the title, had dismissed him when he had tried to advise him not to throw his inheritance away on the gaming tables. He was shortly to leave for Berkshire to help Jasper in his new role as Meg's land agent there.

Meg sighed and closed the ledger she had been reading. Unlike many women in her position, she had taken the trouble to learn about the management of her vast possessions. George had been a trifle concerned that, in her ignorance, she might make decisions without properly consulting him, but she had shown a fund of good sense which had been sadly lacking in some of the men he had worked for.

He had queried the sums of money which had been paid over to Peverel and Jasper, but she had looked him in the eye and said coolly, 'An expense of a personal kind, George, which will not recur, I assure you—' words that she was to recollect somewhat wryly before very much time had passed.

She and Charlotte ate lunch early; a cold collation served on the small lawn behind the house, for the day was warm. It was while they were idling over the tea board after it that James, the butler, arrived.

'Your sister, Lady Wallasey, asks if you will receive her privately, Madame. I have put her in the small drawing-room after telling her that I would convey her wishes to you.' His bow was as grave and as formal as his words.

Being Comtesse, Meg thought rebelliously, inwardly reverting to the hoydenish youngest Miss Ashe again, meant that everyone spoke to her as though she were some sort of grand institution, not a woman at all. She was always wondering what James was really like when he was not treating her as though she were the Empress of China.

'In the small drawing-room, James? I will go to

her at once. I hope that she was offered tea.'

'Indeed, Madame, and cakes. But she declined them both. She seems a trifle agitated, if I may say so.'

Well, there was one good thing about James, he always warned her if anything seemed out of place, so that she might be prepared. As for Hetty seeming agitated; that was certainly not news. All her family appeared to be agitated these days, and she could only hope that her parents, when they came, were going to be an exception to this apparently general rule.

James had not been mistaken. Hetty was pacing up and down the room like one of the caged animals which Meg had seen so recently at the Zoological Gardens. She flung herself at Meg when she entered and gave her a distracted kiss.

Meg extricated herself from her suffocating embrace and cynically wondered what her sister wanted from her. She did not have long to find out after she had bidden Hetty to sit down, and had rung for tea which she at first declined, but then accepted when it arrived. Meg had refused to talk to her until she had composed herself.

'What is it, Hester? What is worrying you?'

'Oh, how clever you are these days, Meg, to see immediately how troubled I am! Oh, I am in deep water, indeed. So deep that I consulted Jasper. . .'

She paused, and Meg, who thought that only a blind fool would not have known immediately how distressed her sister was, could not resist saying, 'Oh, yes, a wise choice. Jasper knows all about deep water. How, exactly, did he advise you to swim out of it?'

'He told me to come to you for help. He said that he had needed assistance recently, and that you had been a tower of strength—although he refused to tell me why he needed help, only that he did.' She paused again, and began to cry—artistically and dramatically. Her distress might be real, but the fashion in which she coped with it was of the stuff of theatre.

'I cannot help you,' Meg said, 'unless you tell me what is wrong.'

Hetty dropped a lacy handkerchief to reveal a tear-stained face. 'Debts, my dear. Debts! Oh, I have been such a fool. I have plunged deep in play of all kind and I am at my wits' end. Wallasey does not know, of course. I should die if he ever found out, but I have not the slightest notion of how I am to pay my IOUs.'

'You know, of course,' remarked Meg conversationally, 'that there is no legal obligation to pay gambling debts. The law does not recognise them.'

'Oh!' Hetty was scandalised. 'Of course I must pay them. They are debts of honour, and those to whom I owe them would let the whole world know that I had defaulted. Where would my reputation be then? Besides, what would Wallasey say? He is always droning on about the need for retrenchment, complaining that when he inherited he had found the estates encumbered because his papa had lost thousands at the gaming tables. He never gambles, and I know that he would send me into the country forever if he knew that I had been doing so, particularly if he ever discovered how much I have lost.'

The youngest Miss Ashe looked at the sister who, before Meg had left England for France eight years ago, had always patronised her. Being only human, she decided that Hetty must pay a little for that.

'What exactly do you want from me, Hetty?'

Hetty disappeared into her handkerchief again. Her sobs grew louder and longer. 'I know that you have helped Jasper, and I have reason to believe that you have done the same for Jane and Phoebe, so why should you not help me?'

'I may be rich, Hetty, but I am not a money well. I take it that that *is* what you want from me? Money to pay for your folly.' She was being harder on Hetty than the others because Hetty had always despised her as the plain sister and had mocked her both publicly and privately. Oh, she would help her in the end, but a little decent gratitude from Hester would not come amiss before she was saved from the moneylenders and the duns.

The eyes which stared at her over the handkerchief were fearful. 'Oh, God, Meg, don't refuse me. I don't know what I shall do if you fail me.'

'Fail you!' Meg's laugh was short. She picked up one of the ledgers which George Paton had left behind. 'Allow me a few moments to examine my financial affairs to discover whether I have the wherewithal to aid you a little—'

'A little!' echoed Hetty.

Unknown to her sister, Meg's account books told a revealing tale of her wealth; not only did she have a vast fortune in what George called the 'immovables'—land, houses, and possessions which could not be sold—but also a tally of riches in cash, specie, stocks and shares which would have made Croesus—the old Greek king, reputed to be the master of untold wealth—jealous. Hetty's gaming debts were like to be a flea bite that would go unnoticed, except to George's shrewd eyes.

'How much, Hetty?' Meg was deliberately curt.

Hetty told her.

'Three thousand pounds. Oh, Meg, I shall love you for ever if you clear them for me.'

'Oh, I do doubt that, Hetty. Love me enough to pay me back, d'you think?'

Hetty began to sob again. 'Oh, Meg, don't be so hard. You must know what a short leash Wallasey keeps me on. I haven't a penny to call my own.'

'All the more reason not to gamble, then. Let me have a list of what you owe, and I will clear your debts for you—on one condition. That you do not play again, for if you do—and you lose—I shall not give you a penny more.'

'Anything, Meg, anything. Oh, you are the best of sisters,' and she made to embrace Meg again, but Meg dodged away. 'No, Hetty. No histrionics, please. Just give up gambling.'

Which, Meg thought, after Hetty had gone, promising to send her the details of her losses, and to whom payment must be made, was not very likely. And after this, who else from her family was left to throw herself on her mercy and demand rescue from Lady Bountiful?

All that was needed to complete the day, she thought wryly, was to have Simon arrive, pestering her to marry him again. After Hetty, she didn't think that she had the spirit left to stomach that.

But it wasn't Simon who arrived to pester her, but quite another pair of visitors: her father and mother, a day early.

'I knew that you would not mind if we arrived before times, Meg. Your father, contrary as usual, said that we should keep to our word, but stuff, I told him, no need to stand on ceremony with Meg.'

She stood back to see Meg the better. Meg was wearing a loose gown of the kind which Cass Devereux often wore about the house. Cass had seen an Indian lady wearing one. A sari, it was called, and Meg had liked it because being loose, she could be at ease in it.

Now her mother said critically, 'Don't you think that your turnout is a little *outré*, Meg, my dear?'

'No, Mother, I don't. Otherwise, I wouldn't be wearing it.'

This calm riposte took her mother aback. The Meg she had always known would have been stridently defiant in making such a statement, not coolly confident.

Oh,' she said. 'Indeed.' She looked about her. 'What in the world possessed you to rent such a barracks as this? You would have been much better off in a little place in Bruton Street.'

'Because I like space about me, mother. I grew accustomed to it in André's mansion in Paris, and I would feel cooped up in a little place in Bruton Street. As it is, here I shall be able to give you a suite of rooms where you and Papa may be privately happy on your own.'

Daunted for the first time in her life by one of

her children, who had now trumped her ace twice, Mrs Ashe looked at her husband. He was indulging in a small secret smile, which he was to repeat at frequent intervals when his hitherto domineering wife came up against her coolly masterful youngest daughter.

Meg smiled, and added, 'I will show you to your rooms; they have been made ready, and were only waiting for your arrival. They overlook the lawns at the back, and the view from the windows is excellent. I will order tea and a cold collation to be sent to you. If you would prefer something a little stronger, Papa, you will find an interesting selection of bottles and decanters on the sideboard in your drawing-room.'

In the face of such kind and carefully organised consideration, Mrs Ashe could find little to say. She did try for a parting shot as they reached the suite of rooms set aside for her and her husband, but her bow and arrow failed her yet again.

'My dear, I understand from one of my correspondents that you have been encouraging Peverel Darrow. That, I must say, I deplore. I do not understand what you are about. His cousin Simon ought surely to be your target. He would make you a most suitable husband and would save you from becoming the victim of gossiping tongues.'

'So he would, Mother. Except that I have not the slightest wish to marry. In any case, out of the frying pan into the fire would be the best description for marriage undertaken in such circumstances. Now, here we are at your rooms and Mrs Hutchings, my housekeeper, has tried to anticipate your every wish.

If she has not done so, pray ring for her, I beg of you.'

All her mother could say was, 'We seem to be a long way away from one another, my dear.'

Meg's parting shot was a deadly one. 'Oh, I thought that you would prefer that, Mother, seeing that so little I do pleases you. The less we see of one another, the happier your temper will be.'

Meg tried to avoid her father's eye as she swept out of the room, Madame la Comtesse de Mortaine in full fig and flower, mistress of all she surveyed. Why in the world had her mother frightened her so in the past? But of course, the youngest and powerless Miss Ashe had been the perfect target for a woman who battened on the fears of the weak.

A week later, seated in Templestowe House's library, Meg was being shown its superb collection of early printed books—or incunabula, as the learned called them—by Templestowe's librarian, Mr Gore, who had stayed with the house, and whose employment was part of her contract with the Earl's estate.

Her dress was a puritanical grey one with a broad white linen collar: over it she was wearing a plain brown holland apron, like those which the housemaids wore when cleaning.

Mr Gore had already complimented her discreetly on her commonsensical apparel. 'Most ladies,' he had said, 'insist on retaining their lightest and prettiest turnouts when they visit me. Most unsuitable wear if one is examining old folios—they shed dust and their calf skin bindings are invariably disintegrating with age.'

Meg wryly wondered how commonsensical Mr Gore would consider her if he were privy to her thoughts. For the past few days she had found herself secretly wondering why she had ever wished that Simon would not call on her. She had expected him to visit her once he knew that her parents were in town, but no. He was staying resolutely away.

She was missing him, there was no doubt about that. Was she regretting that she had refused his offer of marriage? Was she also disappointed that her courses had arrived on time so that there would be no inconvenient legacy of their abandoned evening on the sofa? Meg didn't know.

She only knew that his cousin Peverel, a constant visitor—much to her mother's annoyance, if not to say anger—was becoming less and less attractive to her, but to refuse to see him would create as much gossip as seeing him too often.

Think of someone and you conjure them up, her papa had once told her, so be careful of whom you think! Her lips were curling in a small smile when the ineffable James entered to inform her that Sir Simon Darrow had called and was asking if Madame would receive him.

'Yes, James. And James, show him into the library, not the drawing-room. He might like to inspect the Templestowes' incunabula.'

So, Papa had been right. Perhaps the only time in his life he had been wrong was when he had married her mother. The only explanation she could think of was that when her mother had been young she had been as pretty, but as stupid, as Hetty; and that age, and the disappointments of marrying a poor gentleman, had not improved her.

This was a strict judgement, indeed, and Meg reproached herself for making it, but a week spent listening to her mother's constant criticisms of everything in general, and herself in particular, had been a trying one.

She tried to compose herself whilst waiting for Simon. It would not do to let him know that the mere thought of him excited her, and worse than that, he must never suspect that, since that fatal evening, he had nightly walked through her dreams.

His splendid appearance no longer surprised her. Was it that which made her heart beat faster when James announced him, and he crossed the library to take her hand and bow over it?

He straightened up, and looked about him at the walls lined with oak shelving, at the two tall breakfront walnut bookcases, at the marble busts of Roman Emperors that stood along the room's cornices, and the giant Van Dyck over the hearth, showing the Templestowe family in all its seventeenth-century glory.

'How like you, Meg, to receive me here in the library. I have often longed to inspect Templestowe's superb collection, but he has been either abroad or in the country during my time in London. And now you have granted my wish.' The smile which he gave her was one of pure pleasure.

No reproaches, no sulks, no scowls. Instead, he was pouring over her the kind of diplomatic honey which six years of being an MP must have conferred on him. Meg found herself charmed by him, and responded in kind. 'I'm delighted to learn that I have allowed you to achieve an ambition, Simon.'

Perhaps it was because she was wondering whether he would ever have gone into Parliament if she had married him, that the 'Simon' slipped out so easily. It was as though they were back in those last two years before his proposal when he had taught her to ride, shown her about his home farm, and had advised her on what to read. Before she had changed from a child into a woman, and all the world had changed, too.

With a wife and children he might have been content to be a country farmer all his life. Knowing the success he had achieved as an MP, that would have been a waste.

Now, Meg, she told herself sternly, you are imagining that you had far more power over his life and ambitions than you actually possessed. But the thought haunted Meg a little when Mr Gore came over to show them an early Caxton, with its splendid woodcuts and black letter printing.

A footman arrived with tea for Mr Gore, who retreated to his little study-cum-office off the library to drink it, tactfully leaving them alone.

'I had thought,' Simon began, 'to find you with your mother. I came to pay my respects to your parents—as well as to see you, of course.'

The look he gave her as he said this was a glowing one. The constraints under which their class lived meant that members of the opposite sex could have little time alone together without causing scandal.

Meg gave a short laugh. 'Alas,' she told him ruefully, 'my mother and I are like oil and water these days, I fear. You must remember that when I was a child I never pleased her. Once I thought that, when I grew up, that would change. But no, I fear I please her less than ever.'

'I know.' Simon nodded, and said no more on that, other than, 'On the contrary, though, now you please me more than ever.'

Meg sparked at him almost without thinking. 'Now, sir, you are not to flirt with me. A library is not a suitable place for flirtation.'

'Then tell me which room *is* suitable and let us repair there, for I have a mind to behave as frivolously as I should have done ten years ago and never did. I have a further wish that you would forget your new-found severity and join me in the exercise.' His eyes, his whole bearing, challenged her. Oh, yes, he burned for her as she burned for him. To be near to one another was temptation itself.

And why should she not accept his challenge? Had she not told him that she was prepared to be his mistress? Was he about to accept her offer? And, if he did, if he surrendered to her wishes, would she be glad or sorry? The thought of what being Simon's mistress would mean brought colour to her cheeks.

He noticed this at once. He put both his hands flat on the table between them, and leaned forward until their faces were almost touching. 'You are looking very well today, Madame la Comtesse. Are you well?'

Meg's reply was sturdy. 'Very well. And you may take that to mean, sir, that there will be no legacy of our. . .folly.'

'And would you marry me, Meg—if there were?'

This was plain speaking with a vengeance! But she was equal to it.

'Now that question, sir, I could not answer until there were such a legacy. Until then, the matter being hypothetical, I cannot make an informed judgement.'

'Then you really meant what you said, Meg—that you would be my mistress?'

Although this came out softly, and the door to Mr Gore's study was half-closed, Meg looked guiltily across at it. He had left them alone. Had he heard anything? Were they being talked of?

Simon saw the glance and interpreted it correctly. Was Madame, then, so used to this game of *double entendres* and secret assignations? The thought depressed him. He had not meant to behave as though he were about to take up her offer of an affair, for he still hoped to make her his wife, but he was finding this game of illicit love exciting, to the point of arousing him—even if he were only engaged in the pretence that he might make her his mistress.

But was it pretence? Having shared such delight with Meg, did he want to do so again even without achieving his greatest desire—to marry her? And if he did, if he accepted her offer, would he still not be content until she married him?

Yet if he were the man of honour he thought he was, then should he not refuse all intercourse with her, other than that sanctioned by marriage? And why was this making his head ache, as well as another, vital, part of his body? Were mind and body so intertwined that merely thinking about Meg in his arms could send him into a cold sweat of desire?

Was the naughty madam aware of what she was doing to him? Had Talleyrand, even in old age, been able to teach her the erotic secrets with which rumour said he had enchanted every woman with whom he had ever lain?

And would he kindly stop asking himself questions, which had apparently taken him no time at all, for now his mouth was descending towards Meg's until it was the only part of their bodies which were touching—and across a supposedly chaste library table at that!

Meg savoured the kiss. Was this conquest—or surrender? And who was conquering and who was surrendering? Oh, why was life so full of questions? Wouldn't it be better just to enjoy sensation?

Being so separate, yet so intimately one at the same time, and in this haven where love was usually only words on paper, was strangely erotic, both parties were beginning to find.

An intimate part of Simon's body was beginning to strain against his breeches, whilst Meg was wishing that she was not wearing such a puritanical high-collared gown. Both were cursing their nearness to Mr Gore; and their distance from anything which might be described as a comfortable place to lie down.

What ended the overpowering kiss was the farcical nature of life itself. A woman's voice was heard crying, 'Oh, no, James, I do not need announcing simply to enter the library in order to greet my daughter and her long-time friend. Pray leave me. I am sure that you have other urgent duties to perform.'

It was Mrs Ashe, about to break in on them. Simon, to his astonishment, found that he was quite equal to the saving ploys of the game of illicit love, played out in the wrong place where detection was always imminent. Aware of his betraying condition, he hastily retreated behind a tall lectern where it might not be seen. Meg seated herself again and began to read the noble work of Juliana of Norwich with the most rapt attention.

Mr Gore, who had also heard Mrs Ashe's fortunately noisy approach, discreetly left his study in order to be found on his knees before a tall bookcase not far from the would-be guilty pair. Thus, when Mrs Ashe entered the library, still hectoring James, all was most proper and scholarly—Simon's head being deep in a learned treatise by Isaac Newton.

'So, there you are!' Mrs Ashe advanced on Simon, who, by now respectable again, overt desire having been quenched by her interruption, came from behind the lectern to bow over her hand.

As usual, she could not forbear to criticise Meg. 'What a strange place to receive Simon, my dear. I suggest that we repair to the large drawing-room. I vow that I am beginning to acquire your *penchant* for space.'

Simon looked surprised at this remark. Meg blushed. James, hovering in the doorway, privately relieved that all was decorous, obeyed his mistress's order to arrange for tea to be served in the large drawing-room. That should surely placate her mother.

But it didn't. She roared relentlessly on. 'What in the world has come over you, Meg, to choose such an odd turn-out? You will not credit this, Simon, but the day we arrived here she was wearing some outlandish Indian costume, while today she is disguised as a housemaid. What is the use of your being a Comtesse received at the French court, if all you can do is dress like a servant?'

'What in the world, indeed, Mother? May I point out that you are going the wrong way if the drawing-room is your destination? You are following James, who is making for the kitchens. Knowing you, I cannot imagine that that is where you wish to take tea.'

Meg was not surprised to notice that Simon looked astonished at her shrewish outburst, but after a week of silence, enduring such reproaches, she could not help herself.

He was even more astounded when her mother, blinking back tears, said to him pathetically, in a voice most unlike her usual one, but rather resembling the whining tone which Hetty had adopted when begging for help, 'You see how it is with me these days, Simon. There is no pleasing her. Who would be a mother? Why, if it were not for her father and I, she would never have gone to Paris and married poor André. There is no gratitude in children. None!'

Simon nodded gravely, and remarked as neutrally as he could, 'I suppose that we all disappoint our parents. I know that mine were disappointed in me when I said that I had no wish for the Parliamentary career that they had planned for me. It is one of life's ironies, I suppose, that now that I have achieved it, they are no longer here to enjoy my success.'

This interesting sidelight on Simon's past flew over Mrs Ashe's head, for she began most vigorously to contradict him. 'Oh, no, Simon dear. Both your parents were always very proud of you, I know that for a fact. Meg, though, was always a disappointment until she married André.'

By now they had reached the large drawing-room. Mrs Ashe, seated in its most comfortable chair, droned domineeringly on whilst James and a footman brought tea and Mr Ashe arrived, blinking from the delights of a comfortable afternoon nap taken in his noisy wife's absence.

Mrs Ashe, still discoursing loudly on Meg's failings, leaned forward to say to Simon in what was doubtless intended as a confidential voice, but of which both Mr Ashe and Meg could hear every word—nay, every syllable, 'Of course, my dear Simon, it was always my fondest wish that you and Meg would marry, but the silly child had nothing better to do than marry herself to a Frenchman— and we all know what they are. I suppose that his only saving grace was his wealth!'

To her astonishment, Meg found herself defending her late and unlamented husband, something which she had never thought to do. To such a pass had her mother's stupid spite brought her.

Before the embarrassed Simon could say anything, she remarked dangerously, 'Indeed, Mother, I am not sure that I do know what they are. Frenchmen, I mean. Perhaps you might care to enlighten me.'

Mr Ashe turned a stifled laugh into a cough as Mrs Ashe, for once, struggled to find a suitable put-down for her daughter. At last, 'You know very well what I mean, Meg. You really are impossible these days. Mr Ashe, pray tell your daughter that she is impossible.'

'I had rather not, my dear, seeing that we are living on her generous bounty, both in our own home and in this splendid palace to which she has so kindly invited us. Thanks, rather than criticism, I believe, ought to be directed towards her late husband for leaving her so magnificently endowed. If I, at least, can forgive him for being a Frenchman, surely you must be able to do the same.'

Meg saw both Simon's and her mother's faces change as her father revealed that he and her mother were her pensioners, something which none of the rest of her family knew, for she had asked her father for secrecy in the matter. Annoyed by her mother's baiting of her, he had forgotten his promise.

Even this revelation could not affect Mrs Ashe. After a moment she came out, somewhat sullenly, with, 'Oh, I am sure, Mr Ashe, that I am properly grateful for a daughter doing what, after all, is nothing but her duty. But that does not mean that I am unable to speak my mind when such speech is needed. Speak the truth and shame the devil, *I* always say.'

For the first time Simon was being made aware of the unpleasant spite with which her mother had always treated Meg. He said gently, for he was also suddenly aware of how much Meg must have suffered—and was still suffering—at her mother's hands, 'Oh, I agree that we should always try to be truthful, Mrs Ashe, but my time in Parliament has convinced me that it is sometimes wiser and kinder to be silent. In that fashion, one avoids the unpleasant without perjuring one's self.'

Meg, near to tears, threw him a look of such gratitude that his heart swelled at it. Fortunately, Simon's diplomatic reply had been so carefully couched that Mrs Ashe was uncertain whether he had meant it as a reproach or as praise of what she had said.

So she nodded vigorously, and their later conversation, to Meg's relief, was conducted in all the clichés of polite society.

Before he left, Simon took the opportunity to have a short private word with her. 'My dear,' he said kindly, 'do not take me amiss, but is it not possible for one of your sisters to entertain your mother and father? I have not observed that she is as. . .harsh with them as she is with you.'

Meg's laughter at this was a little strained. 'Pray forgive me, Simon. The subject is not really a matter for mirth, but you must understand that I am only entertaining them at all because Fred Zealand begged me to help them out—my mother's visits to them were putting Phoebe's health at risk. I had forgotten. . .' She bit her lip for she did not want to criticise her mother publicly—not even to Simon.

She started again. 'I mistakenly thought that I could manage to let it ride over my head—and now here I am in the boughs. And there are a pair of metaphors fit only for a bad play at Drury Lane.' She gave another sad little laugh as she finished.

'I see.' Simon stood there helpless, knowing at last how true his love for Meg was, since he wanted, more than anything in the world, to protect her from that world's despite. He was beginning to understand a little why she had refused him eight years ago: that it might have been a reaction against her mother's bullying her to marry him. The thought made him unhappier than ever.

Lust for Meg had temporarily deserted him in the face of her distress. He would dearly have loved to say, 'Marry me, my darling, and I will see that she never hurts you again.' But that would be blackmail of a kind which, because she had been so wounded, Meg would reject. What he did not yet know was that Meg possessed other wounds, which only time and patience would heal.

Meg saw him hesitate and ponder. She wanted to say more, but she had the dreadful belief that, if she lingered any longer with Simon, her mother would follow them and say something so outrageous that the rapport which was slowly growing between herself and the man whom she loved might be damaged by her own behaviour.

She laid her hand on his sleeve, and murmured, 'You must go, Simon. Do not worry overmuch. I think that I am strong enough to bear my mother's presence during the Season. After all, poor Phoebe has had ten years of her, and this is only her first visit to me! I must be strong, for all our sakes.'

What could he say to that? Nothing, only bow over her hand and kiss it, his eyes speaking for him. Meg watched him leave before returning to the drawing-room to find her mother somewhat subdued, and her father looking stern.

It occurred to her for the first time that if her father had been more concerned to care for his children, rather than retreating from his wife's presence to live a quiet life away from her, the history of the Ashe family might have been somewhat different.

But Mrs Ashe did not stay subdued for long. Even before Meg had time to sit down, she resumed her attack on her. 'I am sure that I do not know what has come over you all these days, Meg. Nothing I say or do seems to please. Even Simon's manner to me was a trifle odd. It really is most hurtful when all I am trying to do is promote the happiness of those around me.'

These last words of her mother before she retreated to her suite of rooms left Meg not knowing whether to laugh or to cry. What did remain with her, though, was the look of kind compassion on Simon's face when he had been comforting her.

Chapter Eleven

The ruin which Peverel Darrow had staved off ever since he had left University was suddenly staring him in the face: the moneylenders were threatening to send the bailiffs in. All that was left to him was either a debtor's prison, or flight to the Continent to live a straitened life in Calais, as the late George Brummell had done when his creditors had closed in on him.

One thing, and one thing only could save him: marriage. Marriage to an heiress would solve all his problems at a stroke. The duns would retreat, secure in the knowledge that, once the ceremony was over, they would receive their money back with interest.

Desperate, he had proposed twice in the last week. Once to a young girl of good fortune who would at least be bearable in bed, and then when she had refused him to the fat widow of a filthy rich India merchant who had laughed in his face.

'No title,' Mrs Skinner had jeered at him. 'My poor Thomas left me enough to buy a Viscount at least, and what have you to offer me? Not even a broken-down mansion and a few barren acres!'

'I'm Sir Simon Darrow's heir,' he had protested feebly. 'He is a man of good fortune and large estates, a confirmed bachelor, and—'

'And stuff and nonsense,' she had told him robustly. 'I know all that. Why, he's younger than you are, so even if he never marries you're like to die before him. No, I want a title and lands and I want them now. Money I already have.'

So the low bitch had had him investigated. If that wasn't the outside of enough! All that was left to him was to propose to little Meg Ashe, now the Comtesse de Mortaine. If only she hadn't been told by her bitch of a sister about his blackmailing of her, she might now be his wife. He was sure that, without that hanging over him, he could have won her.

Even so, he might yet succeed. And what a prize she was! Not only because of her money, but because, dammit, he liked her. She would make him a good wife, to whom he would be able to talk, unlike Mrs Skinner, and Charlotte. . .thing. He had already forgotten the young girl's second name.

But if she refused him, what then? Well, desperate men had to employ desperate remedies. He could always try to succeed where Edward Gibbon Wakefield had failed a year ago, and attempt to kidnap and marry her. Wakefield had been caught after he had married his heiress, had been sent to Newgate prison for three years and the marriage had been annulled.

If he could only get her to Gretna Green and marry her, he was sure that the Ashes and his cousin

Simon would not set the law on him, for none of them would—he hoped—wish to see the son of old family friends sent to Botany Bay for marrying an heiress against her will.

He didn't ask himself whether, if he succeeded in getting Meg to Gretna Green, she would agree to marry him—even with the threat of social ruin hanging over her if she didn't. Like many another man, he could not see the indomitable spirit behind her charming exterior. Only his cousin Simon was beginning to understand that Meg de Mortaine had a will as strong as any man's.

Oh, Goddamn everything, that he should be driven to contemplate committing such a crime! But it might not be necessary. Meg might accept him.

She certainly didn't seem to want to marry Simon, although rumour had it that *he* now wished to marry her, which was another potent reason for spiriting Meg away. If Simon should persuade her to marry him, he would surely get the heir who would condemn Peverel to be the permanent poor relation. He would never be Darrow of Darrow Hall.

His meditations were interrupted by his man-of-all-work, Ham Fenton, whom he had sent out earlier with orders to bring back with him George, the footman at Templestowe House, from whom he hoped to gain some more useful information about Meg's life.

'Money for you,' he said abruptly, when George at last stood before him, 'if you can tell me how Madame la Comtesse orders her day and any details about her life.'

George appeared only too willing to oblige. He had already run several small errands for Peverel, and regularly brought him news about Meg's visitors. The latest titbit he had to lay at Peverel's feet was about Simon's latest meeting with her. Part of Peverel's desperation lay in the knowledge that Simon and Meg had spent time together recently— and to learn that they had been alone in the library of all places was a bitter blow.

'Well, almost alone,' George admitted, 'only that half-blind librarian with 'em, James said, and he wouldn't see any hanky-panky, not him. Only half a man.'

'Anything else which might interest me?'

George hesitated, then came out with something which he had overheard James say to the housekeeper. 'Only that that family of hers are like leeches. If any of them want any help from her, she always comes arunning to settle things for 'em, does Madame. Pays their debts, has that 'orrible ma of hers in the house cos no one else wants her, James says.'

Peverel was thoughtful. 'Does she, indeed?' He remembered that Meg had paid him the money to buy Jane's letters back without any demur. *She always comes arunning*, does she, if any of her family are in trouble?

Now he came to think of it, the word was that Jasper Ashe had suddenly paid off his debts, resigned his commission and was working as a land agent somewhere in the country. So who else but Meg could have done that for him? Could this knowledge provide him with the means to trap Meg if she refused his proposal? He questioned George a little more before he handed him his bribe and let him go. A mighty useful traitor in Meg's camp was young George!

What Peverel did not know was that, as he walked back to Templestowe House, young George was feeling the first pangs of awakening conscience. Mr Darrow's money was useful, no doubt of that, but what was he planning for Madame that he needed to know so much about her?

Only that morning Madame had spoken kindly to him, and all the servants were agreed that they had never served a more considerate mistress. He made a private resolution that would hurt his pocket, but never mind that: this was the last time that he would sell information about her to Mr Peverel Darrow. . .

'So you see, my dear, having been such good friends this Season, I thought that I ought to tell you that Jack and I are off to Coverham at the weekend. He says that he has done his duty in the Lords, and is tired of London. Too large, too dirty and the life here too trivial. I most particularly did not wish you to learn the news from anyone else.'

Cass Devereux was seated with Meg on the lawn at the back of Templestowe House. She had brought her children with her, for she was that most unfashionable thing, a loving mother who was rarely parted from her offspring.

'And you are happy to go?'

'Of course. I have to say that I agree with Jack, not just because he is my husband, you understand, but because I, too, love country life. Until I was twelve I lived deep in the Yorkshire countryside, and although Coverham is in Hertfordshire, and the landscape is soft, not wild and rocky, I still prefer it to the town. Jack sends word that he wishes you to visit us when you are tired of London. He believes that you are a country girl at heart.'

Now this was shrewd of Jack, for Meg had said nothing overt to him of her passion for the country life, nor had she told anyone but Jasper of her Berkshire estate. Even her father believed that Jasper's post had been found for him by Meg, not that he was working for her.

Soon she intended to leave London herself and retire to live among her horses and cows. She would have done so before, had it not been for looking after her father and mother on the Zealands' behalf.

'Of course, I shall visit you. I can think of nothing better.' She watched Cass's little son flying his kite so happily and for the first time consciously wished for a family of her own who would run round shouting and laughing, and calling for Mama to look at them. Yes, she thoroughly approved of Cass's attitude towards her children.

'Come soon,' Cass said, shortly before she left. 'The autumn is beautiful at Coverham, full of mellow fruitfulness, as the poet says.'

So Cass liked Keats, too—another bond between them. She would miss her lively, unorthodox presence in the staid ballrooms of the grand and the conventional who made up the bulk of London society. She was faithful to her husband as well, something of which Meg approved.

'I shall leave London as soon as my parents wish to go home. I hope that day will not be long delayed. We are having a grand reunion for the Ashe family before the weekend, at which all of them here in London will be present. Even Jasper is coming up from Berkshire, and Simon Darrow is hoping to look in during the early evening.'

She glanced over to where Charlotte was helping the children to fly the kite, and whispered confidentially to Cass, 'I am hoping that Jasper will soon propose to my companion. He has settled in well in his new position, I understand. I shall be sorry to lose her, but she will be the kind of steadying influence on him that he needs.'

Cass and her children gone, Meg sat down to read the latest novel by the author of *Sophia*. She had only managed half a chapter when James announced that Mr Peverel Darrow wished to speak to her privately. It was really quite odd. Everyone wished to speak to her privately these days.

She had little doubt as to what lay behind Peverel's request. He had come to propose. She had been avoiding him for the last few weeks; with Jasper gone, he had had little excuse to visit her.

Well, he would have to be satisfied with her present turnout—a hoydenish one, because she had dressed to enjoy herself with Cass's children. She was wearing a simple muslin gown, and her hair was loose. With any luck, her informality might dampen his enthusiasm a little.

It didn't. Peverel, staring at Meg's glowing face, at the graceful line of her body, and at her proud carriage, saw nothing of what she was wearing. He saw one thing only, that Meg de Mortaine was a prize worth winning—and not simply for her money. In that moment, he fell genuinely in love with her—he who had never loved anyone before.

To his astonishment, he found that this unlooked-for event made his task of proposing to Meg more, not less, difficult. He was so locked into the habit of charming insincerity that the revelation that he loved her had him almost stuttering as he began to speak.

For the first time, his despair at the notion that she might refuse him was linked to his loss of her, not of her fortune. And sincerity was a trait which he had not practised for years; his tongue stammered over unaccustomed words. Besides, all the words in his vocabulary were shop-soiled by his previous misuse of them.

He had intended to throw himself immediately at her feet in order to display his overpowering desire to marry her. But this ploy now seemed fustian, mere Drury Lane heroics that she would surely despise. How to begin?

Inspiration struck. He would go gently at first. 'Have you had news of Jasper lately? I would dearly like to know how he is coping with country life and country quiet? And for whom is he working?'

This anxious questioning about her brother had the effect of wrong-footing Meg. Knowing Peverel, she had anticipated from him a proposal employing exactly the kind of histrionics that he was so carefully avoiding. Indeed, he was behaving in such a subdued fashion that it did not seem likely that he was about to make one at all.

'Oh, I assure you that Jasper is a happy man. He is working hard, he says, and is finding that he enjoys the rural life. Which is not surprising, after all, seeing that until he joined the Army he was a country lad himself.' She avoided answering Peverel's question about the name of his employer.

Once Peverel would have jumped on that omission, but in the flurry of emotion which his new understanding of his feelings towards Meg had created, he missed it. For several minutes he was reduced to banal chitchat of the kind in which he never normally indulged. The question of how to phrase a proposal that might be successful held him in such thrall that he was quite unable to begin making it!

Meg, indeed, was beginning to wonder exactly what it was that Peverel wished to say to her that he had demanded the privilege of saying it in private. Ten minutes into their meeting, he had said nothing which could not have been heard by Charlotte Hollis.

She decided to broach the question herself, driven, she afterwards concluded, by an intense curiosity as to what the wretched man was about.

She waited until Peverel ended a lengthy and boring disquisition on their recent visit to the Zoological Gardens with the statement that he wished he might be able to afford to join the Zoological Society himself, but alas, his circumstances forbade such a decision.

He cursed himself as soon as he had said this, because it was no part of his plan to dwell on his relative poverty. On the contrary, he was intent on presenting himself as a man of reasonable means. But alas again, an inconvenient truthfulness, usually alien to him, was suddenly breaking out in all directions.

'I understood,' Meg said as he halted to an end, 'that you wished to see me on a private matter. Perhaps my butler was mistaken.'

'Oh, no.' Peverel seized on Meg's statement with avidity seeing that it allowed him a useful and tactful opening to the meat of this interview so far as he was concerned. 'I have a matter of the utmost importance to raise with you.'

Having come out with this, he fell into an unaccustomed silence.

Puzzled, Meg decided to help him out. 'Which is?'

Peverel hesitated, then plunged. 'Oh, Meg,' he exclaimed, falling on to one knee as he spoke, an action not contrived, but coming from the depths of his heart. 'I have fallen madly in love with you. Please marry me,' and he clutched at her hand and began to shower kisses on it.

Unknown to him, it was alas again. He had shown two faces to the world for so long that Meg did not believe a word of this truly impassioned and heartfelt plea. She jumped back, dragging her hand from his, saying briskly, 'Oh, Peverel, do get up, there's a good fellow. You know that you don't believe a word you're saying, so you surely don't expect me to. It's my money you want, not me.'

Peverel was in agony. 'No, no,' he exclaimed, 'not at all. It's you I want, not your money. I love everything about you.' He was dismally aware that even to his own ears every word he said rang with insincerity, however truthful his intent. He had not meant to fling himself on to his knees before her, but the long habit of dissimulation had destroyed in him the ability to speak and act sincerely.

'And if I had no money, Peverel, would you then propose to me?'

Now Peverel knew as well as Meg that this was a question phrased in such a way as to expect the answer no. Peverel's newly found truthfulness where she was concerned plunged him into a further dilemma. Because, even though he loved her, his circumstances were such that, were she penniless, he would never have thrown himself into her way, and would never have learned to love her.

Meg, watching him, was surprised by the varying emotions that chased one another across his usually smilingly placid and carefree face. He wished to tell the truth, but he also needed to win her for two overpowering reasons—one of which was that he needed to save himself from ruin.

He hesitated, and his hesitation told its own tale. 'But I love you, Meg,' burst from him when he saw by her sad dismissive face that his suit had failed. 'Oh, I do, I really do. What do I have to do to make you believe me?'

'Accept,' Meg said, 'that even if I thought you honest in your declaration, I would not agree to marry you. I do not love you, Peverel. Indeed, I do not know whether I can love any man enough to marry him. If you love me, walk away from me without reproaches and without useless words of regret.'

He had failed, and although he still loved her, dissimulation was Peverel's master again. It had to be if he were to survive. Had she accepted him, and they had married, he told himself that he would never have had need to cheat again: that he might have enjoyed the luxury of being an honest man.

But she had not, and he was already beginning to make his plans. The dreadful thing was that the love he felt for her was to drive him on the harder to marry her by any means, fair or foul.

And since fair had failed, foul would have to do.

So he smiled, and smiled. He rose gracefully to his feet, said all the right things, told Meg how sorry he was, and tried to convince her that they could continue as friends—unless, of course, she were to change her mind. . .

But it was plain that she was implacable: there was no likelihood that she would ever willingly accept him. And whatever she had said about never marrying, it was his cousin Simon whom she loved. Simon, who had everything: the title, Darrow Hall, his membership of Parliament, his friends and patrons in high places, the promise of office—and would soon have Meg and her fortune, although, unlike himself, he had no real need of either.

Well, to the devil with Sir Simon Darrow. Whether she willed it or no, she would be Peverel Darrow's bride—and soon.

Chapter Twelve

'**Y**ou may ask me, Charlotte, why Peverel Darrow wished to speak to me privately. I cannot believe that you are not all agog.'

There was no outward sign that Meg was disturbed by the scene which had just passed, but she had an overpowering desire to discuss it with her companion. Charlotte, who was now seated before the glass doors overlooking the lawn, and engaged in stitching a canvaswork bell-pull, smiled at Meg.

'I am supposing,' she said, serenely stitching on, 'that it was yet another proposal.'

'Indeed it was, and an odd one.'

'Oh, and what was odd about it? It cannot have been a surprise, surely? He is up the River Tick, or so rumour says, and doubtless thinks your fortune would help him to paddle out of it.'

'True, and strangely enough, I am relieved to hear that you consider that it was the charm of my money rather than my own charms which drove him on. Which made it all the more surprising when I heard him declare so frantically that he was passionately in love with me. I hardly knew him, he seemed so changed.

'And then, after I had refused him, he changed completely again. He said quite calmly that he accepted my refusal, and hoped that we might still be friends. Friends! Never. There is a reason why we could never be friends. But. . .' and Meg fell silent.

'Sentences beginning with "but" which then break off,' remarked Charlotte serenely, 'always intrigue me.'

'But why do I feel that there was something wrong about the way it ended? Oh, I fear that I am growing fanciful these days. Perfectly behaved though he was, I felt threatened. That was the odd thing.'

Charlotte put down her stitchery. 'Yes, that is odd. One usually feels threatened by bad, not by good, behaviour. Odder still when one contemplates the interesting fact that Mr Peverel Darrow always goes out of his way to be charming to all the ladies.'

Meg was suddenly restless. 'Oh, I must be starting a megrim. I shall be supposing that every bush is a bear, as Shakespeare said. I think it was Shakespeare. . .

'I had better retire to my room to lie down a little before we go to Lady Granville's reception this evening. The party is small, and when I am with her I always feel that I must be very up to the mark, and up to the minute. She may be good fun, and she is always very shrewd. I came to know her well when her husband was the British Ambassador in Paris.'

Charlotte's expression was thoughtful as she watched Meg leave. It was not like her to be so distracted. She might have been describing herself when she spoke of Harriet Granville. If she thought that there had been something strange about Peverel Darrow, then she had probably been correct. The only problem was in what the strangeness might consist.

She shook her head. Speculation was catching and, indulged in overmuch, decidedly led to the megrims—which was possibly what was wrong with Madame la Comtesse de Mortaine, who was usually so practical and down to earth.

A description of both Meg and Harriet Granville, with which Simon Darrow would certainly have agreed. He thought that Meg looked particularly lovely when she entered the Granvilles' large reception room later that evening, to find that Monsieur de Talleyrand was holding court.

Simon had spoken to him briefly and had decided that although he was certainly a monster, he was a charming monster. Had he been monster enough to seduce Meg? That was the question which ran round Simon's brain like a squirrel trapped in a cage.

Meg had dressed herself in the palest green. She was talking to Lady Granville, a woman with a face full of wit and character, but completely lacking in beauty. After a few moments, Meg walked away and Simon could not prevent himself from watching her every move. Being truly in love for the first time, not knowing whether or not that his love would ever be returned, was like living in a kind of hell.

So distracted was he that when Harriet Granville spoke to him about the debate in the Commons that afternoon—she knew that Simon admired her husband's coolly sensible views about the necessity for constitutional reform in order to avoid revolution— he was hard put to give her a sensible answer.

'Oh, it was the usual nonsense,' he managed to say. 'Both sides of the House catcalling, the one at the other. There are times when I wonder how we manage to govern sensibly at all!'

He had said the right thing, for she smiled approvingly at him. 'That was what Granville said when he was an MP. He thought that men of sense ought to get together to agree on policy, not hurl abuse at one another. Imagine a battleship, he said, or a regiment which ran things the same way—nothing would ever get done, and we should lose every battle.'

Simon laughed, and agreed with her. 'True, Lord Melbourne always says that the less Parliament does, the better. It has no business to meddle with the activities of men of sense.'

'And you are a man of sense, I hope, Sir Simon.' Did her eyes turn to look meaningfully at Meg when she said this, or was he seeing subtleties where none existed?

'I hope so, m'lady.'

Apropos of completely nothing she remarked, apparently idly, 'You should not believe all the *on dits* that flow from Paris, dear sir, about the habits of those in good society. Monsieur de Talleyrand, for example, is credited with a reputation that, if the rumours were true, would have a man of his age in his grave in no time. True, he likes to talk to clever young women—as does Granville. But these days, it is invariably only talk. And he also likes to bring cheer to clever young women who are unhappy.'

She was looking at Meg again as she spoke, no doubt of it. And what had she just told him in her clever, guarded way? That the rumours about Meg were untrue—something which he had already begun to believe—and that her relationship with Talleyrand was innocent. More, she had also told him that Meg's marriage had been unhappy, for he had no doubt that Meg was the unhappy and clever young woman of whom she had spoken.

He bowed to her, and said. 'They told me that you were witty, Lady Granville, but they did not tell me that you were kind.'

'I will return the compliment, sir. They told me that you were a sound and honest man, much to be relied on. They did not tell me that you were shrewd. I wish you well in all your endeavours, Sir Simon Darrow.' And yes, she *was* looking at Meg, no doubt of it.

It was also his *congé*, for she was moving on to speak to her other guests, leaving him free to approach Meg. He thought that she looked flushed, a trifle feverish perhaps, but her eyes sparkled and shone the more for it. What was better was that they were sparkling and shining at him.

What a strange mixture of emotions consumed him! Love, lust, a desire to protect her, a desire to share his life with her. And fear that he might never be able to indulge—nay, fulfil was a better word— all these emotions.

'You are in looks tonight, Madame,' he told her. 'You have enjoyed a happy day, perhaps?'

The word 'happy' flew out as an echo of what

Lady Granville had so guardedly told him. Meg looked at his smiling face. Some instinct, she knew not from whence it came, had her telling him of his cousin's proposal that afternoon.

'Which was not exactly a happy moment for either of us, except now that he has had his answer I hope that he will no longer haunt me, for I made my refusal as firm as I possibly could.' She paused and said almost below her breath, 'I tell you this because I know that my association with him made you unhappy.'

Hope stirred in him. 'And you are disturbed by the thought that *I* might be unhappy?'

Meg lowered her eyes as though to examine the fan which she was carrying. 'Yes.'

Hope did more than stir in him. It grew and burgeoned. The desire to hold her, an impossible one to fulfil in a room full of the best society, also grew in him. His eyes were glittering now.

'You are thinking of what I asked you?'

'Yes.'

'And you are ready to give me an answer?'

'Not yet. You must give me time. I have made so many mistakes in my life, you must understand. I have no great wish to make another.'

Hope began to shrivel again. But she had not given him an outright refusal as she had done before—as she had done to Peverel. Hope revived a little, and a savage glee at the thought of Peverel's discomfiture was hope's dark companion. And perhaps he should expect her to hesitate, given what Lady Granville had hinted to him about her marriage.

'We may be friends until you decide—and afterwards, too, I pray.'

'You will always be my friend, Simon, whatever answer I give you.'

Why was she half-encouraging him? Meg did not know. Perhaps with Peverel out of the way, and his suspicions of her dispelled, it might be that they could meet on level terms at last. But always there was that residue of fear about marrying again, which her life with André had left with her.

They were walking along as they spoke, bowing to some acquaintances, smiling at others. More than one man who had become aware that Simon Darrow was in full chase after the Anglo-French Comtesse determined to place their bets when next at their club that they would marry before the Season was over.

Peverel was not present to see his discomfiture completed—Lady Granville rarely invited such as he—but another hopeful lover was. Caro Kenilworth came towards them. She had neither seen nor spoken to Simon since the visit to the Zoological Gardens.

She bowed to them both before looking around the room in order to say sneeringly to Meg, 'I see that your *cavalier servant* is not here tonight.'

'If you mean Mr Peverel Darrow, then pray say so,' retorted Meg coolly.

'Oh, do you have others, Madame, that you need them distinguishing?' Caro's spite was naked. She showed it further by adding, 'You must know that you have lost one of them. Mr Will Osborne proposed to me yesterday, and I have accepted him.

The announcement will be in the public prints tomorrow.'

'Then my congratulations to you both. He is not present tonight, I believe, so you may inform him of my good wishes.' Meg did not let her surprise show, not only because of the disparity in age between Caro and Will, but also because it was so soon after his failed proposal to her.

'No, indeed. Tonight he is informing his cousin, Lord Stanyon, you know, of our happy news. His cousin was most urgent for Will to marry and my name was one of the highest on his list.'

'But why?' Meg asked Simon, genuinely bewildered, after Caro had left, bestowing extreme unction on all about her. 'She is ten years older than he is, and I have rarely seen him speak to her.'

Simon shrugged. 'Stanyon wanted it, I believe. After all, she is not only filthy rich, but owns half of Derbyshire. His lands and hers added together will mean that Will can press for the earldom to be raised to a marquessate, which was always Stanyon's dearest dream. If he couldn't achieve it, then the next best thing is that Will may do so.'

Meg could not prevent a shudder. 'What a dreadful reason for marriage. Oh, I know that our kind do it all the time, but still. . . There was never a sign that he even liked her.'

'Don't you wish to know who was the first heiress on Stanyon's list?' Simon could not prevent himself from saying.

'Who?' And then she knew who it must be. 'Oh! You mean that *I* was?'

'Oh, yes, indeed. You are even more of a prize

in that department than Caro. I will do Will Osborne the honour of believing that he cared for you, but I doubt that he would have chased you so hard if you had been penniless.'

'Which is what I told Peverel,' Meg said, without thinking. 'Oh, dear, I should not have said that.' Her voice was rueful. She looked up at him. Their eyes met, and passion suddenly held them in its thrall.

Simon spoke to break the tension. 'Believe me. . .I would marry you if you possessed not a halfpenny and were in rags. Indeed, I would prefer you in rags. Or in nothing at all.'

And this in a public room surrounded by the cream of society. Bishops, Cabinet Ministers, a Prince—Talleyrand—and two Royal Dukes. To say nothing of assorted dignitaries of every kind. There was even an Admiral present, and the Duke of Wellington, Lady Granville's especial friend, was expected any moment.

Best to pretend that she had not heard his last sentence. 'Well, I do possess more than a halfpenny, sir. Like most present here tonight, I believe.'

'Rumour has it that the Granvilles themselves are not too flush though, particularly after refurbishing the Paris Embassy to their liking,' Simon offered.

'Now, Sir Simon, you are sufficiently a man of the world to know that if Lady Granville is the late Duke of Devonshire's daughter, and Lord Granville's brother is married to the richest and most powerful woman in Scotland, then in their case, shortage of money is no drawback!'

Both of them were seized by the same thought: that Peverel Darrow was not high enough in society's hierarchy for his poverty not to matter. A thought which must have struck Peverel himself more than once.

Meg determinedly changed the subject, as much to show Simon that her slight move in his direction over the question of marriage was a real one. 'I hope that, like me, you are looking forward to the family party I have arranged for tomorrow afternoon. Jasper is coming up from Berkshire and will be pleased to see you, I know.'

'And will you be pleased to see me, Madame la Comtesse?'

She looked up at him, her eyes glowing again. 'You know I will, Simon.'

What heartened him most was that she had dropped the Sir from his name. They stood for a moment, face to face.

'I believe you,' he said abruptly.

Puzzled, Meg said, 'About what, Simon?'

'About Talleyrand. About everything. I believe that you were telling me the truth when you protested your innocence. I even doubt the nature of your involvement with my cousin, despite what I overheard. I believed you even before Lady Granville virtually told me that the rumours circulating London about your life in Paris are false. You will forgive me for thinking otherwise.'

If that did not change the nature of the relationship between them, nothing would. To Simon's astonishment, Meg stood silent while two tears, tears like pearls, ran slowly down her face, to be followed by no others.

They were not touching, and yet, in the truest

sense of all, it was as though they were heart to
heart. Not only that, it was as though they were
alone. The noise of the reception died away. Time
stood still

Meg spoke at last. 'Yes, I forgive you. Though
why you should. . .?' She ran down.

'Change my mind? I have watched you these last
weeks, and the woman I have been seeing is not a
woman who would play fast and loose with her
husband. Or with any man or woman.'

And all that Meg could find to say to that was a
simple, 'Thank you.'

Time began to run again. They were no longer
alone. The noise of the crowded room returned. They
both knew that they ought to separate. They had
been together for far too long.

Simon bowed and took her hand to kiss it in
farewell. 'I cannot wait to see you again tomorrow,'
were his parting words. Meg put the hand he had
kissed to her lips for a brief moment—and then
returned to the mundane world where she must do
her duty, see and be seen, and revert to being the
serene Madame la Comtesse de Mortaine, that great
lady who bore no outward resemblance to the youngest Miss Ashe.

But, inwardly, she had never felt more like her
younger self. Except that this time, if Sir Simon
Darrow came a-courting on the morrow, he would
receive a different answer from the one which she
had given him eight long years ago.

'You're sure that you know exactly what you are to
do, Fenton, and when to do it? Make a mistake and,

at the best, we shall sail in irons to Botany Bay or, at the worst, dance on Tyburn Tree.'

Peverel Darrow had made all his preparations. Usually idle, he had begun a fevered campaign to ensure that he married Meg de Mortaine and saved himself from his creditors even before Meg had turned him down.

He had hoped never to have to put it into operation, but now speed was essential because the bailiffs might be knocking on his door at any moment. He was going to use against her her own generosity towards her family, even though he felt himself to be a cur as he set about doing so.

After all, he loved her and, once they were safely married, he would treat her kindly. Or so he told himself. It was not as though he were going to abduct her solely for her money.

'Trust me, master. Done this before, ain't I?' was Ham Fenton's response. Well, that was true enough, Peverel acknowledged, but Ham's previous piece of villainy had merely concerned his assistance of a minor squire's daughter and the young man whom she wanted to marry, but of whom her parents didn't approve.

Rather than have a scandal, the Squire had glumly accepted the young man and the marriage after the guilty pair, with Fenton's help, had successfully reached Gretna Green and tied the knot, as Fenton always put it.

But this was a different case, was it not? Meg was a great lady, and she was certainly not going to connive at her own abduction. Failure might literally mean death.

'I trust, Fenton, that you have found a reliable lad to deliver this letter for me and who will then disappear, as well as a suitable person to play at being a footman. After that, make sure that the chaise I have hired will be ready to take me to the mews at the back of Sackville Street.'

'Aye, all's ready, master, never fear,' Ham announced reassuringly, before departing to make the final arrangements for Meg's abduction. If this desperate throw succeeded, then he would be in clover as well as his master. If it didn't. . .why, then Ham Fenton had places to hide which neither Peverel nor the law knew of. . .

'You seemed to find Sir Simon Darrow's company pleasing last night, Meg,' remarked Charlotte Hollis the following morning. She had been writing letters and was now busy sealing them.

Meg was contemplating a long list of arrangements that she had just passed on to the housekeeper and to James, all to do with the afternoon party. Her mother and father had not yet come down from their suite of rooms, and she was enjoying a brief respite from her mother's constant complaints.

'I did, didn't I?' was her quiet response, which warned Charlotte that here was a subject on which she chose not to speak. Taking the seat at the bureau which Charlotte had just vacated, Meg began to write a letter to an old friend in Paris.

Her labours were interrupted by the arrival of James, carrying a silver salver which he offered to her. 'A letter, Madame, hand-delivered by a respectable-looking young lad. He said that he could not wait for an answer.'

'A letter?' Meg took it from the salver, broke its seal and opened it. Her name was written on the front in a hand which looked familiar.

It was familiar. The letter was from Jane, and had obviously been written whilst she had been greatly distressed.

'Pray, dear Meg,' she had written, 'of your kindness, I beg you to help me again as you did once before. Oh, I have been such a fool. I cannot speak of this to you this afternoon with all the family present, and tomorrow will be too late. I must see you at once, privately. A friend has generously allowed me to use her home at 4, Sackville Street for a rendezvous with you this morning. Say nothing to anyone, for I fear Vancourt's temper. Come at once, is the sad request of your foolish sister, Jane.'

What in the world could Jane have been doing to lead her to this? Meg stared at the tear-blotted letter, her hand quivering. She looked over at Charlotte, who was now placidly reading. Should she tell her? *Say nothing to anyone*, Jane had pleaded, so she would not. Was it Peverel who was troubling her again? Had he kept back one of the letters?

Meg rose to her feet. She would keep faith with her sister. 'Charlotte, my dear. My letter is from an old friend who has fallen on hard times and wishes to see me urgently before she leaves town.' She looked across at the French clock on the mantelpiece, regretting that she was compelled to lie to Charlotte—but something had to be said to explain her sudden departure.

'I cannot believe that she will keep me long. I am sure to be back well before the family is due to arrive at three.' She looked down at her plain morning dress. 'I need to change into something a little more suitable. Will you kindly arrange for the small chaise to be harnessed and brought round to the front door? No footmen, please, just Jem as my driver. I don't wish to flaunt my consequence.'

Well, the bit about being not kept long would be true enough, for Jane would not wish to explain a long absence from home, she thought wryly as Jem drove her to Sackville Street. She wondered which one of Jane's friends had been ready to oblige her at such short notice.

Jem helped her down—a ragged youth had eagerly run up to hold the horses' heads for him in order to gain a small tip. 'Drive round to the mews at the back,' Meg told him, 'and wait for me, I shall not be long.'

She walked up a few steps to the front door and banged its big iron knocker in the shape of a wreath as vigorously as she could.

The footman who opened it indicated that she should follow him. 'Lady Vancourt is expecting you, Madame,' he told her, polite formality itself.

Meg never quite remembered what happened immediately afterwards. One moment she was walking along a wide entrance hall towards a drawing-room door, the footman before her. The next something dark and heavy was thrown over her head and she was dragged along by a man who was holding her in a cruelly tight grip.

She tried to cry out, but the blanket—she was

sure it was a blanket—muffled her voice, and when she attempted to struggle her captor announced gruffly, 'None of that, now. We don't want to hurt you.'

We? Who could we be? And where was Jane, or the woman who had allowed her to use the house? Surely *Jane* could have nothing to do with this, was her last thought before she was bundled through what must be the kitchen door and the blanket was removed.

Yes, it was the kitchen she had arrived in, but it was empty of all furniture but a grimy table, a broken stool—and Peverel Darrow, sitting in a battered high-backed Windsor armchair before a blackened, long uncleaned, hearth. His expression could best be described as hangdog. A pair of pistols lay on the table before him. The supposed footman had disappeared, and the man who had thrown the blanket over her head turned out to be a servant of Peverel's whom she had seen once or twice before.

Meg fought off the unreasoning panicked fear which was threatening to overwhelm her. She smoothed down her dress, held her head as high as she could, and assumed her most dominant great-lady voice in order to say, 'What in the world are you doing here, Peverel? And where is Jane? Surely she is not waiting for me in what I now take to be an uninhabited house? Is this some kind of strange and unkind joke? And if so, why play it on me?'

She turned towards the kitchen door before which Peverel's servant stood, enjoying her discomfiture, no doubt, and gave him an order. 'Kindly allow me to pass so that I may summon my driver to take me home at once.'

Peverel clapped his hands together in genuine admiration. 'Bravo, my dear. You are, indeed, the nonpareil I thought you. But, alas, I cannot allow Fenton to call your carriage. No, no, I have quite other plans for you.' He rose to his feet and walked towards Meg who stood frozen in sheer disbelief at what was happening to her.

'Oh, Meg, my darling,' he said sorrowfully. 'Why did you not accept my proposal of marriage? We could, I am sure, have dealt so well together, and now. . .'

Dealt so well together. He could not have said anything more calculated to cause Meg to turn away from him, her head still high, her gloved hands closed tightly over her reticule. Even in the midst of the confusion which this untoward turn of events had caused, she remembered only too well who had first said them to her.

Simon.

Simon, who was undoubtedly coming to propose to her this afternoon. Simon, whom she now knew that she loved, and who loved her. And here she was, Peverel's prisoner. By what he had already said, she was sure of his intentions towards her: abduction, and an attempt at forced marriage. And if he succeeded, she and Simon would be parted forever.

Never, no, never. She would never allow it. How, she did not know, but she would think of something. He was still speaking. She must listen to him.

'. . .and now you have compelled me to undertake

this desperate enterprise in order to make you my wife. Oh, Meg, believe me when I say that I truly love you, most passionately love you, but since you will not marry me willingly, then you must do so unwillingly. Although I still hope that you will soon forgive me and come to love me as I love you when you understand what desperate remedies your refusal has forced on me.'

It was true. He was prepared to abduct her—and at the same time had the impudence to declare that he loved her passionately!

Meg flung back her head, and taking the hand which he had extended towards her, she flung that back, too. 'Oh, really, Peverel, this is the outside of enough. You speak as though it is my fault that you are doing this dreadful thing. You have forged a letter purporting to be from Jane in order to bring me here. Your servant has manhandled me, and now you propose—correct me if I am wrong—to drag me to Gretna Green and marry me.

'Well, you are quite mistaken. I shall do no such thing. I will wait for you to come to your senses and send me home. Do so, and I shall tell no one of this fit of madness. I shall go nowhere with you.' She sat down on the broken stool, put her reticule on her lap, and defied him.

All that this achieved was to make him admire her the more for her indomitable spirit—but it could not change his mind. To do so would mean ruin. He felt a cur, and worse than a cur. He was not cut out for this kind of thing. A true villain would have threatened her cruelly, he knew. But he could not do as she asked. Time was wasting. They must be on their way.

'Oh, my dear,' he said sadly, 'my very dear. It is useless. I wish that I could do your bidding, but I cannot. Accept that I mean what I say and come with me, without making an undue fuss.' He picked up one of the pistols. 'I have no wish to threaten you, and I don't want to order Fenton to carry you out to your chaise so that we may all drive north, but I must.'

'And Jem? Is he one of your conspirators, too?'

'No, we have disposed of him, but not harmed him,' and Peverel smiled another sad smile.

Oh, the hypocrisy of him, was Meg's fierce reaction. She folded her arms, and told him, 'I shall walk nowhere with you, you may be sure of that.'

'So be it. But I do not want this—you are compelling me to do exactly what I have no wish to do. Fenton, put the scarf around her mouth, tie her hands, and carry her to the mews.'

'My fault again that you are maltreating me, I suppose,' Meg accused him scornfully before Fenton gagged her and carried her to her own chaise, Peverel following him. Once in, with Fenton as coachman, they drove out of the mews, then out of London to take the road north.

Meg's abduction having been accomplished, the false footman drove Peverel's chaise back to the stables from where Fenton had hired it.

Once they were safely away, Peverel put a tender arm around Meg's shoulders, ignoring the fierce eyes which stared at him over her gag. 'I will remove it,' he said, 'as soon as we are out of London, but if you try to call out or attract attention I shall restore it.'

So far so good, he thought thankfully. And now for Gretna Green.

That morning Jem Potter enjoyed himself at first. But later. . .no such thing. After seeing Madame safely into the house, he had scarcely had time to drive her chaise into the mews, where another already stood in the yard, before a footman came to him brandishing a sovereign. A sovereign!

'It's from Madame,' he explained. 'She will stay longer here than she thought so she has sent you this so that you may get something inside you in comfort, rather than sit out here. There's an inn round the corner. She says be sure to be back in an hour, and not overdo things.' This last was accompanied by a knowing wink.

Well, Madame was a kind soul to be sure. But all the servants knew that, so Jem made certain that he arrived back at the mews when the hour was up. But, Lord, what a turn-up! For on his return he found that both chaises had disappeared, and when he entered the house to find what was up, he discovered it to be empty of both people and furniture.

But worse than that, when, bewildered, and wondering where the deuce Madame and the chaise had gone to without him, he opened the drawing-room door, someone gave him a dirty great blow on the head which knocked him senseless.

He came to with a spinning head and the knowledge that he had the painful task of making his way back to Templestowe House to tell them his dismal story: that not only had he lost a chaise and pair, but Madame as well!

Chapter Thirteen

'You say that Meg left the house at half-eleven of the clock this morning to visit an old friend, and has *still* not returned? How exceedingly inconsiderate of her! But hardly surprising, seeing that she appears to think of no one but herself these days. Even so, I would have expected her to be present to receive her guests.'

Mrs Ashe was at her most dominatingly shrill. Before Charlotte could answer her, she continued in a voice which had the rest of her family wincing, 'And where, pray, did she go? I suppose she had the goodness to inform you of her destination!'

'Well, no,' Charlotte admitted. 'Only that she would be visiting an old friend and would not be gone long.'

'Not gone long!' Mrs Ashe threw up disapproving hands. 'And you have no notion of where she can be. What a way to run a household!'

Jasper came to Charlotte's rescue. 'That will be quite enough, Mama. It is not Charlotte's fault. Nor may it be Meg's. Something must have gone amiss.

241

What, I cannot imagine, but we ought to send for the head groom, in order to find out how many footmen went with her and who was driving her.'

'Oh, I can tell you that,' said Charlotte eagerly. 'She took the smallest chaise and one driver, Jem Potter. She expressly said that she needed no footmen.'

'Stranger and stranger,' sniffed Mrs Ashe who, whilst apparently not liking her daughter, liked the consequence which marriage and wealth had given her.

The head groom, when sent for, confirmed Charlotte's story. 'And young Potter's a highly responsible lad—but who knows, they might have had an accident, but if we don't know where Madame went, then where do we look? The only suggestion that I can make is that we send out as many lads as possible to look for her.'

But where to look? London was so large. Jasper and his three brothers-in-law went into a small huddle with the head groom to discuss ways and means, as a result of which he went to the stables to begin to carry out their plans. Phoebe, always the emotional sister, began to cry at this open admission that Meg might be in trouble, only for her mother to roar at her, 'Kindly stop sniffling, Phoebe. It does not help matters'.

'True enough,' snorted Fred Zealand at his mother-in-law, defying her for the first time. 'And it doesn't help to rail at poor Phoebe, either, so hold your horses for once, pray do.'

What scolding response Mrs Ashe might have made to *that* was forestalled by James announcing

Sir Simon Darrow, whom he had already informed that the mistress had been gone for nigh on four hours, and no one knew where she was.

'Is this true?' Simon began, before looking at everyone's disturbed faces and hearing Phoebe's stifled sobs. 'Yes, I see it is. No search has been made for her, then?' His own voice betrayed his agitation. How could Meg be missing? He had come here determined to propose to her whenever the occasion presented itself, and instead he was being informed that his love had disappeared—had gone no one knew where.

He swung on Charlotte Hollis and asked her a question which, in their agitation, no one else had thought of.

'You say that she went to visit an old friend suddenly. Did someone bring her a message—or had she arranged the visit beforehand?'

'A boy brought her a letter,' Charlotte told him. 'He didn't wait for an answer. Meg read it and said that it was from an old friend who was in trouble and that the matter was urgent. She left at once, saying that she would not be gone long.'

'A letter,' said Simon, with Jasper echoing him. 'Did she take it with her? Or did she leave it behind? And if so, where would she leave it?'

It was typical of Simon, more than one of his hearers thought, that as soon as he arrived he probed straight to the heart of the matter. Charlotte went to the bureau that Meg had been using shortly before she had left.

'She was in a hurry,' she explained as she unlocked and opened it. 'I suppose that there is a chance that she might have left it behind. Yes, I do believe that this is it,' and she handed a piece of crumpled paper to Simon.

Watched anxiously by the whole party, Simon read the letter in silence. Fred Zealand, whose sole contribution so far had been to rebuke Mrs Ashe and murmur 'Good man,' at Simon during his inquisition of Charlotte Hollis, saw his face change as he finished it.

'What is it, Darrow, what's wrong? There is something wrong, I collect by your manner.'

'Very wrong,' said Simon heavily. 'I will have to read it aloud to discover how wrong,' and he did so, beginning, 'This is dated today from an address in Sackville Street. It is as follows.'

For a moment when he ended there was a dead silence, then everyone began to talk at once. Jane sprang to her feet, exclaiming, 'No, I never wrote that. I couldn't have written that. I was never at Sackville Street today. Vancourt will tell you that I never left home until I did so to come here,' and she burst into tears.

Mrs Ashe said angrily, 'This is all some kind of hum, I am sure. And it was very wrong of Meg to rush off on the very morning that she had arranged a family party, even if Jane did write her a letter. She was always an inconsiderate child.'

The dam burst. Jane, drying her eyes, swung on her mother, crying, 'Oh, how can you talk such nonsense, Mother? Did I not just tell you that I never wrote that letter? And Meg inconsiderate! What a story! Were it not for Meg I should be in Queer Street, and so, I believe, would my brother and my

sisters.' She waved a hand at them to encourage
them to support her. 'Is not that so?'

Even Jane might have been surprised at the chorus
of support she was granted. Simon certainly was.
Jane, looking her husband in the eye, bravely confessed, 'What's more, I believe that I know who
wrote that letter. You see, Vancourt, I made a bit
of an ass of myself with Peverel Darrow earlier this
year and wrote him some silly letters. He threatened
to send them to you unless I gave him money.

'If it hadn't been for Meg, I don't know what I
should have done. But she bought him off for me.
Now, since both Meg and I agreed to keep the matter
quiet, and since Peverel certainly wouldn't have told
anyone else about his wickedness, who else could
have known about it? And who more likely to be
able to forge my handwriting?'

She flung herself down beside Vancourt, crying,
'And now she may be in desperate trouble because
she believed that I needed help again.'

Simon stood turned to stone as the true meaning
of the conversation between Peverel and Meg, which
he had so unfortunately overheard, was at last
revealed to him. Oh, dear God, how cruelly he had
misunderstood her. In that, as in everything.

He scarcely heard Jasper saying brokenly, 'She
has also paid my debts, and has given me the hope
of a happy future with my dear Charlotte. I know
that she has done as much for Hetty and Phoebe, so
no more reproaches for her, Mother, ever again.'

'Hear, hear, Jasper,' said his father. 'I should have
silenced you long ago, my dear, where Meg was
concerned.'

Nevertheless, still undaunted, Mrs Ashe opened her mouth to say something scathing about Meg, but caught Fred Zealand's stern eye on her and closed it again. Simple, honest Fred had succeeded where cleverer men had failed: he had been the first to reveal that, firmly treated, she could be silenced.

Simon ignored all this, ignored Mrs Ashe's stricken face, and started for the door, crying hoarsely, 'We waste time. To the devil with my cousin, for that is all he deserves. I am sure that he has abducted Meg to marry her and pay his debts. He has had the impudence to tell me that he loves her. He has several hours start, but I shall go after him at once.'

'Hold on,' exclaimed Jasper. 'I wish to find her, too, but how can we be absolutely sure that it is Peverel who has carried her off—or even if someone has?'

Even as he spoke, James burst through the door, his honest face anxious. 'Sir Simon, Potter is back, injured. He has a strange story to tell. George Newman also says that he has something to confess which might help us, but he will only speak to Sir Simon.'

Potter and Newman's stories confirmed that someone had made away with Meg, although neither of them had any direct knowledge of Peverel's involvement. Added, though, to the evidence of the letter, the likelihood that, as a last desperate throw, he had abducted her was very strong.

Newman was almost the more distressed of the two. 'I never thought he meant her harm,' he said brokenly. 'All he wanted was bits of gossip.' He turned his face away before confessing, 'Particularly about you and Madame. He hated the notion that you and she were friendly. I thought I could earn myself a bit of money for nothing. I suppose I shall be turned away now,' he ended mournfully.

'That will be for Madame to say,' Simon told him, almost absently. He only had one idea in his head. If Peverel had kidnapped Meg in order to marry her he would need to take the Great North Road to York. And Simon would follow him up that road. He would drive to Hell itself in order to rescue Meg.

By far the easiest and safest way for Peverel to take would be the road to Ware, which legend said Dick Turpin had followed, joining the main York Road some forty miles later at Huntingdon. The disadvantage of the mail coach route, which ran via Barnet and Edmonton was that it was so crowded that it carried the risk of his being seen by some friend also travelling north.

If Peverel had gone by Barnet after all, then no matter, Simon would simply have to drive on to Huntingdon in the hope of catching him there.

How fortunate it was that he had come in his two-horse curricle, which would enable him to pick up some of the time already lost. He would be travelling at a greater speed than the chaise—for he had no doubt that Peverel had made off with Meg's carriage.

It was also agreed that Jasper would follow the other route to Huntingdon, in case Simon's guess was wrong. There was to be no mass hue and cry.

'For,' Simon said, 'the less noise we make about this business, the better. If either of us can overtake them and take her to a place of safety before she has been in Peverel's company overnight, then we can save her reputation, otherwise. . .'

'Otherwise,' Jasper said heavily, 'she is ruined.'

'Not completely,' Simon said, 'for today I came to ask her to be my wife, and had hopes that she would agree. If we can thwart Peverel then, come what may, I shall marry her.'

Tigerless, not dressed for a possible long ride north, Simon set off in pursuit of his lost love, privately cursing the Fates who again seemed intent on preventing him from marrying her.

'Have you given any thought, Peverel,' Meg enquired sweetly, 'as to how you are going to manoeuvre me in and out of inns, without my making an unseemly fuss about my abduction, at every place we stop at overnight on the way north?'

Peverel was beginning to think that, even to get hold of her money, marrying Meg would be a great sacrifice on his part. After he had taken off her gag she had never stopped nagging and questioning him in a sweetly reasonable voice, which was unsettling him more than loud recriminations would have done.

'I see no problem there,' he told her stiffly. 'It is in your own interest to draw as little attention as possible to yourself if you are to avoid scandal and social ruin. The sooner we are married, the better for us both—as I am sure you will agree.'

Meg contemplated the passing scenery. They had made very slow time since leaving Sackville Street and the West End behind. Every drover in England seemed to be running their flocks of sheep and cows along the road to Huntingdon via Ware. Several times the chaise had come to a complete stop for some time, and Fenton's leaning down and cursing the offending countrymen seemed to have had no other effect than to slow them down even further. Their final humiliation had come when they had reached Edmonton, a mere seven miles out of London, when geese, ducks, and fowls had not only stopped them, but had almost driven Fenton from his seat, the fowls apparently mistaking the chaise for a suitable place to roost.

'Oh, I don't agree at all,' she informed him cheerfully. 'Social disgrace, so far as I am concerned, is immaterial. I intend to retire into the country as soon as this Season is over.'

'Indeed, you won't.' Peverel gave her an angry glare. 'When you are my wife, I intend to spend the entire Season in London every year—indeed, more than the Season. I detest the country.'

'Which is no more than I would have expected.' Meg put her head on one side in order to stare at him the harder. 'You have the air of exactly the kind of popinjay who considers that the whole of society revolves round him. Now, Simon, on the other hand. . .'

'Damn you, woman, hold your tongue,' he shouted at her angrily. 'I am heartily sick of hearing you prate about Cousin Simon and his perfections. I have had nearly twenty slow miles of it, and enough is enough.'

'Oh, but I like to talk about him. He's such a

noble contrast to your good self. I like that phrase, don't you? It's one the lawyers use. Oh dear, it doesn't really apply to you, though, does it? Not to a would-be felon already half way to Botany Bay!'

Peverel's face purpled. Meg thought that she might have gone too far in her campaign to unsettle him so thoroughly that she might make for herself an opportunity to escape him. She thought that he was more weak than wicked and intended to exploit his weakness. He opened his mouth to say something, but at that moment the coach gave a great lurch and Meg was thrown forward to land on top of Peverel. They had stopped yet again.

This time it was, or so Fenton told them once they had untangled themselves, because a lad had run in front of the horses and had been knocked unconscious. He was now lying on the roadside, being tended by one of the drovers. Another was holding the horses for him. It seemed that the rustics among whom they had been travelling had accused him of going too fast for safety, and there was talk of reporting them to the local magistrates.

'I am sure,' Meg's voice was impossibly virtuous, as she regained her seat, 'that Simon would never have gone so fast in such a mob. *He* would have had more sense.'

'I shall gag you again if you don't stop chattering about him, be damned if I won't,' roared Peverel, before instructing Fenton to get in the chaise and see that she didn't run off, whilst he went outside to try to quell what seemed to be turning into a riot.

Five minutes later he was back—to find that Fenton had pinned Meg back against her seat and had one grimy hand over her mouth. Only her eyes stared defiance at them both.

'Niver met such a troublesome and noisy doxy in all my born days,' Fenton told Peverel. 'What with trying to lean out the winder to scream for help and then offering me money to let her go, she niver stopped talking until I made her. I 'opes as how she's got enough tin to make up for the caterwauling. We shan't git to bloody Huntingdon at this rate, niver mind Gretna Green.'

Meg rewarded him for that by kicking at his calves, and only Peverel's presence stopped him from giving the troublesome doxy such a backhander as she'd not forget in a hurry.

'You're right about not getting to Huntingdon.' Peverel was bitter. 'To satisfy the yokels outside, I've promised to stop at the Fox and Hounds at Ware to find and pay for a doctor for the silly lad we hit, in order to quieten them. I propose that we remain there for the night and leave early before the road becomes filled with traffic.'

Fenton shook his head. 'Best press on, master, in case anyone twigs what we're a-doing and comes after us. We ain't gone very far yet.'

'No likelihood of that. Besides, I'm tired. Stop now and we can order a good dinner. It's been a hard day.'

Meg, her mouth now freed from Fenton's constraining hand, offered him no consolation. 'And several more hard days to come, I assure you, before we reach Gretna. Really, Peverel, is all this discomfort worthwhile, even to get hold of my fortune?'

The look he gave her was one of hate. Contemplating this journey, he had seen himself charming her into acquiescence on it—once she had realised that her case was hopeless. Instead, she had turned into as big a nag as her mother—and even more nonstop. Only the thought of the fortune he was going to enjoy once he had married her, sustained him.

Meg looked out of the window as they inched slowly towards Ware. On the edge of the small town, they came to a crossroads where a signpost informed them that one of the by-roads ran to Coverham. Coverham—was not that where the Devereuxs had their home? She had a fleeting memory of laughing and talking with Cass in happier times.

No time to think of that now. She pondered instead on how to convince the landlord of the Fox and Hounds, when they arrived there, that she was a wronged and abducted woman. Alas, Peverel wisely gave her no chance to do any such thing. Before they even drove into the inn yard he replaced the gag, tied her hands and feet together, and wrapped a large counterpane around her, so that her face was hidden, before bidding Fenton to carry her in.

Loudly shouting, 'Make way, make way, my mistress is taken ill and needs a bed straightway,' he bore her upstairs, an agitated landlady walking in front of them.

Trying to struggle in Fenton's iron grip, Meg found, was useless. Once he had dismissed the landlady, he threw her carelessly on to the bed, leaving it to Peverel to free her from her bonds when he arrived.

Meg, dishevelled and sore, her dignity hurt, as well as her feelings, shot at him, 'I cannot imagine what Simon will do to you when I tell him of this.'

'Too late, my dear. We shall be safely wed before you see him again. I have ordered a good meal for Fenton and myself. For you, gruel—it is all that you deserve and will cool your proud spirit a little. I shall bring it upstairs before we eat. In the meantime, I shall lock you in the bedroom. I do not advise you to call for help. I have told the landlord that your illness has made you delirious—so do not think that anyone will come to rescue you.'

He grinned at her. 'You see, I have thought of everything.'

'Not quite everything. When he catches us up, wed or not, particularly if we're wed, Simon is like to kill you,' Meg told him rebelliously before Peverel left her, locking the door behind him. He had laughed at the notion of Simon, the law-abiding, killing anyone!

Meg was not so sure. She knew of the hidden fires which Simon masked so successfully. She was not, however, prepared to wait for a rescue that might never come. She looked around the room after trying the door. Its lock was flimsy enough, but there was no way that she could break it.

Opposite to the bed was a window. Through it she could see fields stretching to the far horizon in what she assumed was the direction of Coverham. She opened it and leaned out, to see that a small lawn with beds of summer flowers lay below her. At the far end of the lawn was a hedge, and a gate that led on to the fields beyond.

Thoughtfully, Meg closed the window and sat down on the bed to think. The nearness of Coverham had given her an idea. If she could somehow escape from the inn, she might find refuge there with Cass and Jack, even if she had to tramp across the fields to reach them.

She was still plotting when Peverel came back with a tray on which stood a bowl of soup and a large slice of bread. He even knocked at the door before unlocking it, using as much circumspection with her this time as though she were an honoured guest. He had obviously decided to change tactics with her, since threats were unable to silence her.

'You are not feeling too overset, I hope?' he asked her kindly. 'I do regret having to treat you so roughly, but I am sure that you understand that it is necessary.'

'Do not think that you will win me round by being pleasant. I am here as your prisoner, not as your guest. Your absence will be more pleasing to me than your presence,' and Meg turned her back on him.

He placed the tray on the small table before the window. 'Oh, come, my dear. You must know that, despite all, I care greatly for you, even though you have behaved so shrewishly all the way here.'

Meg jumped to her feet. 'Pray forgive me, do. But I regret that I have never been instructed on the correct etiquette to be observed by a lady who has been abducted, has seen her own carriage stolen in order to carry out the abduction, who has been gagged, tied up and carried to her bedroom like a bundle of washing ready for the launderers. The devil take you and your so-called love for me, if this is how you express it. If you truly love me, you will take me home at once.'

She said this as loudly and shrilly as she could, so that Peverel winced at the sound. 'But you must know why I can't do that, Meg. I have crossed the Rubicon. . .'

'And the die is cast, I see. Pray do not speak to me again, I beg of you. Your very voice is hateful to me.'

Nothing was going as he had expected it. He had hoped to win her round with honeyed words, as he had done with other women to gain his way with them. But she had behaved like a fishwife from the very moment that she had found herself in the carriage going north.

Indeed, so noisy was she that he feared that someone might hear them and come to enquire whether anything was wrong, although he had tried to forestall that by telling the landlord and his wife that his own unfortunate spouse was not only sick in body, but in mind.

He had been so charmingly distressed, his luggage which Fenton had carried in was so gentlemanly, and the chaise and its appointments were so luxurious, that neither of them thought to question what he was saying—such a rich and fine gentleman as he undoubtedly was.

What he could do was keep her quiet by leaving her alone while he ate and drank in the inn's diningroom. He had made a point of asking for quarters away from the rest of the guests so that she might not be disturbed. He would put off the task of trying to placate her until the time came when she was so compromised that she could not hope for rescue.

He bowed his way out, determined not to allow her to provoke him into losing his temper again. A good meal, and better drink, awaited him downstairs. The Fox and Hounds' cellars were famous, as all travellers on the Great North Road were well aware.

As for Fenton's dooming that they ought not to have stopped, but should have travelled on into the night to gain an invaluable lead over any pursuers— why in the world should he think that there would be any, given all his careful planning?

Dusk. She needed dusk. Meg had drunk her soup and eaten her bread, surprised to find how hungry she was. Then, remembering the famous coloured print which showed a young woman leaving her upstairs bedroom in order to run away with her lover by climbing down a rope of bedsheets knotted together, she had imitated her, and sat waiting for dusk to arrive.

She was sure that Peverel would not soon return to the bedroom. Food and drink would keep him in the inn's dining-room until she was asleep. For all his faults, she was of the opinion that he would not try to force her—she shied from using the word rape—although, had she proved willing to enjoy his embraces, he would probably have urged her to spend the night with him.

Which was why she had behaved so noisily and shrewishly—to convince him that such a belief was groundless. She opened the window and put her head out. The little garden, as she had hoped, was empty.

She had already fastened one end of the rope to one
of the bedposts, and now she paid it out of the
window, to find that it was still well above the
ground. Giving a great sigh she pulled it back, and
finished it off by adding the bolster case to it.

Oh, famous. It now almost reached the ground.
Next she must climb onto the window sill and begin
to lower herself down—as she had once done on
the trees she had climbed in the gardens at home
when she had been a hoydenish girl. It was as though
the years had fallen away and she was little Meg
Ashe again.

She thanked God that she was still slight, and had
not become puddingy with the years, so that she
reached the ground safely, and scampered, her skirts
held up, across the grass and through the gate.

Where, the good Lord be thanked, there was a
lane and a small sign beside it with an arrow, dimly
scored, and the magic words, *Footpath to Coverham*.
No mileage was given, but what of that. Better to
be on her way to safety—and eventually to Simon—
than waiting to be bundled to Gretna by Peverel and
his odious man.

The only drawback was that a wind had risen,
and there was rain in it, but one could not have
everything.

Simon set a spanking pace on his way north. He
stopped at several posthouses on the road to Ware,
once to change horses—he had no intention of ruining his good cattle by driving them too hard for too
long—but also to enquire whether anyone resembling Peverel and Meg had gone through.

Running through his head was the memory of Meg. Meg laughing up at him; Meg teasing him; Meg, his pretty bird as he had come to think of her, flying free, her own mistress. Oh, if he married her he would never cage her, he would allow her to fly free, sure that she would always return to him, for she was both faithful and true—to herself and those who depended on her, as her family had borne witness. Why had he ever doubted her honour?

Marry her! He had yet to rescue her and, if he were mistaken about Peverel's plans, and his cousin got clean away with her, then that marriage might never be.

Like Meg, on drawing near to Ware, he noticed that he was passing by the road to Coverham, although at the time he thought little of that. Knowing that Peverel liked ease and comfort he was sure that he would stop at Ware.

Sure enough, when he reached the Fox and Hounds and questioned the ostler who came up to serve the highflyer with the splendid curricle, he learned that, yes, a gentleman, answering to Peverel's description, and a lady had arrived in a chaise some hours ago. But the lady had been ill and unable to walk and had been carried in by the gentleman's servant. The gentleman had dined alone and was in the taproom at this very minute.

Simon threw money at him, bade him care for his horses and carriage and set off at the double for the taproom to discover whether his quarry was there.

He was. Peverel sat before the flaming hearth, his booted feet up on a small table, a cigar in his hand, a glass of port by his side: the very picture of suc-

cessful indolence. He did not see Simon until that
gentleman gave a roar, and hurled himself at Peverel
to send chair, table, cigar and drink flying.

'Damn you, where is she? What the devil have
you done with her, you cur? I'll kill you for this!'

All thought of discretion, of smothering scandal
for Meg's sake, had flown out of Simon's head. All
that he wanted to do was beat his worthless cousin
to a pulp. He had him by his lapels, had thrust a
face into Peverel's which was so leonine and threatening that Peverel quailed before him.

'I've not harmed her. I'd never harm her. I
love her.'

'You lie, damn you. You lie,' and Simon shook
his cousin as a terrier might shake a rat so that
Peverel's teeth chattered and tears came into
his eyes.

'I say, sir,' quavered a young gentleman, standing
by the bar. 'Hold on, there. What's to do that you're
in such a pother?' He appealed to the landlord.
'Ought we not to fetch the constable?'

Still holding Peverel in a vice-like grip, Simon
bellowed at the youth. 'Who the devil asked you to
interfere in a private quarrel? If I want a constable,
I'll send for one myself. I'll deal with this cur—
privately. Landlord! Is there a room I can use to
question this malefactor and decide whether to start
him on his way to Botany Bay?'

Peverel knew that the game was well and truly
up. He had never seen Simon behave after such an
abandoned and ferocious fashion before. Here was
a man he had never met. And he remembered Meg's
prescient words: 'Simon is like to kill you.' He had

laughed at them, and how wrong he had been to do so.

'I want no trouble in my house,' said the landlord sturdily. 'Will the gent you're aholding so cruelly agree to speak to you privately, though?'

'He'll agree to anything I ask of him, won't you, Peverel?' Simon snarled at him. Unable to speak through a combination of fright and shock, Peverel was only able to nod his head in the landlord's direction.

'There, you see!' Simon was triumphant. He twisted Peverel round, bent his arm up behind his back and shoved him into the room off the snug, indicated by the landlord, where he flung Peverel into a chair.

'Now. Don't lie to me, damn you. I'm prepared to let you go to save scandal if you'll tell me where she is.'

'Upstairs. She's upstairs,' quavered Peverel. 'I haven't hurt her. I swear I haven't. I love her.'

'And a damned odd way you have of showing it.' Simon bared his teeth, before saying, 'Now lead the way. Take me to her room. Try to trick me and I swear to God I'll have your blood.'

If Peverel did not know his cousin, Simon scarcely knew himself. From the moment that he was certain that Peverel had made off with Meg he had had only one idea in his head. To find her and give Peverel the beating of his life.

They had reached the bedroom. 'L-l-let go of me,' Peverel stuttered at Simon, 'and I'll unlock the door. I swear to you that she's safe and sound—asleep by now, probably.'

Only she wasn't. The room was empty. Rain was beating in through the open window, drenching the sheets which Meg had used to make her escape. Simon's pretty bird had flown.

Chapter Fourteen

'Safe, is she? Damn you, Peverel, you couldn't even abduct a helpless young woman without making a botch of it.'

Beside himself with rage, hope having been succeeded by fear, and the knowledge that Meg was somewhere out there in the rapidly darkening night, caught in the pouring rain, Simon dealt Peverel such a fierce blow that he was thrown backward over the bed, stunned.

He leaned forward to seize his cousin again by the lapels of his smart coat. 'I've a mind to beat you insensible, here and now, except that I haven't the time. I have a duty to find my poor darling, who has escaped you only to be caught in a storm. But I warn you, if she's harmed in any way when I find her, you'll pay a heavy price.'

And then he was gone, storming down the stairs to try to find his lost love. Peverel followed him, feebly crying, 'Only let me come with you. Oh, dear God. I never meant this to happen.'

Simon had reached the front of the inn and was

making for the lawn at the side before Peverel caught him. Fenton, alerted by his master's shouts, ran out of the room where the ostlers, grooms and postillions had been drinking, in time to see Simon, whose arm Peverel was now pulling on, turn and give him a mighty blow which had him reeling, but still hanging grimly on.

'What the devil's up, master?' cried Fenton, putting up his fists preparatory to attacking Simon. 'Let him go, damn you.'

This inapposite statement had Simon turning on Fenton, shouting, 'Damn you for a fool. *He*'s hanging on to me.' When Fenton struck at him, Simon, hampered by Peverel, swung his booted foot at him to catch him cruelly above the knee and below his midriff.

Fenton fell to his knees, screaming, 'Damn you, you've ruined me.' At the same time, Simon, beginning to be secretly surprised by his own violence, freed himself from Peverel, whom he threw to the ground to join Fenton. That done, he ran through the streaming rain towards the lawn which Meg must have crossed to leave the inn. Common sense told him that she could have gone no other way for fear of being seen. What more likely than that she had left through the gate?

Like her, once through the gate he saw the signpost saying Coverham—and the green lane which led to it. No doubt she thought that safety lay that way, but what she could not know was that the big house where Jack and Cass Devereux lived was over five miles away.

What to do? He could still not be sure that she

had fled in that direction, although the likelihood was strong. He stood for a moment, debating the matter, then Peverel caught up with him.

They stood face to face, water streaming from them both. The savage expression on Simon's face frightened Peverel into crying out in a vain attempt at mitigation or justification, 'Only let me help. Let me try to find her, too. I never meant this to happen. I swear. I never thought that Meg would be so daring, so rash as to put herself in danger.'

Simon was minded to strike him again, to roar at him that *he* had put Meg in danger, but in this desperate pass only common sense could help.

'Dare I trust you?' he asked grimly. 'If I take the path to Coverham, thinking that she has gone that way—will you scour Ware to find her? And if you do, may I have your worthless word that you will return her to the inn until I come back to claim her? If you try to abduct her again, I'll see you hanged or transported, on the word of the Darrows whose name you have shamed today, even if I have to follow you to Hell to catch you.'

Numbly, all his usual easy bravado gone, his face bearing the marks of Simon's fists, Peverel muttered, 'I promise. Dear God, what a mess, what an unseemly mess. What have I done?' He hung his head until Simon roared at him again.

'Be off with you. On a night like this, we've no time to lose. I'm for Coverham, and you, you do as I bid you.'

He stayed a moment to watch Peverel make off in the direction of the front of the inn before starting

on his own long walk. There was no driving a curricle or, indeed, any other form of carriage, along
the narrow track. Pray God he found her before
long—or before anyone else did.

Meg, wet through, shivering, her teeth chattering
involuntarily from time to time, was huddled in the
lee of a hedge. The rain, which had not been heavy
when she had left the inn, had grown more and more
so as she walked along the track. The wind had got
up, too, and she was walking into it, which made
her progress slow.

Tired, weak through lack of food, and soaked to
the skin, her light dress clinging to her so that walking was difficult, she had finally given in to
exhaustion when the track became a mud bath and
she had lost one of her light shoes. She had no idea
how far she had walked, and there was no sign that
she was drawing near to either Coverham village or
the big house just outside of it. Either place would
be sanctuary.

Lightning, which lit up the whole landscape to
reveal that she was still out in the open with no
houses near, was followed by a crack of thunder.
The walk to Coverham, which had seemed to offer
her salvation, had turned into something quite different. It might even have been wiser to have remained
Peverel's prisoner.

Just as she was beginning to stand up, in order to
trudge a little further in the hope that she might find
a barn or a hut to shelter in, Meg saw a man walking
up the lane towards her. Mixed emotions ran through
her. Another human being might offer her assist-

ance—or he might offer her something worse. She moved further into the lee of the hedge to hide herself until he had passed, but even as he did so she was overwhelmed by an almighty sneeze.

The man heard her, and turned his face in her direction so that she saw it for the first time. It was Simon! By what miracle had he arrived here? At the very moment that she recognised him, Simon called, 'Meg? Is that you, Meg?' and ran towards her.

It would not be exaggerating to say that they flew into one another's arms as recognition was followed by relief. Wet through, water running from his hair, Simon was kissing and caressing Meg, and she was kissing him back. 'Oh, my little love,' he exclaimed brokenly, whilst stroking and comforting her. 'Thank God that I have found you. Say that you are not hurt?' His loving attentions caused Meg to burst into tears for the first time on that dreadful day.

She muttered through her tears, 'I am quite wet enough without crying as well, to make matters worse. Apart from that, I don't think that there's very much wrong with me—although I do feel very strange. But how in the world have you managed to find me?'

'No time for that now, my darling. Later. Now we must try to find immediate shelter, and then. . .' he looked around him '. . .failing that, either return to Ware or press on to Coverham.'

Even in the circle of his arms the rain seemed to be able to find her. Meg shivered. 'How far are we from Coverham? I thought to find sanctuary there, but I seem to be no nearer to it than when I started out.'

Simon was making calculations in his head. He reckoned that they were slightly nearer to Ware than to Coverham, but to return her to Ware would risk courting the leers of the crowd in the Fox and Hounds and creating a scandal which would hurt her—the innocent party—the most.

On the other hand, to take the slightly longer route to Coverham would mean that they would not only find the sanctuary Meg had hoped for, but discretion and sympathy. Coverham it must be, and so he told her.

'Do you think that you are able to walk so far, Meg—over two and a half miles?'

What would she have done if he had not found her? Meg's shiverings were fuelled by that thought as well as by the cold and the rain. Without him she might have been unable to go on—and so she told him.

'Never!' Simon was robust. 'I know your gallant heart.'

'The worst thing is that I have lost one of my shoes, which will slow us down, I fear. It is difficult walking with only one.' Meg was trying hard not to sound stupidly complaining, but the resolution which had sustained her all day was being watered down by the relentless rain.

'Then take it off, my darling. I know the path is muddy, but it is soft and not stony, and it will make walking easier. Do you remember taking off your shoes when you were a little girl? And on being reprimanded, you always said that you preferred walking without them!'

Meg was struck by this. It called up memories of the hoyden which she had once been and one in particular, which she had sternly repressed ever since she had left England to become a French *grande dame*. 'So I did. I had quite forgot. What a nodcock I am.'

Walking without shoes was odd, she found, now that she was a grown woman, but more comfortable than with only one. Simon slowed his usual rapid pace, and together they progressed slowly towards the warmth and shelter of Coverham, like a wet Adam and Eve trying to find Paradise, not leave it behind.

Back in Ware, Peverel scoured the town and the roads leading out of it for any sign or news of Meg. He stopped the few people still about, continuing to use what was now a useful fiction to save her reputation: that she was his disturbed and ailing wife, who had run away from him and must be found. Like Simon and Meg, he was soon wet through.

Constantly with him was the knowledge that he, and he alone, had brought them all to this pass. Misery and remorse—new sensations for him— warred in his breast. Even his impending financial ruin seemed a faraway thing, of little note beside the dreadful knowledge of what he had done, and of what he now knew he was: a criminal and a coward who had hurt the one person whom he had professed to love.

Not professed! No, never, he *did* love her, and that one fact alone brought him face to face with the reality of himself and his life. And what he saw was shocking him into a long-belated penitence.

They were not far from Coverham when Meg began to flag. She had been walking more and more slowly, saying nothing to Simon of how ill she was beginning to feel, how exhausted. He constantly asked her if she wished to rest, but she always told him no. She was not sure that, if she stopped, she would ever be able to go on again.

The rain had ceased, which was a boon, and the moon had come from behind the clouds—to reveal that they were almost at the great gates which opened on to the gravelled drive which led to Coverham House. To their right was the road which led to Coverham village. It was at that point, with refuge almost in sight, that Meg's overtaxed mind and body gave way.

She suddenly clutched at Simon's hand, heaved a great sigh, and muttered, 'Oh, Simon, I feel so strange.'

Alarmed by the weakness of her voice, which had previously sounded so strong, Simon stopped, and put an arm around her. 'What is it, my darling?'

'I don't think that I can walk any more.' The gates and great house in the distance wavered before her; the very ground beneath her poor muddy feet seemed unstable. Finally everything, gates, house, ground and feet disappeared into the dark, and only Simon's sustaining arms saved Meg from falling unconscious into the mud.

He lifted her up to carry her: his precious burden. He kissed her white face with the great blue smudges under her eyes, and stroked her wet hair, loose and streaming down her back. He would carry her to the ends of the earth to save her, let alone to the doors of Coverham which drew ever nearer.

She was even lighter than he had thought, a frail vessel to contain such a dauntless spirit. Only the elements had conspired to prevent her from completing the journey herself.

Panting, dog weary, but sustained by the knowledge that Jasper Ashe had been decorated for carrying his wounded lieutenant to safety far further than this, and in worse conditions, Simon walked at a smart pace until he reached the gravelled sweep before the house.

At the bottom of the steps leading up to the huge front doors, Meg opened her eyes again, and began to try to struggle out of his arms. She had no notion of how far he had carried her, but, 'Set me down,' she croaked at him. 'You cannot carry me all the way to Coverham.'

His answer was to hold her to him even more lovingly. 'Oh, but I can—and have. See, we are here. I am going to set you down for a moment, so that I may knock on the door and try to wake the house.' He gently laid her on the top step before stripping off his sodden jacket—his caped greatcoat had been left with his curricle—and rolling it to make a pillow for her head.

Meg, now beyond anything but lying still, watched him hammer on the door again and again with a giant knocker in the shape of an imp before it opened and a querulous voice demanded to know, 'Who the devil is making such a damnable noise when all decent folk are readying themselves for bed!'

They had reached sanctuary.

Chapter Fifteen

'How is she? Tell me how she is?' Simon was frantically accosting the doctor outside Meg's room on the following morning.

Welcomed by Cass Devereux the previous night—her husband was visiting Woburn for a few days to discuss country matters with the Duke of Bedford—Meg had been put to bed immediately, and Simon's wet clothes had been exchanged for some of Jack's country wear.

After that, Cass had arranged for him to be fed, saying briskly when he demurred a little, 'Jack always says that the mark of a good officer is to see that his men have an excellent meal after battle or hardship. I can't feed Meg, but I can feed you, and then, and not before, you may tell me why and how you have arrived here.'

He did feel better when he had eaten, and then the whole sorry story came tumbling out. 'I thought that to bring Meg here might cut scandal off at the knees. No *on dits*, you see, if she has been staying with you. As for hubble-bubble at a posting inn in

Ware—who's to tell? Both Peverel and that criminal of a man of his risk transportation or worse if the true story came out.

'No, we are both your guests, and since you tell me that you have no others here, your servants may talk among themselves, but that is all. Your own reputation, m'lady, is spotless, so your word will not be questioned.'

'Call me Cass, pray do. And yes, I believe that you have done the sensible thing by coming to Coverham. But what of your cousin? Is it right that he should go scot-free after what he has done?'

'No, but consider the alternative and the damage to my poor, innocent Meg if the true story became known. It would cling to her always, and there would be those who would put their finger by their nose, and say, "No smoke without fire." Besides, I have given Peverel the fright of his life.

'He may not, in any case, remain long in England. The duns and the bailiffs are after him. Calais is his destination. Had he not done this to Meg, I might have helped him, but now. . .' and he shook his head. 'He has punished himself.'

'True. And we must both hope that Meg is better in the morning.'

She did not tell him that Coverham's doctor, roused from his comfortable bed in the West Wing, had privately told her that he thought Madame was suffering from more than exhaustion. 'She has a fever, I fear. But we shall know more in the morning.'

She must let Simon have a night's rest after his

labours—and trust that daylight might find Meg better.

But alas, she was not. And so the doctor informed Simon as kindly as he could, 'Madame's fever is worse. She does not know herself, nor where she is. I have given her opium to help her to sleep. Only time and cooling draughts will help her. If she grows worse, I shall bleed her to bring the fever down.'

'By no means,' Simon exclaimed. 'It has been my experience with both men and horses that bleeding does indeed bring the fever down, but weakens the patient to such a degree that they are unable to fight the illness and frequently die in consequence. Only if her life is in immediate danger will I agree to her being bled.'

'Pray who are you, sir, to make such a decision for her which goes against all medical practice?' The doctor was a trifle frosty at having his authority challenged.

'The man who hopes to become her husband when she is recovered—which I trust will be soon.'

But Meg grew no better. As she lay on her bed, she knew nothing of what was happening in the world outside, that Peverel had come to Coverham to discover whether Simon and Meg had reached there.

Despite what he had said to Cass, Peverel had looked so miserable and was so unlike his usual conceited arrogant self that Simon had arranged to give him a little money to make his forced flight to the Continent more comfortable. Peverel's servant was to go with him, relieved that he was not on his way to Botany Bay.

Jasper Ashe had finally arrived at Coverham after

a fruitless journey to Huntingdon, after which he had backtracked to Ware to hear from a bemused landlord of Simon's arrival and departure, and Meg's flight. Coverham, Jasper had thought, was their destination. He had been allowed in to see Meg before returning to London with the news of all that had happened.

Jack Devereux had come home in the meantime; and Simon was camped outside her room, suffering with her, refusing to leave to take up his life in London until she was well again.

He had been allowed in once to look at her. She lay silent and semi-conscious in the great bed, her face whiter than its sheets. He had wanted to stay with her, but both propriety and the doctor forebade it. A chair in the corridor was his place, vacated only when Cass insisted that he dine with her and Jack, lest he fall ill himself.

Not only were she and Jack surprised by his behaviour, but Simon himself could only wonder hazily what had come over him. Where had the coldly impassive, the almost stolid man he had always been, gone to? He had scarcely known himself from the moment that Meg had been in danger. He had helped to save her. And now she was in worse danger than ever, and from that he was powerless to save her.

On the next day she took a turn for the worse. Her fever had risen and she was delirious. Simon could hear her from his post in the corridor. The doctor was sent for, and came from her room, looking grave. Distraught, Simon seized him by his lapels, much as he had seized Peverel. 'How is she?' And then, 'She is in danger, is she not? You must let me in, I must see her. Immediately.'

The doctor tried to struggle free, saying loftily, 'It would be neither wise nor seemly. You would only endanger yourself, and all for nothing. She knows nobody.'

Their raised voices frightened the servants who were nursing Meg. One of them ran to fetch Cass. Simon saw her coming, released the doctor and cried, 'I must see her, Cass. Tell him to let me see her. I don't care whether I endanger myself, or breach the proprieties. If she is so ill that she is despaired of, all the more reason for me to see her.'

'Let him in,' Cass told the doctor quietly. 'If she is so ill, then it would be the greatest kindness to allow Sir Simon to be with the woman he intends to marry.'

The doctor shrugged his shoulders. 'Very well, m'lady, but on your head and his be it. I cannot take responsibility if my orders are countermanded.'

Simon stayed no longer. He was in Meg's room, on his knees, her hand in his. Her eyes, brilliant with fever, were turned on him, but she did not know him. She was speaking, but not to him. She was in the past, with the man she had married, and what she was saying to him came nigh to breaking Simon's heart.

He kissed the hot hand he held and tried to reassure her. It was most plain that she was reliving a life which had been desperately unhappy. For a moment she seemed to be soothed by the sound of his voice—and then she was in the past again, reliving the troubled years of her marriage.

In her delirium, Meg was back in de Mortaine's chateau. Her husband was with her, telling her that he had married her because she was a stranger to his country, who had no one but her aunt in Paris to whom to turn, to tell of the long agony of her life with him. Of life with a man who thought only of himself, and condemned his wife to a living hell.

To try to soothe her, to quieten her, for she grew more and more agitated, Simon used his voice exactly as he would have done if he were trying to gentle a horse—and it seemed to work. He kissed her hot hand—only for her to withdraw it.

She tried to sit up, so he took her in his arms, her hot body burning against his cool one. One of the servants brought her lemonade and he held the glass for her to drink from it. She thanked him prettily—but still had no notion of who he was, only that he was being kind.

The doctor came in and said sourly, 'If the fever breaks, which I doubt, she will sleep and recover. If not. . .' and he shrugged his shoulders. Simon took no notice of him. All he knew was that he was with Meg, that he loved her, that she had suffered, and that if she lived he would make it his business never to let her suffer again.

Later, in the evening, he had his reward. Meg was still in his arms, the sweat pouring down her face and body, but suddenly she reared away from him, and said in the most melancholy voice, 'If only I had married Simon! How stupid I was not to realise that it was him I loved, not some imaginary Prince

Charming. I behaved like a child, and as a child is punished, so am I being.'

'No, no,' he told her earnestly—although he knew that she could not hear him.

'It was I who was wrong. I was careless in my manner to you when I proposed because I did not then understand how much I loved you. I don't think that I understood what love was. All I could think of was that I wanted a wife and that you were convenient. It was only when you refused me and I had lost you that I realised what I had done, and how much the youngest Miss Ashe had meant to me.'

After that she seemed to recover a little, as though, somehow, through the mists of the fever, she had grasped what he had said, although her hair and body were still as wet as they had been on her long walk through the rain to Coverham. Simon laid her down, but still held her hand in his: the contact seemed to comfort her. Later, when Cass came in to suggest that he rest a little after his long vigil, he shook his head at her.

As night fell, so Meg fell silent. She turned her head away from him, and began to sleep. The hand in his grew cooler, and her breathing, which had been noisy, quietened.

For a brief time Simon was afraid that the doctor's gloom had been justified, and that she might be dying but, as the night wore on, he lost his fears and, tired out with watching, fell asleep in his chair. Cass, looking in on them again, refrained from disturbing him lest she disturb Meg; they both looked so peaceful together.

*   *   *

In the morning when he awoke, Meg was awake, too, and fully conscious. Her first words to him were puzzled ones. 'Is this Coverham, Simon? And why are you sleeping in a chair by my bed?' Her voice was weak, but clear, and it was plain that she had no memory of her long days of suffering. Later, she was to tell him that her last recollection was of falling against him almost at the end of the green lane, at the first sight of Coverham.

The nurse, who had come in earlier, ran to fetch the doctor, to tell him that Madame's fever had broken, that she was conscious and was recovering. Simon bent over Meg to kiss her gently on the brow. 'You have been very ill, my darling. We almost despaired of you.'

Meg looked up at him. 'And how long have you been here, Simon?' she asked him, for she could see the stubble on his face, the growth of beard the result of his long watch, and the shadows under his eyes, which told of weariness and worry.

'They only let me in to be with you yesterday, and that because you were so ill, and I made such a fuss. Oh, Meg, my darling, we all feared for you, but I do believe that you are over the worst.'

The eyes on him were bright, but no longer with fever. 'Did I dream that Peverel kidnapped me, that I ran away from him, and that you came to save me?'

'No dream, my darling, but that is all over. Now you must get better.'

She turned her head to kiss the loving hand which held hers. 'Oh, Simon, when I was a little girl I always dreamed that one day a brave knight would come along to rescue me—from what I could never imagine. It was the rescuing which was important, not the reason. And now I have my brave knight, who rescued me and brought me safe to Coverham.' Her voice ran out from very weakness.

'Dear Meg, I was a very belated knight. For you had rescued yourself before I reached Ware. Did you ever imagine doing such a daring thing when you were the little girl, whom I now know I have always loved?'

There, he had said it to her in tones so tender that Meg could not doubt him. All the way along the green lane before he had arrived to help her Meg had been regretting one thing, and one thing only: that she had refused him again. In her delirium, she had relived her time with André and had run from him, trying to find a saviour—whom she now knew was Simon. They had found one another—and this time she would not refuse him if he were to renew his offer.

'But I would never have reached Coverham on my own,' she told him tenderly.

He kissed her for saying so. 'You were my brave girl, forever and always. And what is even better: you are my generous girl who secretly helped the family which had always scorned her—and asked no thanks for it.'

Meg shook her head at him. 'Oh, I was not really brave. I think that I was only able to escape because Peverel was not really a villain—only weak and stupid. A true villain would have treated me even more harshly and made sure that I would never have had the opportunity to escape.' She made no answer to his words about her generosity—she had no wish to discuss it, and Simon respected her the more for that.

'True enough, my darling,' he told her tenderly, 'that Peverel was a weak fool, and I must thank him for his folly—if I ever see him again. But it still took courage to escape into the black night.'

Simon saw that the effort of talking had tired her, but the look of love on her face determined him on what to say and do next. They had lost too much time. He would make sure that they would lose no more.

'There is something I must ask you, Meg, before the world arrives to part us again—but only temporarily this time, I hope—'

Exhausted though she was, Meg struggled into a sitting position, saying earnestly, 'Before you ask me your question, Simon, there is something I ought to tell you. It is about my marriage. No one but André and I knew the truth of it.

'I married him because he was handsome and had been brave: a true Prince Charming, I foolishly thought. The man I turned you down for. But, oh, what a mistake I made. Young he might have been, but he was old and jaded in all the vices of life. So much so that our married life was a mockery. I thank God that my aunt, who helped to make the marriage, did not live to learn the truth of him.

'And when he decided that a young and untried woman was no longer to his taste, he resumed his old ways and treated me most cruelly. Oh, he did not beat me, but he had a vicious tongue and used it to demean me daily and to tell me all the details of his wicked life. He died in a duel caused by his seduction—nay, his rape—of the wife of his best friend, but not before he had tried to destroy my reputation.

The irony of it was that he had no relatives—they had all died in the French Revolutionary Terror—so that his wealth and his estates came to me. But the price I paid to inherit them was a terrible one. The very idea of marriage seemed hateful to me after André's death.

'But those who truly loved me knew the truth. And there you have it. I refused the good man who loved me—and married a roué instead. To survive I became hard and unfeeling myself. Until I met you again.'

The eyes she turned on Simon were grave and loving. Meg thought that she owed him the truth and, weak though she was, must tell him that truth before he proposed to her.

Simon took her in his arms and held her to him, his lips on her hair, telling himself that he must be gentle, that she was still weak from her illness. Though she needed love, that love must be restrained, not powerful.

'Oh, my darling, you are as honest as you are true,' he told her. He knew, from what she had revealed in her delirium, that she had not told him all the horrors of her life with André de Mortaine. But that knowledge was a secret for him to keep. It was enough that she had confessed her folly—as he had confessed his.

'Before I ask you to marry me,' he said, 'let me say this. That had you accepted me all those years ago, I do not believe that our marriage would have been a happy one. You were too young and I was too proud, too sure of my own rectitude, too certain of the rightness of my own judgement. What was worse, I knew nothing of true passion, the depth of love of a man for a woman—until I lost you for the second time.

'When I first proposed to you, I thought of marriage as a kind of bargain between us, as a convenience, a mere continuance of a long friendship, and nothing more. But life has chastened us both, and at the same time has offered us a second chance.

'Meg, my darling, before the doctor arrives to send me away, will you make me a happy man by promising to marry me? This time I make the offer with love in my heart, and respect for the brave creature that you are to survive such a marriage, and my cousin Peverel's villainy.'

'Oh, yes, Simon, yes. I offer you my love unconditionally, the past forgotten and forgiven. The present and the future must be ours.'

Meg was in his arms, where she had always wanted to be, and where she had feared that she might never be. Before them lay fulfilment and a shared life. Her face was flushed, not with fever, but with returning health. Weak she might be, but not so weak that she was not able to enjoy Simon's gentle caresses.

Cass Devereux insisted on accompanying the doctor to Meg's room as soon as she learned that Meg's fever had broken and that she was on the way to recovery.

She also insisted on entering Meg's bedroom

before the doctor did. What she saw there had her shutting the door again, and saying to the doctor, 'I should leave your examination of Madame for a little, sir. I think that the medicine she is receiving at the moment will be as helpful as anything that you might prescribe for her.'